THE MORNING OF THE FOURTH DAY

a novel

Myron 'Bud' Wheeler

WEB

Requests for permission to make copies of any part
of the work should be mailed to:
Wiley E. Bean, Publisher
P.O. Box 97
Grand Ledge, Michigan 48837

Library of Congress Catalog Card Number 94–094263

Wheeler, Myron
The Morning of The Fourth Day

1. Wheeler, Myron
2. Fiction
I. Title
ISBN 0–9637650-0-0

Printed in the United States of America

Revised Edition

THE MORNING OF THE FOURTH DAY

a novel

Myron 'Bud' Wheeler

July 1, 1994

To Al Dalimonte

Bon chance toujours

PROLOGUE

'fate is the hunter'

Ernest Gann

June 18, 1815
Belgium

Rain fell, gentle but steadily across the plateau of Mont St. Jean—all night and into the early hours of the morning—leaving in its wake a wet and soggy field; horses and cannon would become mired in mud—mobility lost.

One of the master military and artillery geniuses of all ages was unable to open his well planned 'game of chess'. Late, at 11:35 o'clock in the morning, on one of the longest days of the year—five hours late—the first shot was fired and the battle began.

The field would have been carried—the victor vanquished—notwithstanding the sunken road of Ohain, undisclosed by the shake of a peasant's head.

The enemy's rescue—the Prussian Army of Blücher—arrived in the early evening and saved the battle; that which would have been lost, had the contest been joined as planned.

Wellington, the Iron Duke—now destined to become Prime Minister of England—filed his report of victory to a waiting world from the nearby village; a place called Waterloo.

July 30, 1991
Dead Horse Lake, Wyoming

On the night of the third day—Will Dean was away from camp.

WYOMING

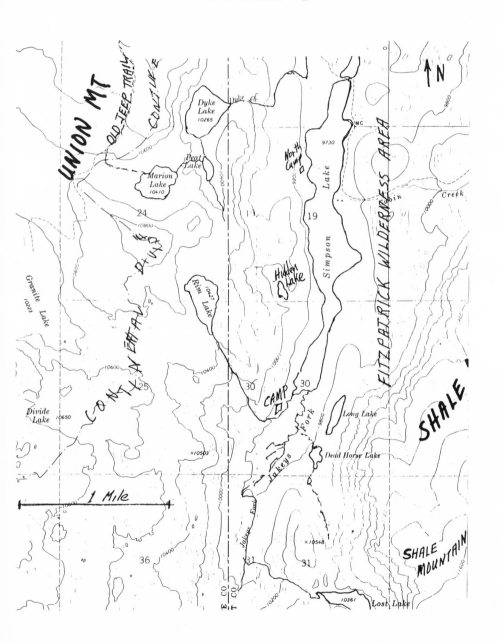

BILL OF FARE

PART I
'things happen—we call it fate'

PART II

'things didn't work out too well
for 'Ole Brer Possum' either'

THE SNOW-IMAGE

'But the common-sensible man saw nothing . . . they know everything—oh, to be sure!—everything that has been, and everything that is, and everything that, by any future possibility, can be. And, should some phenomenon of nature or providence transcend their system, they will not recognize it, even if it come to pass under their very noses."

Nathaniel Hawthorn

1

Walden Ridge

October 13, 1989
Prentice-Cooper State Forest
Marion County, Tennessee

It was late in the afternoon when Lee parked his new, though dusty, GMC Sierra pickup truck at the south side of Mullens Creek. He had driven a short distance east of the old Kelley's Ferry Road roadway, now known as Mullens Cove or River Canyon Road. The meandering Tennessee was shielded by the escarpment from the northeast breeze blowing along the top of Walden Ridge. Cool air, settling slowly to the river valley—a welcome change from the earlier heat of the day.

Chattanooga, eight miles easterly as a crow flies, lay out of sight; blocked by the south loop of Walden Ridge and the northerly thrust of Raccoon Mountain. To the south, Lookout Mountain, on a clear day, surveyed the scenery of five states.

It was a beautiful, cloudless, early fall afternoon and bass fishing on Mullens Cove had been enjoyable, but contrary to predictions of the bait vendor at R & R—Bait & Tackle on Nickajack Lake, unsuccessful. The two brothers, on a break from their Hayters Gap, Virginia daily routine, had energy to burn.

"Okay, big brother, here's the wager. You get out here and walk up Mullens Creek to Ransom Hollow, then up the hollow to the top. Your back pack and the shotgun weigh about twenty pounds. I'll drive around the east side to Ritchie Hollow, park the truck south of Joe's cottage and hike up the north side of the hollow. The north fork to the top'll bring me out about a mile due east of where you should be. My pack's about thirty pounds, so no trail hiking either. Agreed?" Lee asked.

"Sounds good, Bro."

Lee continued, "When you're on top, start for the pond east of the jeep-trail road-crossing. Take off your pack if you want to, since I'll be lightening up for the stalk. Every sixty paces or so, stop and in an audible voice—no whispering mind you—say a word or a number in your recorder. For every one of your codes that I record in mine, before you spot me, I get twenty bucks—up to a hundred. If you spot me before I record five, you get a hundred from me."

1

"You still think you're that good?" John questioned his forty-one year old brother.

"John, we're the same height, build, hair, eyes and everyone says we've got the same Virginia hill-country accent. But you're three years older and twenty pounds fatter! Besides, I've stayed alive in some real tight places doing things a lot tougher'n this. I've still got a few tricks others've taught me, to pass on—if you get rid of that gut!"

"Don't you worry about my gut," John retorted. "I'll get rid of it after the six pack in my back pack!"

"Another thing, Bro, don't get startled and blast me with that buckshot loaded deer-slayer. Not that I couldn't duck 'em!" Lee quipped. "But, if you see anyone who looks like a ranger, you'd better lay it down and walk away. We can always find it later."

"Good idea, Lee. They wouldn't like a twelve-guage with buckshot in here this time of year. Bow season, and me with no license."

Though three years older, John was well aware of Lee's occupation over much of the last twenty years. In matters of the field, he was more than willing to listen, learn and defer to his kid brother. Never close as youths, later events had welded them in a tight, protective bond.

"Okay, let's sync our watches, check our voice recorders and radios," Lee advised.

The equipment checked, John climbed out of the truck, put on his back pack and walked to the driver's side. "How much time do you want, Lee?"

"Oh, gimme an hour. Let's say you start from here at five-thirty, it's about an equal distance to the top. This is the worst road I've ever seen! Last time I drove it I almost got sick!"

"You won't. I'll see you at the pond and you can give me your hundred!" declared John, with a laugh.

As Lee drove the twists, turns, dips, hills and obstacle course of the narrow road to Ritchie Hollow, his mind went back to other stalks. John had no chance. He wouldn't take his money and finally he'd be able to convince him just how much he could still learn. Even with his great skill and years of experience stalking game throughout the Smokies, John was still an amateur. Hunting wild game, with all their great protective assets, was nothing when compared with a life or death stalk of a trained professional killer; animals lacked logic.

Both familiar with the area, John would have been shocked if he knew Lee lay silent, some fifty yards down-wind as he climbed the last few yards toward the jeep trail. The trail, forming approximately a two mile westerly loop off the top ridge road, was still some two hundred and sixty feet below the westerly edge of the top. The steep part of his climb over, it was time for a cool beer. There was no rush, since all he had to do was spot his brother before he could record the five codes—no problem.

Time for a leak thought John. I'll just whip out my johnson and drain a brew at the same time. He had just finished both when the sound of the hated off-road toys of the suburbanites, carried on the northeast breeze, reached his ears. Forgetting Lee, but not the past, he moved slowly to the middle of the trail and waited. His mind was in turmoil and with hammering heart, he clicked to 'off' the deadly, semi-automatic shotgun's safety.

Three, four-wheel off-road vehicles, two side-by-side and one to the rear, pulled to a stop some twenty feet away. In the shaded light of the late afternoon, he knew the large one to his left would be their spokesman.

"Hey, man, what's the problem? You a warden?" asked the tall, well muscled young man.

"No problem. Just you pricks," John answered.

Lee remained frozen. He could hear voices, but with the idling engines, could not make out the words. From his position he wasn't able to tell if John was in the trail blocking them or not.

"Well then, just let us by and we'll be out of here," the young man politely requested.

"Where're ya from?"

"What's it to ya?" the rider demanded, his voice rising in pitch.

"Don't get smart, shithead. I asked a civil question!" John snapped back.

"Well, asshole, it's none of your goddamn business. This is state land and we've got a right to be here!" he angrily retorted.

"Maybe! But who the hell owned it before the state stole it? Do ya know that?" John yelled, his rage boiling.

"Listen you fat hillbilly, you aren't going to shoot all three of us. There're game wardens all over this forest. I'm a senior in law school and I know our rights. So get the hell out of our way!" he demanded.

"Here're yer rights you sonofabitch!" snarled John. His pent-up hatred exploding as the shotgun's blast reverberated through the hills. Fifteen, thirty-three caliber lead spheres of double-ought buckshot—traveling at a velocity of twelve-hundred feet per second—ripped through the young man's chest. The impact—obliterating his upper heart and shattering his spinal column—was the devastating equal of multiple simultaneous hits from a thirty-two caliber pistol.

The second blast, a blended roar on the heels of the first, slammed through his young wife's right breast destroying her heart and both lungs before she could even turn to her dying husband. Knocking her to the ground on her side, the buckshot left her twitching in the final throes of death.

The third blast caught her fifteen-year old kid brother in the shoulder as he spun out of his vehicle in an attempt to escape the horror. Running down hill he could hear the killer reloading, yet following close behind. Tripping, he landed on his back, only to look up into the muzzle of the shotgun aimed at his face.

"Don't kill me!" he begged, shaking in fear.

His quivering, terror-stricken plea for life went unheeded, cut short for him without sound or pain, as the top of his face and head was shredded into the soft, leaf-covered soil of Walden Ridge.

Knowing John was still in the high-pitched state of a killing frenzy, Lee waited—close, but behind a tree. John, on his knees continued to shake, his sobs slowly subsiding.

"John—John—John, it's me, Lee. Are you okay?" he softly asked.

"Yeah—I guess so," John replied, in a voice still rasping from the massive jolt of adrenalin.

"John, stay right here," Lee ordered, moving him slowly over to the tree. "Don't move. Stay absolutely frozen, no matter what happens—I'll handle things."

John nodded his head in silent obedience.

Lee shed his pack and placing all John's gear in his, removed his outer shirt, put on his gloves and raced to the hated all-terrain vehicles. Parking them several yards off the trail, but in a neat row side-by-side, they would tell any observer their owners had gone for an evening stroll. With little difficulty, he located and pocketed the four empty shell casings and their plastic wad columns.

Carefully he checked the carotid arteries of each, not that it mattered, and grabbing the big one with a skill born out of intensive training, baptized in the fire of southeast Asian combat, rolled the corpse onto his shoulder and carried it to the side of the boy. And with a pen knife, swiftly left his mark— old habits were hard to break. Quickly he made the round trip with the body of the young woman and marked to match her husband, they now lay together in the silence of the dead.

Successful in the hike down the escarpment, they had entered the truck when it hit Lee, "What'd you do with that beer can?" he asked.

"Oh shit! I must've thrown it in the brush when I heard 'em coming. Shit—shit—shit! What do we do now?" John asked. "My prints are all over it!"

"I don't know. Ever been arrested or printed that you can remember?"

"Not that I know of. Registered for the draft, but don't recall ever having been printed. No, not that I can remember."

"Well, we sure as hell aren't going back. Those kids are going to be missed soon, if not already. They'll have a tough time in the dark, but they'll have dogs in there looking for us in a hurry."

Heading south on I-27, after leaving the Signal Mountain loop of the Tennessee River, they picked up I-24 to I-75 and the three hour ride to the Abingdon exit from I-81, just north of Bristol, Tennessee. "John, when we get home," said Lee, breaking the silence, "everything we have with us except the radios—we didn't use 'em—goes in garbage sacks and the dumpster down at Brumley Bridge. Even the shotgun. Understand?"

"Yes."

"I mean everything. All fishing gear, boots, shoes, clothes—absolutely everything—and then in the morning we clean the truck inside and out. I don't want a speck of dust or mud to be traced to that area."

"I understand," John quietly agreed, as silence again became their sole companion.

12:30 A.M., Saturday
Hayters Gap, Virginia

"John, let's get the hell out of these hills. It'll just get worse and you, well both of us, are going to be in deep shit. I've always wanted to check out the Rockies. I've heard there's a lot to see and do in western Wyoming."

"I guess so, Lee. But do you want to know something?"

"What?"

"I hate to say this, but I don't feel too bad. And to be perfectly honest, it felt like I shot the bastards who killed Mom and Dad."

"John, I've killed and done far worse to so many for Washington— Nam, Rhodesia, Angola, Afghanistan—so maybe I'll just decide who the enemy is for awhile. Let's get the hell out of here. Go west young man, go west! There's something I've gotta tell ya. I was in the bank the other day, First Bank and Trust Company in Abingdon. You know, the one with the big white pillars. I was talking to the manager about our valley here. And you know that parcel down toward Brumley Gap?"

"Yeah?"

"It's been sold. And get this, the buyers are going to develop a damn camping area for weekend vacationers from Bristol!"

"*Déjà vu*," John whispered.

"Right."

"This is one of the most remote places in Virginia, it's not even on the new state map! What the hell—Mars?—the Moon? Hell, they'd even have off-road vehicles there!" John groaned.

"John, you can always get a job at any GM dealer in the country. My job at Highlands Community College is a 'come or go' deal. Hell, all I do is tutor French. The land money is still in Dominion Banks around the state. I'll let Colt know I'm out west, in case they want me to contact some dealers. We've got more money'n we'll ever need, and we can live off the land for a couple of years. Wyoming—Montana in the summer and then we can go down to New Mexico or Vegas in the winter. What the hell, you've always wanted to go out west and I've always wanted to visit the Green River area in Wyoming. It's where the old-time trappers had their big rendezvous. Now they hold one every year—sometime in July, I think.

"We can always make money off those dumb tourists. Put 'em to sleep and lift their wallets! It's so damn easy when you know the right buttons to push. No pain, no headache, just a momentary blackout. I'll teach you. The rich tourists got the Highlands and we'll get some of it back."

"Christ, Lee, I've never heard you talk this much! Gettin' your motor runnin'?"

"Yeah. Guess I miss the hunt—no adventure. Want to get back in shape—run the mountains, get my kick back. I felt good today, but not as good as when I was still a 'merc'. The specialty jobs I do now are more like a consulting physician. Maybe I'm addicted to adrenalin!" Lee exclaimed.

"With you, Bro," John cut in. "Both of us need ta get rid of a few pounds. Man was I ever pooped when I got to the top of Ransom Hollow."

"John, I've got an idea. You know how some stamp collectors are?"

"No?"

"Well, they specialize and that's what we could do. We won't touch anyone unless they're lawyers, but with those bastards, it'll be open season!"

"Did I tell you the big guy who was giving me the lip was in law school?"

"No shit! I heard him talking, but I was too far back to make out what he said."

"Yeah, he said he was a senior and he knew what his rights were. I said, 'here're your rights you sonofabitch' and nailed him with fifteen of Remington's finest in the middle of his chest. Picked him right outta his seat and the second nailed his chick. Didn't realize it was a girl until you told me. Then there was no turning back. Just winged the little guy and had ta run him down. The poor damn kid, I feel real bad about him. Shit, I forgot. Hell, it's all right here on my little ol' Dicktamite voice-activated recorder, if the blasts didn't bust it. Here, let's listen."

"Boy—wow!" exclaimed Lee, as the tape ended. "That sure escalated fast. You pushed each other's buttons in a hurry! I'd better burn that tape."

"I'm sorry about the last one, but one blast in the head ended it."

"It would," Lee replied, suddenly very quiet.

"What's the matter, Lee?"

"John, do you realize what day yesterday was?"

"Friday. Why?"

"It was October thirteenth. Twenty years ago to the day that it happened. Did I ever tell you I saw the photos of Mom and Dad?"

"Oh—Christ! How the hell'd you do that?"

"It was easy. Remember, I was still in peak condition and just went in. Heck, a jail's no problem for me. I checked the sheriff's file one night. Horrible! Oh God! Why? Mom . . .," he started to sob.

Absorbed in grief, they went back—back in time—twenty years back.

Some wounds never heal.

————————

How is it possible that good people are capable of doing evil acts? Some would claim it must be a bad childhood—blame, like a painted scarlet letter, a yoke around their parents' necks. While others might cast fault on genes or chromosomes or refined sugar—too much of this, too little of that.

Perhaps there is nothing so complex to ferret out. Perhaps, in an imperfect world, combinations in the Rubik Cube of life just work their accidental conspiracies to hex the minds of innocents. Perhaps there is *evil* lurking in the hearts of all.

Mackintosh Highlands

When you're in love with a beautiful woman,
        you watch your friends,
            everybody wants her . . .

Even Stevens

March, 1968
Frederick County, Virginia

Like a slumbering Rip Van Winkle, time and change had simply driven past the six-hundred and seventy acres of one of the most beautiful valleys in the vicinity of Winchester, Virginia. In addition to Bogue Creek, it had two multiple spring-fed streams and three crystal clear ponds; one created by a dam was, in reality, a small lake.

To all who knew its rugged yet serene terrain, it was a 'beautiful woman' and the wrong 'everybody' wanted her. The mostly wooded land was not financially productive and the tax base, while reasonable, gave it a method of evaluation of less than would normally be expected.

The large tract of land was, as it had been for many generations past, in the same family and was now owned by Mordecai Mackintosh along with his invalid wife Elizabeth, known to their intimate friends as 'Beta'.

"Lee, come to the study with me if you will. There're some things I'd like to talk about."

"Sure, Dad. I'm just glad to be home now. I know it's rough. Mom's health—God I love her—both of you," and with tears in the eyes of both, Lee hugged his father. He knew they might argue about Viet Nam, but love him and their Highlands, he did. To lose his mother and their Highlands would be devastating. "Dad, the truth. How much time does she have?"

"Son, her doctor said several years and you'll be home long before she goes, so don't worry about that. I know how much you love your mother. It just seems as though somehow John and I always did things together and you were a little closer to her. We both love each of you as much as humanly possible. You know that, don't you, son?"

For reasons Mordecai could never figure out, Lee occasionally seemed cold. John, three years older than his only sibling, enjoyed the hunt, while Lee, *too good* with his twenty-two, appeared to enjoy the kill. He had noticed a few instances of a mean streak toward small animals when Lee was younger. His example of kindness and an occasional comment didn't seem to take hold. There may have always existed a subtle closeness to John that Lee sensed and resented, even if only subconsciously.

"Of course, Dad. I think it's just that John's spent so much of his time in the Highlands and I've been gone a lot. What'd you want to talk about?" Lee asked.

"Well, nothing much, not about losing the Highlands."

Mordecai, now seventy years old, took his Springfield '03 down from above the fireplace mantle, running his hands over the smooth stock and carefully sliding his thumb along the side of the bayonet. It had been his constant companion when, as a twenty year old marine, in June of 1918, he'd taken a stroll through a very bloody, but long forgotten place called Belleau Wood.

"You're about the same age I was at Belleau Wood. But, I suppose your weapons are a lot different now, aren't they?" he asked, handing the rifle to Lee.

"Yes sir!" Both boys out of love, not duty, often replied to their father with a crisp 'yes sir'; at least whenever the requested task or adventure was something they wanted to do. I don't want to tell him what I've been taught, at least not the details, Lee thought.

"It's different now, Dad. I'm Special Forces and we go into the field in teams of three. The object is to not make noise, so we fight with our hands, knives, and cross bows," he explained, leaving out the deadly *garotte* and a few other bloody tricks.

"I know, son, but somehow it just doesn't seem right. It's kind of like if an outside army had come to help in the War of Northern Aggression, on either side. It was our dance, not England's or France's."

"Dad, let's not argue. You know we have to stop communism!" he exclaimed, a little tension rising in his voice.

"Maybe, but sometimes I wonder. Our boys over there dying to win a body count. I'm getting sick of watching the Generals, who always seem to be saying we're winning, but send more boys and equipment. Maybe this outside threat is a little like what Marx said about religion. If we didn't have it, we'd invent it. If we didn't have a threat, the military factories would close wouldn't they?"

"I don't know, Dad. I suppose it was easier in World War I and II, maybe even Korea. I haven't been there yet—maybe—I'll try to keep an open mind. Here's John. Let's change the subject and have our meeting with Mom like we planned," suggested Lee, as he handed the rifle back to his father.

"All right, Lee. A good idea. Just come back to us son. Keep your butt down and your powder dry!" he exclaimed, placing his rifle above the mantle, in it's place of honor beneath the gleaming *Claymore*, the treasured battle sword of the 'Mac an Toisich', and together they met John and headed for the large parlor.

Only fifty-eight years old, her slender body rendered more frail by bone cancer, but with eyes bright and sparkling, the ever cheerful Beta took off her audio-book earphones. Reaching out, she took the hand of her guardian angel Mordecai, who, leaning over, planted a warm, passionate kiss on her loving lips.

"What brings my handsome trio of macho males to this fair lady's bedside?" she asked.

"Oh, Beta, what a spark you have! Let's see if you can lighten up the clouded countenance of this sad group. You know why we're here. The decision has to be discussed. Do you feel up to this?" he asked.

"Certainly, love. I'm just happy you men deem it proper to include a mere Southern Belle," she replied demurely. "Say, have you called me Beta all these years because it's only the second brightest star in a constellation?"

"Of course not! And Southern Belle my arse! The boys should've seen you splitting wood, building the dam and downing sour mash in your youth!" he exclaimed.

"Hush, hush. Don't give away our secrets. Make 'em pay if they want our history, my dear!" she chided.

Each of the boys gave her a warm hug and pulled up the chairs for what they knew would be a long session.

The decision had been made by Beta and Mordecai to fight the condemnation proceedings, Virginia's taking of the beautiful Mackintosh Highlands. One evening together in the parlor, a few weeks before Lee came home from training at Ft. Campbell, Beta had asked, "Are you sure they'll really want to take our land?"

"Well, Beta, let's face it, I know the highway people. Harwood's worked his butt off as design engineer and he's paid his dues. He wants I-66 completed and I'd wager he'll get it. He's been chief of design long enough and my guess is he'll be the next commissioner."

"What affect will that new environmental protection law have, if it's passed?" Beta asked.

"I don't know for sure, honey. Those groups fighting sixty-six will undoubtedly try and use it, but John's tough. It'll be the main link from the District of Columbia out to the Shenandoah Valley."

"But why do the parks people want our land so badly?"

"Can you imagine a better place? The people in the suburbs want to play in the hills and they're the ones with the money and toys. With the growing off-road motorcycle craze, the people need hills to roam around in. My thirty-five years with transportation doesn't influence the people in parks, maybe just the opposite. Besides, I'm retired over five years now and when you're out to pasture, you've got no more power!

"The fact this property has been in the family for six generations won't count for anything according to our lawyer. The offer's not bad, it's just I simply can't give up without a fight. It's not right to take private land like this for parks, just because you've kept it nice and made it into an ideal site. Not when other people are willing to sell land that could be developed like ours."

"Mordecai, I know you want to fight and I'll support you of course. I can't imagine a stubborn Scot ever giving up land without a fight." And so they embraced and the decision was made; it had been made in their genes. There was nothing they could do or that they wanted to do, other than fight.

Now it was up to Mordecai to explain. Both knew the boys would agree, but like their ancestors before, they also knew the verbal history would help the boys to understand.

John rose and started for the study. "Yes, John, please bring it," said his father. John continued and carefully lifting the *Claymore,* pondered as always, if only it could speak. Returning to the parlor, John carefully handed the revered weapon to his father. The *Great Sword* of the Highlanders and in more recent times, namesake of an even deadlier device, one that knew neither friend or foe nor adult or child. It was a sword swung in circles with both hands as the Highland Scots rushed their enemies.

"I know you boys have heard much of this before, mostly in one ear and out the other. But some day, so you can pass it on to your children, if you ever have kids and make me a grandpa," he admonished them both, "I wish you'd write this down, Lee. Then we'll have a record of this meeting. In ancient times clan poets, the *Bardi,* memorized clan history using poetry. Written records were forbidden, but we won't worry about that!"

"Sure, Dad," replied Lee, knowing one of his special talents was an uncanny ability to quickly learn other languages, and with his excellent skill of shorthand, he could both listen with understanding and record at the same time.

"First," said Mordecai, settling into his favorite easy chair, moved from his study into the parlor to be near Beta, "your mother and I've decided to fight. In spite of local support, we're not likely to win. I'm sure the lawyers I'm going to send you to will be confident of winning. But times are changing. Power is no longer in these hills or in the country anywhere. Nor is it even in the cities. It's in the suburbs where the people with money live. They work in the cities and want to play in the country. They want these Highlands, but we don't want to give up without a fight."

Mordecai stood and gripping the mighty *Claymore* in both hands, felt its power surge through his still strong, though slowly weakening muscles. Tears welled in his eyes as the thrill of the memories of past days of glory raced through his brain and filled his soul; Culloden—1746; Battle of Worcester—1651 and back, even to the great and horribly bloody Battle of Harlaw. It was there, in 1411, that Clan Mackintosh, with support from their adjacent neighbors, the powerful Clan MacBean and other great clans of the mighty Clan Chattan Confederation, fought the Red Comyn.

"From before the time of the Red Comyn, we've always fought, either against invaders of our lands or in recent times, for our country in other places."

"They had commies back then?" laughingly interjected a playful John, to the chagrin of his sometimes over serious father.

"I was wondering about that too, Dad!" added Lee, grinning from ear to ear.

"Well of course not!" the patriarch of the family exclaimed. "They were a clan that can be traced back to William de Comyn, Chancellor of Scotland in the twelfth century. His son John, was called the Red Comyn and he probably had a lot of red hair and beard. A very powerful family of Badenoch. The fighting was over various land disputes and Comyn opposition to Robert the Bruce, who became King of the Scots, with Confederation support. The facts, like so much of the past, have been lost in the mists of history. Truth shrouded in the fog of literary inventions. We won however! My sons, there are many, many books in my study ye can read, would ye want," he spoke, in the southern accented Gaelic that he occasionally went to, "but I'll give ye a bit of our past.

"I know from the word of me ancestors that this sword was taken from my great-grandfather's grandfather, whose name was Malachi Mackintosh. He fought for Lady Mackintosh at the *Rout of Moy*, but it was at the Battle of Culloden where he was captured. Legend has it, that for some unknown reason he saved the life of an English officer. The officer arranged to have Malachi's sword returned to him by the captain of the prisoner ship that brought him to Old Fort Monroe, on the north shore of Hampton Roads. From there, he came here and while obviously hostile to the English, was able to get this grant. Although the Old Tory, Lord Fairfax, blocked a substantial portion of his request.

"As you know, your mother on her mother's father's side, was a MacBean. Her Bean paternal ancestor, though a staunch Presbyterian, fought against the British invader and was captured by Cromwell's forces at the Battle of Dunbar, in 1650. He was brought to New England as a prisoner of war and some of his descendants migrated to this area. We met and were married forty-two years ago."

"Why don't you tell 'em about Cousin Gillis, honey!" Beta exclaimed with a grin, knowing how sick he was of hearing about Cousin Gillis.

"Oh my, Gillis! Gillis! Gillis!—I should've named one of you Gillis! Oh well, all right. At the Battle of Culloden in 1746, Gillis MacBean became a bit of a hero. The word is he was huge—many of the Beans are. Anyway, Gillis was a scourge to the English. Swinging the mighty *Claymore* in his huge right hand, usually a two hand sword, and wielding his great Targe on his left arm, he cut down at least fourteen of the Hanoverian forces. They finally rode him down with their horses and left him for dead. But he was able to crawl off the field to an old shed, where he died the next day."

"What's a Targe, Dad?" Lee asked.

"I wish I had one to go with the sword, but I don't. It's a round shield, and at six-foot eight inches, I imagine Bean's shield was big. They're round and have an iron disc in the center, with a sharp, tapered steel point coming out of the disc that could kill an enemy. I've a picture of one on the Crest Badge of the MacBeans. Remind me and I'll get it out later and show you.

"After Culloden, the English went through the Highlands and killed all the clansmen they could find. I've read they even killed the women and children, and if true, it was genocide. In 1746 they banned the wearing of all Highland dress. About forty years later the law was repealed and the trews, doublet and hose, and the Tartan kilt could again be worn. The Gordon Highlanders took the heights of Dargai in 1897, blowing the pipes and wearing the kilts!" he exclaimed.

"Anyway, your ancestors were always willing to fight for what they believed in. Malachi's son Mordecai, who I was named after, fought with the Virginians under Washington in the War for Independence and then fought the British again in 1812, when they burned Washington. My father Jeremiah, fought for Lee in the War of Northern Aggression, while only a teenager.

"As you can tell from his letters, my grandfather was opposed to Virginia's secession and opposed to the war. When the ordinance was passed in 1861, my dad volunteered to go and fight. Fathers and sons don't always agree on wars!" he added, smiling at Lee. "They had a couple of slaves who were more like members of the family. In the hills, slave owning was very limited— not like the plantation system. Jeremiah fought under Beauregard down at Manassas, but you've lived and breathed that history— nothing more to be said. He made it or we wouldn't be here! I was born in '98 when your Gramp was fifty-four.

"Good lord, boys. We've been around these hills a long time. It was your half-Creek Indian cousin, Chief William Mackintosh, who helped Governor Troup of Georgia get nearly five million acres of Creek Indian land down on the Chattahoochee in 1825. He was killed that spring by some Creeks who'd opposed the Treaty of Indian Springs.

"You know, taking land by force or with beads is nothing new in our history. Maybe we reap what we sow! When the Cnerokees were driven out of northern Georgia to Oklahoma in 1838, almost four thousand of the eleven thousand or so that started, died on the way. It isn't a pretty page in our history, especially since most of them were peaceful Christian farmers, just in the way of the whites!

"Boys, we can't stop the invasion of the tourists with their mechanical toys. They'll swarm over these hills like flies, leaving a trail of plastic, beer cans and other debris I'll not mention in front of your mother."

"You mean condoms!" said Beta, laughing at his embarrassment.

"Beta, don't you talk about things like that," he scolded. "Anyway, I can't stand the hassle myself. Lee, you're going to Langley for a special class and then to Viet Nam, right?" he asked.

"That's an affirmative. I'll be there about six weeks, back here for two and then fly to Nam for field duty."

"Well, boys, your mother and I want to fight and maybe, just maybe, given the history of the Hooper Furnace, we might win. But it's doubtful. Our lawyer prepared a power-of-attorney to give John complete authority to hire Hannibal and Draco of Washington, DC, to represent us.

"John, you can negotiate with 'em to pay their fees out of the proceeds of the taking,if we lose. The State has offered us three-hundred thousand now and the money'll be paid over to us if it's determined they get our land. If we win, we can borrow on a long-term note, up to one hundred and twenty thousand from Dale, at Commercial Bank in Winchester. This should be enough to pay the lawyers and get the place ready for a bed-and-breakfast setup. We've already done the paper work and it's covered in the power-of-attorney. Also, we have the ten-thousand dollar retainer the lawyers want when you meet with 'em. If you can, set up an appointment in D.C. when you're going to take Lee to Langley. It's always easy to get an appointment with lawyers when they know you're bringing in a ten-thousand retainer!" laughed Mordecai.

"Who are these lawyers, Dad?" Lee asked. "They any good, or just big and expensive?"

"Who knows," Mordecai sighed. "They always think they're good! They were recommended. It's not usual to take private property for recreational use. Similar cases have been upheld in other states, but it's never been done here that our lawyer knows about. Public issues get expedited through the courts, and we should know soon, one way or the other, if we lose the Highlands. If we lose, they get the land immediately, though sometimes there's some leeway. Then a local jury trial is set to determine the value of our land."

Located on the easterly edge of the Appalachians, some twelve miles west of Winchester, it would be approximately a one and one-half hour drive, via Interstate 66, (if the partially constructed super highway was ever completed), from the crowded urban sprawl of the District of Columbia. Already a park-like valley—an ideal parcel to form yet another recreational facility for the crowded urbanites.

Privately known as Mackintosh Highlands and to the public as the Hooper

Furnace Farm, she would surrender her private virtue to the all powerful suitor *the public good,* to be hereafter known as Sleepy Hollow.

Constitution
of the
United States of America
Amendment V

No person shall . . . be deprived of property without due process of law; nor shall private property be taken for public use without just compensation . . ..

Condemnation Proceedings
Eminent Domain

The power to take private property for public use.

Black's Law Dictionary.

Due Process of Law

The established legal procedures whereby someone gives up something they do not want to give up to someone who wants what they do not have. Usually at a great cost to both sides in attorney fees and conducted under the guidance of a judge.

Wise Sage

Determination of Necessity

A trial before a judge, without a jury, who decides whether or not the State has a legally valid reason to take private property.

Damage Trial

The owners' opportunity to have a jury of their peers decide what the property being taken is worth.

It was the family's plan to develop the spacious, brick family home—built for an earlier time of large and extended families, together with household 'help'—into a bed-and-breakfast. The grounds, carefully maintained by John—

a planned rural retreat—to provide sufficient income to supplement the couple's meager social security and Mordecai's state pension.

Dropping Lee off at Central Intelligence Agency headquarters in Langley, Virginia, John headed for the District of Columbia.

The saga of the transfer of a substantial portion of the value of their property to the pockets of the corporate law firm began when John, holding a Power of Attorney from his father and invalid mother, walked through the heavy plate-glass doors of Hannibal and Draco, the Washington, D.C. based mega-firm, on the advice of a friend of a friend.

The huge firm had offices located in several major market areas around the country and like a fast-food franchise, maintained numerous branch offices in cities where courts and their judges were located. It never hurt to be in a position to make substantial contributions to the judicial campaigns of those lawyers who wanted the security of a steady income, long vacations, extensive medical plans, a generous retirement program, and power.

"Well, Mr. Mackintosh, to recap our conference and agreement. First, my co-counsel, Beth Tripp, will work with me on the case only when necessary. Second, we'll contest the 'taking' of your parents' land, that's the Determination of Necessity, through the Virginia courts, but not to the United States Supreme Court. Third, fees for these proceedings and preparation will be billed at $100.00 per hour office time and $140.00 per hour for out-of-office time for each attorney hour. Fees to be secured by a first mortgage and a lien on the proceeds. Fourth, I sincerely hope we don't, but if we lose on the necessity issue, the $300,000.00 payment from the State is to be used to bring all fees and costs current. Fifth, the damage issue, or value of the land and buildings, will be a jury trial and handled by our firm on a percentage-contingency basis. As we explained, to cover a contested trial that might result in a minimum verdict of the State's offer of $300,000.00, we will prepare and go through this trial on a one-third contingency basis of any money received over $240,000.00."

"Is that standard?" John asked.

"Yes," Henry Simpson, one of Draco's many junior partners, replied. "Usually attorneys take one-third of everything over four-fifths of the offer. This means we'd have a guaranteed minimum fee of $20,000.00 for handling the damage trial," he added.

"I guess we've gotta trust someone."

"You can trust us. We'll do the best we can," Simpson added, winking at his good-looking co-counsel.

The best for who, thought John. But not having much choice in the matter—those were the terms of two other firms he'd called on his own—he signed the detailed agreement and shaking their hands, left for the Highlands.

At frequent coffee breaks, the topic usually discussed by the two attorneys handling the case consisted of parties they were certain to have after the new state park was built. These coffee breaks, of course, would be billed as a 'conference with co-counsel re: value' at the hourly rate of $100.00 per lawyer.

The attorneys, both in their late twenties and each married to others, would, on a pleasant spring evening, after normal billing hours ended, spend four hours viewing the premises. Twice paying particular, lingering attention to secluded and conveniently placed fallen logs. Since this was time out of the office, it would be billed at the hourly rate of $140.00 for each and result in an entry on the final total billing hours as—two attorneys, view of premises—4 hours——$1,120.00. The law firm's policy, as did many large firms, required each attorney to submit time-billings for work on files, totalling at least sixty hours per week.

Home from the CIA *special* school, Lee, nothing more than a silent spirit, practiced his field skills mastered at Fort Campbell. He followed, watching in cold, silent fury the laughing, fornicating coupling of the two city lawyers, there to view the premises. They did not seem too concerned about the property; touching each other, but not touching the land they were supposed to preserve for his parents.

Since the least, under the law, the damage-jury could return as their verdict was the state appraised value, it was an absolute feeding frenzy for the sharks in the money filled pool. A hint from the State condemnation attorney, over cocktails in a Georgetown lawyer-bar, assured the Mackintoshs' attorneys that at the courthouse steps, another twenty percent would be a reasonable settlement, was well received. The 'Mackintosh feast' was a foregone conclusion. Besides, wouldn't the old couple's final share be sufficient to provide a cubicle in a state-sponsored low-income, old-age, death-house, known as Serenity Retreat, Incorporated?

The determination-of-necessity lost, it was easy to convince John, after the failed appeal, that the final offer should be accepted. All possible billing, except the paltry time of trial, had been entered and a trial might not gain the known twenty percent. One third of everything over $240,000.00, together with the horrendous fees incurred on the determination-of-necessity proceedings would be enough, even for these rapacious attorneys.

3:45 P.M.
Monday, October 13, 1969
Mackintosh Highlands

The check, after deductions to cover the twenty-seven page billing on the determination-of-necessity and the lawyers' percentage of the final settlement, arrived three days before the scheduled bulldozer. The old family estate would be too expensive to be cared for by state workers.

Mordecai, home from meeting with Beta's doctor, sat and pondered what he'd learned. At most Beta had a few months of excruciating pain, and they had to be out of the house within the week. Their Highlands to be known as Sleepy Hollow, a park misnamed; an off-road vehicle mecca for the power hungry suburbanites. The thought destroyed him. Lee was in the field and out of contact.

Slowly he opened the registered letter from the law firm. He assumed it was the long overdue check and a billing explaining all their *work*; that they lacked the courage to deliver and discuss it in person, was apparent. Shock—disgust and shock at their obviously fraudulent charges—filled his soul. The now necessary rest-home for Beta's final days, would quickly take the remainder. There would be nothing left for John and Lee, with only empty loneliness and near poverty for himself. With no loving, laughing Beta and no little grandchildren, there was simply no point.

Walking into his study, he first loaded his old double-barreled twelve-gauge shotgun and bowing his head, said a long prayer. Finally he rose and reaching up, rubbed his hands along the edge of the gleaming *Claymore*, leaving a trail of blood dripping across the Springfield he had willingly used to fight for his country. He turned and slowly entered the quiet parlor. Walking across the room and bending over as the tears poured, pressed his lips to his only treasure; his sleeping and heavily sedated, beloved wife, Beta. His heart breaking, *the song* was felt in his soul; *'O'flower of Scotland, when will we see your like again . . . the hills are bare now, and autumn leaves lie thick and still, o'er land that is lost now, that was so dearly held . . . but we can still rise now . . . and be together again. O'flower of Scotland . . .'.*

Breathless, John found strength to scream in agony at the sight of the body of his bed-ridden mother, instantly after finding his kindly old father. Heads devastated by the twelve-gauge shotgun blasts, that moments before had crashed, two hundred yards up the valley to where he, out of sheer habit, had still been working.

The horror of the scene in the great parlor would be etched forever in his brain. Slowly John returned to the dining room, to find on the table the meager check for his parents' share of their valley. Mackintosh Highlands existed no more.

Rage. His rage simmered deep and insidious—John changed—hate took over and John, twisted by forces beyond his control, became that which he had never been. Kindness became hostility—warmth became coldness—a smile was rarely to be seen. The feeling of total helplessness seeped into every pore as slowly, a good person became a hateful person. A seething loathing of lawyers festered in his soul. And, like the rising pressure in a riverboat boiler, one day it would explode.

The closed-casket funeral brought out a large percentage of Franklin County. Just a tragedy in the hills, it was not mentioned in the Washington Post. There were no lawyers from Hannibal & Draco, PC.; the pathetic sprig of flowers—a business expense.

The long, powerful, one-arm hydraulic steel claw of the red and white, state-of-the-art, Link-Belt Speeder LS-5000 back-hoe, like some giant prehistoric monster, was devouring the family's lovely residence as the funeral procession passed on its way to the couple's final resting place in the old family cemetery. The operator—not seeing the procession, nor hearing the sad yet powerful dirge of *Mackintosh's Lament,* played by eight pipers and four drummers of the Mackintosh-MacBean, Tartan clad Scottish Band—continued the feast.

An urban recreation park. Progress.

———

Absorbed in the past, Lee's mind took him back to a time not yet forgotten.

3:00 A.M., October 16, 1969
A remote valley . . .
South Viet Nam

Night in another venue. While his parents were being buried on the opposite side of the world, the home tragedy unknown, Lee practiced his skill. The *garotte* of the sentry was quick, indefensible and silent. The deadly wire pocketed, he unsheathed his knife. The blended steel blade - tempered—hardened—honed to a hair-splitting edge at the ready, he stealthily crept forward. The modern tool—like its ancient, knapped flint ancestor, thirsting again to commence its barbaric chore. Like a shadow he glided from sleeping VC to sleeping VC, leaving behind only a trail of gurgling Vietcong blood, so the world, he was sure, would be saved from communism.

A hero's welcome to be received, at least in Frederick County and hopefully at Mackintosh Highlands. He knew without doubt he would make it out and back to his mother and father; he was a survivor.

Two more weeks of hell would pass until in the early morning fog, he heard the thump-thump-thump of hope. "Run you bastard, run!" a voice screamed. Racing between hostile fire he leaped, grabbing the rising skid with his good right arm, just as the tail boom swung away and was pulled into the arms of rescue. "Pilot hit in leg—losing control," a voice yelled in his ear. They knew what he and the others had been through and rescued all they could; most they couldn't.

November 1, 1969
Camranh Bay

Inside he screamed, his face was stone, but his Special Forces comrades, who had seen just about everything, froze. His eyes conveyed pure hate, not the cold acceptance of his duty as an IT; this was different. Lee rose out of the folding camp chair and leaving the papers for all to see, walked slowly out the door and toward the bay.

"Jesus!" exclaimed the Captain. "They buried Socket's parents while he was in the field. Shit here's a copy of an attorney statement and it's a fuckin' book! We'd better watch the poor bastard."

"Watch him, my ass. For Christ's sake, he can do whatever the fuck he wants. There'd be no fuckin' way to stop him except to shoot him. He could kill himself or you before you could sneeze, if he wanted to. He's got a brother back home, so let's see if we can get him the fuck out of here. Shit, he only went in on an intelligence mission and should've been out. He could've at least flown home for the funeral, but instead the poor bastard got cut off by the storm and spent three fuckin' weeks in hell." Lieutenant Stevens declared.

"John's letter says for Lee to pick up mail being held in Abingdon, Virginia," said Captain Storms. "Maybe we can help the poor bastard. Right now he's ready to waste somebody!"

October 14, 1989
Hayters Gap

John, sobbing over the relived past, slowly quieted.

"John, I never told you about those two lawyers that handled Mom and Dad's case, did I?"

"We talked about the billing—should I say stealing and then about the accident. What about 'em?"

"It was right after that school I went to over at Langley . . ."

"You've never told me about that, that's for sure! Why not?" interrupted John.

"It's over now—no need. Back to those two scumbag lawyers. I'll never forget that day. What a sight! It was the day they *came*—no pun intended—to look over the Highlands. It was just before I left for Nam and I'd gone for a hike around the Highlands—afraid it might be my last chance—wearing my camouflage gear. Kind of practicing for field duty, when I heard 'em laughing and snuck up on 'em. The girl had on hiking shoes, knee socks and a pleated skirt, which I thought was a bit odd. But then I realized she was dressed for the sport!

"When his fingers weren't in her, his tongue or his dick was! They were unconscious of everything but each other. Got so close I could've counted her curly hairs! Was downwind and could even smell her. It was the horniest thing I'd ever seen. Was younger then and must've jerked off three or four times! She was sure built nice. Wanted to jump into the action, but kept my distance. Part of our training was to stay put—even if your best friend was being tortured—unless, of course, you could help without compromising your mission."

"That must've been somethin' to see. I'm getting a diamond-cutter just hearin' you describe it, Lee!"

"You've read Wambaugh, too?"

"Yeah, about the hard-on, blue-veiner and the diamond-cutter. Quite a way to describe 'em!"

"John, I met an old First-Sergeant in Nam who said he'd rather work it in soft, let it get hard and listen to their ribs crack!" Lee laughed, as John broke up laughing. Lee continued when the laughter, a welcome relief from their grief-saturated memories of the past tragedy, ended. "You know, that little romp around the Highlands by those two scumbags cost Mom and Dad over a thousand dollars as I recall."

"Boy, it's too bad you couldn't 've gotten to 'em before they were killed in that car crash."

"John, I guess after today—yesterday afternoon, I mean—well, didn't you think it a little strange the way their car went off the road and they were burned so bad they had to be identified from dental records, and just after I got home from Nam?"

"No. I just thought it was poetic justice. Don't tell me?"

"Yeah—you got it. It was poetic all right. Classic revenge. Just like Poe's, *The Cask of Amontillado.* I told 'em who I was, what I was going to do, and why I'd never get caught. I'd followed 'em to the motel. They were still in such heat for each other, the old forbidden fruit, they never heard me come into the room. Showed each of 'em what I'd been taught at Langley while they were raping our parents' assets. Before I started my *professional* detail work, I gave both of 'em a taste of what raping ass-sets was all about! I was able to do everything just right, and they each let go in time to set up the car. I made sure they were still breathing."

"Jesus! I don't think I want the details," John sighed.

"You don't," whispered Lee. "I told 'em their last party was a gift from both of us for what they'd done to Mom and Dad. It was something I'd been conditioned for. You couldn't 've watched."

"I suppose you're right," John replied. "Lee, your idea of going West is good. Let's get things wrapped up over the next few weeks. Set up the accounts so we can draw on 'em and head out. We could spend Christmas in

San Diego or someplace warm and try to put these memories to rest. Even the hills around here are a constant reminder. What do you say?"

"It's all right with me and the sooner the better. Since I'm not teaching that course in military history this year, we could leave any time. But, let's not have it look like we're running. We'll talk up the new park with the police chief—let him know about our contacts—where we're headed."

"Good idea. Lee, I'm crashing. I'm exhausted."

"Can sure understand, Bro. You know, I think I'll just clean up a lot of this gear. That may be better'n trashing it, which might look suspicious. The shotgun won't have to go, since I got all four shells and the wad columns. There's no way to trace buckshot, without the liners. See ya in the morning."

Lee worked as a professional; there would simply be no evidence. Only a beer can that might be explained, if ever connected, and marks that couldn't. Oh well, shouldn't have haves, like the past twenty years, were down river.

He worked, slow and methodical, his mind scrolling over the last twenty years. So long ago and yet, just yesterday. Where's it all gone? Why so fast? Why haven't I ever told John how it happened?

Well, he sighed out loud, maybe it just brought out the pictures of Mom and Dad too vividly. Those and the photos my brain took. If I tell John— maybe when we're out west—I can put *Phoenix* back in the ashes. Nobody should be conditioned to do such things—not to children—not to children— even if they're old enough to set traps and carry ammo.

Maybe I haven't told him because I really am afraid of Orlov. Christ the son-of-a-bitch was fast! How he got away from me in Afghanistan blows my mind. Oh well, I promised her—I know she could hear me—that I'd get them and him. Maybe she'll forgive me—vengeance is mine sayeth the Lord— one of her favorite verses. Oh well, two down, one to go. If only there was some way to get in—he'll never come out of Russia again, at least it's not likely.

My un-magnificent obsession! Maybe we can go to Taos and look up the old man. He may have a little more information on the bastard. Orlov— Chuikov—whatever. It's just not fair any one person can be that smart and that goddamn good. And so tall and so goddamn good looking to boot. I'll say this for him, the bastard does have class!

Shit, if old Marshall Vasili Chuikov acknowledged him before he croaked, the son-of-a-bitch'll have the whole goddamn Red Army covering for him along with every goddamn man, woman and child from Poland to the Pacific, as well as the KGB!

I don't care if the bastard did smoke 'em at Novosibirsk. He can take his damn *summa cum laude* and his damn *avtomat Kalashnikov* AKD-74 5.45 millimeter folding stock and cram 'em up his ass; silencer, banana clip and all. Would sure like to find the son-of-a-bitch some day. I'll cut his goddamn nuts off—at least I'd try.

Too wound up to sleep, Lee walked over to their kitchen file cabinet and pulled out a map. Spreading it on the plank table, his eyes scanned western Wyoming. Slowly he drew his index finger along the route of the Oregon Trail. Independence Rock, west along the Sweetwater River, Split Rock Mountain, beacon to the western travelers, trail of the Pony Express—'go west young man, go west', he thought with a deep sigh. He continued on—South Pass and north to Pinedale—just west of the continental divide and site of the Green River Rendezvous. New territory—Vegas in winter, Bridger Forest in the summer—a new hunting ground. Well, I may as well turn in, it's been a long day, he sighed, and folding the map, headed for the sack.

Things are just going to get worse, thought Murphy. I'd better keep these men on my 'watch' list.

2

Sweetwater

Monday—October 1, 1990
Split Rock Mountain
Sweetwater River Valley, Wyoming

The warm fall breeze, too gentle to disturb the absolute quiet of the valley, brushed softly across their cheeks. Turning to each other, their fingertips touched, the silence broken only by the sparkle in her pale blue eyes. For a short while, the world went away.

The huge pile of rocks, some fifty yards northeast of the reststop, with its hidden trails and caverns, provided a private escape. "Gosh, Trish, that was something! I'll bet we're not the first couple to take advantage of those rocks on a warm fall afternoon."

"I don't suppose anyone could see us from the highway. At least they wouldn't get pictures from a moving car! I imagine we weren't the first."

"I think we just invented a new cocktail. You remind me of a demure Southern Belle, with a lot of kick, and you turned this Scotsman into butter! We can try it out tonight. Southern Comfort and some butterscotch schnapps. We'll call it 'rapture on the rocks'!" exclaimed Will, with a laugh. "You know, it's kind of eerie standing here at this nice, safe, highway rest stop looking out over this valley. The Pony Express route, Butch Cassidy—all that western lore. One of the largest mass migrations in history, at least in our country."

"Will, they could see Split-Rock if they were going out West or coming back to the East for days. We'll hop in the van and be in Fort Washakie in an hour! It's hard to imagine travelling by wagon train."

"It's hard to imagine life in those days, period! No running water, no television! I brought copies of letters one of my great-great-grandfathers wrote and one from his nephew, with me. They went through South Pass on their way to the gold rush in 1852. I wanted to go to some of the places they saw, but we're not going to have time."

"Was he a Dean?"

"No, Trish. His name was Enos Wheeler and he was my maternal grandmother's paternal grandfather. His son, George Wheeler, was just a little tyke when his dad left, about my grandson's age. Isn't he something?"

"He sure is a little busybody—just like his dad and his dad!"

"Who, me? At least he's got his mother's curly red hair. And while we're speaking of genes, you know, of my sixteen great-great grandparents, Enos is the only one I have letters from. Probably the rest didn't go anywhere! Let's get in the van and start for Fort Washakie. This would be a good place to read 'em."

"Okay."

"Here, they're short—I highlighted the important parts. They're like a voice from the past. The first three are to his wife Mary, and the last to her, is from his nephew. The style and spelling are strange, but they tell the story better'n any movie—the nitty-gritty."

Trish read, while Will drove on.

Letter #1:

St Joseph. April the 23
1852

My dear wife.

I now have time and opportunity to inform you of my health. which is good. I left Galena on the 10day of April on board the good ship Doctor Franklin bound to St Louis. Landed safe at St Louis on Monday the 12th of April after a run of 2 days ...

We had a good time on the boat with a jovel lot of passengers. Had a race with another boat called the Danube. we run by her ... passed several flourishing towns. St Louis is a large town with a good deal of business. There is a good deal of emigration this spring from the South. A steamboat blew up at St Louis a few days before I arrived. Killed one hundred and 75 passengers and officers and crew.

We will now fancy ourselves at St Louis. The spring is late. fruit trees are in bloom. all nature looks green the 13 day of April. We now leave St Louis. go on up the Missouri river on board the good ship Sarznack bound for St Joseph. We now have some 3 hundred passengers aboard. We find her to be a miserable old boat with a hard Captain and crew. They have a good deal of trouble with the passengers. however we come along up to Lexington and found a steamboat there blown up that killed lots of passengers. however I did not learn how many there were. all Mormon passengers ...

April 27. 1852

Jesse and Marvin did arrive the 26. They are well. Had a very hilly bad muddy route from Galena to St Joseph but they have done well by the team ...

We are now in a great hurry as there are some cases of small pox and colera at St Joseph ...

I should like to see you very much and the children. I feel anxious to see them. I know they have a good mother and that is a consolation to me (you must excuse poor spelling). I am tired of doing nothing. I want to be on the road.

Yours with respect.

Letter # 2

May the 26, 1852

My dear wife,

I will now tell you how we prosper on our journey. We left St Joseph May the 4 and now 22 days travel from civilization. Still we are not alone. We are amongst the thousands of others, some better and some not as well off as ourselves . . .

One man has his wife and family along. We have passed some Indian toll bridges. They have some bridges across small streams from 1 to 2 rods wide and claim from 2 to 4 shillings toll. Some of the emigrants have had trouble with the Indians. One company, rather than pay the toll of 4 shillings went to work to build a bridge to cross on, whilst at work the Indians shot amongst them, killed two of the men and wounded others. The Emigrants run off and the Indians plundered their wagons and made their escape. The emigrants went to fort Kearney and entered their complaint to the soldiers and the soldiers went to the chief of the tribe and told him to give up the Indians that committed the act or they would kill the whole tribe. We have not learned what they did.

From St Joseph to fort Kearney 294 miles, from Kearney to Laramie 337 miles. We passed Fort Kearney the 18day of May and all is well. We have had no trouble with the Indians or anything else. We keep watch ever night . . .

The next we come to is Scott's Bluff. It is so called on account of a man by the name of Scott being killed there. Those bluffs have the appearance of some city or fortification at a distance. We have now passed all these wonders. I have not much more to write about. I should like to hear from you and the children, and kiss little Charlie too. We travel hundreds of miles and see nothing . . .

Letter #3:

My dear wife,

We are now camped on the West side of the Green River and calculated to lay up for the day, and I now take this opportunity, my dear wife, to inform you of my health. It is good . . .

We left Fort Laramie on June the 1st and traveled at the rate of 25 miles a day through the most miserable, barren looking country I ever saw. The road, however, is good the country is worth nothing, only for a road to California. We have seen plenty of bad water, alkali and saleratus. We passed independence rock the 10th of June. I was on top of it. It is 125 rods long and 125 feet high. The mountains rocky ridge along the Sweet Water runs for 30 to 40 miles. The next we come to is Devils Gate, a gap in the rock which the Sweet Water passes. The passage through the gap is about fifty rods and the perpendicular walls on each side are about ten feet apart and 400 feet high. We are now in sight of Wind river range laying off to the right, covered with ever-lasting snow . . .

We have crossed the summit of the Rocky mountains and have struck the waters that flow into the Pacific. The altitude of the pass is 7000 feet above the sea . . .

I would like to be with you a little while and see the children to tell them that their Pa will be home by and by and bring them gold, you know, to please them, but you can't tell them when nor I either. I have no more to write now. I will finish this letter at Salt Lake so good by.

June the 27. 1852

We have arrived at Salt Lake and in good health and find the city much larger than we expected and the people much more friendly. It is a healthy place and is watered with mountain streams in every street. Salt Lake city contains 1440 lots of 1 1/4 acres each, laid out in blocks with streets 8 rods wide and it contains about 3 square miles or something less than 2000 acres of land. The buildings are generally adobe or sun dried brick. The population of the city is between 5 and 6 thousand . . .

I for one feel just as well as ever I did in any country, but the Mormons tell us that we will have trouble enough beyond here, but we got in company with enough now to slay all the Indians that care to call on us. We have guns and revolvers enough to shoot 200 balls without loading in our train and we think we are safe but can't tell what may come. We have been here since the 24th and will leave the 28th, on Monday.

I have been to the bath house yesterday and had a good wash. The water was luke warm right from the spring and is mineral water.

Now I have not much more to write but would tell you to be careful of the children. I would like to see you and them and all our friends, so good by all as you can't expect to hear from me very soon again as it is 800 miles from this point through . . .

Yours with respect.

A letter from Marvin Wheeler.

April the 24th 1853

I now take this opportunity to write a few lines to you. I am well and enjoying myself as well as could be expected. I hope that these few lines will find you the same.

I received your letter April the 5th. You said that you wanted me to write to you if Enos and Jesse said anything about dying. Jesse didn't say anything about dying nor about his burial. I burried him the best I could. I had a grave dug about five feet deep and wrapped him up in his blanket and a buffalo robe and then filled the grave pretty much full of brush and then trod on the dirt. I did that so the wolves couldn't dig him up.

I talked with Enos about dying about two days before he did and he said that he would get well. I couldn't make him believe any other way. He wanted me to drive along until we got to the Mormon station and there we would lay up. I drove along until the night before he died. I had Herman Coon talk with him the night that he died. He gave up then that he should die. He said that he wanted to be burried the same as Jesse was. I then burried him the same. He wanted to see you and the children, and he would be contented.

I hope you won't get the fevor for California, because it is a hard old place as ever I have seen yet. I have seen more strapped men since I have been here that I ever saw before.

I want you to write about all of the four and all the particulars, my respects to you all.

Marvin Wheeler.

"Sad, isn't it?"

"A real tearjerker, Will. So matter of fact, he took sick, died, got buried— we moved on! He would've been contented to see them. Do they know where he died?"

"The other records indicate the Humboldt valley area, I'm not sure where, but about two or three hundred miles southwest of Salt Lake City, in Nevada. There obviously was correspondence between the date of Enos's death and the letter of April 24th from Marvin to his Aunt Mary. Enos and Mary had three children, George, who was one of my great-grandfathers, a daughter Loraine, and, of course, 'little Charlie'. I don't know what became of Loraine or Charlie."

"In the letter, he says they were going from Fort Kearney to Laramie. Will, Laramie is nowhere near the Platte. Did they leave the river?"

"I don't think so, Trish. I wondered about that. He did say they left Fort Laramie and in those days, forts on the frontier were usually built near water. Why don't you check the map along the Platte and see if there's a Fort Laramie."

Moments passed as Trish scanned the map. "Oh yes. Here, about sixty miles up river, a small town on highway twenty-six. Here's the place—Fort Laramie National Historic Site. You have to cross the Platte to get there."

"Then I'd be inclined to believe they went to Fort Laramie and then headed west across, as he described, 'the most miserable, barren looking country I ever saw'."

"I guess it doesn't matter much," said Trish, with a sigh. "Nothing more from Enos except his letters and the genes he left behind."

"You know, honey, most people will say that their mother is the most important force in their life. If that's true, tracing your genealogy is an exercise in forgotten significance. How many people could possibly give you the maiden name of the mother of each of their sixteen great-great-grandparents?

"Those copies of the letters were given to me by a cousin who lives west of Jackson. A grandson of George. He's in his eighties now. Some of my ancestors on both sides, settled in Jackson County between the 1830's and 1850's. Of course I can trace my maternal line to Wheeler, but one of my other relatives had a greater impact on my life than most of my direct ancestors."

"How was that?"

"George married a woman by the name of Samantha Horton Kimball who, of course, is one of my great-grandmothers. That Lincoln rocker in my den with the carved-rose headpiece belonged to her mother. Samantha's sister had a granddaughter a few years older than my mother, who I always called, Cousin Marguerite. She was an absolutely beautiful redhead and a very talented pianist. She was an organist for the Michigan Theater, in Detroit during the days of the silent movies. Before my time! Her husband, Eduard Werner, conducted the Scandinavian Symphony Orchestra in Detroit, and he was a Wayne County Prosecutor during the 'roaring twenties'.

"They didn't have any children and when I was young, I'd spend a week or so every summer with them. Eddy, that's what Cousin Marguerite called him, would take me fishing on the Roscum River in Canada and tell me war stories of the twenties and his cases for the Detroit Street Railway. They believed in complete abstinence, and during Prohibition, a lot of whiskey was sent to the bottom of the Detroit River! For several years he was President of the Detroit Federation of Musicians. I went to the state band-shell a few times when he guest-conducted the Detroit Symphony Orchestra."

"Are they still living?"

"Oh no. Cousin Marguerite died in the late '50s. Eduard wanted me to go to Wayne State, but I went to GW instead. I don't think he was too happy with me, because he was awful lonely and wanted us to live in the area. Choices! He was a 33rd degree Mason and passed away a few years ago at the Masonic Home. Cousin Marguerite and Eduard are the ones who steered me to law and classical music. They had a Grand piano in their living room, and I'll never forget the way she could play. It was so beautiful. I could sit and listen to her play for hours. There was a lot of Tchaikovsky and Hank Williams in my youth!"

"You do have an odd assortment of tapes."

"I've always been torn between spending *A Night On Bald Mountain* or going up *On Top of Old Smoky*!" Will laughed.

"You make your living with words, don't you, Will?"

"I guess so. They were friends with people at WXYZ and that's how I got the photograph signed by Brace Beemer, the *Lone Ranger*, that's hanging in the lounge. Eduard was a good friend of Fred 'Hap' Gaertner, editor of the Detroit News. I got to sit in a front-row box-seat, when 'Prince Hal' Newhouser was pitching for the Tigers! They'll probably never vote him into Cooperstown because he pitched during World War II. But hell, he won 26 games in '46, won back-to-back MVP awards, and no American League pitcher has ever done that! Enough of *This Is Your Life*. Let's stop at Fort Washakie and visit Sacajawea's grave, then spend the night in Dubois."

"Spend—again, so soon—ooh!" she grinned.

"Damn, you're still in that frame of mind?"

"Well, it was kind of one-sided up in those rocks."

"We'll see—maybe they sell oysters in Lander."

"Perhaps I should look for a younger man?"

"What a pity—youth is wasted on···"

"The young," Trish finished.

"It would be interesting to retrace the route. Maybe we can do it someday," said Will.

"Do it? I hope so!" rejoined Trish, with a grin.

"There you go again!"

"I hope so! This time, please play Franz Liszt's *Les Preludes*."

At five-foot two, the slender blond in her early forties, possessed a keen mind and a quick wit. She enjoyed and easily laughed at, but was never the butt of dumb blond jokes.

Some five miles from the highway, to be found only by inquiry at the Trading Post, on a barren parcel of land past a row of cotton-wood trees, sprawls the still expanding Indian cemetery.

At the end of a well worn foot path, wending its way among lesser stones—one treads lightly over the graves—stands the modest granite monument. Flanked by two smaller, one in memory and one the marker of her sons, it spoke to those who cared, simple, yet eloquent in their simplicity:

SACAJAWEA
DIED APRIL 9, 1884
A GUIDE WITH THE
LEWIS and CLARK
EXPEDITION
1805–1806

A small monument to an incredible young woman—beautiful—brave—intelligent. Forgotten. Her name on an occasional street corner, a lake in North Dakota and a short stretch of expressway in downtown Buffalo, New York.

After a few moments of silence and a photograph shot into the setting sun, the couple returned to the Trading Post. "Hey, Trish, take a look at this brochure. Wow! Doesn't that look fun! Mountain—horseback—wilderness trout fishing. Boy, this is something Burr and I've been talking about for years!"

Reading over the brochure, Will handed it to Trish as she climbed into the passenger seat and they started their journey to their evening destination. "Well, you've heard the commercial," she replied, "just do it."

"Maybe next summer. If we don't plan it, it'll never happen."

"Who would be going?"

"Well, it's Burr's idea—then Sam, George and probably two of Sam's brothers-in-law, Kevin and Tom."

"Do I know Kevin and Tom?"

"You may've met them. Kevin Smith is mister-fix-it for Motor Wheel. A traveling trouble shooter. And Tom Tanner is an insurance claims supervisor. That would be six. Just the group size the outfitter wants."

"Proving city boys can take care of themselves in the mountains, right?"

"No, not really, Trish. They've all had lots of experience in the field. I'm probably the only one that grew up—got older—riding horses. Tom was a long-distance competition shooter in NRA matches. Burr's a Nam veteran. Special Forces I think. He won't talk about it though. Kevin's tough and George can sure take care of himself. He'd die to save his friends. And you know Sam. He is one tough cookie! He saved my life in Alaska at great risk to himself. Nobody watching and no cameras! It's a hell of a lot tougher to be a hero when nobody's around! I'll never be able to repay him."

"I think you're right. I remember that tale, and you are one lucky person to be here. Now fasten the seat belt, just like you should've been wearing your life jacket!"

"Yes, dear. Anyway, as I was starting to say, all of us, except Burr, have gone on fishing trips together in Canada. He's the only outsider, but hell, he can get along with anyone. We wouldn't be trying to find ourselves or solve problems. Just a fun vacation of mountain fishing, saddle sores, hangovers, wet clothes, bugs, cold eggs and warm beer!"

"The male, macho, bonding thing, right?"

"Hell—do you want us to find some girls to take along?"

"No, that's all right. If you go, Will, just come back safe. Don't forget, your daughter's getting married in September."

"Trish, I'd better warn you because I'm sure you'll hear about it. Usually, when we go in the field, I spend a night out by myself."

"Why?"

"Oh, just to get away. The silence is its own symphony. You've got a better chance of seeing game when you're away from camp."

"Isn't it a little risky?"

"Not really. It just sounds risky. If you're prepared, and know how to keep a fire going, you're pretty safe. Things happen that can be kind of funny."

"I'll bet there's a story coming!" Trish laughed.

"A short one—I promise. Sam, his brother-in-law Hank, and I were in the White River Forest of Colorado in October of '81. My ex ran over to Meijers while we were packing and got me a small tent—I'd forgotten mine—for my night out. I'll cut this short. Sam and I hiked way up on this mountain, and then he went back to the base camp at Snell Rock. When I put the tent up, there was a sheet left over that I didn't realize was a rain shield. I thought it was a ground cloth!"

"Let me guess!" Trish exclaimed.

"Of course! About midnight—drip—drip—drip! Freezing water right in my face and splashing on my rifle! I crawled out of this damn—you've got to be an engineer to put it together in the sunshine—pup tent and in the pitch dark, got the shield over it. Am I having fun! About two in the morning, I woke up and it was light in the tent. So I got up and dressed to head back. Instead, it had turned colder and was crystal clear out, with about two inches of fresh snow blanketing everywhere."

"What did you do?"

"It was so beautiful—the moon and a billion stars were out—that I hiked the rest of the way up to the peak. And, it was a sight like I've never seen in my life! It made the damn tent worth it!"

"Just be careful, honey."

"What the hell could happen trout fishing? Break a leg I suppose. Nothin'
to worry about."

"It sounds fun. While you're gone, I'll try to find something to do."

"Maybe I won't go!"

"Oh sure! Like you're going to worry about me. Will, I've heard about
your escapades!"

"But have you seen any pictures?"

"No."

"Rumors don't count! Ask Hart, they had pictures!" Will laughed.

"Maybe you could lose a few of those pounds around your waist and
give the outfitter's horse a break!" Trish laughed.

"I'm not in such bad shape for a fifty-five year old lawyer."

"What do you weigh now? One seventy-five? Where's the lean, mean,
hundred and fifty-six pound machine you keep telling me you were five years
ago?"

"Okay—okay—okay—I'll work at it. No, maybe I'll ask the guide if
he has a mountain trained Clydesdale!"

"You know, Will, if you lost some gut, your ticker could concentrate
on pumping blood to other body organs," Trish chided.

"Now that's an incentive!" Will exclaimed, glancing over at Trish with
a fresh look of lust, as they approached the small Wyoming town of Dubois.

Wednesday
Slough Creek
Yellowstone National Park

"Will, I was reading those handouts on Wyoming. The trail from Ft.
Laramie to South Pass was the Overland Trail and the route used by most of
the emigrants going to California."

"Part of geography class slept through, honey!"

"Listen to this, '. . . in 1867 gold was discovered in South Pass, and
South Pass City became the largest community in the territory'. Wow! I bet
you never knew this! 'Esther Hobart Morris, a resident of South Pass City, led
the fight for women suffrage, and in 1869, the Territory of Wyoming became
the first governmental body in the world to grant women the right to vote. A
statue of her stands in front of the state capitol in Cheyenne'."

"For sure I'd never heard about that!" exclaimed Will.

"Your great-great grandfather, rolled right past the gold and never knew
it was there. Isn't that something!" Trish exclaimed.

"Trish, this has been a great vacation!"

"It sure has. But I can't believe I was up while it was still dark and hiking among mule deer in a Wyoming—or was it a Montana—fog?"

"We were in Wyoming, but we'll go through a corner of Montana at Cooke City and then back into Wyoming to Cody."

"Honey, what would we've done if we'd run in to a bear?"

"That's really no problem. They're usually afraid of humans and they run away."

"Oh, sure! I've read about bears attacking people, especially in the parks. And we should've had bear-bells on so we didn't surprise them. Right?"

"Right."

"Well, what would we've done if one started for us?"

"That's easy, Trish. I take the walking stick and stand my ground, while you run away as fast as you can."

"What about you?"

"No problem. You'll feed the bear and he won't be hungry for me!" exclaimed Will, bursting into a belly shaking laughter.

"Funny, funny. I'm serious."

"Trish, remember when I said let's go back, turned around and walked toward you?"

"Yes."

"I smelled one. The wind'd shifted just enough and I caught a whiff— a benefit of not smoking. They've got a fairly strong, rank smell. The only thing you can do is get up a tree, or play dead, even when they're mauling you. Doubt I could play dead, but I'll bet I'd climb fast!

"When Sam and I were in Alaska, we'd hiked up a feeder stream and came across fresh tracks of a sow with her cub. We spotted a pile of scat— that's bear poop—and when I broke it open with a stick, steam came out. We made a u-turn and got the hell out of there. The only smart thing to do when a mother's guarding her cub. If you kill a bear without a license, it'd better be chewing on you!"

"Have you ever gone bear hunting?"

"No. I don't believe in shooting things you're not going to eat."

"I guess it helps if you know a little about the outdoors."

"Sometimes. You can't run to a phone and dial 911. There's an old Russian saying—of course it doesn't help when you're crapping your pants— 'if you're afraid of the wolf, stay out of the forest'."

"Fools rush in . . .?"

"Right."

"Trish?"

"Yes, Will?"

"Would you mind if on our way back, we went up to the National Park at the Little Bighorn?"

"Of course not—if you want to. But I thought you went there a few years ago with your family?"

"Yeah, in the summer of '78. That's why I asked if you'd mind—knowing she and I'd visited there."

"Of course not. But why on earth would you want to visit a remote place like that again? Isn't once enough?"

"Normally I'd say yes, but to explain why is going to take a bit, if you're really interested. So let's have breakfast first and start for Cody. The Park Service has an exhibit at the Little Bighorn showing the events leading up to the battle, including Washita River. The massacre there of Black Kettle's Cheyenne in 1867 or '68 was committed by Custer's regiments of the 7th Cavalry, and Wounded Knee was carried out by the 7th in 1890. Maybe I can come up with a good enough reason. Something's pulling me and I'm not sure what."

"Will, this looks like a neat restaurant—let's try it out."

"Golly, Trish! That's a first! You wanting to eat this early."

"I don't want you to turn in to one of those bears! Sometimes I think you'd rather eat than . . ."

"Don't say it!" Will interrupted. "I can do three meals a day!"

"Darn! What a pity!" exclaimed Trish, with a grin.

Parking the van, they entered the small, rustic, family restaurant and were made welcome with a piping hot carafe of coffee. The crisp morning hike and early departure from Slough Creek had rendered Will ready for the touted 'Mountain Man' breakfast.

"Honey—how can you get by with just a fruit plate? I'm starving!"

"It's just habit. It's how I've conditioned myself. Do you want me to eat like you do?"

"Well—no. I just can't seem to cut back when I'm travelling. A grapefruit breakfast doesn't seem right when I'm on vacation."

"Boy! Look at this headline, Will. Things are really heating up in the Gulf."

"I hope there isn't another war. It's so damn easy to get into 'em."

"Men and killing. They always seem to find the right words to justify it. Honor—duty—country—religion. More weeping mothers."

"Fathers weep too, Trish."

"I know—I know. You don't nurse the babies though. Somehow everyone seems proud of the hero's death."

"I know what you mean. They'll give the Pericles speeches, pin medals on the living and hand 'em to the mothers and widows. It'll look good on TV. It filters out the screaming and the stench."

"A great topic before breakfast!"

"You brought it up, Trish. Heroes are one thing, but no one's comfortable around the cripples."

"Handicapped, Will, handicapped."

"I know. I'm sorry. I take out the garbage, but a sanitation engineer picks it up. Just look at Uncle Richard. I love him dearly, but I'm embarrassed to take him to a restaurant. You can't drape a medal around his twisted neck telling the world he sacrified a perfect body shooting down Nazi planes in North Africa. Totally disabled for fifty years!"

"He seems happy living at your sister's."

"Yeah—she takes good care of him. He'll probably out-live me!"

"Maybe Saddam will pull his troops out," Trish, always optimistic, hopefully declared.

"If he doesn't, it could send a lot of parents picking poppies."

"What?"

"In Flanders field . . ."

"Among the crosses row on row," Trish softly whispered. "I'll bet you're glad Zach's out of the army."

"For sure, Trish. He's on inactive status, but they could call him up in a hurry. His unit at Ft. Bliss, the Third Cavalry—one of Patton's outfits—just went through desert training in California. He's trained in heavy equipment and might have to go."

"How about Mark?"

"I doubt he'd get called up. The Navy'd be a big part, but he's been out several years. They shouldn't have to call up electricians. But I'm not too worried. If Saddam doesn't pull out, Bush isn't going to get into a World War II tank battle. I'd bet he'd just hit him with high technology."

"Well, I guess you don't have to worry about William. With the munchkin to raise, it would have to be an all out war to draft him. Was he ever in the military?"

"No. He should've gone marines! Dad—air force, Mark—navy, Zach—army,—we'd have 'em covered! Family get togethers would've been something!"

"William is *quite* a young man. They really made me feel welcome."

"I believe all my kids like you, Trish. You weren't on the scene when I left. I don't think they blame anyone. What they don't seem to understand is my leaving. Why now, after so many years. Hope I can explain it to 'em some day. It may be easier for younger children to accept. I just don't know. Divorce is tough on everyone. They miss the big family gatherings as much as anything. They were good times. I'm sure your kids miss the gatherings too."

"They do. Will, I think I can empathize more with your daughter's feelings, having been there, than the boys. She may have a difficult time accepting me because of conflicting loyalties."

"Well," reflected Will, "Tanya'll be so damn busy in law school she won't have time to worry about what her old dad's doing."

"That may be true, but the feelings are still going to be there. Have you heard anything from Tom?"

"Not lately. He's marching to *his* drummer. Fathers and sons," said Will with a big sigh. "There seems to be a zillion reasons to love and as many to hate. Maybe sometime we'll be able to straighten things out."

"Do you think Zack will be going to college?"

"I believe so. He had a real good record in the army. Enough about my kids, Trish. I just hope your son and daughter can accept me."

"They will," Trish replied with a warm smile.

"Ah! Here comes food! End of family problems," declared Will in anticipation.

Breakfast was a dim memory, Cooke City long out of the rear view mirror, and most of the scenic drive down the Sunlight Valley over, before the wind, blowing through the grass with its scattered white crosses, jarred Will's memory. "Trish?"

"Yes?"

"Are you really interested in why I want to go back?"

"Go back where, honey?"

"To the Little Bighorn."

"Of course I am. This sounds like a history lecture on the way, but if you think it's important, then share it with me."

"Well, I think it's important. Like Steve Biko thought it was important the blacks in South Africa have a true history of their culture."

"What in the world is the connection, Will?"

"I've read a bit about the frontier and I know if you'd read about it, you'd be raising the same question. So here goes Will Dean's theory of American Indian History 101. Let's give the class something to think about. Listen up students! General George Armstrong Custer, from Monroe, Michigan—dashing hero of glorious cavalry charges that saved Lincoln's ass on more than one occasion—wasn't massacred at the Little Bighorn, he was punished for what he did at Washita River!"

"Good God, Will, don't drive off the side of the mountain! What in heaven's name makes you say that?"

"If you start from the premise the Indians were dumb savages, just bucks and squaws to be shot for sport from railway cars, then the statement is ridiculous. But if you can accept the fact that Thomas Jefferson and James Madison studied the Iroquois Nations Confederation—that held together six nations with a representative form of government that lasted longer than the United States has been around—as well as Locke and Rousseau, to create our Constitution, then it may make sense."

"Wow, that was a mouthful!"

"I'm on a roll, Trish, look out! There's no dispute about Custer himself and units of the 7th Cavalry carrying out the Washita River Massacre, and this was Indian country. They'd been around these plains a long time and the different tribes—there's white man's language again—Nations, may've been well aware of what was going on. When Custer's vanity put himself and some of the 7th away from forces that could've supported him, he may've given the Indians an offer, to even the score a little, that they couldn't refuse! And remember, at Washita River, a lot of women, children and old men were killed. While at the Little Bighorn, it was soldiers out doing what soldiers like to get medals for!"

"What makes you think it was punishment, rather than just killing all the soldiers they could?"

"You nailed it, honey, and that's what's troubled me about the battle. You see, Sitting Bull just wanted to go to Canada, and they did. Maybe they didn't want to fight General Terry, or Crook, or Gibbon, or, maybe nobody. But with Custer out there with only five companies—about two-hundred and sixty men hanging out to dry—it was just too good to be true. And here's why I think it may have been for that reason. The only soldiers close enough to help Custer were about a hundred and twenty under the command of Major Reno, and about a hundred and ten under Captain Benteen, some three miles away. They were engaged by the Indians, but apparently only in a holding action and no attempt was made to wipe 'em out."

"But why do you want to go back?"

"Since I was there, they've gone over the battlefield, literally inch-by-inch, and I'd like to see if anything more's been discovered. If Custer was being punished for gunning down Chief Black Kettle at the Washita, it makes the Indians look a little better and Wounded Knee a little worse. And if I was an Indian child, I'd enjoy reading an honest history book.

"I think that was what Biko was trying to say to the people of South Africa. I'm probably going to be wasting our time and gas money, but it strikes me as one more incident where the Native Americans have taken a bad rap. And, if my theory's right, they don't deserve it. Maybe they didn't have a written language to preserve history from their point of view. But that doesn't make it right for the other side to distort history. I guess nobody's going to appoint me public defender of the Indians, so I'll just rest my case!"

"Take me there, Will. I'd like to feel it, too."

Their white-knuckle visit to Sheep Mountain and the ancient Medicine Wheel over, Trish headed the van for Montana while Will studied the map of western Wyoming. "Trish, the Dubois area is where Butch Cassidy hung out and over South Pass is the Green River. The Green River Rendezvous site's about sixty miles up river from where Enos probably camped."

Murphy gave a shudder as Will reached down and picked up the fishing vacation brochure.

"You know, honey, now's the time. If Russtovitch and I don't do a mountain trout trip next summer, we'll just keep putting it off and never go."

"Like I said, 'just do it', Will," Trish replied with a warm smile at her significant other.

Something is wrong thought Murphy; a terrible mosaic is falling into place. There's a bitter cold breeze blowing out of the northeast; sweeping across Superior and heading this way. Burn the brochure, Will, burn the brochure.

Thank God birth certificates don't come with crystal balls.

3

Marquette

December, 1990
Maximum Security
Marquette Branch Prison
Marquette, Michigan

Marquette, named after French missionary, Jacques Marquette, is located on the south shore of Lake Superior, approximately one hundred and fifty miles northwesterly of the Straits of Mackinac. The city, built along the west shore of Presque Isle Harbor and Marquette Bay, has two well protected, shipping and boating harbors.

To the west the terrain rises quickly, its trees and other vegetation covering in most places, ancient bedrock, the Negaunee iron formation. Known to the experts as *hematite* - Fe2 O3 and *magnetite* - Fe3 O4, this ferrous-oxide rich chert, was the building block and treasure of the Iron Age. The pits—daily destination of miners ever mindful of the November 3, 1926 cave-in at the Barnes-Hecker killing fifty-six—were in the domain of, but unused by, the Stone Age *Chippewa* and *Ojibwa* Indians.

Discovered again in 1841 by the white man, geologist Douglas Houghton, the federal government, in anticipation of an iron ore mining rush, negotiated another of its long litany of Indian Treaties. This time the *Chippewa* and *Ojibwa* Indians, with no concept of owning land, *willingly* ceded all their territory west of the Chocolay River, and south of *Gitche Gumee*, the 'shining-big-sea-water'.

By 1857, the Iron Mountain Railroad was hauling ore to the newly built Presque Isle Harbor ore docks and by the turn of the century, Marquette County was supplying one fourth of the United States' iron ore.

Rapid population growth resulting from the mining industry, together with overcrowding at Jackson and Ionia prisons, led to the decision to build Marquette Branch Prison in the 1880's. Completed in 1889, it was designated as the incorrigible prison and until 1981, Branch Prison as it became known, was the only maximum security prison in Michigan. As such, it housed the most dangerous and assaultive prisoners. The State of Michigan has never had the death sentence and the word, Marquette, at least for down-staters, became synonymous with a tough prison, a place for hard-cases.

39

Located on eighty-three acres of land donated to the State by a local businessmen's association, the prison is bounded on the east, by Marquette Bay; the south, by the south city boundary; the north, by the Carp River and west, by the hills.

Guy Gerlach was one of Branch Prison's six hundred and thirty-four Level V, maximum security residents. Gerlach needed maximum security; if he didn't, the rest of North America needed maximum security from Gerlach. There is no point in searching his history to try and find reasons or explanations to understand Gerlach; they always can be found. He is here. He exists, and change has not been possible, remaining, like a cartoon character, 'I am what I am said . . .'. And the *am* for Gerlach is evil; pure—clear—clean—undiluted—unmitigated and unredeeming evil. A cold and calculating self preserving stop at nothing do anything to anybody even myself to achieve my goal or my pleasure evil. An evil so pure that a finger print could rot oak evil.

That pure evil could sail under such false colors defied both logic and reason. In fact, common experience dictated against this insidious inconsistency. For Gerlach was handsome—lean, light brown hair, blue-eyed and in possession of a smile that could melt an ice palace. Yet, like a modern day *Potemkin village,* his appearance was a phony front. A tool to disarm both male and female; gates normally shut to strangers swung open. Evil should look evil. It should travel with bear-bells to warn of its approach. It should not lurk, as it did with Gerlach, beneath a microscopic layer of body tissue.

To say Gerlach enjoyed inflicting his barbaric savagery on others to serve his purposes or pleasures, would leave out his willingness to inflict such savagery on himself to achieve a goal. To hang himself in the hope of being rescued, so as to escape from a hospital, was viewed only as a suicide attempt by one jurisdiction and not recorded. His drinking Drano, while in a deputy's custody and then escaping from the hospital, went unrecorded, since he was recaptured and convicted of the more serious felony, 'breaking and entering a dwelling'. A second, this time successful, phony hanging to escape from a hospital, again went unrecorded as an escape since there was a grand auto theft and interstate Federal prosecution.

Gerlach's first visit to Branch Prison, in 1972, was as one of Marquette's, Level I, two hundred ninety-eight guests in minimum security. At that time his only escape attempt known to Michigan authorities was a rather dumb and botched county jail attempt. He had no *known* record of violent crime, and was due to be released on parole in a very short time.

He walked away from minimum security and leaving a trail of blood, abducted and brutally murdered a young woman from Negaunee; murdered a teenage party-store attendant in Wisconsin; murdered a deputy sheriff in Benton Harbor, Michigan; and following his conviction of murder in the first degree, rode back to Marquette in a prison van.

In Michigan, conviction of murder in the first degree means mandatory life in prison; no parole, no early out for good behavior. Life, mandatory until death do us part life. Only with the rare commutation by the Governor or new evidence—such as somebody else did it, 'we're sorry', could you get out. Or escape.

Guy knew he would die near the cold shores of Gitche Gumee, unless he could pull off the unheard of, a solo escape. Michigan knew there would be no parole, Guy knew there would be no commutation or new evidence and North Americans, if they thought about it, would pray.

The mistake, if there was one in dealing with Gerlach, was not the fault of the prison staff. It sprang instead from two, possibly unavoidable circumstances. First, the error of omission; there was simply no record of the risks Gerlach would take to get outside. He was more than willing to chance death in the hope of success. And second, the prison system itself. To deal with inmates who have no hope of ever being released and yet provide the very least of basic needs, there developed a system of reward and punishment.

Gerlach was simply one among equals. They would not be in Level V unless they were considered extremely dangerous and escape risks. The maximum security area is tight; a compact, walled and steel rectangle of three and a half acres within the thirty-five acres of developed prison property. Inside this confine, certain services, such as laundry and training facilities, were contained. Not all of the Level V residents were in for life and of those who were, some by good behavior, could be rewarded with work in the laundry or other facilities within the wall.

Branch Prison tried—they tried in good faith. They did not want anyone to escape, but they had a *system*, and no system is perfect. If it were, Christa would be teaching school and the other Challenger astronauts about their work and play. *Thetis,* mother of *Achilles,* couldn't, NASA couldn't and neither could the State of Michigan make a perfect system.

Gerlach was evil, but shrewd. He learned from his mistakes and he knew he would eventually escape, only the rest of the world did not. There had to be a chink in the armor. He knew how the system worked, he would eventually find a way. Like *Paris,* he would look carefully. *Achilles*—invincible, unbeatable—the killer of *Hector,* had to have a weak spot. And, like *Paris,* he would find that weak spot and shoot his arrow through the gap in the sheet of steel between himself and North America.

The years would pass without infractions, he would follow the rules. No insubordination, no hostility toward the 'man'. In the class-for-life of incorrigibles, Guy was one of the betters. He knew one basic truth, he'd have no help from outside. With no family, and no money or friends—life's frequent handmaidens—escape would require inmate assistance, security staff off-guard, a chink in the armor, good physical fitness and incredible luck.

He could be in control of physical fitness, unless weakened by disease; he could develop inmate assistance and by good behavior, lull guard security.

He firmly believed a chink was always there or could be created. Given his view of heaven and earth, luck fell on the good and the bad like an equal opportunity spring rain creating flowers and floods. His good luck would simply be someone else's bad luck.

Years passed and an extremely fit and endurance conditioned Guy waited. He was willing to do whatever had to be done. He could be a king or a queen and he took care, in any manner and with whatever methods, of those he thought might help or were friends with someone who could help. Lines of communication were carefully nurtured, favors cheerfully granted. To maintain his credibility he collected his due, it was expected. As a proven cop killer, he already had status among the residents. The perks and the stability did not however deter him from his goal, he wanted out. He enjoyed the adrenalin highs of crime and he wanted women. There was plenty of sex in prison, but he couldn't have women and they were the grass on the other side of the fence he wanted to graze on.

The longest days have launched the great invasions of history; Napoleon into Russia, June, 1812; Hitler into the Soviet Union, June, 1941; and the Allies onto the beaches of Normandy, June, 1944. On Friday, December 21, 1990, in the darkness of one of the shortest days, a 5'10," 160 pound *Homo sapien*—known to the State of Michigan as #48325, to his parents as Guy Gerlach and his cell mates as Big Guy—would be launched against the human beings of North America.

When the time came, it came quick and Guy was ready. He had to strike while the iron was hot.

———

Wednesday evening, December 19, 1990
Guy Gerlach's Maximum Cell
Branch Prison
Marquette, Michigan

Something was nagging Guy, he couldn't get to sleep; like a sense of presence, there was something going on, but he couldn't put his finger on it, so he talked.

"Joe, did you see that sheet on the history of this hole?" he asked.

"No," his cell mate replied.

"Well, you should read more. Man these days are borin'. I'd like to've been here in the good-ole-days!" he exclaimed.

"Why?"

"Hell, Joe, there was a lot of good shit goin' down then. In 1928, they stabbed Warden Catlin and the Deputy Warden, a Fred Menhennett. Both died.

Can you believe that! They got the mother-fuckers in the auditorium. Just imagine the high! I'll bet everyone was fuckin' or suckin' that night!

"Then in '31 a Dr. Hornberger, or somebody, was shot to death in a botched escape, and in '39, a bunch of prisoners kidnapped the Warden, the Deputy Warden and two of those asshole parole board mother-fuckers. They caught 'em all, but the prisoners were lily livered. They didn't waste anyone. No balls!

"In '50, they took Governor G. Mennen Williams himself hostage in the kitchen! That was a bad scene 'cause the Governor's mother-fuckin' bodyguard'd snuck in a pistol and killed one of us! The fucker'd hid the gun from security. Wasn't that a cheap trick? God damn it Joe, I've got it!" he exclaimed.

"Forget it, Big Guy. This is level five and no one gets out."

"I know and it's because they always try to escape from prison. Escape into the prison—to level one."

"Look, Guy—you're in forever. Two convictions of first degree murder in Wisconsin and you blow away a pig in Michigan. You're here to be the bungee or the bungor for the rest of your natural life, so forget it."

"Joe, I know the system and don't mind doing my turn, no big deal. Food's good, TV, and all that shit. I've gotta get out, period, and I don't give a fuck what happens. I gotta have some cunt. So listen, the laundry carts go to level one, right?"

"Yeah, but they're airtight and locked," Joe answered.

"Joe, gimme a fuckin' break. I drank Drano to get to a hospital from a Sheriff's jail and goddamn near died, but the dumb fuckers did their *Good Samaritan* deed and saved me, right? I got up and walked out of the hospital like I fuckin' owned the joint.

"Hung myself in a goddamn jail in New Mexico, five goddamn minutes before cell check, and the dumb pigs cut me down and sent me to emergency. Walked out of there and drove away in the BMW of the fuckin' doctor who saved me!" laughed Guy.

"Ha—Christ, you're something else, Big Guy. The guys you do in here ain't gonna miss you, hung like you are. But I am—I'll help. Where'll you head for if you make it out?"

"Well, I've done time with the feds in New Mexico—weather's warm and dry. They can take the whole mother-fuckin' State of Michigan and all five of those cold mother-fuckin' Great Lakes and stick 'em, water, sand and dirt, up their asses for all I care.

"They'll never, ever get me back here alive. I'll leave so many cunt dead, some state will fry me out West, but I ain't goin' to die of old age in this cold-ass state," he vowed. "First, I'll go to Flint to get my girlfriend back from that shit-faced lawyer she's been fuckin'," he lied. "Then, it's bye-bye Michigan—hello mountains!" The dumb lawyer can have the stupid bitch, he thought. Thinking to himself he would never be back, there was no point in sharing his detailed plan with Joe, so he continued the subterfuge.

"Highway 41 east to the bridge is my only way. I'll get out aways, hide the bodies of whoever I get and hole up somewhere. Then I'll use some skiers to get me across the Bridge and south. Here's how I'm goin' out and I need your help.

"My job in the laundry is how I start out. The Hundred Year Centennial is Friday and Saturday. Thursday night the laundry'll work a night shift and clean laundry'll be shipped out to the level one dorms at about five in the mornin'. Get a message to Dorm A to unlock their laundry cart and have several residents standin' around. Have someone distract the supervisor. And oh, get me a shank, not a horse mind you, and a car door jimmy if you can. I blend in, start carryin' laundry, and out the door—snap—just like that!" he laughed.

"It might work," Joe replied, thinking to himself he had parole coming if he kept his nose clean, but he did owe Guy. And, he was dead if Guy found out he didn't help. Someone would get him, that's for sure he thought.

"They'll lock me in after five o'clock count and before shippin'. The cart'll wait in the hall and they'll distract the supervisor. There's only one of him and a bunch of us. The cart goes through the Sally Port a little after five and they're supposed to be shook. But what the hell, I'm caught and back in solitary beatin' my meat, I'm dead, or I'm out 'ridin' the range once more'!" he sang, laughing with glee at the thought of pussy.

"If Murphy don't fuck with me, it's Detroit City, well Flint, here I come!"

"Who the fuck's Murphy?" Joe asked.

"You don't know that mother-fucker?" Guy asked, incredulously.

"No."

"He put ya here!" Guy exclaimed. "You didn't wanta be here, did ya?"

"No."

"Okay. I'll let ya in on Murphy's Law. One, if anythin' can go wrong, it will. Two, nothin's as easy as it looks. Three, and this may get me, everythin' takes longer'n you think it will," Guy explained. I've done my homework, he thought. Everyone in max is checked on the hour, and the extra laundry shift could work either way, longer or shorter.

His plan was good, and like one of Newton's laws of physics, for every action—an equal and opposite reaction; Guy's good luck would be someone else's bad. Knowledge heals; it can hurt. Guy read and had knowledge—some. *The Mining Journal*, Marquette's daily paper, had shown the 1990–1991 Marquette County Snowmobile Trail Map.

From advertisements in the paper and from the map of the snowmobile trail, he knew that by simply running across the shallow Carp River, in winter only a trickle, he could run west on the groomed trail along the north side of Mt. Marquette and pick up the trail's business loop. This would take him to the two-hundred and four room, five story Holiday Inn, on the south side of U.S. 41. His time for this three and a half mile run should be well under twenty- five minutes. He would be missed at the six o'clock head count, a twenty-five minute grace period. Give Murphy ten minutes, and he had fifteen minutes before the sirens sounded. The State Police would be immediately notified, and within another five to ten minutes, road blocks in place.

With Lake Superior as a natural barrier to the north and east; blocking U.S. Highway 41 west of Brookton Corner's and again, southeast of the prison; and by blocking county roads 492 and 553 in an arc between the U.S.-41 blocks, the net would be closed.

Sirens throughout the city would immediately notify all a breakout had occurred. Doors would be locked and weather permitting, the State Police chopper, if in the area, up. He would be caught or freeze, but once west of Brookton Corners, they could color him gone, unless Murphy shifted sides.

The newspaper was full of information. Friday, December 21, 1990 would be the last day of school until January 2, 1991. Many families would leave for the south—snowbirds seeking sunshine. Others would be heading west and southwest to some of the best ski hills and vacation packages in the midwest.

For some, the lure was Iron Mountain, Michigan and the action at nearby Pine Mountain; until recently, the greatest man-made ski jump in the world. Where just to watch those few fearless jumpers was a thrill in itself. To even stand on the top of this run was to make the pulse of mortal men and women race.

From the newspaper, Gerlach was aware that across Highway 41 and opposite the Holiday Inn was the Elias Brothers' open-all-night Big Boy Restaurant. He was also certain a few families would be taking their children out of school at least one day early. He could predict that some of these early bird gets the worm types would be heading out from the Big Boy, in their spacious motor homes and vans, with happy tummies from the breakfast bar, hot mugs of coffee and wearing their latest winter togs. He would enjoy the fruits of their labor, as well as whatever else they had to offer.

Laying back on his cot, with pleasant thoughts of the Friday morning ahead, he whispered to his cell mate, "Joe, I know you'll help me. Do you want me to do ya?" he asked.

"No," Joe replied. "You're the one who needs a good night's sleep, and walking over, bent his head down, bringing his mouth to Guy's name sake.

———

Thursday, December 20, 1990
8:00 P.M. Eastern Standard Time
The Palomaki's
West Ohio Street
Marquette, Michigan

"Well, little lady, it's off to bed for you. It's up like we planned at five a.m. and out of here in thirty minutes!" Hannes spoke lovingly to his only child and, needless to say, co-holder of his undying love and affection. Born on the 27th day of April, *Huhtikuu,* in 1978, to the first generation Finnish couple, Merja, named for her birth date, but known to all as Mia, was a blithe spirit.

"Dad, I saw you take your jumpers out. Does that mean you will?"

"Maybe. Ted said it's well-groomed, and it depends on the wind. We'll see in the morning. Now off to bed with you. Mom and I are tired."

"I'll bet," she said, with a hint of a knowing grin.

"Out of here, before I get you! You little imp!"

"Me thinks our little girl is not so little anymore. What do you think, my little ski-pole warmer?" he whispered to his wife, Kreeta.

"Well, my big slope-jumper, she is twelve, and sometimes you do grunt and groan!"

"Can't help it dear. It's your fault, you're just too erotic! Come on, I'm horny."

"How can anyone be too erotic?" she asked. "I'm horny too, but let's wait a bit, it'll whet your appetite. Hannu, are you sure you still want to jump?" asked Kreeta, a tone of concern in her voice.

"Yes, if I can. I'd like a shot at it and might get lucky tomorrow. My balance is still good and Ted said the slide was as good as it's ever been. Just think of it, three hundred and ninety-nine feet. I'd have to break it by six inches!"

"Oh, let's go to bed—you can do a lot better than six inches!" she whispered, doing a shimmy that gave her shapely breasts a bounce and headed for the stairs.

If ever there was a perfect husband and father, Hannes might be it. Kind, but not doting; loving, but not possessive. A fan of Kahlil Gibran, he knew we share love, but do not own it. He knew neither his daughter nor his lovely wife were his possessions.

Their devotion was earned by his love and kindness, not by fear or apprehension. Mia generally minded her father because he rarely commanded. He was open minded; a trusting optimist with great faith in the human race. Hannes and his like-minded wife and companion Kreeta, taught at nearby Northern Michigan University. Avid skiers, both downhill and cross-country, they were pictures of Finnish health and vitality.

Kreeta, thirty-one years old, five foot five and a hundred and sixteen pounds, was blond, blue-eyed and trim; as was their charming twelve year old daughter. She was an instructor in Greek and Roman history at the School of Arts and Science, while Hannes, at thirty-two was of a more precise nature, a mathematics professor. No wimp was Hannes however, he was in superb physical shape; skilled and brave in an area few humans could ever be.

Palomaki, in Finnish meaning fire-hill, was an appropriate name, for Hannes was a ski-jumper. The family, and all present, would feel vicariously that awesome moment when a jumper, like a bolt of fire, would leave the hill and fly further than any human without a parachute.

Literally millions of people, young and old, male and female, have jumped from planes, yet only a handful could put on those two-hundred fifty centimeter or longer slabs, glide down a snow-ice covered runway and shoot into space, at nearly seventy miles per hour, for an uncertain landing, hundreds of feet away.

Knowing the next ten days were going to be crowded, Hannes, a gleam in his eye, followed his willing and ready soulmate heading for their warm, cozy waterbed. At thirty-two, doing it three times a night meant something different than going to the bathroom. Hannes, a little out of breath and still shaky—both had made a fantastic double journey to the bursting stars—lay warm and close to his loving wife. A few moments passed before the spell was broken by her soft whisper, "Hannu, I just get scared. How long are you going to jump?"

Vanity, oh vanity he thought with a sigh. In those occasional duels with vanity, he was justifiably proud of his father, one of Finland's crack, white-uniformed, ski-equipped riflemen at the heroic defense of Summa during the Russo-Finnish Winter War of 1939. If he could just break the Austrian's record, a poem in his honor might be entered in the *Kalevala,* the Finnish national epic, and maybe help put in their place those few smug, condescending Swedes who still harbored disdain for the Finns of northern Michigan.

Vanity, my main selfish fault he thought, what can I say. "Well, maybe I should think about it a bit more," he answered. "It's a great thrill, it's one hell of an adrenalin rush! I'd be scared to death if you or Mia would do it. But she'll be wanting to jump the Monster someday and she's good. We can't deprive her of that, can we?"

"No, I suppose not. I'll just die as she comes down that slide, though."

"Listen, honey. We'll have breakfast at five-thirty or so in the morning as planned. With the roads and traffic it'll probably take about an hour and a half to drive to Pine Mountain. We can check in at the resort and get our gear around. I told Ted—he's the Hill Captain this season—I'd check in with him at about nine o'clock. Wind should be down and we'll see how I do. Then maybe I'll give up on the record and put my old boards to rest over the mantel. How does that sound?"

"Darling, you do whatever you want. I'll always love you, even with a broken back!" And reaching down after that morbid thought, found it might be time to get some sleep.

It was one of life's simple mistakes. Hannes over-looked a fact he was well aware of—Pine Mountain was on Central Time. It mattered.

5:32 A.M., Eastern Standard Time
December 21, 1990
Dorm A—Minimum Security

Ahead of schedule, Gerlach quickly climbed out of the laundry basket and suppressing a shout of elation, bent over and picked up the bottom layer of towels. From behind, an unseen hand slipped a razor sharp shank, its handle well taped, and a car door jimmy into his right hand, hidden beneath the towels. As he walked toward the door, the supervisor, his back turned, was laughing at another of a trustee's hilariously funny jokes, usually at the expense of the 'man'.

The door closed silently behind him and since no one cared much about minimum security, especially at this time of day, no one saw Gerlach as he crossed the Carp River and headed at a fast, steady pace for the Big Boy.

5:33 A.M.
Elias Brothers—Big Boy Restaurant

Hannes pulled his Chevrolet Beauville van into the right hand slot facing the east end of the restaurant. A few spaces to his left, the steps led up to the front entrance. The sleek, blue, Michigan State Police car—with its gold light-ening-bolt accented, dark blue shield—parked by the steps, gave the family a warm sense of security.

Hannes and Kreeta were stepping out of the van when Mia, a little slow at this godforsaken hour, slid the right side, middle door lock open, after her father had hit the electric lock button to lock all the doors. As they shut their doors, she quickly climbed out, shut her door and hurried to catch her parents. It never occurred to any of them that the side door was left unlocked.

5:54 A.M.
Elias Brother -Big Boy Restaurant

Bad luck rained unseen on the Palomakis, while only good luck washed the brow of Evil. Out of breath, Gerlach opened the unlocked storage shed to the east of two garbage containers. The shed's door, less than twenty paces from the passenger side of the Palomaki van.

A dim light disclosed, among various supplies and clothing, a set of dark green coveralls, some brown-jersey work gloves, a black, knit wool hat and several rolls of three-inch wide duct tape. His sweat-soaked prison blues discarded and wearing the green coveralls, hat, gloves and with a roll of tape, he walked over to the brown and white van. Checking the ski rack, he noted two pair of regular down-hill skis and the long jumpers in their vinyl case. A smaller set of down-hills interested him; was it a girl or a boy? I guess it doesn't matter he thought, as he checked the side door. Finding it open, he entered the darkened van and thinking he might need it later, hid the car door jimmy.

Luck is with me—Murphy, keep up the good work—with a State Police car parked a few spaces away from the van, I would never have dared to open the door with a jimmy, he thought. Quickly he searched the pockets of the front doors and seats for weapons and finding none, moved to the rear seat. Well hidden behind the middle seat, located directly behind the driver's seat, Gerlach waited for a family he didn't know and sirens he could expect.

6:11 A.M.

Hannes, carrying a thermos of hot coffee, walked around the front of the van, unlocked the passenger door and held it for Kreeta. Seated, he handed her the coffee and hit the electric switch to unlock the other doors. Shutting hers, he headed for the driver's side and climbed in. Mia, who had stopped to talk to Bob, the night manager, ran around the van as Hannes shut his door, turning off the dome lights. Mia opened the side door, entered the dark rear, closed the door and getting in the middle seat behind her dad, buckled tight her seat belt. All secure, they started west on U.S. Highway 41 and then heard the faint sirens signaling a breakout.

"Well, no need to worry!" said Hannes, smiling at Kreeta, as she reached over and gave his arm a loving squeeze. Picking up speed on the divided, four-lane highway they soon passed Brookton Corners and in his rear view mirror, Hannes saw the flashing lights of a police car as it turned, it's headlights directed back to the east.

Shock—a sledge hammer to their chests—adrenalin pulsed through their blood streams as the cold, strong, male voice, reached their ears and registered instantly their horrible plight. "Just do exactly as I say, keep your eyes on the road sir and drive at a steady pace. Your little girl's life depends on it. All of you—stop whimperin' young lady—no one's goin' ta get hurt. I only want the van. You're very lucky. There ain't no reason for me to hurt any of you, if you do exactly as I say. Do ya understand?"

Helpless, but with his mind racing, Hannes murmured "Yes," as did Kreeta. Mia just continued to shake.

"First, so this nice young lady who looks pretty strong and healthy to me, don't do somethin' stupid and get herself hurt, I'm going to restrain you— just some tape around your arms.

"Man, just sit still and face straight ahead! I mean it!" he shouted at Hannes. "Now, where was I? The tape." Putting the shank between his teeth, he quickly taped Mia's wrists to the seat arms. With the seat belt on, there was nothing she could do.

Totally helpless, Hannes drove as ordered.

"Would you please turn the radio to WDMJ?" Guy politely requested. The early morning ski report was interrupted as Gerlach took the hot coffee from Kreeta and, turning on the overhead light, showed them both the razor-sharp shank; a short knife, it was all he would need. They had no weapons— they trusted. There were no pistols in their pockets, in the van doors, or in their house. As did most, they relied totally on their tax dollars to protect them and their daughter.

Drinking some hot coffee, he moved back beside Mia and looked her over; his lust rose, but he would contain it for now.

"You'll never get away with this," Hannes spoke up, his voice returning from the speech freezing shock.

"You're probably right, but I have nothin' to . . ." he was cut off as '. . . we interrupt this program to bring this special bulletin. An inmate has managed to escape from the Branch Prison. Prison authorities have confirmed that Guy Gerlach has become the first and only person to ever make a solo escape from level five, maximum security, in the prison's one hundred year history. Authorities say Gerlach had himself locked in an airtight laundry box by his accomplices and was unlocked in a minimum security dorm.

'Gerlach was in for mandatory life after his conviction of first-degree murder for killing a down-state police officer. He was also convicted in Wisconsin of murdering a Negaunee mother of three and a Wisconsin teenage boy, following a walk-away from level one in the early seventies. Gerlach, a white male with light brown hair and blue eyes, is five-foot ten and weighs a hundred and sixty-five pounds . . .' informed the announcer, his calm voice a counter-point to the stark terror felt by the Palomaki family.

"Sixty," Guy interjected.

'. . . and is considered armed and extremely dangerous. More details will follow. We now return you to our regular programming'.

Mia, crying, was the first Gerlach turned to, "Listen young lady, I don't want that shit," and holding her nose, he popped one of her gloves in her mouth and placed a strip of tape around her head and the glove, holding it securely in place. Her cries of agony could no longer be heard.

Taking advantage of the dark and her total helplessness, he slowly unbuttoned the top of her blouse and reaching his left hand inside her brazier, squeezed and rubbed her young breasts. First he had to secure the man; he could be dangerous. Jumpers had guts and he wasn't going to take any chances. Reaching between her legs, he rubbed the innocent Mia and whispered in her ear, "Later."

"What're your names?" he asked.

With no response given, he decided it was time to talk tough—no more 'please' and 'thank you'. "Listen, you pricks. I can kill ya both right now, put your bodies in back, drive myself and your charmin' daughter, who'll certainly be good company, that is until I'm done with her. Or ya can do exactly as I say and answer my questions. Do ya understand?" he demanded.

"Yes," they both answered, knowing now, without a doubt, he could and would; he had nothing to lose.

"Now, names?"

"Hannes—Kreeta," they said together. "Our daughter is Mia. She's only twelve," Hannes added, terrified for his helpless daughter.

"What street da ya live on?"

"West Ohio."

"Well, well, let's see. Graveraet middle school, the old Marquette brownstone high-school. Corner of North Front and West Ohio. Right?"

"How did you know that?" Kreeta asked, somewhat amazed.

"Phone 225–4302. For Christ sake, lady, it's a landmark. I've been in that stinkin' hole for sixteen years! What's your last name?"

"Palomaki."

"Well, well. Kreeta Palomaki, Professor in the humanities."

"Instructor."

"Sorry. Let's see, Dr. Hannes Palomaki, Professor of Mathematics, Northern Michigan University. Co-author—'Chaos Theory—Real or Fancied', 1989. That's kind of appropriate isn't it!" he sadistically laughed. "Local ski-jumper most likely to break Kogler's record. How's that?" he queried.

"Not bad," Hannes muttered, in a tone of bitter hate, his mind racing to come up with a plan.

Enough, Guy thought, like'em I won't hurt'em, I know all about hostage defenses, keep'em talking and they won't kill you. "Now, both of ya, do exactly as I tell ya or it's all over. Capice?"

"Yes," they both replied.

"Pull over at the side in that cleared area—do what I say and be quick.

Hannes, slide your seat back as far as it'll go. Kreeta put your arms folded on the dash and your head down. Hannes, your arms behind your back—do it!"

Hannes, his heart pounding with adrenalin, sped fast forward through his options. How could he give up to this evil force that had invaded their world without a fight? If only the knife was at my throat and not Mia's. Pray and obey.

Their captor's guile provided the gossamer thread of hope leading Hannes, out of fear for Mia, to surrender his strength and power; his last opportunity to come to the rescue of his beloved wife and precious daughter or to defend himself. Quickly, Gerlach taped Hannes' wrists together; taking no chances he wrapped them over and over, no human could break these bonds. "Now turn and put your feet between the seats and stretch your legs out as far as you can." He removed Hannes' shoes and socks, then taped his ankles. "Now back here," he ordered, and dragging the helpless Hannes like a sack of flour, placed him on his back, on the bench seat, with his head to the passenger side.

With a brutal blow to the side of the head, he stunned Hannes and forcing one of his gloves into his mouth, quickly taped his face, but tragically, left his eyes and nose uncovered. Helpless, Hannes could now see and hear, but do nothing except groan in agony. Gerlach now had absolute rule. The knife and her maternal instincts to protect Mia would control Kreeta. "Keep your head down, Kreeta," he again ordered.

Opening Mia's blouse and pants, he again rubbed her breasts and this time he went inside her pants and her. Hannes, twisting and groaning in hatred only received sharp stabs in both of his thighs, no arteries—but more than just a typical prison 'hello'—Gerlach cut to render Hannes' legs useless. There would never be a record for Hannes Palomaki.

Gerlach stripped naked, his rigid penis a frightening sight to Mia, who looked in horror and curiosity. She had no idea they could get that big. She had only seen one little boy's stiff and by accident her father's naked, but limp.

Opening what looked to be a man's travel case, Gerlach dressed in Hannes' pullover and a pair of sport slacks. He put on Hannes' shoes and socks, secure in the knowledge that unless Murphy switched sides, Hannes wouldn't need them. With his penis still out of his slacks he again rubbed Mia. Aware that time was his biggest enemy, he climbed into the driver seat and headed for Duluth. "Kreeta, you can set back now. Hannes and Mia are both fine."

In the dim light she could see Guy rubbing himself, a flush came over her, she had never seen such a thing. Certain now he would take more than the van, she prayed he would just leave Mia alone and let them live. She knew she would have to follow his orders to stay alive and just possibly, their luck might change. Something might go wrong and she would be able to stop what deep down inside she feared might happen. There was always hope; a deer might cause a crash, a tire blow out. Many things could happen allowing her to gain control.

"What are you going to do with us?" she asked.

"Not much," he lied. "Where were you headed, the Monster?"

"Yes, and if we're not there by eight in the morning they'll be looking for this van."

"Don't bullshit me, you couldn't possibly get there by eight. Not on that north-south road and traffic—you're lyin' again. I know all about jumpers. Let's see, last night Hannes called Ted, the Hill Captain, 'How's the track?'. 'Oh, fine'. 'Great! I'll check in with you say—nine o'clock, give us time for breakfast, drive down, check in at the resort, unload and walk over'. Not bad hey? Don't lie to me anymore, okay?" Gerlach also overlooked the abnormal east-west Central Time Zone change, of Michigan's upper peninsula.

"I guess," she sighed.

"I'll level with you. I'm—we're—goin' to Duluth, that's ninety-four miles from Ironwood. It's one hundred forty-seven to Ironwood and we're out fourteen—that's about two hundred twenty-seven miles all told. East-west road is clear and dry so I'll hold it at between sixty and seventy, not too slow—not too fast, put it on cruise and kick back."

He had three hours until they were missed—at the earliest—later if Murphy held steady, but he had to drive and if stopped, he had to have control. She'll never jump out and leave Mia, she can't beat me and the hot coffee's out of her reach. Talking softly he gave her no choice, "Take off your jeans and your sweater, bitch, and come over here and go down on this or I'll stop, tie you up and do Mia." She'd do just what he was forced to do his first time in prison; do as you are told.

To Hannes' agony, the new moon's silence and her daughter's mortification, she nursed him to his climax while he rubbed her bare breasts and then, reached his fingers deep into her.

Hannes' humiliation deepened as he soiled his jeans and urinated. Tears streamed down his face as he could see how things would end, unless—Ted. God, he prayed, oh God, please help us, what have we done? What has Mia done? Show mercy God, he implored.

The new moon, having risen at 4:02, Eastern Standard Time, shed no light and like Hannes, could only watch in helpless silence. Throughout history it could only light or pass in darkness as the spectrum of human evil and good unfolded beneath its vigil. Today, the moon thanked its creator for being unseen—embarrassed at being unable to help this innocent, stricken family. Only fate or other humans could, or would, intervene.

Finished, Kreeta pulled her blouse down and getting back in the passenger seat, put her jeans on, too embarrassed to look at Mia or her Hannu, helpless in the back. "Well, that was sure good for me. Was it good for you?" Gerlach asked, a leer on his face.

In total degradation, with tears streaming down her face, she clenched her teeth and refused to respond to his sick question.

"We'll do it different next time," he taunted, and increasing his speed, raced as fast as he dared for the Wisconsin border.

8:40 A.M. Central Standard Time
Pine Mountain
Kiwanis Ski Club Headquarters
Office of the Hill Captain

Ted Malgadi, 1990–1991 ski club Hill Captain, having checked the new wind gauge and the ski slide, returned to the warm club headquarters.

Pine Mountain Ski Slide, known as the Monster to ski jumpers, began its long and colorful history in 1928. For many years it was the highest artificial ski jump in the world. With a height of one hundred seventy-six feet and length of three hundred ninety-five feet, it had a reputation in the ski jumping fraternity as one of the better one-hundred-twenty meter hills in the world.

Ted knew his friend Hannes still had the great leg strength required for the in-run transition and the landing-hill transition, those periods when the tremendous 'G' forces are produced as the skier is forced through the curved plane of the hill and at landing. He knew Hannes' balance and timing were still at a level where, if the hill and the wind were at their optimum, a record could be set. Today was good—he could feel it—Hannes will be happy.

Ted was there the day in 1980 when Armin Kogler had made that awesome jump. Built like his friend Hannes, at 5'10" and weighing about 160 pounds, the Austrian Air Force jet pilot had broken the hill record he had previously set, of three-hundred and eighty-five feet, by some fourteen feet.

Conditions today were as close as they had ever been in the last ten years. It wouldn't be official since it wasn't in competition, but it would be known; it would count in Hannes' heart and in the hearts and souls of all Finns. Wow, a couple of good jumpers down the track and my buddy may have a crack at it. Guess I'll walk up to the resort and talk to him, he thought and was about to leave when the phone rang.

"Ted, I hate to ask you, but we're out of milk and you know what it's like around here in the morning. Could you please run a couple of gallons home, honey?"

"Okay," he sighed. She's a good wife, just too damn fertile—six kids he thought with a grin, remembering the antics of his twin three-year olds. To hell with the Pope! He sends me milk, I won't get a vasectomy!

Yelling the catch phrase of the day, "I'll be back," to his assistants, he started out for the one hour chore. It's too bad my radio is on the fritz, I could listen to the news on that escape and weather reports, he thought, as he pulled out of the lot.

8:45 A.M. Central Time
West Bound—U.S. Highway 2

Past Hurley, Wisconsin, the van on cruise at sixty-eight miles per hour, Gerlach could wait no longer; it was time to be serviced again. With no choice, and following his direction, Kreeta lowered her vagina on the head of his erection. Gasping at its huge size and with nothing but agony and hate on her part, she gritted her teeth as he thrust deep inside. It ended quickly; broken and without feeling she dressed and resumed her seat, tears streaming from six eyes.

Satisfied for the moment, Gerlach pulled to the side of the road. Under his absolute control—her fear for Mia would keep her from running—Kreeta relieved herself while their tormentor removed the rack with skis and threw them in the deep powder snow.

Back in their seats he began to push his speed, I'll test ole *Murphy* he thought—*Murphy* refused to budge. Good luck, bad luck, there was simply no opportunity and nothing *Murphy* could do to help the innocent Palomakis as the van rolled without hindrance through snow blanketed forests and scattered villages of northern Wisconsin.

———

9:45 A.M. Central Time
Kiwanis Ski Club Headquarters
Pine Mountain

Shutting the door behind him, Ted turned and looked around the room. "Where's Hannes?" he asked, of no one in particular.

"Haven't seen him. Maybe he's out checking on the hill," Mary replied.

Taking his binoculars, Ted headed out to find the friend he knew he could set his watch by. At five minutes after ten, he entered jump headquarters, "He's not out there. Something must've happened."

The ten-twenty news brief came over the radio and once again reported the escape, "At five-thirty this morning, a prisoner by the name of Guy Gerlach became the first person in Michigan history to make a solo escape from Level five, maximum security of the Branch Prison."

This time, with Hannes late, it registered, "Oh no!" yelled Ted. "Shut that off, the phone quick!" Realizing the emergency, Mary hung up on her caller. "Quick, get me the Marquette Big Boy," he asked with urgency as the operator came on.

"The number is 228–8588, repeat. . . ." Hanging up, he immediately called and got a busy signal. Knowing about the snowmobile trails and Hannes' habit, his frantic tries continued to be blocked by the busy signal. Fear sunk in deeper as he punched in the number for the fourth time.

"Good morning, Elias Brother's Big Boy. May I help you?"

"Yes. Do you know Hannes Palomaki?" he asked.

"No," a voice replied.

"Please get me the manager . . ., Mary, run up to the resort and see if they're there."

"Hello, this is Bob. May I help you?"

"Bob, Ted down at the Monster. Were Hannes and Kreeta in this morning?"

"Ya, that Mia too, she's a little knock-out that one. Why?"

"What time did they leave?"

"Oh, heck six-ten or so. He said they were heading down there," answered Bob, in his heavy Finnish accent. "Oh my God! They're not there yet? That guy that got out—oh my God! Not the Palomakis," he groaned.

"I'm going to call State Police," said Ted, as he hung up. His mind raced, he'd go west, probably Duluth; maybe south on forty-five to eight and St. Paul, a lot further—no Duluth.

––––––––––

11:24 A.M. Eastern Standard Time
State Police Headquarters
Negaunee, Michigan

"State Police. May I help you?"

"Yes, get me the Captain please."

"Are you kidding? We're tied up here—no way, not now!"

"Christ—this is Ted, at the Monster, and I know who that bastard's got!"

"Wait just a minute," replied the desk officer.

"Ted—Hansen here. What've you got for us?" the Captain asked.

"John! It's Hannes—Hannes, Kreeta and Mia! I think that bastard's got 'em!"

"Oh no—oh Christ! How do you know that?"

"Look at your map, John! Bob, at the Big Boy, said they'd left at six-ten. The bastard gets out, runs the Carp River snowmobile trail to the business loop. Good shape, twenty minutes—gets there, maybe six to six-ten, and nails 'em! Hannes told me last night he'd check in here at nine. You know Hannes, that means nine! They're in a ditch, a hospital or kidnapped! I figure he'll head for Duluth. They're in a brown and white, Chevrolet Beauville van, with skis on top."

"Ted, just a minute, did Hannes mean Eastern Standard Time or Central?"

"Well, he left the Big Boy at six-ten. That would mean they'd be here by eight o'clock Central Time. He told me nine o'clock. It must be he had another errand. Maybe I panicked. But I still think something's wrong!" Ted exclaimed.

"Okay. We'll do what we can—I'm in touch with all units. I'll get back to you. Thanks, Ted."

Hanging up the telephone with a sigh, Ted settled back in his chair, totally helpless and unable to render any assistance to his good friend and jumping partner, Hannes, or his lovely wife and daughter. And with a premonition of his worst fears, tears began to well in his eyes as he bowed his head and prayed.

By eleven thirty-two Eastern Standard Time, all State Police and Sheriff, Upper Peninsula patrol units, had been notified. By ten thirty-five Central Time, the State Patrol Headquarters of Wisconsin and Minnesota were notified; at ten-forty Central Time, the City of Duluth was notified. Everyone but Gerlach was an hour behind schedule.

10:08 A.M. Central Time
Richard Bong Bridge
Superior, Wisconsin

Gerlach was now confident he could get away. One of his prison companions, a former interstate trucker, told him all about trucking and had described the truck terminal in Duluth. An independent, likely a produce hauler, was most apt to be empty for the run back south. It would set high on its tires and empty, the driver would not be getting paid for the return trip. A driver, seeking a ride south for pay, would be a welcome passenger.

If he had to, he could call the local truck broker to locate a southbound trucker with a load going out of Duluth, but this would be more risky since the police might think to check. Once he had a ride, he would be passed from truck to truck as a California bound driver, a common practice among truckers.

Gerlach knew he was running out of time if the Palomakis were missed and calls were out. He would have to get off the main highways and ditch the van. He could stroll away to the Arrowhead Truck Terminal on Carlton, approximately eight blocks northeasterly of the US-2 and Interstate 35 crossing. All he had to do was follow '2' through Superior and cross St. Louis Bay on the ultra-modern, Richard I. Bong Bridge and he would be out of Wisconsin.

"Hey, bitch—see that car!" Guy exclaimed. "That's a Mitsubishi headin'
for Bong's Bridge! Ain't that the fuckin' shits!"

Only her desire to save her family could force her to break the cold-
silence of her burning-hatred, "So, what's the point?"

"Lots of time to read in prison. In World War II, Bong, a twenty-two
year old kid from Poplar, Wisconsin, became the best of the rest. He was a
real 'top gun'. He shot down forty confirmed jap airplanes, had seven more
probables and eleven damaged. The all time American ace!

"They were mostly jap, Mitsubishi A6Ms, produced by Mitsubishi Heavy
Industries in 1940. They were the fastest and most maneuverable plane in the
Pacific. The japs called it the *Reisen Kanjikisen*, which meant 'Zero Celebration, Carrier-based Fighter Airplane'. The name comes from the twenty-six-
hundred year celebration of the ascension to the throne of *Jimmu*, the legendary
first emperor of Japan. Nineteen forty was the Zero Year celebration.

"Bong was able to shoot 'em down with the Lockheed Lighting P-38,
developed in '42. Was ordered home after his fortieth confirmed kill. Married
his college sweet-heart, in February of '45, and died that August testing one
of the new P-80 jet fighters. Now, Mitsubishis go across 'his bridge' taking
their owners to work. Kind of ironic, don't you think?" he asked. Fear of
impending doom, not made lighter by his history lesson, sealed Kreeta's terrified lips.

Across the bridge, he drove over Interstate 35 and continued on to West
Duluth. Turning left on Grand Avenue, Guy drove slowly, searching for an
area to park the van. At the next block, on his right hand side and across from
the Diamond Tool and Horseshoe Company, he found the ideal place. No *dia-
mond-day* or *lucky-shoe* for them, he thought, and pulling into the lot from the
back alley, parked the van and shut off the engine.

Kreeta, a kind, loving and trusting person, was burdened by an inherent
disadvantage. Blind to the future and ignorant of their captor's brutal battery
on Hannes, she had been unable—when released under the knife's deadly vigil—
to make a ferocious, maiming attack on Gerlach that might have been a viable
option.

She knew to lose an attack would bring certain death and leave Mia and
her Hannu to Gerlach's mercy. Seated to the far left and turned slightly toward
her, he had maintained an ever wary watch. Belted in her seat, with her left
arm taped to the rest during the drive, there had been no opportunity. She made
the bitter choice—she would obey and pray.

"Kreeta, I want you naked on the floor, then I'll tie and gag you. Hannes
can bang on the van sides and someone will let you out. I'll be long gone, so
just do as I say. Now strip and lie on your back between the seats." With no
choice and fearing the worst, but praying he would let them live, she stripped
and gritting her teeth, waited. "One more time," he said, mounting her and
then, with a swipe of his wrist, ended her agony.

As Gerlach, to complete his rape, took Mia, Hannes—shaking in fear and hatred—closed his eyes and prayed. *A vision—out of body—in a sparkling white gown—the Saint Lucia Festival princess—radiant in her natural beauty— her wreath aglow with candles—made whole—as if on an escalator—ascended in stately glory the staircase to Heaven.* Mia's total fear could not mask her extreme pain, and, as he had her mother's, *evil* ended her short existence. The angels screamed and took them to their bosom.

Hannes, helpless and frozen with fear, eyes tightly shut, heart hammering violently, could only twist and groan as the razor sharp shank made a half circle around his throat. Gerlach froze as a woman crossed the lot, entered the car beside them, slowly backed out and drove away.

10:21 A.M. Central Time

Gerlach, putting on Hannes' warm jacket, climbed out, locked the doors and walking to the side of the empty parking place, tossed the door-jimmy on the ground. That'll throw the mother-fuckers off my trail, he thought, and strolling across the parking lot to Grand Avenue, headed uptown toward Carlton. With over a thousand dollars of their vacation money in his pocket, he began to whistle, 'Oh what a beautiful morning', absolutely exhilarated and without remorse as he reminisced over his early morning trip. He knew it would be easy to catch a ride with a south-bound trucker. Arizona winters and Wyoming summers, he thought, in happy contemplation.

10:42 A.M.
City of Duluth
Patrol Car #7

Officer Gronsky, a ten year veteran of the force, with his young rookie partner learning the ropes, slowly turned his white, Chevrolet Caprice patrol car, left from Nicollet Street onto north-bound Grand Avenue and headed toward downtown Duluth. The call, received only five minutes earlier, had sent shivers up the back of his neck. Instinct and quick calculations of time and distance put his nerves on edge. "Keep your eyes peeled, Alex. That son-of-a-bitch could be in the area."

Well familiar with West Duluth, it hit him as he passed Taco John's on 46th and Grand. He had never seen a van that color parked in the lot across from Diamond Tool. "I'm going back. Let's check out that van," said Gronsky, reaching for his mike. "Central—Car 7 back to Grand and 47th. Would you give me that Michigan van plate again? EJ-1203. Okay—hang on—it's here. Send a backup unit. Ten-four."

"Okay, Alex, let's go," he ordered. And pulling their new, Glock 9-millimeter semi-automatics, proceeded to the silent van. The young officer, new on the job, looked in first—the veteran didn't want to—turned and violently retched.

This is hideous, thought Murphy. The equilibrium is disturbed. 'He's vexed God'. He must be stopped. I'll keep watch on this matter.

The calls went out. Evil was on the loose.

4

'. . . birds of a feather . . .'

Saturday evening
February 16, 1991
Lansing, Michigan

Pulling his '79 Olds winter-beater into the drive, Will climbed out to face the bitter cold, dark, early evening. As he shut the car door, Burr walked out of the house, turned, kissed his wife and three youngest children goodby and headed for the car. "Where does Sam live, Will?" he asked, as they shook hands.

"He and George live on Tecumseh, north of the Grand and a little east of Waverly. About a ten minute drive from here," replied Will, backing out of the drive.

"Have either of 'em ever been married?"

"No. They're confirmed bachelors. Sam's fifty-four, a year and a couple weeks younger'n me and George is around forty-five, I think. George—last name Prep—is a hell of a good cook, and Sam—last name McCord—about the worst cook I've ever met! I could tell cold, mushy pancake and lumpy potato stories for hours. When we hunt, I cook!"

"Can you believe it, Will! Wyoming this summer! Hey, why don't you fill me in on these guys. I've heard how Sam saved your ass in Alaska, but that's about it."

"Okay. Sam's about to retire. Been a teamster and driven a route most of his working career. Spends most of his spare time helping family and friends. He'll put on a new roof—paint—rebuild a house—you name it. I've known Sam a long, long time. In spite of driving, he loves to travel—lookin' forward to seeing the world."

"You said George is a trucker?"

"Well, he takes a semi to Detroit once or twice a week. He's in charge of purchasing produce for Michigan State and that's a bunch of salad shooters! George doesn't hunt much—of course none of us hunt like we did when we were younger. George likes to cook, read and fish, and probably in that order. He's a very kind, gentle person. Just don't piss him off. I've never seen him angry, but he's tough. He'd go to the wall to protect his friends.

"Then there's Kevin, who's in his mid-forties. He and I get under each other's skin occasionally, because we both want to do things our own way. We've adjusted. I'll tell you this, the man's a damn genius! He works as a trouble-shooter for Motor Wheel. Runs from plant to plant in the US and Canada fixing machines others can't, and making things run smoother."

"Does he have a family?"

"Yes. He's married to one of Sam's sisters and they have a daughter that'll be getting married soon. Kevin's a strong family man—God—family—country. He isn't blind and realizes more than machines need fixing."

"Will, it sounds like you trust these men a lot."

"I do. Burr, you've been in the army. If you pick your team, you know where they stand. But if it's by an assignment, you pray. Right?"

"That's the God's truth!" exclaimed Burr.

"Well, these men, by family and friendship, are all picked. In the field, shit can happen and you never know from where. In a blink your life's in someone else's hands. Sam's proven that. I just hope I wouldn't fail."

"We all hope that, Will. How about Tom?"

"Tom's married to another of Sam's sisters. Health has been a recent problem—his ticker. They did some vascular pipe cleaning and a valve adjustment, so he'll take it easy. He just turned sixty, has grown children and several grandchildren. He loves to travel, reads a lot, and is really looking forward to retirement. As a claims supervisor, he's had to cover disasters around the country. He's done a lot of arson investigations."

"How do you two get along, with him in insurance and you suing people?"

"Oh, he kids me a little, but he's never taken a cheap shot because of lawsuits or criminal cases I've handled. He really believes in the system. Tom was born and lived in Portsmouth, Ohio, just across the river from Kentucky. He's very quiet and soft-spoken, but don't let that fool you. The man's a crack shot. Has a bunch of trophies from shooting in NRA competition. Long distance matches. One thousand yards with a thirty-ought six, using iron sights! Doesn't hunt much any more, but if you heard one shot, you'd find him cleaning out a trophy buck!

"In a quiet, smooth way, he gets the job done. The man has a great sense of humor. You'll hear some stories of claims he's handled, that'll crack you up!"

"Well, I'll tell ya, Will, I'm really looking forward to this trip. Six days in the mountains, trout fishing and horseback riding. Can you believe it? Six days with no telephone beeper or problems to solve!" exclaimed the nearly ready to retire, telephone company trouble-shooter.

"I know," replied Will. "Now the kids are gone and no dog to take care of, traveling's a lot easier. Trish and I had a great time out west."

"I'll bet you did!" exclaimed Burr, with a grin.

"Private matters, old boy, private matters," Will replied, with a laugh. "Here's the house. I know you'll like these troops. They're all confirmed non-smokers. Die-hard—don't you dare blow smoke in my space—fanatics. I was three decks of Luckys a day. We're like a covey of reformed hookers!" exclaimed Will, as he parked in front of the one-story, white, ranch house.

The two were met at the door with a firm handshake, their coats taken and the introduction of William 'Burr' Wolf, to the tight, family group, completed.

"Will," inquired Sam, as seated with the others around the oak, kitchen table, he clutched a hot cup of coffee in hands toughened from years as a route-man for Nabisco, "did you get in touch with the outfitter?"

"Yeah—well, his wife. They received our money order. We're paid in full and confirmed to start out early Sunday morning, July twenty-eighth for a place called Simpson Lake. No idea where—up in some mountains."

"Did she say how many'd be in camp?" asked Kevin.

"She mentioned Bob's brother—don't know his name. They take four or five pack horses, furnish all the food and do the cooking. You wash dishes, Sam!" exclaimed Will.

"Your ass! You can't cook any better'n I can—you sausage!" Sam retorted.

"Alright you two, alright—war stories for camp," ordered Kevin. "Say, Will, how'd it go in Cincinnati?"

"Bullshit!" exclaimed George, "I don't want to hear anymore about that damn case. I'm sick of it! Oh, go ahead, Will. Just don't put us to sleep."

All in the gathering were well aware of Will's eight year struggle against the team of four, high-powered firms defending Noel Cain, another attorney, a psychiatrist and three other medical doctors.

The so-called 'surrogate-mother' business, no longer legal for money in Michigan, had precipitated one of the most highly publicized disputes in the country. Certainly it was the most public case Will had ever handled. The third federal judge to handle the case, had, over a period of six years, granted defense motions, piece-meal, that resulted in his clients case being dismissed without ever having their day in court.

Appeal had been taken to the Federal 6th Circuit Court of Appeals in Cincinnati, and Will had argued the matter on Valentines Day, the preceding Thursday.

"Okay, George—I'll keep it short," promised Will. "But first, this so-called 'surrogate-mother' phrase is just plain bullshit. A woman has a baby—insemination or the old-fashioned way, she's the mother. It's her baby. She may be a surrogate-wife, but she sure as hell's a mother and it's her child. If she has other children, it's their half-brother or half-sister that's being sold!"

"Well," interrupted Tom, "it's what everyone seems to call 'em."

"Am I wrong, Tom?" questioned Will.

"No—I guess not. It is her baby," Tom conceded.

"Tell us about Cincinnati," said Sam, knowing Will could jump easily to an aside and he'd have to keep him on course.

"Great, great city. Stayed at the downtown Ramada Inn, a hop-skip'n-jump from the Federal Building. I was so nervous when I started my argument, thought I'd piss my pants! It went fine though. My partner, the former Mrs. Dean, had prepared a hell-of-a brief and the presentation went smoothly. I hope!"

"Hell, Will, it's her and her husband's baby. I still don't see how you've got a claim" declared Tom.

"Tom, you sound just like an insurance adjuster!" exclaimed Kevin, jumping to Will's defense.

"I was for thirty years," he replied. "You'd better explain it, Will."

"Keep it short, Will," admonished George.

"Okay, but listen you guys, no lawyer jokes and talking law-law-law crap on this trip. Is that a deal?"

"That's a deal," promised Kevin, as the others nodded their agreement. "Now explain your case without a lot of legalese and gobble-de-gook jargon!"

"Here goes. We claim the defendants had a duty to make a safe program. It was a new venture. The purpose was to have a child by a semen donor, who wanted a genetic heir. Don't you think these business-for-money experts should know how long a woman must go without sex to assure none of her husband's sperm were lurking around, ready and able to nail her egg?"

"That would seem basic to me," ventured Burr, in his first sortie into the discussion.

"Well they didn't," continued Will. "None of 'em were fertility experts and the longest any of 'em believed sperm could fertilize was seventy-two hours! Our expert is the University of Michigan's top gun on fertility. He says studies conducted by the Catholic Church clearly show that under ideal conditions, the little devils can fertilize an egg for up to ten days! That's why they call rhythm-method-people, parents!

"My clients never had a chance. Given the time sequence involved, there was a risk of exposing a conception of theirs to whatever disease the donor might have, if any. And the worst-case scenario happened."

"But, how can you possibly show the virus causing the birth defects came from the donor?" inquired Tom.

"A very good question, Mister Doubting Thomas! The infectious disease expert—who by the way, was not someone we hired—had been called in when the baby was born, long before lawyers got involved. It's his opinion, *with a reasonable degree of medical certainty,* that the cyto-megalovirus—CMV—came from the donor. Remember, when they inseminated the woman, they used fresh semen they knew had not been tested for anything! We wouldn't have done that to a registered Hereford cow!"

"Wow!" exclaimed Tom, a bit more receptive.

"Anyway, when active, CMV would only appear as a common cold to an adult. But, in a primary infection, she'd have no immunities. If near the time of conception, it can cause catastrophic defects to a developing baby."

"Were they testing for that disease?" asked George.

"No. But maybe they should've been. But that's not the point. Proper advice could've precluded a conception of their's being exposed to *whatever* disease the donor might've had. With only the donor's sperm in place—it's the donor's baby! Our case in a nutshell," said Will.

"When'll you hear from court?" asked Sam.

"I hope before I die of old age!" exclaimed Will, with a laugh. "Now, no more law crap."

"You ever speechless, Will?" asked Tom.

Will, contemplating how to answer, was rescued by Sam, "You bet he's been speechless."

"When, Sam?" asked Will, doubting that he ever had.

Bursting out in a good belly laugh, Sam began, wiping away tears of merriment. "We were in Newfoundland—our 1972 trip—and after Will'd shot a bull . . ."

"He's always shooting that," laughed Kevin. "Aren't you, Will?"

"Anyway," resumed Sam, "Will was down to his last bottle of scotch—he drank Glenlivet back then—when his guide asked him if he could have a drink. Said he liked scotch and water. Will said sure. Well, the guide, a lanky old codger in his mid-sixties, who'd already worn Will's butt out tramping over hill-and-dale, takes an eight ounce drinking glass, fills it to the top with Glenlivet, walks over to the corner and sticks his hand in the drinking bucket. Then he shakes the water off his hand and snaps his fingers at the scotch. One damn drop splashes on the top of Will's last booze and the guide downs it. Everyone in the tent burst into laughter at the look of horror on Will's face. He was speechless!" exclaimed Sam.

"Will, I thought you only drank Jack Daniel's?" questioned Burr.

"That's right, Burr. But that was before my trip to Lynchburg," replied Will, with a grin.

"Here comes another one," laughed Tom. "Burr, you ever been to the Jack Daniel distillery in Lynchburg?"

"No."

"Well, it's quite a place. A guide herds you around in groups of ten or so and takes your picture in front of Jack Daniel's statue. Later, they mail a copy to each member of the group. Will's got a letter from the distillery apologizing for the film's not developing! Ever since, Will only drinks Jack. Guess he feels he owes it to 'em!" exclaimed Tom, with a smirk.

"Rumors—rumors—rumors, but still no pictures," replied Will, with a chuckle.

"Someday you're going to run out of luck, Will," Tom declared.

"Talk about luck and things not working—a buddy of mine, a kay-mag, was in a North Korean rice paddy when an incoming mortar shell hit. They all hit their bellies in the mud, but it was a dud. When they examined the round, they found the E. I. du Pont markings! Their mortars were a millimeter bigger than ours, so they could fire our rounds, but we couldn't use theirs. The Chinese gunners were pros."

"What's a kay-mag?" asked Kevin.

"They were K-M-A-G. It stood for Korean Military Advisor Group. But they'd blouse their pants, put on their red scarfs, olive green hard-hats and tell the girls it stood for Korean Mountain Airborne Guerrillas! They didn't want to tell the ladies they did CID dirty work."

"Were you in the Korean War, Will?" asked Burr,

"Oh, no. I met the guy when we worked on a job a couple years after it was over."

Tom, Sam and Will, air force veterans and Burr, army, regaled George and Kevin with war stories, old and new. The evening of congenial friendship and laughing comradery—often spicy—demonstrated that Burr would well compliment the group's mountain adventure.

George and Sam, heading for a visit with family and friends in Oregon, meant that two vehicles would have to embark in July for the journey west. Time flew and the five months to departure passed quickly. None could be aware—ignorance of the future was certainly one of life's greatest blessings—of dark storm clouds brewing in the southwest corner of Wyoming.

9:15 P.M.
Thursday, February 21, 1991
Pinedale, Wyoming

KEN'S
LONGHORN SALOON
Liquor/Food/Live Music

Like a lonely outcast from a herd of sheep, among a few stunted pines beyond reach of the town's sidewalk, sat the one-story Longhorn Saloon. The bar, a favorite of the locals, was located two miles west of Pinedale on the south side of State 191 and a few yards west of the New Fork River. Parked in front, as if a row of guarding sentinels, stood the usual odd assortment of pickup trucks, most of them four-wheel drive. The only thing they had in common was a generous coat of dust, barely legible Wyoming cowboy truck plates and the west's mandatory gun racks—filled—in the rear windows.

By no means did the Longhorn give the appearance it catered to, or wanted a traveling station wagon with a load of hungry children. The ever-present owner, who lived in a small apartment in the rear, watched. Kenneth Jordan, age fifty-five, was the father of five sons and two daughters, all grown, living in the mid-west and busy raising his thirteen grandchildren; he could only watch.

Ken, at five-foot seven, one-hundred forty pounds, and the survivor of jaw bone surgery for cancer, was too frail to control or participate in the occasional, rowdy activities and male macho tests of strength. Non-judgmental, always an understanding listener and gentle counsel to their various problems, he was truly loved in the purest sense, by his steady, regular customers. Control over the activities was left to the most sober of these. And they responded to a wink or a nod from Ken, who, while not interfering, would, on rare occasion, seek to modify behavior too exuberant or dangerous.

The regulars only desired a local bar in which to have a little good, clean fun—dance—drink—shoot pool—talk about sex—hunting—fishing—stupid people in Washington—the big city Blacks, and to watch and enjoy Betty Lou. And Betty Lou was something to see—beauty in motion. Trim, brunette, flashing brown eyes and two of the finest—'way up firm and high'. At five-foot one, ninety-eight pounds, little Betty Lou was a spark and an occasional special treat of safe sex for those regulars who accepted her terms. They were simple; cash, no romantic involvement, only when she wanted, and physically, she controlled the action.

A former legal secretary from San Francisco, she had left her job, tired and fed up with pompous lawyers who wanted to play without pay and billed their clients at atrocious rates, which always seemed to include those quickies spent with her. Nevada for a brief stint was financially rewarding, but did not give her any control. At the Longhorn there was no percentage to Ken, he didn't want it, nor did he partake. Content in his own relationship, he enjoyed the good business of the bar.

As in all small bars, there was in the rear corner, a juke box. Its turning, white-mirrored ball catching and casting the blue and pink lines of light in motion. A Rowe AMI, it held two hundred songs, most of which the cowboys, guides and local mountain men enjoyed. There was however, one rather out-of-place record occupying a blank space and only to be played by Betty Lou. The locals knew if any tourist should happen by accident to hit B-5, a wooden nickel went into the jar; Betty Lou wanted to keep track.

In the opposite rear corner, on the other side of the small bandstand, a round oak table sat beneath the dim light of a dusty, imitation Tiffany. With space for six, the seat in the shaded corner, was the chair of honor for the sport of Betty Lou. Hanging from the middle rafter, an old-time, black, cast-iron dinner bell with a rope through an old wood pulley attached to the side wall, within Betty Lou's reach, should she want it to ring.

Betty Lou, during her weekly shift of Monday through Friday nights, was like Ken, a favorite and well-protected friend of the ever present regulars. There were usually one or two men with an extra fifty, plus any tip, who would enjoy the slow rhythm of *Black Velvet*, always to follow the appropriate cue of Betty Lou's high-spirited dance to the fast, jitterbug beat of B-5; Bob Segar's *Betty Lou's Coming Out Tonight.*

Slowly, Lee backed his GMC pickup alongside a battered, but still functional Ford. Familiar with the vehicle, his only concern was whether he would again be forced to withdraw. Without hesitation the two brothers climbed out, locked their doors and headed for the saloon. John's desire to talk to and be with Betty Lou, if she was still working, would not be denied.

It was nice to be known, if only on a casual basis, and they were warmly greeted by the friendly owner, the ever present handkerchief at his twisted jaw, "Hi, guys. It's been a while. The same? Jack on the rocks?"

"Sure, Ken. How've you been?" John replied, reaching out to shake his hand.

"Fine, fine—same old wreck!" answered Ken, with a friendly smile.

Just then, both were grabbed from behind by a bouncing Betty Lou, "Hi, guys! Long time! How are my two favorite virgins? I mean Virginians!"

"Hey, Betty Lou!" exclaimed John, giving her a big hug. "We're official cowboys now, truck plates and all. We bought that place in Rock Springs we were renting last year. No more nonresident hunting and fishing stuff. It's too damn expensive!"

"Let's get a table," interrupted Lee.

"Where?" Betty Lou smiled. "Back corner yet, Lee?"

"Well, maybe. I know John's in a hurtin' state!"

"Give me a couple of minutes to hit the tables. I want to talk a bit about last fall. Lee, I'm real sorry about what happened."

"Hey, Lou, not your fault," Lee quietly answered and, turning, followed John to the round table.

By the pool table, the Ford's six-foot three, well muscled, but brainless owner, looked at Lee walking past, giving him a cocky smirk. Totally ignorant that death—or any stage between—was slowly passing by. There would be no trouble; Lee would spare the idiot, at least in Ken's saloon. Believing Lee to be a coward, it would be more than a year later before he would read and understand how close he had been to dying, or much worse, one last November evening.

"John, I know you like Betty Lou, but . . ."

"Hey, Bro—I know what she is—she's a super person who enjoys her work. I don't want to get married and probably never will. Any woman as smart and sharp as our mother would never be contented with her role. And I don't think I'd ever be happy married to today's woman. So don't worry, we're both alike on that one. Enjoy 'em and forget 'em. Right?"

"Thou doth protest too much, Bro!" quipped Lee.

Betty Lou, with a big smile of sincere friendliness, walked over, "Well, guys, bring me up to speed."

"Nothing much, Betty," John began. "Vegas and San Diego this winter, and we also spent some time down in Taos. We're on our way to Jackson for some downhill, and we wanted to stop by and see you and Ken. We plan on spending some time this summer camping up in the Pinon Ridge area of the Tetons—lots of lakes. We may try the Bridger Wilderness area. My Bro here wants to conquer Battleship Mountain. Right, Lee?"

"We'll see."

"Lee, about last fall, I know you're not afraid of that idiot. There won't be any trouble. His friends are going to get him out of here after this game, okay?" Betty Lou implored. "Besides, one of you'd better make that bell ring. It hasn't for a long time!"

The bell rang when Betty Lou's was rung. Later that evening, a happy and confident John was rewarded with B-5, Black Velvet and a ringing dinner bell. A joyful and satisfied Betty Lou used the money to buy the delighted regulars a round from a smiling Ken, who started to pour as she headed for the rope.

"Betty, we're going to leave a little early tonight—another hour or so. We've got a room down at the Pine Creek and plan on leaving bright and early for Jackson Hole. We've got reservations at the Virginian for Friday through next Wednesday. We're both ready for some downhill at Snow King."

"All right, John. I won't take it personal!" Betty Lou laughed, giving him a hug and a long, warm and very wet kiss.

"Not too mushy there, you two," Lee chuckled, as Betty Lou broke away to wait on the other patient and envious customers.

———————

Friday, 6:00 P.M.
February 22, 1991
Jackson, Wyoming

"Boy! Lee, you missed it!"

"What was that, John?" Lee asked, toweling off and still wet from the shower as they watched the credits roll to the sensuous beat of the background music.

"Well, there must be a town not too far from here by the name of Dubois. I guess some stripper called Geeoh, or something, went bare-ass in a bar, the Rams Head I think. Anyway, some uptight, asshole preacher got all hot and bothered about it and wants the bar's license and the owner's ass. He's worried about the town's children. Why the fuck don't he keep his brats out of bars!"

"Hell, John, you're always readin' about some preacher or scout leader messin' around with little children. Those preachers are famous for not being able to keep their peckers in their pants. They always seem to get uptight over anyone else having a little fun!"

"Dubois can't be too far, Lee. They showed a scene of la Grande Te- tons—ole big tits! Maury Povich said it was 'just a bend in the road'. Probably only a bar and a gas station. Let's get our map out and take a look. Here, look, Bro, it's only eighty-five miles over to Dubois. The Togowotee Pass looks easy and we can be there in a couple hours. We can have dinner—they must have a restaurant in the burg—and check out the action. How 'bout it?" John asked.

"Sure, why not. Sounds like something different for a change. We've spent all our time west of the divide, so it'll be a change of scenery. Let's go for it."

The town of Dubois—nestled in the valley of the Wind River, flanked by the beautiful Wind River mountains to the south and the Absarokas to the north—could best be described by what it isn't. Thankfully, for a break from the real world, it isn't Atlantic City nor Paris nor New Orleans nor the smog-blanketed City of Angels.

Small, with a population of only a thousand-seventy or so souls; quiet, clean, friendly and safe. Its welcome mat was out for those who could enjoy the pleasures of the surrounding area. Bathed in crystal clear air and watered by clean, cold mountain streams, it sparkles in the valley at an elevation of sixty-nine hundred feet, like a magnetic diamond drawing trout fishermen, hunters, photographers, hikers, riders, and in the winter, snowmobilers for high mountain trails without parallel. It does provide a few establishments for those who might, on occasion, enjoy a more boisterous evening's entertainment than watching the electronic pacifier.

The uneventful drive, a pleasant respite from the day of down-hill skiing on the steep slopes of Snow King, ended as Lee parked down the street from the Ramshorn Inn. A short stroll brought them to the entrance. "Shit, John, look at this poster—August, 1989! Well, we might as well go in and check it out."

"Welcome to the Ramshorn, boys. What could I get ya? Name's Leigh," greeted the friendly bartender.

"How about a couple Jack on the rocks," said Lee with a smile, "Black Label if you've got it, please."

"Sure—comin' right up."

"What's with GiO? We just saw her on television, over in Jackson?" asked John.

"She was something—danced on stage only two nights, but she sure made Bert Crow's bar famous! The *Current Affairs* you saw was a re-run. They've done it several times. Sell you a video?"

"No thanks," John replied. "We'll just have a couple more drinks. We may want to check out the Rustic Pine. Our truck's over that way."

"Okay. But it's a lot more fun here," Leigh declared.

With the constant crowd of new faces resulting from the national publicity, Leigh would have no memory of ever seeing the two strangers from Virginia.

"Lee, can you believe it! They got all riled up over a dancer on stage! I don't think they're ready for couch dancing!" laughed John. "Do you?"

"I doubt it. That preacher'd have a cardiac if he saw some of the shows we've seen in Vegas or San Diego! My God, I hope he stays out of the Longhorn!" Lee exclaimed. After a few minutes of watching the pool table, well reserved by the row of stacked quarters, they left and sauntered down the wooden sidewalk to Jepson's Rustic Pine Tavern. Filled with snowmobilers, they brushed elbows, but didn't make waves.

Moving to the end of the bar, Lee noted that a dinner had been brought in from an adjoining restaurant, apparently part of the same building. "John," Lee suggested, as his brother returned from the toilet, "we can get some steaks next door—how does that sound? We can get drinks and hustle chicks later."

"Great! Let's go. I'm starved. Say, this town's a heck of a lot more 'an a bend in the road! It may be a little isolated, but this is a neat place!" Together they left the bar for the restaurant side and were quickly seated next to a table with two couples. Orders taken, they sat in silence over black coffee and without being obvious, listened to the adjacent conversation.

"Gary, how've you been doin' on cats?" the younger of the two men asked.

"Not so good. The dogs had one on the go last week up in Ten Sleep, but that's a long haul. I'm not going back. They've been seeing a lot of cougar sign over in the Gypsum Creek area of the Bridger. I think I'll try the area, maybe next season. How're you doin' on bookings, Bob?"

"We just filled up on fishing—got a good bunch," the woman with the outfitter answered, apparently his wife.

"Where're they from, Linda?" Gary asked.

"There's six of 'em and I just know about the one who wrote. He called last weekend about his precious money order. Sounded friendly. An attorney by the name of Will Dean. Guess they're all from the Lansing, Michigan area."

A look of interest flashed between the brothers and Lee began to scribble meaningless lines along the bottom of his placemat.

"These six are the last before we start the first sheep hunt. We'll put 'em in at the south end of Simpson. You've got the north end reserved don't you, Gary?" asked Bob.

"No, but I don't think there're any outfitters going up except us. We'll stay about a mile and a half north of you among those lodge-pole, if I'm even in there."

"No problem. Plenty of space and fish for all," said Bob. "While we're up there, I'll be able to take a ride to the top of Shale and check out the Bighorn herd. Say, Gary, did you get the portable phone you were talking about a couple of weeks ago?"

"Yeah. We tried it out when Jenny and I went on the snowmobile safari last week-end. Neat! You should get one. It'll fit in the saddle bag real easy, an' man, you can call anywhere!" exclaimed Gary.

"They seem too civilized. Next I suppose you'll have a portable TV up there!"

"Good idea, Bob!" laughed Gary, in reply.

"Linda, do you ride up to Simpson Lake from here?" inquired Gary's wife. "That's a helluva ride for dudes."

"No, Jenny," Linda answered. "We'll take two trucks and the big horse-trailers up toward Union Pass, and then out south toward the Moon Lake trail. We pack in on that trail to the Whiskey Mountain trail. Cross at the north end of Simpson and then cross back to our site at the south end. It's only a three to four hour ride and it gets 'em adjusted to the horses."

"Don't it worry you bein' up in the mountains with six strangers, camping out?" asked Jenny.

"Oh hell—not her!" Bob jumped in, his voice a little loud and slightly slurred. "She can shoot that pistol she keeps in her saddle bag with the best of 'em. Don't forget, she's part Indian. She's got a knife taped to her calf, night and day."

"Hush, that's my secret," whispered Linda.

"Are you thinking what I'm thinking, Bro?" John quietly asked.

A slight smile and a nod was Lee's only reply.

"They're coming in on Saturday, July twenty-seventh and we'll take 'em in first thing Sunday morning. They've paid in full for a six day trip!" Bob exclaimed.

"Must be nice to be able to do that for a few fish," said Jenny.

"Oh, it's not so expensive. They're probably all middle aged, over-weight, under-worked dudes. Two of 'em are retired I guess. 'Let's take a break in the mountains' white-collars," Bob replied. "Our livelihood depends on 'em, whether we like 'em or not!"

"Let's hit the bar side and dance—what say?" said Linda, as she slid her chair back and stood up.

Tall, lean and good looking, John's eyes could not help penetrating the rear of her tight jeans. Lee showed more interest than usual, but his mind was on that lawyer. Checking his notes as he slowly ate his steak; Will Dean, we have a date. In my mind you're just like the son-of-a-bitch and whore who stole our land and murdered my mother and father; vengeance is mine sayeth me.

"John, let's not go back to the bar. Let's just head back to Jackson—
I want to think this over. Okay?"

"Sure. I'm with you, Bro. Whatever. You covered me, I remember.
Me thinks you have a plan!" Paying their bill with cash, as they generally did,
the two left for the Virginian and a good night's sleep.

4:00 P.M.
Wednesday, July 10, 1991
Pine Creek Motel
Pinedale, Wyoming

"You know, John, we could use a third person. We certainly don't need
any help, but it might be handy to have a scapegoat, just in case."

"Well, we aren't going to walk up to someone on the street and say
'hey man, how'd you like to hit a camp of tourists—say, shoot five or six;
torture a couple of lawyers, rape and carry off an outfitter's wife!"

"Oh, I don't know—if they were all lawyers we might have to draw
straws!" laughed Lee.

"Lee, since you started planning this caper, you're the happiest I've
ever seen you."

"Things have been a little quiet for a merc. We lifted a few wallets in
Vegas and I did a couple of lawyers in Reno, but nothing like this. We're
really going to have to be in shape for this one. I mean combat ready and you
are going to get with it, Bro!" Lee warned. "A daylight hit on a camp of eight
is going to take some doing!"

"Wasn't picking up that hiker a kick?"

"Not really—what risk to me? We just started to chat. I was friendly
and completely non-threatening. Gave her my best French accent, '*Oui, tu est
chic type*' and she opened up. Hell, I wasn't going to do anything until she
came out with that, 'I'm a lawyer from Washington, D.C.', bullshit. Gave her
a gentle one side of the head, just like Billy Jack to that prick in the park.
Popped 'em while she was out and brought her in. Think of the fifties we've
saved!"

"Lee," said John, laying down the TV schedule, "let's watch *America's
Most Wanted* and then go out to the Longhorn. The Rendezvous crowd'll be
comin' in this weekend, and it's going to be wild around here. I know Betty
Lou'll be going into hiding, 'cause she doesn't like those rowdies."

"All right with me, Bro. I'll turn on the TV."

'We take you now to Marquette, Michigan . . .', the announcer intoned.

"Jesus—what a bastard, John. That guy's a real sexual-sociopath!" Lee
exclaimed, as the program ended.

"Boy, we could sure use him!" John exclaimed.

"They think he's in the Southwest—tracked him through truckers to Arizona. The son-of-a-bitch even did the last trucker who gave him a ride, just to buy a few more hours!" exclaimed Lee. "That's one face I'll not forget. A big part of my training was in spotting certain individuals."

"Tell me, Lee, how do you go about picking out one certain face in a crowd?" asked John. "I'd know if it was someone I was around and then saw 'em on television. But the next day, to spot a total stranger?"

"You're right, and without a photo in hand it can be tough and easy to make a mistake. Let's walk down to the post office, see if they've got one and I'll give you some basics. It's a lot like how easy it is for you to spot a squirrel when the leaves are still on. You don't look for squirrels, but for lines and motion that're not supposed to be there.

"For instance, they said he was five-ten. Well, he can't get shorter, so you check for lifts that'd be uncomfortable or out of place. You don't pay any attention to hair. It can always be changed. And take eye color for example— tinted contacts can change eyes, so you look for contacts. But, the most important thing will be his mannerisms. He knows he's wanted and his eyes, unless he's a real professional, will be darting all over the place to see if anyone's staring at him. Especially whenever he's anywhere near a television set. If that program was to be shown on a bar set, he'd be out the door."

"Lee, if he's out West and trying to stay away from television sets and wanted posters, he'd be spending most of his time in the boondocks. If he wants to see some action and night life, what better place than right here during the Rendezvous with all the strangers coming to town?"

"Hell, John. Let's just go down to the Longhorn tonight and pick him up!"

"Wouldn't that be the shits!"

"Sure. And pick up some Colorado lottery tickets too, Bro!" said Lee, with a laugh.

"Well, here we are. Let's see if the good ole U.S. of A'll be any help. Bingo! Lookee here, John. That's our man! Let's get a copy an' maybe we can be public servants an' do our good deed. Let's pick up a few things over at Faler's and go get something to eat."

With a copy of the wanted poster in hand and their shopping over, the brothers began the stroll to their favorite restaurant. "John, you know we've got a couple of hours, suppose I might as well tell you how it happened."

"Lee, you don't have to. I know Nam still bothers you."

"Oh, not so much anymore. It was a long time ago and after working in Afghanistan, Orlov's been on my mind. He was there. He did a number on a young man whose sister I was, shall we say, close to. I wasn't able to get near him, and then had to leave. You think I'm good in the field? Well, maybe so, and my little trick is something, but there's always someone better!"

"I find that hard to believe, Lee."

"Well, there is. Let me tell you about Orlov. We knew he was out there. We called him Nads, 'cause he always took 'em—didn't kill, most of the time. Just went for information and left 'em something, I should say, left 'em without something, to remember him by. I was out working alone. By the way, this was after I'd gone back to Nam for the second tour and a few months before it all fell apart. I was working in what had been called the Phoenix Program.

"I'd gone up north to an area in the highlands where the trail crossed out of Laos and back into Nam. Was living off the land and eating native so I wouldn't smell like an American. I'd sacked out in a small, well hidden little valley with a lot of tree cover and away from any of the hostiles' camps. When I woke up, just before day break, there he was. He'd taken a dump and must've farted, which woke me. A person is vulnerable when they're sleeping, eating, screwing or taking a shit!"

"That's for sure," agreed John.

"Anyway, while he was wiping off I moved to a few feet downwind of him. There was just enough light to see. He was resting on one knee, his left, and his right knee was on the ground. I could tell he was Caucasian and spoke a couple of words. My crossbow was aimed at his chest and with treated bolts, he didn't stand a chance, or so I thought! The nerve agent works instantly. Any hit is fatal and without noise.

"Mind you, I didn't know who I had. When I came to, all I remembered was a blur. There I was, staked out and scared shitless. His Russian accented Vietnamese made me think it was him and realized if he let me live, and I thought he might, it'd be as a eunuch.

"He wanted to talk, but his English was almost as bad as my Russian, so we struggled in Vietnamese for a couple of minutes. Then he said something in French. It was like old home week, and then of course, I knew immediately he was Nads. He told me his name was Sergei Orlov. Said he was sick to death of the Vietnamese and wanted to get the hell back to some borscht and smell like a real Russian. We kept quiet, 'cause if the VC found us, I was dead meat. And he wanted to talk. I sure as hell wasn't in any hurry to have my nuts cut off!" Lee laughed.

"No shit! I can relate to that, Bro!"

"Anyway, he was just as dedicated to communism as I was hostile to it. I asked him if he was going to kill me. He said he should, for all the trouble our *phung hoang* program was causing in the area, but hell no and proceeded to give me a history lesson, right there in the forest. He said we couldn't win. That we were doing the same thing and making the same mistake Navarre'd made."

"What'd he mean by that?"

"Well, he wasn't going to give me a condescending lecture on something he could assume I was aware of. Do you remember *Dienbienphu?*"

"No, Lee. I only remember the name and that the French lost there, none of the details. What about it?"

"The French General, Henri Navarre, completely under estimated General Vo nguyen Giap's ability to equip four full divisions and to move heavy guns over the mountains. As a result, the French got their asses kicked and lost over ten thousand prisoners to the Vietminh."

"Did he convert you?"

"Not hardly. But he did point out it was kind of stupid for Caucasians to be killing each other. He said it'd be kind of dumb for Russia and the United States to duke it out so the Orientals, he called 'em 'slants', could divide up the spoils. He reminded me how Catherine the Great had refused to help her cousin, King George, during our War for Independence. Said it was because her royal cousins in England and Germany—Germany did send Hessian mercenaries—laughed at the difficulty she'd had in suppressing Pugachev's Revolt in 1773."

"Was that true? I know you're a history buff, Lee."

"Oh yes, Orlov knew what he was talking about. He told me how she'd organized the League of Armed Neutrality between a group of shipping nations in 1780, to protest British treatment of neutral shipping during our fight for independence.

"Then he went on about how two Russian fleets had 'shown the flag', one at New York and one at San Francisco, during our Civil War. I told him I'd never heard of it and I'd studied the war in detail 'cause my grand-dad fought for Lee.

"He said one of his buddies told him about it because his grandfather, a seaman from St. Petersburg, was on the Admiral's flag ship, the *Alexander Nevskii*. He said six ships under the command of Rear-Admiral Lisovskii, including two clipper ships, sailed into New York harbor. He said that maybe we deleted history as much as they did. He also reminded me about the trip the Tsar's son, the Grand Duke Alexis, made to Fort McPherson, Nebraska, in 1871, to go on a hunt with Buffalo Bill.

"Anyway, Orlov claimed that the appearances by the Russian fleets may have been a factor in England staying out of the War. Remember, England needed cotton for its textile industry and cotton needed slaves. Forget the bullshit about states rights. Let's face it, states rights did mean the right to buy and sell slaves. He pointed out Tsar Alexander II had emancipated the serfs in 1861 and supported Lincoln, who was considering emancipating the slaves.

"Once when I was in New York, I checked Coast Guard records and the bastard knew what he was talking about. He knew more of our history than I did! He even had the number of ships and the Admiral's name right! This really is a fascinating page in American-Russian history. The *Alexander Nevskii* and another clipper ship sailed into New York harbor in September of 1863, followed by the other ships over the next few days. They were docked at the

Brooklyn Navy Yard and completely re-stocked and outfitted. The officers and men were treated like royalty.

"The Russian Pacific fleet, consisting of four corvettes and two clipper ships, under the command of Rear-Admiral Popov, sailed into San Francisco harbor in October of 1863 and checkmated the Confederate's *Sumter* and the *Alabama*. It's easy to remember his name because of the vodka! There's no doubt but those events sent a strong message to England to stay neutral in the Civil War."

"Lee, I know you're on a roll, but let me interrupt you, if you don't mind?" asked John.

"Sure, no problem. What is it?"

"Well, I was just thinking. Didn't the British build the *Alabama* and *Florida* for the Confederacy, in England?"

"Oh yes. They were built at Birkenhead in 1862. I think the British constructed about ten ships in all, either in England or at other British ship-yards. The *Alabama* was one hell-of-a fighting ship. Captain Raphael Semmes and his men captured or sunk around seventy ships, Union or merchant ships bringing supplies, between 1862 and '64. The *U.S.S. Kearsarge* finally sunk her off the coast of France, near Cherbourg I believe, in June of 1864."

"Lee, wasn't there a tribunal or something, after the war, concerning ships built by the British?"

"Yes. The Alabama Claims Case. Britain submitted to arbitration by a five nation commission in Geneva. It was that or possibly lose Canada to the United States in a fight over fishing disputes and territory claims in the North-west. There was a lot of pressure to annex Canada after the Alaska purchase."

"What'd they decide?"

"They awarded the United States over fifteen million in gold. More than twice the cost of Alaska!" exclaimed Lee. "You know, John, the Russian fleet under Popov, had been given orders to stay out of any fight between the Confederate ships and the Fort. But if they got past the Fort, and in position to shell San Francisco, they were to be sunk. Out-gunned, Semmes backed off. Discretion's the better part of valor!

"But, back to Orlov. There I was, staked out and Orlov sharing a break-fast of dried fish, rice cakes and tiger eyes with me in the middle of the fucking jungle in southeast Asia, talking over the history of Russia and the United States in French—and me waiting to have my nuts cut off!" laughed Lee, and continued. "Orlov was no dummy. He said that Russia, in spite of putting Sputnik in space, was still a third-world economic disaster. He believed if we'd ever stop fighting, Russia and the United States could be the biggest trading partnership in the world. He said the Russian people hadn't forgotten our con-voys to Murmansk during the Great War."

"Lee," John spoke up with a quizzical look and tone of voice, "just what the hell are tiger eyes?"

"Tiger eyes!" Lee replied jokingly. "They make you tough! No, they're the nut or fruit of a small lime-colored shrub. They've got a peach-fuzz on 'em and when they're ripe, they split open and look like a cat eye. Taste a little bitter, like citrus, but are very high in protein. We'd chew 'em or cook 'em or mix 'em in with other food, like fish or rice or snake meat."

"I'll stick to beefsteak and pistachios!"

"John, you don't see me going to Vietnamese restaurants, do you? Back to Orlov. He told me his father was a Russian general at Stalingrad who'd fallen in love with a Red Crescent nurse during the battle. He said he was born in Alma Ata. That his mother'd been raped, tortured and murdered by fundamentalists in the early sixties, in Kabul."

"Do you believe what he told you was true?"

"Yeah, I really do. I don't think he thought it mattered 'cause it wasn't likely I'd get out of the jam I was in alive. Maybe he wasn't even sure about whether or not to let me live. He was very open, yet pensive. Remember, the shit both of us were doing was tough, even when you've been conditioned to do it. I mean real tough, wake up at night tough."

"Did you ask him anything about his training?"

"Yes, I was just coming to it. I asked him how in hell he took me so quick and easy. He asked me if I remembered Roger Bannister's four-minute mile. I said I did, and he reminded me how everyone'd said it couldn't be done. Once someone does it, others are bound to. Now they all do it, if they want to compete.

"Well, this was his story. I'll tell it as best I can. Remember, John, someday I'll cut his nuts off if I can, but to tell you the truth, this Orlov—who'd be forty-eight sometime this summer—is one extremely tough cookie. He's smart, sharp and tough—and I mean mentally and emotionally—as well as physically. I honestly don't think I could take him—unless I got lucky—but I'd try. Pretend you're staked out and you know you're going to lose your nads. Pretend I'm Orlov talking."

"Happy thought!" laughed John. "I'll try, Lee."

'After Stalingrad, my mother went back to Alma Ata where I was born. She married a fundamentalist who couldn't deal with her liberal views and beat her on a regular basis. How I hated that bastard. He was cruel to me because of my Russian father. She became active in the party and was able to get away.

'My mother was such a warm and high-spirited woman. She had the coal black hair and the flashing dark eyes of her Tartar-Kazakh mother. She spoke Turic as well as her father's Russian, and taught me both. We lived in the city of Alma Ata, which is north of Lake Issyk Kul, not too far from China's Sinkiang province. My grandfather was a medical doctor there and it's where she received her nurse schooling.

'After I was born, she completed her medical training and became a doctor. But it was her playing the *dombira* so beautifully that I remember about her the most.'

"What's a dombira?" asked John.

"That's just what I asked!" exclaimed Lee.

'It's a lute-like Eastern instrument,' Orlov explained and continued. 'They needed doctors in Korea, so in '50 she took me with her to Harbin, Manchuria where she worked in the burn clinic. A lot of pilots get badly burned, so do a lot of others. Your side likes to use napalm even though it's banned under the Geneva Convention.'

"North Vietnam didn't sign," said Lee, shifting roles.

'Big deal—so use it!' Orlov, rejoined and continued. 'It was in Harbin, as a young boy, where I learned what you saw, or should I say, felt! An old man—a Korean *sensei*—was my mentor. He was a real master. He also taught me those knots you are tied with. The kick and the follow through blow that knocked you out have been a real life-saver. How would you say it, an ace?'

"An ace-in-the-hole," John answered.

"Good, John. That's exactly how the conversation went! I told him it's a card game we play."

'Anyway, there was conflict brewing in Afghanistan between the Marxists and the Fundamentalists. So after Korea, my mother was sent to Kabul to work for the party and I was sent to Moscow for training and lots of it. Socket, I am sure you have met some neurologists in your schooling. In 1965 I was notified of her death and shown photos of my mother being worked on. Fat, ugly women with bad breath are shot, but the beautiful ones pay a much higher death-tax before they are allowed to let go.'

"Orlov's voice broke with a flood of tears. It's odd how strangers can share intimate details. Like the first he could let it out and share this horror. Showed me her picture. God, she was the most beautiful woman I'd ever seen! Reminded me of Ava Gardner. Strange as it was, having heard what'd happened to his mother, I felt a bond, even though I knew what he was going to do."

'To say the least, I have been dedicated to my work. My first assignment in '68 was in Prague, to obtain information on the revisionists. And now we meet.'

"What happened then?" John asked.

"Well, he said he was sorry, but rules are rules and he had to stick to his rules. He said he had to leave and might as well get it over with. I told him that if he didn't kill me, I'd hunt him to the ends of the earth if he cut my nuts off. The bastard just laughed and whispered, '*bon, ça m'empêchera de m'endormir*', a phrase that means about the same as our 'that'll keep me on my toes'."

"What happened?"

"No memory of anything. He put me out, but before he did, I remember asking him about the kick. He said 'you already know—like Bannister, now that you know it can be done—just work it out'. I knew then he'd made up his mind to let me live. Wasn't looking forward to losing my nuts, but didn't want to die either. Can still do it—just a complete vasectomy—no way to retie the tubes though!" Lee laughed. "When I came to, my sack was clamped and the family jewels were gone! He'd left me a small tube of medicated salve and a note pinned to my shirt. He'd also cut one wrist loose."

"What'd the note say?"

"It said '*Bon jour et bon chance* Socket Mackintosh'. Well, it sure as hell wasn't a good day—having lost my nuts. But I did have good luck and got the fuck out of there. I felt *that* donation for the cause was enough for one trip," laughed Lee, in spite of the painful memory. "How the hell he knew my real name is beyond me! I carefully cut one of the knots loose without untying it, so I could study it later. It's truly an amazing knot!

"Well, after Nam, my work as a sales rep for Colt Industries has let me have time off whenever I needed it for special jobs. They've got no idea of my advanced training. Whenever I'm needed out of the country, I'd just be in Miami—sell a lot of guns there—and go out to Homestead. Good ole Air America can drop me just about anyplace. French papers, passport and another name have given me complete freedom of movement, world-wide, with no record anywhere. I've never even held a US passport."

"Any idea who Orlov might be?"

"Maybe. I was able to get photos of most generals who were at Stalingrad—should say the Stalingrad theater."

"Hell, Lee, I haven't got the foggiest notion where it is."

"John, with the cold war going on, it's a blank page in American history books. About the only thing kids know, is fear of being sent to the Russian front was the worst threat Colonel Klink could make to Sergeant Schultz, in *Hogan's Heroes*! Anyway, I went over every photograph with a police identity expert. Nothing. Then I got to thinking—this guy was good, real, real good. Maybe his father was also smart and as good, and then it hit me. There're always promotions, especially in times like those were. So I went back to my source, obtained photos of all the marshals and went to the expert again. There he was! Given the dark hair and a Tartar-like moustache, I had Sergei Orlov. Of course I can't say he was his father. Probably Orlov can't either, unless they'd met and he'd acknowledged him."

"Who was he, Lee?"

"He might not mean much to you, John, but to a history buff who's read some of the details, beyond the Russian official sources, he was a hero and a leader of heroes. Former Commanding General of the Russian Sixty-Fourth Army. It was Marshal Vasili Chuikov himself. He was brilliant—brilliant, brave and promoted to Marshal after the war. His tactics in carrying out Stalin's basic strategy made him one of the great heroes in a time of thousands of heroes. The army he commanded was one of Stalin's 'strategic reserve armies' and was called the 1st Reserve Army before it was sent into battle. Another thing about Chuikov, he was so popular and such a hero at Stalingrad, that after the war, the KGB 'retired' him to write his memoirs. His base was the military and not the party!" Lee exclaimed.

"John, Sun Tsu, a Chinese military expert, wrote the first known work on military strategy about five hundred years before the birth of Christ. He wrote 'All warfare is based on deception. Hence when we are able to attack, we must seem unable'. Whether history likes him or not, Stalin had *ten fully equipped armies, half a million men,* in reserve between the Don River and the Ural Mountains that not even the Russian generals at Stalingrad knew about! They weren't used until after the Germans had committed themselves fully to the battle for Stalingrad.

"I'll tell you something, Bro. Waterloo was fought in one day on a two mile front. Gettysburg was fought in three days on at most, a four mile front. Stalingrad was fought by the *creme de la creme* of the German Army, in a battle that lasted for months, on a three hundred mile front!

"If Hitler could've taken Stalingrad and the great tractor factory there, he would've been able to cut the Volga river pipeline of the Caspian oil fields and stop the wealth of food and material from the Caucasus. The Third Reich would've controlled Europe—the Urals to the Atlantic. They could've concentrated their forces on England and we might not've had a chance. It may've taken a strong leader like Stalin to checkmate a man like Hitler. The Germans lost almost as many men as we lost in both theaters in all of World War II! Do I sound like a history professor?"

"You were! Just don't give me the whole fuckin' war!"

"Marshal Chuikov was born January 31, 1900, in a town called Seredryannye-Prudy outside Moscow, and died March 18, 1982. That information may give me some leads. Well, if Chuikov is his father, and he's a dead ringer, at least I have a photo—not that I'd ever forget the man who cut off my nuts! I'll track him down some day. But it'll be tough as long as the KGB's around to protect him."

"Lee, what if Orlov's not around?"

"Oh, he's around all right. Governments always need some intelligence experts who can do dirty work. Remember when those Soviet officials were kidnapped in Beirut a couple of years ago?"

"Yes—as I remember it they were released within a few days for some reason."

"Right, John. Forty-eight hours. And the reason, I'll wager, was Orlov—Nads."

"What makes you think so?"

"I don't know for sure, but the word on the street is that the Mossad— Israel intelligence—identified the family who had 'em. This'd be an extended family with lots of relatives. KGB took over, grabbed a couple of their young boys and brought 'em to Orlov. He sent 'em home castrated with a note he'd castrate two more boys a day until the officials were released unharmed. It took forty-eight more hours and cost six little boys their nuts! Remember— this is a society where you can have several wives and being potent, is a prime value. Carter pronounced important as 'impotent' and the Shah of Iran never forgave him!

"If you castrate an adult he can still have sex, just no children, but if you do it to a young child, it's my understanding he won't develop normal male traits. He could always sing in the boys choir!" Lee laughed. "I want that bastard, and the old man you met in Taos has given me a clue. He said they'd found out Orlov loves to fish and has a friend who runs a camp on a remote, far-east Siberian river called the Uda, about twelve-hundred miles north of Tokyo. Supposedly they have some of the largest salmon in the world, Tai-men, that grow to be over a hundred and eighty pounds."

"I heard only part of the conversation, I'd gone to the can. Tell me about those fish."

"The old man believes the fish will lead me to Orlov. He believes when Orlov retires, he'll fade into Siberia and go after the record. That he won't settle for any ordinary fish. The *Hucho hucho,* that's the Latin genus and spe-cies name for *Taimen,* spend their whole life in the river. They don't migrate to the ocean like other salmon. He said they can live to be at least fifty years old and grow to be monsters."

"Wow! I'd sure like to hook into one of those."

"So would I, John. But there's just one minor problem."

"What's that?"

"The KGB! Remember, I told you he said 'good day and good luck Socket Mackintosh'. That means the KGB knows everything there is to know about me. It also means they know everything there is to know about you, brother of mine! In case you've forgotten, they're a little bit touchy about the Far East. I think they shoot first and fingerprint last. Don't forget Korean Flight 007 that strayed off course in '83. You really don't think the Committee for State Security is going to let the two of us go on a fishing trip in Siberia, do you?"

"I suppose not. Probably the closest we'll ever get is a Sunday morning good-old-boy television trip. Lee, you mentioned some 'program'. What was that?"

"It was the Phoenix Program that Orlov brought up. He thought what we were doing was diabolical. He said 'at least we only hit our enemies'. I told him we never knew who the enemy was. If they were, we got information and if they weren't, then we showed 'em the VC couldn't protect 'em."

"That is a little sick!"

"When the anti-war people and the press got a hold of it, the CIA said they'd stop it. But what they did was change the name from the Phoenix Program to the *phung hoang* program. It meant the same thing, but the press never picked up on it. Isn't that one for the books! It's kind of like the theme music for *The FBI in Peace and War*. It was the march from *The Love For Three Oranges,* composed by the Russian, Prokofiev, in the 1930's. Hey, John, it's after nine. Let's end this history lesson and hit the Longhorn!"

"Lee, why don't you take up Betty Lou's constant offer? You know, back in the corner she'd never know."

"John, if they can't see that's one thing, but I know and that's the problem. Come on—let's go."

"Okay," sighed John, heading for the door as Lee paid their tab. It was nine thirty-five when the two brothers, their history lesson and dinner over, walked into the quiet Longhorn Saloon—light outside—most of the locals were still working.

Ken, waiting on a customer seated alone at the bar, smiled and waived. Two pool shooters paid them no attention and nowhere in sight was Betty Lou; she was either in the bathroom or gone. Disappointment clouded John's face when suddenly his brother's grip of steel on his elbow brought him to a stop. The look on Lee's face answered his unasked question and together they walked, casually ignoring the stranger, to the other end of the bar.

"Ken, how are ya?" Lee spoke in greeting. "My brother wants to buy some of your Colorado lottery tickets!"

"How many?" asked Ken, with a grin, knowing it must be a joke. "Jack on the rocks?"

"None, and yes. Just a private joke about lottery tickets. John thinks he's going to get lucky with Betty Lou," Lee answered.

"She here?" asked John.

"In the powder room," Ken answered, bringing their drinks and picking up the five Lee always laid out for the four dollar tab. "Thanks," he added.

Lee nodded down the bar with a questioning look at Ken, who, with a shrug of his shoulders, cued him it was the stranger's first visit. Picking up his drink, Lee sauntered over with a friendly, open look and posture. "Howdy, stranger. Name's Lee. Shoot pool?" he asked, extending his hand.

"Some," the stranger replied, without offering his hand.

Lee quickly, but without showing offense, dropped his. "Why don't we challenge these dudes to partners? My big brother down there couldn't line up two balls with a straight edge!" he laughed. Knowing full well how easily he could win, with or without a partner—unless of course his partner knocked in the eight ball by accident—it was simple to make the game appear close, but lose.

"Come on over. What's your name?"

"Troy," replied the stranger.

"Come on over, Troy. I'd like you to meet my brother. He's in heat over the waitress. Her name's Betty Lou and I think you'll like her. Betty Lou, this is Troy—Troy, Betty Lou. Better watch it though, she'll break your heart. Right, John? This is my older brother, John. John, this is Troy."

"Glad to meet both of you," said Troy, a little more relaxed.

"Excuse me," said Betty, as a group of six men came into the bar. "I'll get those guys and then come on back," she promised, smiling as she saw them head for the round table.

Seated between the two brothers, Guy suddenly felt trapped and not without reason. "Guy," said Lee in a cold, strong, but quiet voice, "don't make a fucking move until you've heard me out. Trust me, even you don't stand a chance, so just stay calm and you won't get hurt. I could kill you in self-defense. I've got a picture of you in my pocket, okay?"

"Okay," he murmured, his voice tense.

"We need your help. We're not cops and we both hate lawyers. Savvy?" questioned Lee, quietly.

"I agree on that," an extremely nervous Guy replied.

"We also want you to try out a toy we've got back at camp," added John.

"What kinda toy?"

"A she-toy," Lee whispered. "A wind-up attorney she-toy!"

John spoke up, "I hate to share Betty Lou with anyone, Guy, but you've got to get to know her better. Maybe then you'll trust us a little more. You game?"

Guy, a bit more relaxed, smiled and nodded his willingness to go along, "I don't think I got much choice, but it sounds like something I'll enjoy!" he declared.

"Good. Wait here," said John, as he left the table and headed toward the waitress station.

"Betty, will you do us a favor?"

"Sure, John. What?" And listening closely, a smile came over her face as John explained.

"No—problem!" she exclaimed. "He's not bad looking." God, what a gorgeous hunk, she thought to herself, but I'll bet John's going to get jealous. By the time Betty Lou finished her dance and the sights and scenery she'd flashed at Guy, he was the proud possessor of the grandest of diamond-cutters Betty Lou had ever encountered. With the condom well stretched, it was clear to those who observed that this was a journey she would not soon forget.

Betty Lou played a double to Black Velvet's single. Any momentary feelings of passion she may have felt for Guy were as one-sided as those of a masturbating *Peeping Tom*. Guy's deep thrusts were to him nothing more than stabs with a blunt dagger into the heart of those who had real friends. He could care less if he gave her pain or pleasure; his release always felt good to him, no matter the target.

After twice ringing the bell with vigor, something Ken had never heard, and serving free drinks to the now busy bar, she returned to the round table. "Wow! That was something to write home about!" she exclaimed. "I never did buy that crap about 'it's not the size of the sword, but the skill of the swordsman'. That's what small- peckered men preach! Big Guy should be your name, not Troy!" she exclaimed.

"Well, Betty," he said without smiling, "name's Troy, but you can call me Big Troy if you want."

"John, stick around awhile. You can have me, on the house, without a shower cap. I like you and trust you. Okay?" she whispered in his ear as the two of them walked to the end of the bar.

"Sure—Betty, I know business is business."

"John, that was business at your request don't forget, and fun. But you're for fun, *and like*. I really mean it," she declared with sincere feeling.

Knowing he held a special standing made it possible to deal with Guy and smiling, he returned to the table to congratulate him. It was in the early dawn that the trio reached their camp. Most of the evening and the three a.m. breakfast, had been spent in planning the hit on the Simpson Lake camp; now only a little more than two weeks away. Big Guy, his lust only partially satiated by the vibrant Betty Lou, was well ready to ravage the helpless camp prisoner.

———

Saturday, July 13, 1991
Gypsum Creek camp

"Daylight in the swamp, men," said Lee, shaking both by the feet, signalling the start of a new day. "Coffee's hot. We've got some planning and getting-in-shape to do."

While it occurred somewhere with each new dawn, it nevertheless seemed incredibly tragic to Murphy, who certainly understood good and evil, that such moments of beauty on this great planet, could be equally shared by both. As guardian of this venue, often falsely accused of helping evil, I cannot intervene by stopping trains or adding cannon to armies. I could have tickled the deer's nose, but would it really have helped? Now and then there are little things I can do; sometimes make it rain, a puff of air to nudge a movement, and occasionally make someone take a second look. Not much, but I never intervene to save people from their own folly. I had better stay alert and keep an eye on this affair.

Dawn, breaking the grey light of a star-filled night, harkened a new day in the crystal clear air and quiet solitude of their Gypsum Creek camp. "Where the hell are we?" asked Guy, now awake and sipping a piping hot cup of coffee beside the small, smoke-free cooking fire. "This is my second day here and I ain't got the foggiest fuckin' notion where I am."

"You're in the Wilderness Area of the Bridger National Forest," Lee answered, "at a lake about ten thousand feet above sea level. I don't know if it has a name. To our east, about a mile away, is Sheep Mountain. To the west and also a mile or so, is Gypsum and then about two miles to the south is Battleship Mountain. All three of 'em peak at around eleven-thousand five-hundred feet."

"If you were an eagle," said John, slow to come awake, "it'd be about a twelve mile flight to Simpson Lake, but one hell of a tough hike from here."

"When we looked over the topos," said Lee, referring to the 7.5 minute topographic maps, "this appeared to be a good place to check out, and it turned out better'n we expected. We've even had other campers down on the lake, but they never knew we were here. We stay quiet, use sign language and our two-way radios a lot."

"He's pretending he's in Rhodesia," John laughed, softly.

"How 'bout her?" Guy asked.

"She's been conditioned—never utters a sound—just bangs a couple of rocks together, only once, if she needs something. She knows better'n to leave the cave, but we take good care of her. We take her to the lake, and she stays fairly clean. She won't eat very much, but she does like trout," John answered.

"We believe there were cougars in the cave this spring, but they've stayed away since we've been here. They'll probably be back when winter sets in. This is certainly as beautiful a place as we've ever seen. I can just imagine what this valley was like a couple hundred years ago," Lee speculated. "We'll stay here until I go over to scout out the scumbag's group. I'll go over and check out the area the weekend of the twentieth. That way we'll have a camp-site located for the night of the hit, and I'll have a position set to film 'em on their way in."

"Lee, why don't we all drive up the Union Pass Road and make sure we have an open trail, at least to a site to hide the truck a little closer to the Divide. That way the two of us can help you clear any trees or rocks out of the way?" John suggested.

"That's a good idea, Bro."

"I thought you said that both camps were in wilderness areas?" asked Guy. "And hey, why don't you guys use horses like everyone else out here?"

"First question first. They are, but we'll be driving in from the north-west and stay well clear of the forbidden zone," John answered. "Now about the horses. While Lee and I are from Virginia and have always been around 'em, we've just never ridden 'em, at least I haven't. Lee?"

"No and I don't know why. Our folks had work horses, but they got rid of 'em before we were old enough to ride and we had a small tractor we used. That's how John got started in engine work. Out here, once you get in shape, you can actually move around in these mountains quicker on foot. The horses need trails most of the time and use switch-backs, while I go straight up and straight down!" Lee added.

"What about the girl?"

"We don't have to worry about her, Guy. Like I said, she's been well conditioned and won't budge. She knows better. Doesn't she, Lee?"

The grin and a nod confirmed his confidence in his ability to modify human behavior, "I think she does," he whispered in reply.

"Lee, why don't you tell Guy about that poison you told me about a while ago?"

Having made up his mind about Guy's expectancy of life—as an actuary would say—he thought to himself 'why not?' and began. "Am I not to be left with any secrets?" he laughed in mock seriousness. "Okay. Listen up, Guy. You ever heard of a Stonefish?"

A negative turn of Guy's head cued Lee to continue. "Well, it's a small fish that lives in the coastal waters of southeast Asia. It has spines and often it'll have bits of seaweed or plant material on it that make it almost impossible to see. In Latin it's called the *Synanceja horrida* and horrid it is! A lab in Virginia, near a city inside the beltway called Langley, used it to develop a poison we used in Viet Nam. If a person was cut by a blade treated with it, death was certain—virtually instantaneous. Of course a quick death is the best you can hope for, especially if it's in your sleep, as Kenny said! It didn't get its species name *horrida* because of instant death. The toxin, unaltered chemically, which, by the way, has no antidote I'm aware of, causes absolutely unbelievable agony before death. If you inject a person with some of the toxin, anybody watchin' would throw their own children to pitbulls to avoid it," said Lee, in quiet summation.

"Wow," Guy muttered, realizing Lee knew what he was talking about and was not bullshiting him. "I think I'll watch where I wade!"

"He learned some pretty good shit from a mad Russian while he was in Nam. Maybe someday he'll show you what good ole Chuikov taught him."

"What was his name?"

Giving a deep sigh—well no harm in that—thought Lee, knowing what he had planned for Guy, and began, "His name *is* Sergei Chuikov. You pronounce it 'chewy cough'. Like chewin' a cough drop. It's spelt C-h-u-i-k-o-v."

"Let's change the subject. John'd mentioned a lake, high up on the east side of the divide, that the old jeep trail went down to. You don't want to drive that far?" asked Guy.

"I think the trail has been completely blocked. And since we don't want anyone to know we're in the area, we won't drive above Flat Lake," Lee explained. "I believe the lake you're thinking about is called Marion."

5

Fitzpatrick Wilderness Area

'. . . when a system in equilibrium is subjected to stress it tends to a new equilibrium that opposes the effect of the stress . . .'
Henry-Louis Le Châtelier—French chemist

Thursday, July 25, 1991
Lansing, Michigan

The first day of the horseback-accessible mountain, trout-fishing trip was to begin at 6:00 a.m., Sunday, July 28, 1991 from Dubois, Wyoming. The carefully planned journey, dreamt of for years, began as the Chevrolet van and Buick Riviera entered westbound Interstate 69 and headed for the *Windy City*. Six middle-aged men seeking respite and vacation from the stress of their modern-day work world, in the clean air and crystal clear waters of the high mountains of western Wyoming. Unknown as they left, their refuge would be in the no-motors quiet of the Fitzpatrick Wilderness Area; a part of the Shoshoni National Forest lying just east of the Continental Divide. Their camp, six-hundred and eighty feet below a lake named Marion.

The sixteen-hundred mile journey became eighteen-hundred so a few of the party could view for the first time, four faces carved in stone, a pillar of rock known as Devil's Tower and on a desolate hillside, the grave of an old Indian woman.

First to interrupt the smooth way west was one of Wisconsin's finest, near mile marker eighty-nine, warning that racers were always welcome on the track at Elkhart Lake. A long and entertaining breakfast at Blue Earth, Minnesota; the obligatory buffalo burgers at Wall Drug, following a quick drive through the Badlands of South Dakota; and thirteen extra pit stops to grant mercy to a few weak, uncoordinated bladders, would complete the diary of the unexpected.

The oldest of the group, Tom, was in line for story telling time. Recently recovering from heart arterial roto-routing, the sixty year old insurance claims manager began, "Some of the stuff we see is unbelievable, but this is the funniest I've ever heard. The guys up ahead have heard it, so I won't have to tell it again. It's known in the office as 'the case of the flying fist' and I swear to God it's true. At least the facts were sworn to in statements taken under oath. It was a claim filed by a woman passenger injured in an accident that happened when the driver lost control of his car and went across a ditch. They'd got to fooling around, if you know what I mean, and as they were driving down this back country road she was giving him a hand job.

"You know what the bumper sticker says—'shit happens'. Anyway, they were going along at a pretty good clip, both the car and her hand on his johnson, and then came the moment of truth. As his climax started he shut his eyes, apparently arched his back and pushed on the accelerator, just as the road turned to the left to go over a bridge. The car continued straight up an incline, went airborne—as he came in midair—and the car crashed on the opposite side of the stream. The creek's, not his! She sued him for losing control!" he finished, as they broke into laughter at the thought of the scene described.

With Will at the wheel, the van, loaded with gear, transported westward the humorist claims-manager Tom; the communications executive Burr—soon to be known as Tex; and Kevin, the trouble-shooter for the auto-parts manufacturer still in business. The meetings at Sam's had developed a smooth rapport. George, at the wheel of Sam's Riviera, held point on Interstate 90.

All except Tex had been on fishing trips together. Sam and Will, friends for many many years, had hunted New Mexico, Colorado, Alaska, Newfoundland and of course, Michigan. Without Sam, Will would be dead. The Dudes would leave their tales of adventures past to the mountain campfires. "Hey, Will, call ahead and have George stop at the next rest area. Got to take another piss break!" Kevin requested of the driver.

"Christsakes, quit drinking beer, or we'll never get there!" Will admonished. Reaching for the CB, he hit the transmit button. "Hey guys, guess what, it's pee-pee time for ole puckered pecker again! You all want some advice for an old man?" he asked.

"Go for it," came the reply.

"Well, number one, pee every chance you get! Number two, take advantage of every erection, whether you're alone or with somebody! Number three, never never trust a fart!" he laughed, as they all roared in approval.

Kevin, his bladder's plea for relief having been granted, took the wheel of the van as Will stretched out on the bench seat for a short nap. A few miles of silence was broken by Burr as he pondered the rapid passage of time. "You know, this vacation is going to be over so damn fast. We spend six months planning it, getting our gear around, the meetings over at Sam's, talking about it with all our families and friends, and then the time'll go so fast and bam! It's over, we're on our way home!"

"What? What? Did I miss something?" asked Will, in an excited voice, coming out of his slumber. "Is it over? Hell, I don't remember any of it. I've been diagnosed as having advanced CRS! Did I drink too much whiskey and do the whole damn trip in an alcoholic fog? Are we headed home already?"

he asked, peering out the window at darkness, trying to figure by stars, the direction they were headed. "Did I catch any fish?"

"What's CRS, Will?" asked Tom.

"Can't Remember Shit!" came the reply. "Come on you guys, tell me what the hell happened. Did something happen out there I'm not going to want Trish to hear about? You know guys, this isn't funny, I'm serious! Come on guys, what happened? Did I fall off my horse and land on my head?"

"Relax, Will, the best is yet to come and we'll take care of you. Do you have any money for bail?" asked Kevin. Sometimes they couldn't tell if Will was kidding or cold-dead serious.

"Will," spoke up Burr, "with your imagination, why don't you write a book?"

"He can't write! Can you, Will?" laughed Kevin.

"Just enough to endorse checks!" the butt of endless lawyer jokes retorted to his good, but constantly needling friends.

"That was good! Watch it, Kevin, he's shifty!" Tom chipped in. "Why don't you? You've had some good cases."

"Well, Tom, I'm not done yet, so I don't know what case is worth writing about. The real cases don't seem as exciting as the fictional ones."

"Heck," spoke up Burr, "you've had murder, rape and that product case in Detroit. The rape case you had in Detroit a few years ago would make a good story."

"I'm getting tired of lawyers books and I think many people are. They're either 'who-done-its', or 'I-did-its'. In the real world there're damn few 'who-done-its'. The police aren't always wrong or stupid. Usually the trials are about 'what was it that the right who did'."

"I think you're right," said Tom. "What about the 'I-did-its'?"

"Those are mostly ego trips," Will answered. "Every good case I've had, couldn't have been won without a lot of help and some of 'my' best ideas came from my own clients."

"I agree, Will. I read one a few years ago where some famous lawyer wrote about his life in court and as I remember it, he had an 'I' in almost every sentence," said Burr.

Tom, deciding it was time to change the subject spoke up, "Hey guys, we agreed only one lawyer joke per person on the whole trip. We all want to get away from our work, and don't forget we promised Will over at Sam's house that we wouldn't be talking about law."

"I agree," said Kevin. "The only problem is almost everyone, one way or another, has to deal with the legal system and generally it's in a conflict situation. Hell, if you're a witness, a victim, get a divorce, have kids that get in trouble, a property dispute—I hope not accused of a crime—no matter your occupation, everyone has opinions and convictions about the legal system!"

"Long speech, Kevin!" Burr laughed.

"It's true," he replied. "Look at television, if it's not sports, it's a law or cops program. Someone should do a study and zap every single program that mentions the subject in any way. Shit, there wouldn't be much left!"

Will, listening in silence, tongue gripped tightly between his front teeth, was determined not to speak, since it was his occupation, no matter how tired of solving people-problems he sometimes got.

"Let's try to not talk about it and maybe we can shield the poor bastard from all this law-law-law shit for a week or so. How does that sound, Will?" Burr inquired.

"That'd be nice," Will replied, with a nod and smile. "Why don't you put on Johnny Horton's tape, Kevin. We can shoot some of the Iron Duke's best in New Orleans and go 'North to Alaska'. I imagine you're all getting tired of listening to my Anne Murray collection."

"Amen! You got a crush on her?" asked Kevin.

"Just one of my secret fantasies!"

"You know, guys," Tom began, "not to change the subject, but it's too darn bad Cody is so far out of the way. The Buffalo Bill museum there is something else! Have any of you ever been there?"

"I haven't," replied Burr and Kevin, in unison.

"We stayed at the KOA campground east of town a few years ago when we took the kids to Yellowstone. We visited the museum twice. Spent the better part of two days in Cody, as I recall," Will replied. "Took in a rodeo— it's a nice town."

"Isn't that Winchester gun collection something! And the art and Plains Indian exhibit, I thought it was just fantastic!" Tom exclaimed.

"Tom?" questioned Will. "Can you imagine Cody and that Cheyenne chief, Yellow Hand, going out in the river and fighting it out with knives to settle a dispute, instead of the two armies fighting! It's too bad they can't do that today, there'd be a lot less war!"

"You're right. And I'd forgotten about the Grand Duke Alexis, the son of Tsar Alexander, coming over to go buffalo hunting with Cody. That's kind of hard to imagine, isn't it? He gave Cody a sable, ermine and snow-leopard carriage robe they have at the museum. I'd say it's probably one of the most beautiful blankets ever made, unless you're a vegetarian!" Tom exclaimed.

"Just think of it, the son of the 'Tsar of all the Russias' coming to the United States to go hunting with an Indian scout! How'd you like to have that on your resumè?" exclaimed Burr.

"Speaking of Indian scouts, have any of you ever been up to the Little Bighorn battlefield, the national park there?" asked Will.

"No, not me," replied Kevin and Tom, together.

"Neither've I. Why, Will?" Burr inquired.

"I think something fishy's going on," Will answered.

"How so?" questioned Burr. "It's a long way out of the way and we didn't go up there."

"It just happened our family went there in the summer of 1978, then Trish and I went there last fall when we were out here. Christ, I goddamn near got thrown out of the park office!"

"How in hell did you manage that?" asked Kevin.

"Shit, I asked one damn question and the goddamn clerk acted like I'd stepped on his nuts!"

"What the hell'd you ask him? If his wife was still selling blow jobs?" said Burr, exploding in laughter.

When the outburst of laughter subsided, Will began, "No, I simply asked why they'd removed the exhibit that explained how Custer and some of the 7th Cavalry had carried out the raid that massacred Black Kettle's Cheyenne at Washita River in 1868."

"Why do you think the Park Service would do that?" asked Kevin.

"I don't know unless it's politics over the Supreme Court's decision that the Black Hills were stolen from the Sioux. The court ruled they're entitled to a hundred and twenty million or so in damages."

"You know," spoke up Burr, "I read where the Sioux refused the money— they want the land. And Senator Bradley, the basketball great from New Jersey's bill to give 'em federal land in the Black Hills was narrowly defeated. If the U.S. can delete Washita River from Custer's resume, you make him look better and Crazy Horse worse. Don't forget the 7th Cavalry carried out the massacre at Wounded Knee in 1890, maybe to get even."

"Well," added Kevin, "you can change the future with an eraser easier than with a lie."

"I think the Indians at the Little Bighorn were well aware of Washita River and had a golden opportunity to kick Custer's ass. Maybe the Park Service for some reason would like everyone to forget Custer's role at the Washita," added Tom. "I don't think the American Indians were as dumb as a lot of people want to believe. That Shawnee, Chief Tecumseh, was one hell of a smart dude from what I've read. And from what I've read about Crazy Horse, he kicked General Crook's ass at the Rosebud and just completely out- smarted Custer. And I'm from Monroe! Hell, the house Custer lived in is just down the road from where I lived!"

"Kevin," Will spoke up, "we won't solve the American Indian Movement question today, so why don't you get Sam on the radio. We might want to stop at the next town. I'm getting a little tired and it's about time."

"Good idea, Will. Sam?" Kevin radioed ahead.

"Yes, my son?"

"Will wants to stop at the next town."

"Fine, my son. What's it called?"

"Blue Earth," Kevin answered.

A sharp, nasal, staccato "*naio mota mota shita itanda*" came over the CB in a voice that sounded like Sam's.

"What the hell was that!" exclaimed Burr.

"Oh nothing," answered Will. "Sam still cusses me out in Japanese. It's what a Japanese man would say to a close male friend in a situation where you or I would say, 'what the goddamn hell took you so long!'. Literally it means, 'what have you been doing that slowed you down'."

"How do you say it?" asked Kevin.

"Phonetically it's pronounced 'nah-eee-o mo-tah mo-tah she-tay i-tan-day'," Will explained.

"Do you speak Japanese?" Burr inquired.

"Oh hell no, just bits and pieces. Hey, there's the exit, let's get a late-night snack. I'm hungry!"

Thursday, July 25, 1991
Gypsum Creek Camp

"If everything goes according to plan, you're going to have to take three of 'em to the east edge of the camp. Do you think you can cover 'em, Guy?"

"Heck yes! Long's it's understood if they don't do exactly as I order—pow!"

"No problem," John replied. "Just have 'em lay face down and tie their wrists behind their backs. When you hear the signal we've got the other five secured, just pop 'em in the back of the head. Lee, why don't you show him your rope trick?"

In his mind, Lee had decided it wouldn't matter what secrets he shared with Guy. He was sure John would agree, but it could wait until sometime after the hit; it might be an interesting challenge. "Okay, this is a special knot that works very well to restrain a person, yet is quick to untie. We'll use 'em when we tie up the mountain man and the tourists, but the broad and Scumbag get another trick."

For Christ's sake thought Guy, how fuckin' dumb do these stupid mother-fuckin' hillbillies think I am? "I think I can fuckin' manage to tie someone up," he declared, with an exasperated tone of voice.

"I'm sure you can," said John. "The question is, how quick, how secure and with how many hands? Show him, Lee."

"First, Guy, take this cord and tie John's hands behind his back. Lee watched as Guy wrapped the cord in a double loop around each wrist, drew them together and secured them tightly with a standard, figure-eight knot. Guy worked fast, as fast as his method would allow and it would take John, if he even could, quite some time to escape. But the knot took quite some time to tie.

"There, let's see you beat that!" Guy challenged.

"That was good and it looks secure, but it was a little slow and you had your eyes on your work for quite a while. Here, let me show you something. John, stand in front of Guy and flash a series of finger counts. Now, Guy, put your hands behind your back when I tell you to, holding one wrist with the other hand. I'm going to hold this stick out in front of you so you can see only one of my hands is free and I'll count John's signs, okay?"

"Yeah, I got it."

Standing in front of Guy, Lee showed him the stick in one hand and a three foot long piece of cord in the other. "Okay, now put your hands behind your back gripping one of your wrists, like I told you." Stepping around behind Guy, with the stick still in Guy's view, Lee counted John's finger signs. "One, four, two, five." Guy felt a tug as Lee stepped back in front of him, no more than four seconds had lapsed, but probably less. Struggling to free himself, Guy finally gave up. With a snap, Lee released him and handed him the straightened rope.

"Who the hell taught you that?" Guy exclaimed.

"Oh, it came from a wrinkled old man who lived a long way from here," Lee quietly replied.

"Did he teach you any other magic?"

"Well, I'd say I learned from one of his students something more important than rope tricks—to respect my elders. Often they know things you don't. That's how they got to be elders! John, why don't you and Guy practice the knot until both of you can do it blindfolded with either hand and then I'll time you. You'll see that it's so simple, you'll wonder why it's unknown. Wait, why don't you practice with the cord you'll be using, it handles differently. Just a minute and I'll go and get some out of the tent.

"John?" Guy inquired. "Has he got any other little tricks as good as that one?"

"He's got a couple I know about and maybe he'll show 'em to you someday. I'm not sure myself what all he's capable of doing. He went through a lot in Nam. Here he comes and pay close attention Guy, he hates to have to explain things twice. He believes a lot of ignorance is self-inflicted. That it's caused by television and people not reading anymore."

"Okay, listen up. Don't pull hard on this or jerk on it, because this cord is so thin it'll slice through your skin and sever the arteries and veins of your wrists."

Taking a piece of the cord, Guy examined it, "It looks like a child could break it. What the fuck is it, anyway?"

"It's made with a fiber called *Aramid*, marketed by DuPont under the trade name of *Kevlar*. There's another brand I'm aware of called *Arenka*. These fibers have the same breaking strain-point as steel fiber of the same diameter. It's four times stronger'n steel of the same weight and you couldn't break it by pulling.

"Okay, students, this is a piece of cord, got that?"

How fuckin' stupid does he think I am, thought Guy as he nodded his head in the affirmative.

"These are the ends of the cord, got that?" Lee continued.

Christ, thought Guy, nodding. John just smiled, knowing what was coming next.

"Guy, the look on your face shows some impatience. Do you know what the section of the cord between the ends is called?"

"No, I guess not," he replied, his face flushed with anger at being called and caught without an answer. Books on the art and science of ropes and knot tying were not allowed in prison. It was one of many gaps in his self-taught and over-rated education.

"It's called the *bight* and it's the portion of cord the knot is made with. You could devote a career to the study of knots if you wanted to. I've been told the number of knots is endless, but you only have to learn one, so let's get started."

I should have paid attention to that old Portuguese cellmate of mine a few years back, thought Guy. At least he taught me the hangman's knot and I learned how long it takes to hang someone. God that was fun watching the old fart twist and jerk.

The knot, like the concept of the wheel, was simple and like most unknowns, only the discovery was difficult. After showing Guy the layout of the knot on a flat surface and giving him several opportunities to create it, Lee began. "Good, now here's how you create the loops and twists with one hand. I'm goin' to try an' slow this down in order for you to see it. Watch close. The energy of the moving cord helps to make the loops themselves, so here goes."

Having gone over the twists and turns, Guy, with excellent hand-eye coordination, was able to rapidly master the trick. John, already familiar with the knot, was forced by the competition to improve his speed. "Very good," Lee praised them both. "Now this can best be done when the person you're restraining can be forced to grip one wrist with the opposite hand, but it can also be used to stake a person out. However, if you don't want 'em to bleed to death and exit quickly, you've gotta use a different knot or a different rope.

"The knot ends up working like a pair of handcuffs, except as you pull on it, it tightens up. Yet, unlike a standard running knot, it doesn't loosen when tension is released. But you can release it, just like a draw hitch. I discovered, quite by accident, how to make a handcuff out of a single sliding knot I'd been introduced to. You know what 'they' say, necessity's the mother of invention! Guy, maybe if you get interested in the science of knots you'll come up with a miracle knot and be famous!"

———

July 27, 1991
Gypsum Creek Camp

"Well, Guy, you've had a couple of weeks to get in shape for this. Do you think you're ready?" John asked.

Always in good physical shape, and having worked harder than either of them, Guy was supremely confident of his physical ability. He was convinced in his mind he could take either or both the Mackintosh brothers. "I think I'm ready," he replied, with a sneer that put John and Lee on edge.

"Do you think you're quick enough?" John asked.

"I think so."

"Why don't you show him your little trick, Lee?"

"Naw, not now." I'll show the prick, thought Lee, this bastard couldn't be delayed by a plea for mercy anyway.

"What's his trick? He didn't do Betty Lou last night and man, she's sure as hell's one trick!" Guy exclaimed, swelling once again at the memory of his last trip to the Longhorn.

"He's quick with his feet. It's something he perfected in Nam. Lee can kick a card out of your fingers before you can drop it, and from a kneeling position!" John challenged for Lee.

"Fuck, no fuckin' way man! I seen a lot of kick shit—the French sabot-fightin'—but no fuckin' way. Not from a kneelin' position! I'll bet you fifty on that!" he challenged. Ropes are one thing, but this is my field he thought.

Some people are slow learners when it comes to evaluating their opposition. Vanity, like the Great Barrier Reef, can break many a seaworthy ship.

"Lee?" asked John.

"Okay, John. I'll try, but let's get it straight Guy—one time? Two out of three—or double or nothing on the second, if I win?" questioned Lee.

"Shit man, I'll drop it and it'll be double or nothin' for you if you want your fuckin' fifty back! How far back, twenty feet?"

"Hell no! John, would you please draw a line and we'll check him out. The rule, Guy, is you pretend you've got a pistol and I'm on my knees begging for my life. I'll nod when I think I'm close enough to beat you. If you think you can let go of the card before I can kick it out of your hand, nod affirmative and the wager's on. Okay?" Lee asked.

"Fair enough," a confident Guy accepted.

"Here, set this cap, loose, on the top of your head. Okay, now pinch the card tight by one corner so if I kick it out, the corner'll be bent and you lose." Lee knelt on both knees, his arms raised in surrender and begging him not to shoot, inched closer to the card wielding Guy. Lee raised his left knee and lowering his arms for better balance, shifted his weight to his powerful left leg. His muscles were taut and ready to propel him up and forward. At approximately six feet, he knew he could take the over-confident Guy and nodded the challenge.

Guy shrewdly watched Lee's face of stone and his intense eyes for a telltale sign. Certain the fifty was in his pocket and already spending inside Betty Lou, he acknowledged his acceptance. To drop the card before motion was to lose. He held it tight—though willing if necessary—there'd be no need to cheat.

Guy heard Lee's sharp, abdomen-tightening cry, saw and tried, but the total of his perception and reaction time was too great. He felt the whack and puff of air as Lee's right foot, only a blur of motion, sent the bent card fluttering to the ground, far to his right. Unseen, either a hand or a foot shot over the top of his head, flicking his hair in passage and sending the hat beyond the card, rolling in the dusty grass. In silent awe he handed the fifty to the stone-faced Lee, and walked back to the campfire.

"Guy, don't feel too bad," said John, in consolation. "That's his special trick and as far as I know, he's the only one in the world who can do it. Let me tell you something else. Except for me, I don't think anyone, other than a couple of his special-forces comrades, has ever seen it. Anyone else is dead! Let's go and say good-by. He'll be gone on surveillance for the next three days.

———

Sunday morning
Simpson Lake

The journey west, meeting the outfitter Bob, his wife and partner Linda, the camaraderie, conversation and companionship of the evening at the Rustic Pine ended the prologue.

"Will," said Bob, handing the reins of the white blazed gelding to the Dude, "I hope you can ride. They said you could. Baldy's going to be difficult—he wants to run. He'll dance a lot and do a little side stepping, but hold him in. If he bolts, the pack horses may break and we'll have a mess," Bob instructed.

"I'll do the best I can," Will replied. "I noticed he just has a leather chin strap. Does he take the bit, Linda?"

"No. He's a tender mouth, so just keep him reined in and that should do it," she answered.

"Okay."

The adventure began as each mounted their horses and fell in line for the three hour ride to Simpson Lake.

By the time they climbed the plateau at the southwest end of Simpson Lake and headed for the grove of trees shielding the camp site, without knowing it, they were well preserved in all their glory on video. Sore from several hours ride, either climbing or descending, rest and a cool brew were the primary goals of all; except Baldy. Prancing sideways, he wanted to measure Will and the plateau. "Bob, can I let this damn horse out?" Will asked. Not sure what Bob's reply would be, he relaxed the reins enough.

Bob hesitated, but Baldy didn't. Like a bicycle, you never forget, thought Will as the horse headed north, quickly gathering speed. Baldy, as had Charlemagne, the fast and high-spirited, American-Bred, buckskin, saddle-horse of Will's youth, wanted to show his mettle and test his rider's. Leaning forward, hat in his right hand and reins in his left, they raced at a ground-devouring gallop straight toward the north edge of the plateau. Shifting his balance hard to the right, with his thighs and a steady, firm pressure on the left neck-rein, Will guided Baldy through the sharp right turn and back along the easterly edge of the plateau.

The three-quarter mile run, enough for Baldy and Will, ended at the stream some sixty yards due south of camp. At a trot, Will and Baldy, each with a better understanding of the other, returned to their companions. They would be saddle partners—not friends—with mutual respect, for the days ahead. Linda, caretaker of her treasured horses, greeted them, "We weren't sure there for a minute, Will. If you'd gone over that bank, you wouldn't be doing much fishing this week!" she exclaimed.

"Wasn't too sure—either!" Will breathlessly replied. "Was prayin' Baldy—knew what he—was doin'—not tryin' to—commit suicide!"

"Why the hell are you out of breath, Pierre?" chided Sam. "The horse did all the work—you sausage!"

"Just out of shape. It's been thirty-five years since I've had a ride like that. Wow!"

"Come on show-off," said Burr, "have a beer. We've got some fishing to do. Hell, it's only noon."

Lee, once again a mercenary, a silent and unseen shadow, moved from his well-hidden filming site. Travelling south and west, he crossed Jakeys Fork, the main inlet forming Simpson Lake, through the tall willows. Walking northwesterly through the pines, he crossed a small creek draining some of the southeast side of Union Peak and running west to east, at a point approximately one hundred yards above and to the southwest of the camp. No need to even be careful he thought, the noise made by the hated city tourists was enough of a guidon to assure his success. Moving in close to camp, he would be able to study the tourists and the outfitters who brought them here in detail.

From his camera site, located near a sharp turn and steep drop in the trail, he had been able to take excellent close-up footage and capture voice of each of the eight riders. It was apparent that Bob and Linda, both lean and nearly six feet tall, were in superb physical condition. Each, likely to have pistols and Linda with her hidden knife, could be dangerous. This was their backyard.

It was also clear the scumbag lawyer, Will Dean, could ride, but so could many other out-of-shape goose pickers. He was certainly no threat, nor were any of the others as long as they weren't wearing hand-guns. The rest of today, all day Monday and Tuesday morning; ample time thought Lee. The campfire bullshit tonight and tomorrow will provide book on all of them. Surveillance at breakfast tomorrow and Tuesday will provide the morning routine critical to planning the Wednesday morning attack. Moving in close, closer than anyone could ever imagine, he made himself comfortable and with small pad and pencil, began to take notes. The hours passed and soon they were all at the evening meal.

"Gosh, Bob, that was some trout dinner!" exclaimed George. "Are we going to eat like this every meal?"

"You dudes catch 'em," Linda replied, "and we'll cook 'em!"

"It's a good thing you guys stayed on Simpson," said Kevin. "We didn't do too well up at—what's the lake we were at, Bob?"

"Dead Horse," answered Bob.

Kevin continued, "Sam and I tried to fish, but Bob and Will skinny-dipping must've scared 'em away."

"It's a wonder you didn't freeze your nads," spoke up Burr.

"I can't find 'em yet," laughed Will.

"You won't need 'em up here anyway. We should've left you in Blue Earth!" exclaimed Sam.

"Hell, she was sharp, but not dumb. He'd never've got to use 'em there either!" laughed Kevin.

"You know, guys," said Tom, "this has been one heck of a trip already and it's only the first day!"

"Amen," they nodded in agreement.

"Bob and Linda, what've you got planned for us?" asked Burr, now known as Tex.

"Well, Tex, tomorrow, if the weather holds like this and the reports are good—with rain maybe late Wednesday afternoon—I thought we'd hit some mountain lakes around here. Then early Tuesday morning, I'd like to take you to the top of Shale Mountain. It's about a three hour ride, but worth it. It'll be cold and very windy, but you can see the Tetons, the Absarokas and the other mountains in this range. We should see plenty of Bighorn and you can ride through glaciers. It's just one heck of a nice place to visit, but I wouldn't want to live there!" he laughed. "Let me give you all a little geography lesson now so you've got a general idea of where you are. It's easy to get disoriented in the mountains, especially if it's cloudy.

"First, we're in the Wind River Range of the Rocky Mountains, east of the Continental Divide and a part of the Shoshoni National Forest. West of the Divide, in the Teton mountain range, is the Bridger National Forest, and the area of both forests adjacent to the Divide is designated as a Wilderness Area. No motors of any kind are allowed in here."

"How about my electric shaver?" Kevin inquired.

"No question about it my man, you're a violator!" he laughed. "Think of the area as a huge horseshoe opened to the north with Simpson Lake about in the middle of the valley and to the south or the toe of the shoe. The shoe is formed by four mountains with the Continental Divide following the crests around us and dividing Fremont County from Sublette County. Bill Sublette was a mountain man and was among the first men in this area, . . ."

"Ah—what?" interrupted Linda.

"First non-American I mean, he wasn't an American Indian I mean. That better?" he asked Linda, who nodded in the affirmative with a warm smile. "Back to the geography lesson. Union Peak's about four miles northwest of us and to the south of it, rises Three Waters Mountain. Swing easterly and at the toe, south of us, is Square Top and to the southeast, about three miles away, is Shale's peak. Shale Mountain is huge! Its gradual north slope drops to the north, almost to a line parallel to Union Peak. The high spot of Shale is Burro Point, and the view there is unbelievable!"

"You guys'll see some scenery that'll take your breath away," said Linda. "This is a quiet area—no motors of any kind!" she said, with lots of emphasis, grinning at Kevin. "They don't even fly over, unless it's an emergency. Why don't you describe a few of the lakes in the area you'll be fishing, Bob?"

"Good idea honey," he replied. "The ones we'll be fishing are all at various elevations and all in the horseshoe. They drain down to Simpson, or to the north, along with Simpson, into the Wind River. As you've seen, Simpson has a lot of Brook trout, so does Dead Horse. Above us, in the hidden valleys of Union Mountain, we'll fish Rim, Peat and Dyke lakes. They have Cutthroat and some Grayling. Near those three lakes and a little to the west, is Marion Lake. It has some real nice Golden, but they're hard to catch and we'd have to fish for 'em at night. To the south of us, up Jakeys Fork, are Pinto and Sandra Lakes. About right straight across from us, due east and just a bit higher is Long Lake. Then straight south of Long Lake, in the canyon above, is Dead Horse Lake and above it, Lost Lake."

Linda spoke up, "I want to ride back to town. I've got to get some Miracle Whip . . ."

"You're what?" George exclaimed. "You're going to ride all the way back to Dubois to get some Miracle Whip! Maybe we could do a commercial!"

"Oh, I've got a short-cut and I want to check on that sick horse. I'll head out when you start up Shale. So we'll be on the same trail for awhile, then I cut to the northeast. I should be back late Tuesday afternoon in time for dinner," Linda declared.

"Excuse me, partners," said Will, getting up and heading for the woods, "I shall return!"

A few moments passed before Bob broke the silence. "Hey, guys, how many of you brought pistols? You saw me miss the coyote on the way in. Could any of you hit it?"

"Guns? Us? We're fishermen!" exclaimed Sam. "Oh come on Tom, show him your nine-millimeter. Kevin, dig yours out. Where's Will?" Sam asked.

"I think he went to take a dump," George answered. "He told me he didn't think he'd bring his."

"Just you two?" asked Bob, looking over the dudes' two handguns.

"What would we need 'em for?" asked Kevin.

"Just to scare away bears, since there aren't any robbers up here. But Linda and I always have one in our saddle bags. It just makes us feel a little less vulnerable I guess," Bob replied.

"Well, happy campers, I'm going to hit the sack, it's been quite a day. Burr, you'd better take some nose plugs or burn some incense. Will's dangerous in close quarters! Aren't you, Pierre?" Sam asked, of the returning Will.

"Russtovitch, 'a farting horse will never tire, a farting man, is a man to hire'," Will rejoined.

"What's this 'Russtovitch' and 'Pierre' bullshit?" Burr asked, fairly new to the group.

"Oh, it's just their pet names," George explained. "Sam's full name is Samuel Russell McCord and it goes back a long way. They've hunted around the country too much. You should've saved the camera and let Pierre drown, Sam!"

"That's a story for another time—let's hit it," suggested Kevin, heading for his tent.

"A good idea," said Linda, standing up. "We'll start breakfast a little after daybreak."

———

Monday afternoon
Rim Lake

"Will, you take a lot of kidding. It seems as though everyone always has a lawyer joke all set to go. Do they bother you?" Bob asked.

"No, not really. You know, Bob, the nice thing about a lawyer joke is they're always safe and you can tell 'em anywhere in front of anybody. Hell, a fat female blond-headed black Polish Jew, will laugh at a lawyer joke! My dad told me to be a dentist. Everyone needs 'em, they're paid by insurance and they don't have to deliver babies at three in the morning. A lawyer will always piss off their clients. If you win, they were right all along—who ever thinks they are wrong—and you obviously over-charged 'em. And God help you if you lose! Hell, they were right and you were stupid!

"You know, people are always carping about some crud who gets off because of some technicality. Hell, like my grandfather always said, 'it all depends on whose ox is getting gored'. I've defended several cops and if you ever want to see someone insist you make the prosecutor dot the i's and cross the t's, it's a cop. They've got that *Bill of Rights* memorized when it's their fat in the fire! I've never understood why people get so pissed off at lawyers. Shit, except for the crooks who cheat their own clients, lawyers just do what their clients want 'em to do.

"But back to that trout. I'm real glad he was just in shock and recovered. I think I've had enough killing to last a life time. Of course I'll keep on fishing, which is probably a little inconsistent!"

"Were you ever in the military?"

"Yes, I enlisted in the Air Force in January of 1955, shortly after the Korean War was over, at least officially over. They were still having a lot of problems with Syngman Rhee and his government in South Korea that we were interested in, but it's the killing I did as a kid that bothers me. Maybe I was *too good* with my twenty-two. Bob, the old ghosts don't want to go away. It seems in the middle years of family and work they stay hidden, but in a later, less hectic time, they float around with haunting images. My memories of my youth—say eight to eighteen—when I lived on the farm, are mostly of killing."

"How so?" Bob asked

"Well, there was a two cent bounty on English sparrows and a box of twenty-twos cost fifty cents. So, if I didn't miss, I could make fifty cents in a couple of hours," Will replied. "And a movie only cost a quarter! On the farm, my dad and my grandfather raised chickens, sheep, pigs and beef cattle. All had to be killed for sale. I raised hundreds of rabbits that were like pets, but I had to kill and dress 'em out for the stores in Lansing. Never could bring myself to eat 'em!

"The muskrats I liked to watch playing in the ponds in the spring, the beautiful mink playing on his slide that went into my Victor number one trap. The crows—literally hundreds I shot over a stuffed Great Horned owl—the pheasants, stray cats, the Spitz that dragged me off my bike, the extra baby kittens we couldn't keep. They'll all be there to greet me! Now it seems like a lot of killing for a young boy. At the time, it was just natural and needed. It didn't bother me then, *maybe* I even enjoyed it. But it does now and I'm really torn about hunting."

"I think I understand, but it's my livelihood," Bob replied. "Hunting—guiding—it's a way of life out here, with the lakes, clean air, quiet, peaceful—only the sounds of nature."

"You know, Bob, hunting a Bighorn would be a real physical challenge—all the rest, 'lions, tigers and bears, oh my', you can get to 'em fairly easily. They can kill you, which is a fear, but not a realistic fear. When's the last time you heard of a hunter being killed, especially when they're backed up by a professional? But sheep—that's another story, you can kill yourself just trying to get near 'em! I swear their eyes are better than our binoculars."

"You're right, Will. I hardly ever put my glasses on Bighorn without finding a lookout already watching me. They usually stay put, but the moment you back up and get out of their sight, they move to another spot," replied Bob.

Bob is a professional; a lean, tough, mountain man who knows the high country and its most wary big game. There was no doubt but that all of the 'dudes' were impressed with his abilities in the mountains. "Bob, I can see it now. I shoot a Bighorn—he'll knock me down at the gate to Fire Lake—the moose'll whack me with their hooves—the dogs, squirrels, cats, rabbits, muskrats, chickens, pheasants, crows, pigs—all tear, peck, pull and chew. I just wonder which one'll get my pecker and my cajones?" he laughed. "I'm glad the Cutthroat lived, I suppose he would've turned into a shark in my nightmares!"

"Oh, hell," Kevin spoke up, laughing. "You know he'd grant you professional courtesy! Let's start back, it's about time to eat."

"Good idea," Will replied. And the three, on a separate jaunt to fly-fish Rim Lake, headed down to their Simpson Lake campsite.

Monday evening

"Well, Linda and Bob, now you've heard our life stories—condensed. We're just ordinary people, each with different backgrounds and adventures. We've all had to get up and go to work every day like most of the rest of the people in the world. We've had a few vacations along the way and now Sam is retired, Tom will be soon and I might in a year or so. That's about it," said Tex, who had just finished the last of their brief biographies.

"Sam," Linda spoke up, "you mentioned being in the Air Force. When were you in?"

"I joined in 1954 and got out in '58," Sam replied.

"What did you do?" asked Bob.

"Well," Sam began, glancing at Will, "nothing exciting, I worked a little in communication. They gave me a top security clearance and sent me to the Far East, Japan. But not to change the subject, that reminds me of something. When I joined I went through basic training at Sampson in New York and then they shipped me to Warren Air Force Base in Cheyenne. Man that place was wild in those days!" Sam exclaimed.

"How was that?" inquired Linda.

"In the summer of '54 they held their crazy Frontier Days celebration and ran herds of wild horses right through the middle of town! As I remember it, a couple of people were killed and eight or so were sent to the hospital! But I believe they stopped that tradition."

"Things were a little crazy in those days!" exclaimed Tom.

"Is this the first time you six have been together on a trip?" asked Bob, forgetting to ask Sam what he did in Japan.

"Yes," replied Sam. "And if Will doesn't stop eating beans and cabbage, it's his last trip!"

"Come on, Russtovitch, stop picking on ole Pierre. At least he doesn't use worms and bobbers!" laughed Will, in his own defense.

"Yeah, but what's this I hear about his not using flies either?" asked George. "Come on, Kevin, let's hear the true story of the Monster Cutthroat of Rim Lake."

"Here goes," Kevin began. "That's a real beautiful lake, of course aren't they all! It's one of those all of us went to late Sunday afternoon, after the swim in Dead Horse. This time it was absolutely still with a glass finish. You could see bottom and the trout swimming around. They were jumping, feeding on bugs and flies and I couldn't get 'em to hit on spinners at all. The water was so clear, apparently they could tell the artificial lures."

"We didn't do too well—this was the first time I'd ever used a fly-rod," said Will.

"There's always a first time," said Linda, with a wicked grin.

"Bob, go ahead and tell 'em what Will was doing," laughed Kevin, at the thought of Will's utter frustration with the fly rod.

Bowing his head in surrender, Will confessed, "I was helpless."

"Okay, you guys, listen up, since there's only one lecture per camp on the joys of fly fishing. It's the ultimate sport up here!"

"Oh, I don't know about that!" laughed Linda, obviously in a playful mood.

"You'd better do your duty tonight," said Tex, with a laugh.

"First the basics—of fly fishing," Bob again began, looking at Linda with a friendly scowl. "As Kevin said, in this crystal clear water, when it's still, the trout can tell the artificial lures and even worms, with or without bobbers!" he laughed. "You've all seen how you work out the fly line with a forearm and wrist action. Well, Will did that fine, but then he lost his technique. Didn't you Pierre?"

"I've been told that before!" Will grinned in reply, as they all had another good laugh.

"Pass that butterscotch schnapps," said Bob. "That's good shit! Well, the Cortland fly line floats and it's very easy for the trout to see. The smart ones, the old ones with experience, aren't going to hit a fly anywhere near the end of that line."

"How do you hook 'em then?" asked George.

"One step at a time my friend! Tied to the end of the floating line is a piece of fine, tapered, nylon line about two feet long that's called the *tippet* and the trout can't see it. At the end of the *tippet*, is the fly with a small barbless hook. I don't remember what kind of fly we had on, do you Will?"

"Hell no, they all look alike to me. I can't imagine it makes much difference to the trout, if they're feeding. Like, 'oh shit, here comes a squirrel fly, I ate 'em for supper last night. I think I'd better just wait for a red-tip thistle!"

"I agree," said Bob, continuing. "Will's problem was that as he let the line out to drop to the surface of the water, he was picking a sight point *on* the surface. As a result, the Cortland laid out nice, but the lighter weight *tippet* with the fly, is stopped by the air resistance and dropped at the end of the floating line, like a cobra snake settling down in it's basket!"

"One goddamned cast by the professor of fly-fishing and up came the Great White Cutthroat of Rim Lake!" exclaimed Will.

"Man, you should've seen it!" Kevin exclaimed in amazement. "That line settled to the water as the tippet rolled out and the trout must've seen the fly coming. When it was near the water, the trout exploded up through the surface and I swear, took it in the air!"

"I think you're right, Kevin. It can happen awful quick sometimes. I'll let you guys in on my secret and Will's problem. All you have to do is aim for an imaginary point about three feet or so above the surface. Then, as the Cortland settles down, the tippet and fly have time to roll out with the fly extended away from the end of the visible line. You take over, Kevin."

"Bob set the hook, handed the rod to Will and caught the rest of the action on the video. It was a heck of a nice fish with a blood red 'v' under it's throat. I'd say it was about eighteen inches long."

"A true fisherman!" laughed Tom. "And it'll get an inch longer every time we hear the story!"

"It was quite a thrill," said Will. "Maybe I can catch one myself before we leave. How big was that Cutthroat anyway, Bob?"

"Oh, I'd say it was about sixteen to seventeen inches. It was a nice one for this altitude. We'll catch him again someday and whoever does, I hope they'll let him go. It was a male, probably about twelve years old, that just got out-smarted this time, but he'll be even more wary from now on. The Wyoming record is around forty-one pounds, but not up this high. An old one, an *Oncorhynchus clarki*, that's the Latin genus and species. You dudes didn't think I could speak Latin, did ya? Surprise! Surprise! By the way, the Cutthroat is the Wyoming state fish."

"*Ovis canadensis canadensis,* that's our Rocky Mountain Bighorn. *Felis concolor,* that's the cougar. You want more?" he laughed. "We make our living up here, so we study 'em and we take care of 'em. It's the outfitters up here and the Wyoming Game and Fish Department employees who feed and take care of the sick sheep. We protect their habitat and work to save 'em, not the do-gooder anti-hunting wimps from the lowlands. They come up here when it's nice out, but we're up here in the spring and freezing rain! Hell, one of the outfitters caught pneumonia and died. Another's horse slipped on some icy mud and he'll spend the rest of his life in a wheelchair. I'll bet that never made the do-gooder press!" said Bob, ending his speech in a somber mood.

George spoke up for all, "I think you'll find this group appreciates what you and your friends must go through."

"You know, I could eat another sandwich," joked Will, intent on testing the outfitters. "The insatiate cormorant, soon preys upon itself,' said who?"

"Shakespeare," Linda replied. "But I believe he was talking about vanity."

"Hey, guys, 'tis not wise to underestimate thy opposition! Linda, an A for Bill and an A-plus for vanity. That would've nailed a lot of English lit' majors! How about one more try?"

"Give it your best shot!"

"I'll bet these mountain streams held a lot of *Castor fiber,* didn't they?"

"You're right, they did trap a lot of beaver in this area."

"I give up! I give up! There's your Scrabble partner boys!"

"Well, dudes. Shale Mountain at the crack of dawn. Then more trout in the afternoon. Good night all," said Bob. And getting up, they started for their tents, bringing to an end the second day of their adventure.

————

Tuesday afternoon
Gypsum Creek camp

John and Guy, alone with the helpless young woman, had nearly three days to develop their friendship. In spite of their joint effort at knot tying and survival workouts, it was clear to John that Guy was truly an evil person. John was certain only Guy's desire to engage in the sport of the hit had allowed him the thrill of each new daybreak.

The young captive had provided some common sport, but even in that, Guy's arrogance, deep seated hatred and brutal violence did not set well. I'll keep an appearance of friendship he thought to himself, but this bastard has got to be stopped. He could only imagine Guy's brutality to that innocent family in Duluth and the horror and pain the little girl had suffered through. His thoughts were interrupted by Guy's question.

"John, I don't like lawyers, but why does Lee hate 'em as much as he does? Is it somethin' you can tell me?"

You aren't going to be around much longer, so I might as well, thought John. "Sure, why not. Did you ever see the movie, *The African Queen*?"

"Yeah, I also seen a few in prison."

"Remember the scene where the leeches were all over Bogart's legs and body?" asked John.

"Sure. Who wouldn't remember that?"

"Well, while some lawyers were stealing our parents property, Lee was in Viet Nam fighting for his country and following orders. You've seen the scar on his left arm?"

"Yeah, I seen it."

"Now, just imagine this," John began, ignoring Guy's grammar. "Lee was trapped in a large, marshy area surrounded by Viet Cong and had to stay under water breathing through a hollow reed. His body was covered with leeches. They were in his nose, his ears and everywhere else they could get to. Big bloodsuckers and little bitsy bloodsuckers and in-between bloodsuckers! While he was under, the Cong were jabbing their bayonets into the water trying to find him. One went through his left arm and he had to reach across his body with his right hand and hold his arm tight, while the soldier pulled the blade out, so the blood wouldn't give his position away. He had to stay down until dark to save himself from some very hideous torture. He sewed himself up and was able to get to a chopper a few days later. It was then he found out our parents were dead. Blames the thieving lawyers!"

"Jesus fuckin' Christ," muttered Guy. "He must be one tough mother-fucker." The distant sound of the familiar pickup truck was a welcome intrusion into the tragic past and current solitude of their Bridger Wilderness camp. They could expect Lee to complete his hike up in about an hour and John would be ready with a pot of hot coffee.

"Hi, men. How's it going?" Lee asked, in greeting.

"Fine, Bro. But we're itching to get on with it," John replied. "How'd you do? Are they in camp like we expected?"

"Right on schedule and exactly like we heard it planned at the restaurant! I'd kill for some hot coffee though! I ate good, just enough of theirs along with some delicious Golden I caught and grilled at Marion Lake. All in all, it was a fun three-day trip. There's a group of six—an outfitter, his assistant and a couple with two children—camped at the north end of Simpson. They shouldn't be any problem, since they're about a mile and a half away and sleep in late."

They won't be any problem for me, thought Guy, to himself. Those children will be my dessert after I take care of these fuckin' hillbillies.

"Lee, I know you've said this was my venture to plan. So, here goes the basic strategy—what I think we should do. We make the hit, do our thing, put the tourists in their sleeping bags, zip 'em up tight and close their tents. We pack out the camp meat and her mountain boy covered with the tarps on two of the horses. We don't take any equipment or food that can be traced to their camp, okay?" John asked. Lee and Guy both nodded their approval and John continued, "We only take their cash since we don't need any of their other shit. After we pack up the truck, we load her in, then dump his body in the gully Lee found on the west side of the Divide."

"Why in hell are we botherin' to haul his body out?" Guy queried.

"Good question, Guy. But stop and think about it. If the mountain man's found dead in camp, they'll know immediately it's an outside hit and all hell's goin' to break loose. I want to be in the Apache Forest in New Mexico before they even start looking. If they're both gone, it may mislead 'em for awhile. I want to cover the minutiae of this operation," John answered.

"There you go again, John, using those highfalutin' words," Lee admonished.

Ignoring his brother, John continued, "We then take the horses a short distance toward the base camp, on the east side of the Divide and turn 'em loose. They'll find their way back to camp and stay near the other horses."

"John?" Lee interrupted. "Why don't we kill the two horses so they're short two in camp? That would make it look more like something bad happened, the outfitters panicked and took off."

"Great idea, Lee. By the way, I'm open to any suggestions," John replied. "The group's not due back in Dubois until late Friday afternoon. By the time they're missed or someone should find the bodies, we'll be long gone. It's not likely anyone'll think to look over the Divide for quite awhile. The weather report predicted rain for late Wednesday afternoon or Thursday. It'll wipe out our tracks and make it almost impossible to find us. I can't wait to watch that fuckin' lawyer squirm!" John exclaimed. His hatred for attorneys, like his brother's, knew no limits.

"Well!" exclaimed Lee. "I can't wait to tickle his horse's tail!"

"You're going to tickle his horse's tail? And just what the fuck's that supposed to mean?" queried Guy, assuming he would learn a little more from Lee's unending bag of tricks.

You're dangerous enough, thought Lee. I'm not about to show you. "It's the *cauda equina,* the horse's tail. The area of the first lumbar vertebra where the spinal cord nerves branch out to all parts of the lower body. It can get real exciting!" Lee exclaimed. "Scumbag'll be squealing like a stuck pig!"

"You and John can have your fun. While you're toyin' with him, I'll be doin' the bitch. Maybe all three of us'll be squealin' at the same time!" exclaimed Guy.

"If you agree on the basic strategy, the tactics are up to Lee. You've been there twice and can brief us on the details. Okay, Lee?" John inquired.

"Sure. But we haven't got a lot of time, so why don't you start going over the video. I set this up at a sharp bend and drop in the trail, a short distance east and above Simpson Lake. The sun was coming through an opening that made it easy to film 'em and no way could they see me. The mike was set real close so we've got good voice, both here and in camp. First in line is Bob, then Burr, who they also call Tex or Adorable. Then it's Kevin, Linda, Sam, George, the scumbag Will Dean and last, Tom Tanner. Why don't each of you run that section a couple of times."

"Any of 'em got guns?" asked Guy.

"Both the outfitters, Bob and Linda, and watch it with her because she's got her *sgian-dubh*."

"What the fuck's a ski-en dew?" asked Guy, now wary of Lee's never ending surprises and hating to show his ignorance.

"Tell him, John," said Lee, with a grin.

"It's a small, razor-sharp knife Scot Highlanders carried in a sock sheath, on the outside of their right calf. They used it to administer the *coup de grâce*, by slitting the throat of a mortally wounded soldier, friend or foe."

Maybe I'm part Scot, thought Guy.

"Back to the others. Kevin's got a 9 millimeter, but it's always in his saddle bag. Bob and Linda keep theirs in saddle bags. The last in line, Tom, has a .45 caliber Browning semi-automatic. None of 'em carry 'em in body holsters, so I don't see how they'd ever do 'em any good.

"I also learned that Tex, who doesn't have a gun as far as I know, was in Special Forces. He should be considered the most dangerous of all, even without a gun and out of shape. He'll always be a threat because of his 'memories'. We're not talking about playin' a basketball game. We're concerned about a few seconds of explosive, adrenalin-drenched muscle, coupled with the knowledge of what to do. But I'll tell you one thing, if they all had guns and were wearin' 'em, there's no way we could make this hit! Not unless we wanted to sneak 'around at night and cut their throats. That'd defeat our whole purpose.

"The last in line, Tom, has had heart problems. But he's a former NRA shooter—I didn't get what competition, rifle or handgun. So we have to consider it's handguns. Sam, fifth in line—the scumbag's hunting buddy—is probably the toughest of 'em all, but he'll break. Kevin, third in line and George, sixth in line, are about six foot, lean and both appear to be in very good shape.

"Scumbag's seventh in line, with that silly purple hat and stupid grin. He's fifty-five years old, five-seven and about one seventy-five pounds. Probably the best rider among the tourists. He had no problem in a ride around the plateau. He doesn't have a gun and he's got bum wrists— hockey and car accidents according to campfire bullshit. He was in the military, probably Korea or shortly after, but he didn't talk about it around the campfire. So I don't know what branch."

"How'd you find out?" asked John.

"The way he tucked in his shirt—a military tuck."

"Did you film in camp?" asked Guy.

"Yeah. I filmed in three segments. The ride in, the breakfast Monday morning and then a section on the camp Monday forenoon, to show the layout and tent location. I'd like you to get each identified in your mind with segments one and two first. There's a blank run after each so you can stop and rewind until you're satisfied."

As they reviewed the tape, Lee filled his coffee cup and sat down on the log bench, mentally going back to Monday forenoon. Filming the tents when Linda'd gone for a ride alone, he'd resumed his well-hidden site waiting for the noon lunch. He hadn't planned on any further filming, but when Linda returned and came to the campfire with a towel and bar of soap, he'd reached for the camera.

The ubiquitous telephoto video camera; privacy forever lost. A scene of utmost intimacy, even if unknowingly shared with a happenstance witness, now captured in close detail—preserved—reviewed—still—slow motion—reverse action—prints obtained—to be shared with all who might, for whatever need or reason, gain access. In pure innocence, Linda, standing on a reed mat had carefully and in a state of private bliss, bathed her slender, milk-white body. Her well tanned face and hands the only witness marks to her rugged 'mountain man' occupation. Not since his encounter with Orlov had Lee been aroused to this state over the sight of a naked woman. Relief would not go begging and he'd completed his self-gratification. Reflection on the previous morning passed, Lee spoke as Guy set the camera down. Obviously, he'd only seen the tents. "Oh, John, I forgot, there's a short segment after the tents you might want to look at. Take a look and show Guy. I'm sure he'll be interested!" declared Lee with emphasis.

Driven to a peak of sexual lust by the sight of Linda's most intimate bath, her privacy forever stolen, Guy could no longer wait. "I'm goin' over and give yer camp bitch another poke. Do either of you want any more?" Guy asked.

"I don't," said John. "She doesn't have any moves."

"Me neither," added Lee. "I'll just finish her when you unload."

The helpless young woman made no sounds when Guy brutally entered her weak, lifeless body. Just three weeks before she had been a beautiful, physically fit and tragically innocent law-school graduate, unarmed and alone on a mountain hike. Her hopeless agony ended when Lee deftly snapped her neck as Guy groaned out his orgasm.

"Guy, if you'll start digging a grave over in that small depression, I'll start digging a deep hole over by the big rock. We'll cover her with a bunch of sticks and then fill it over with a few inches of dirt and stones. That way the coyotes can't dig her up," he suggested. "We'll put some hot coals in the bottom of the hole I dig, add the video, her things, then more coals and fill it with dirt. They'll never find anything but her body, if that. Okay?"

"Yeah, Lee," Guy replied with a surly tone ignored by Lee. Jesus, I hate nigger work, he thought as he started to dig in the hard, rocky soil.

Lee, with a yip of a hunting coyote, signalled John to join him and signing, asked him to bring the other spade.

"Lee?" asked John, taking a break from his turn. "How 'bout a back door? Have you thought about it?"

"Of course!" Lee exclaimed, in a whisper. "Guy'll go down with the two horses, the outfitter and the little AR2."

"What about the girl? And oh, by the way, do me a favor and don't pop her eyes. Okay?"

"Sure. John—John—John, 'O ye of little faith'! Remember Friday night when I went to the can and that idiot Hanson and his buddy followed me in?"

"Yeah, what happened?"

"Nothing happened, but after he was done shootin' off his mouth about what a cowardly fuckin' faggot I was, he told his friend he was leaving for a few days to scout some areas to bow hunt Bighorn. He said he was going by himself and would be back Thursday or Friday."

"So how's that goin' to help us?"

"It's a variation of *Let's Go Play At The Adams*. When I 'talk' to him, I'll confirm he went out alone and if he ran into anybody. When they find him in his cabin with the dead girl, they'll also find a note he'll write in remorse. He'll get drunk and take an overdose of Valium. It's doubtful they'll look close enough to find any marks, but they'll find the nine-millimeter with his prints on it. I may even let him use it to go out easy, so he doesn't have to 'talk' to me anymore!" said Lee, with a quiet laugh.

"Lee, here comes the lazy bastard. God, I'll be glad when he's down. I can't stand the asshole!" Betty Lou'll forget him, John thought to himself.

Without ceremony they buried the used-up young woman and as previously planned, began cleaning up camp and packing for the trip over the top to their temporary waiting site.

Tuesday, July 30, 1991
Evening of the third day
Simpson Lake

"Well, happy camper's—it's been great. I like you all, but it's time for my night out."

"Whoa! Wait a minute, Will. What do you mean?" asked Bob. "You're my responsibility."

"Mine too," added Linda. "This is a partnership operation."

"Do you want to come with me, Linda?"

"Whoa! Whoa!" laughed Bob. "Not without me!"

"*Menage à trois,* under stars," said Will, grinning.

"Manage what?" Bob asked.

"Just an old French phrase," Tom answered.

Sam spoke up, "Oh, don't worry, Bob. I've been telling you for three days he's whacked! Now you know it!"

"Well," Linda interjected, "this is Wyoming—land of freedom. Worst that can happen is a bear will eat you. And wow, the way you eat, that'll save a lot of money on our food bill! It's a good thing we've been eating trout as it is!"

"Good God, Bob, let him go. The way he farts, I'll at least get one decent night's sleep!" Burr exclaimed.

"Where do you want to go, Will?" asked Bob.

"I'd like to take Baldy and ride up to Dead Horse canyon. There'll be a full moon and it's crystal clear out. If a rain blows in, I'll be able to get under that huge rock. Hell, it's almost a cave."

"You and Baldy both could get under that one," said Kevin.

"If you go, Will," said George, "you know we can talk all we want about you!"

"Christ! I hope we can find something better than that to talk about!" exclaimed Tom, with a laugh.

"Well, guys and gal," said Will, "we've been gone now six nights, counting tonight, and this is our third day in camp. It's been one hell of a trip already, with a ton of good memories. I can't imagine a more fun or closer group—eight and no tension at all."

"Unless Linda walks out of our tent tonight!" laughed Bob.

"I'll pee in the sleeping bag, honey," she promised.

Will began again, "I propose we have a toast—go around the camp fire and hit on whatever comes to mind, more as less as it happened. Tom, why don't you start?"

"Here's to Blue Earth!" Tom exclaimed, with a laugh.

"Here—here," the dudes replied in unison, breaking again into laughter.

"What the hell is blue earth?" asked Bob.

"That's another story!" exclaimed George.

"Here's to women who think I'm adorable," said Burr, and everyone roared in laughter at the Rustic Pine incident the Saturday night before.

"Here's to worms and bobbers!" toasted Sam.

"Boo—hiss!" chided Will, as the others cheered.

"Here's to Golden eagles soaring above Dead Horse Lake and the wind blowing through long brown hair!" said Kevin. And on that one, a look of curiosity passed over Bob's eyes.

"Here's to riding through glaciers, and herds of Bighorn rams on top of Shale Mountain," said George, as they all cheered.

"Here's to Cutthroat trout and Bob knowing how to work my fly rod!" said Will.

"You landed him!" Bob exclaimed.

"Here's to George's horse knowing her way home with an empty saddle," said Linda, laughing at the memory of George dejectedly plodding across the valley.

"Here—here," laughed George, along with the rest.

"Here's to Will and Baldy getting that damn dead tree to break loose!" added Bob.

"Here's to Linda and Bob, two of the greatest mountain men and guides we could ever hope to meet. May you live long, happy lives, have lots of mountain children, and put up with us next year. We love you both," Will spoke softly.

"Here—here," said the dudes, finishing their drinks.

"Well, gang, I'll see you at breakfast. Linda—Bob, I'd like about three eggs-benedict with Canadian pea-meal bacon and lots of sauce, a side order of blueberry pancakes with hot maple syrup and some crisp sausage!"

"You're the God damn sausage!" exclaimed Sam, getting up to help his hunting buddy head out. Together they saddled Baldy and tied Will's sleeping bag behind the saddle. "Pierre, do you want to borrow Kevin's pistol?"

"No. Baldy'd raise all kinds of hell if a bear or cat came into the area, I'll be fine. Sam, I've got to tell you something. I brought my Mauser with me, but I didn't want to show it around. Hell, I can't hit much with it and I don't want to embarrass myself. Don't say anything about it, okay?"

"Sure. Hell, never hurts to have an ace-in-the-hole not everyone knows about. I don't think we've seen everything Burr's got either."

"See you in the morning, Russtovitch." And shaking hands, the two lifelong friends parted.

————

Dead Horse Lake

Away from camp, the silence alone was sufficient reward for Will's customary night out. His site for the night was at the edge of a small, trout filled lake, known for some long forgotten reason as Dead Horse Lake, located in a box canyon above the Simpson Lake valley. It lay approximately one mile southeasterly of camp, five to six hundred feet above and from the rocks on its east side, gave a fantastic view of two-mile long Simpson. The long and narrow Simpson drained north into Moon Lake; feeding then into the clean, clear waters of the fast-flowing and incredibly beautiful, Wind River.

Flowing southeasterly to the Wyoming town of Riverton, the Wind turned and headed north to become known as the Bighorn River. The Bighorn, along with numerous companion tributaries, formed the great Missouri, known to many as Mighty Mo. Draining the east side of the Continental Divide of the Rocky Mountains and the High Plains of the Northwest, Mighty Mo joined— if not itself being joined—the Mississippi at St. Louis, some two thousand three hundred miles away.

In earlier times, the beautiful valley had been a popular site often visited by various nomadic hunting families of the Eastern Shoshoni Indians. Prior to the mass migration of the westward pushing white man, they ranged throughout the high mountain country of western Wyoming, and the adjacent mountains of Utah, Idaho, Colorado, Montana and the border area of Canada. It was easy to understand how the Shoshoni—with the waters of their mountains flowing by the Snake to the Pacific; the Saskatchewan to the Atlantic; the Missouri to the Gulf of Mexico and the Green to the Colorado and then to the Gulf of California—believed that they lived on the top of the world.

Enjoying the solitude of the peaceful evening, Will went back in time— two hundred years earlier—and imagined the young native American, the beautiful Sacajawea. Daughter of a proud chief of the Agaiduka Shoshoni, Chief No Retreat, she was captured and held as a slave by the Hidatsa. Gambled away to the French trapper, Toussaint Charbonneau, she became the key guide for the Lewis and Clark expedition to the Pacific Ocean in 1805.

Will's mental journey was broken by the feeding sounds of a cow moose and calf appearing at the swampy end of the lake. A great place to visit, but a hell of a tough place to make a living he thought. To the east and a thousand feet or so above the canyon floor, the Golden eagles were again soaring in unison; one of natures best aerobatic displays.

From the vest's left side pocket, he removed the Jason Perma Focus 7 x 21—2000 binoculars. The seven ounce glasses have a field of vision of 7.5 degrees, which, when translated to understandable language, meant that at a thousand yards, with a field of fifty-two and a half feet per degree, the user would see an area three-hundred ninety-three feet wide. The 7 x 21 meant that an object viewed would be seen seven times larger than with the naked eye. The objective lens, that farthest from the eye, at 21 millimeters in diameter, would deliver adequate light to the eye for daytime viewing. Designed with automatic focus and a black, non-reflective finish, they were easy to use with one hand and would not be readily observed from a distance.

A direct descendant of Sir Isaac Newton's *Optics*, published in 1704, they were the latest in modern technology and like many electronic wonders of the twentieth century, would give a double meaning to viewing the splendors of nature in the time of the rising sun.

The Golden eagles now out of view, he scanned the ridges of the mountain east of him in the ascending line of the evening sunset, "Wow, look at those Bighorn sheep!" Will exclaimed to Baldy, his only companion for the evening. To the southeast and high above on an outcropping of rock, at the west edge of Shale Mountain, bathed in the last bright light of the setting sun, stood two Bighorn ewes, each with a pair of lambs; a sight to behold. What a wonderful and stress-free vacation this has been for all of us; we may even be able to face the real world he thought. Will finished the last of his paper sack of trail mix as the fading day shifted to the soft light of evening. The full moon and stars filled the sky as night approached and the third day came to an end.

Nights alone in Colorado, Michigan, and the terrifying night spent on Will's Hill, in the Wilderness Area of central Newfoundland, had well prepared him for this cool, clear night out. He felt for and removed the .380 caliber *Mauser-Werke AG* seven-shot, semi-automatic pistol from the right side pocket of his camera vest. It's not much good for anything except at real close range, he thought. Maybe I could scare off a cougar or a bear if one came around. I'm a little ashamed to show a weapon I don't think I can hit much with, at least Sam knows I've got it.

With Baldy tied on a long grazing rope, Will snuggled down in his warm sleeping bag. He knew that the long day's ride and the fresh mountain air were better than any sleeping potion; except one he thought, thinking of his girlfriend in Michigan and Linda with the warm breeze blowing through her long brown hair, on their second trip to Dead Horse, Monday afternoon. Too tired to stay awake for any productive fantasies, Will drifted off into a deep and restful sleep.

———

Evening campfire
Simpson Lake Camp

"Boy, we can sure talk about him now," declared Bob, and they all laughed. The ease with which the Dudes and the mountain man and his wife, Linda, had gotten along, created a relaxed atmosphere among all. While of different worlds, the evening in Dubois and three full days of living in the rigors of mountain camp life, had quickly removed many of the barriers created by the privacy of a walled room existence.

Camp life, more like the open style in the circle of the tepee, developed an easy readiness to kid and joke, even quite ribald at times, among the old and the new found friends. The eight, at least for this very special week, had formed, without even being aware of it, a tight, caring and protective clan.

"Where's Sam?" asked Burr.

"I'd guess he's at a nature call, it's his time," George answered.

"Does Will have a pistol with him?" Bob asked.

"No, I don't think so," George replied. "He had a real nice Smith & Wesson .357 magnum, but it was stolen."

"I thought I heard him say he had some kind of Mauser?" Tom questioned.

"He does. It's a .380 semi-automatic, but he told me at our final get-together he didn't think he'd bring it because he couldn't hit his prostate if he stuck it up his ass!" George added, as they all broke into laughter.

"Why does he go out for a night?" Linda asked.

"Probably to abuse himself!" laughed George.

"Well," answered Sam, returning to the campfire, "I think he just likes to be alone. He's a total non-joiner at home and it's the way he lived as a kid."

"Does he take booze with him?" Bob asked.

"No—never. It's more like getting close to nature. Hot, cold, wet or dry, it doesn't matter to him. Will knows there are bears out there so it's kind of a challenge to be alone. No tent usually—just his sleeping bag. He'd never dull his senses with alcohol, not out in the wilderness. Of course, you saw him on stage at the Rustic Pine Saturday night!" Sam added.

"Boy, he was into it then!" Kevin exclaimed.

"It was the Jack Daniel's. Heck, he couldn't even do the Texas two-step!" exclaimed Linda.

"When Kevin, Will and I went up to Rim Lake and Will caught that Cutthroat trout," Bob started . . . .

"You caught and he landed, you mean!" interrupted Kevin.

"Right. Anyway, he said he didn't think he should kill any more," Bob continued. "He said he'd done too much killing and at too young an age. It was starting to bother him. Said he'd have nightmares now and then about some of the animals he'd had to kill as a young kid on the farm."

"Boy he sure opened up to you," said Sam. "He hasn't even told me that. Although, I know he started hunting English sparrows for a two cent bounty with a BB gun when he was eight years old. But, let me tell ya something. You two don't have to worry 'bout Will being out in the field alone—he'll be back," Sam declared, in a steady, strong voice.

"What kinda shot is he?" Linda asked.

"Wait a minute, I've heard these stories before, I'm going to make a beer run to the creek. Who wants what?" asked Kevin. The orders placed, Kevin headed out as Sam cleared his throat.

Bob stopped him before he could begin, "You're not going to bullshit us are you, Sam?" he asked.

"No. I'll tell you what I've heard and then what I've seen with my own eyes and these eyes are very good. At least they were when I witnessed what I'm about to tell. You've heard he started on sparrows, first with a BB gun and then with his grandfather's single-shot bolt-action twenty-two. Bullets cost a penny a piece so he could double his money if he didn't miss. He's usually very careful in his shot selection.

"His mother told how one year he killed his limit of eight rooster pheasants, all on the wing, with eight shots using his dad's Savage, single-shot, 16 gauge shotgun. That's some kind of shooting, if it's true and I've no reason to doubt it. He got his first rifle, a Remington bolt-action—a model 512 repeater—when was twelve. He's not much of a target shot, but seems to have an uncanny ability to hit things in motion. One of his sons, Mark, told me he was with him several times deer hunting and has seen him kill three whitetail on the dead run, and never missed a shot! Now for what I've actually seen. But, I wouldn't say these things if he was here 'cause I don't want to give him a bigger head 'an he's already got!

"Twenty years ago, we were hunting in the wilderness area of central Newfoundland. Steadman Wentzel, a great outfitter, had put us in at the headwaters of the Grey River. It was late in the afternoon of the last full day of the hunt. Will and I, with our guides, were in camp. I'd shot my moose and Will's guide was sick, so we played cribbage and stayed in the area near camp. By the way, the people in Newfoundland were wonderful to us."

"Is that the year Will double-skunked you at ten cents a point and you threw the board in the fire?" Kevin asked.

"Yes, but I skunked his goddamned ass six straight times in Colorado a few years later!" Sam retorted.

"Back to what happened at South Lake camp. Later in the afternoon, Will and his guide went for a short hike up a hill directly behind camp. Damned if they didn't spot a bull feeding on a plateau about a mile south of camp. They ran back to camp and the four of us—only Will and I with rifles—got the boat. We rowed south to a small hill we could climb, to see across the river to the plateau. Moose have fantastic hearing. The damn bull must've heard us, because he was standing broadside, head left, ass right. Head swung around and ears cocked toward us like TV satellite dishes!"

"What kind of rifle did Will have?" Bob asked.

"He's got an old, converted, military rifle. It's a 30–06, fitted at the time with a Redfield range-finder scope. He was shooting 180 grain Nosler Partition bullets my brother-in-law, Hank, had loaded for him," Sam answered and continued. "I'm glad he can't hear me now 'cause I'm always ragging on him, claiming I shot the bull with my .300 magnum! To tell the truth I've never seen anyone put a scope on target and shoot as quick as he did! That damn Nosler bullet streaked almost four-hundred yards across the plateau at about twenty-five hundred feet per second and literally swept the bull off his feet! I couldn't believe it! I've never seen anything happen so damn fast in my life!"

"Wow! Where'd it hit him?" Linda asked.

"After we dressed him out, we found the bullet went between his left ribs, through his heart and lodged on the inside of his right shoulder blade. Will has the mushroomed bullet."

"That must have been some shot to see!" exclaimed Bob.

"As you know, a heart shot may or may not be a good shot. He was probably aiming for the front shoulder. But like Paul Harvey says, do you want to hear 'the rest of the story'?" Sam asked.

"There's more!" exclaimed Linda.

"You bet your sweet ass! Oops," Sam stammered, his face turning red.

"Take my word for it boys, it is!" added Bob, and they all had a good ribald laugh.

"Back to central Newfoundland. We went down to the boat, rowed across the river and climbed the short distance to the plateau. Let me explain something about hunting in that area. First, the guides don't carry rifles. The plateau was covered with a short, dense brushy growth that's very difficult to walk through. You usually walk single file in narrow caribou trails. Another problem is tough vines that grow across the trails. They catch the toes of your boots and it's as easy as not to be tripping. For that reason, the guides, when they're in the lead, won't let you have a round in the chamber. If you come upon a moose, you'd better be able to load your rifle in absolute silence!" Sam exclaimed. "Of course with a bull down, we were loaded.

"Now here comes the good part and I swear to God it's absolutely true. That bullet went through the lower part of the heart without being mushroomed and didn't hit any valves or arteries. All it really did was knock the bull off his feet and totally piss him off! I was directly behind Will, with the two guides behind me, as we walked onto the plateau. That damn bull was standing there and before even Will could shoot, he was charging at us with a full head of steam and death in his eyes!" Sam exclaimed and pausing, caught his breath. "I'd tripped on a vine and was laying on my side. Will had him in his scope, but didn't want to shoot while the bull was charging, since he wouldn't be able to refocus in time due to recoil.

"Will'd read that most of the time moose'll stop their charge, go up on their hind legs and smash you with their front hooves—lot like a horse. Well, we're all screamin', 'Shoot, Will! Shoot!' And he's standin' there with a charging moose fillin' his scope, wishin' he had open sights and prayin' the damn moose'd read the same book he had! The bull went up on his hind legs and Will shot him through the throat, right below his head. He dropped deader'n a hammer not fifteen feet from where Will was standin'! Will's heart was racin' so fast he couldn't even talk. Can you believe a lawyer being speechless?" And with this comment, they all had another good laugh. "But I'll give credit where it's due, he took the charge and never budged an inch! A year's meat at his feet!"

"If Oswald could, why couldn't Will've shot sooner?" asked Burr.

"Don't get Will goin' on that! Three shots on a moving target at ninety yards in six seconds! With a four-power scope on a twenty-two dollar bolt-action he'd just got!" exclaimed Sam. "Will goes bonkers. Says it's impossible. Claims Mossad *kidons*—assassins—tried, but couldn't duplicate it. With iron sights, 'shooters' keep both eyes open. Don't squint like amateurs, so you don't lose your target. With a scope, you've gotta close the eye you're not using. After the first shot, you've gotta find the moving target which is off-scope due to recoil. Will oughta know! He's shot bolt-actions for forty-eight years. He calls the one-bullet theory, the *Waltzing Matilda* bullet! Guess you just got Will's lecture!" Sam laughed.

"Back home, the moose is a lot more famous than Will. A local actor made some TV commercials for a business called *The Stereo Shoppe*, where he talks to the stuffed moose head," George interjected.

"Have you seen him make other tough shots?" asked Bob.

"Yes. Not as dramatic, but far more difficult," Sam answered. "Pass me the Harvey's, George, if you will please. Thanks," said Sam continuing. "It was seven years ago when Will and I were in Alaska. We were on a two week rafting trip down the Coleen River—far northeast corner of Alaska. We were just south of the Continental Divide and west of the Yukon Territory. Roger Dowding, one of Alaska's best known bush pilots, had flown us up from a village on the Yukon, called Circle.

"It was the first day and before we'd started down river. This was a drop trip—just the two of us. We were countin' on game and only brought a little freeze-dried to go with whatever we could get. Our first camp was set up between the Coleen and a small feeder stream full of Grayling. And we didn't use worms! Will had his .357 pistol and I had my .300 magnum, Winchester bolt-action with a scope. I was after a trophy caribou, but all Will wanted was a young bull for camp meat and for the Indians in Circle.

"In the late afternoon we spotted a small group of caribou runnin' along the bank, across the river from us. They were about two hundred yards away and runnin' inside the group was a young bull, mostly hidden behind some cows. Will asked, so I handed him my rifle. How in hell he did it I'll never know, but he shot over the back of a running cow and picked off that bull with a high shoulder shot. He never touched any of the others!" Sam exclaimed. "Later I got my trophy bull and we had a raft full of meat to give the Indians."

"Do you think it was luck?" Bob asked.

"I don't know," Sam answered. "If it was, he always seems to have it.

One of these days he'll run out! I'd sooner think it's instinct. If it's in motion, he nails it," Sam added. "And now, the rest of the story!"

"There's more?" Linda queried.

"Just a small point for you shooters. Will had never shot that rifle in the field before! How does that grab you?" he asked.

"It must've been luck and he'll probably run out sometime," said Burr.

"He almost did. Sam, why don't you tell 'em about the river incident?" questioned George.

"You happy campers wanta hear more Will Dean stories?" asked Sam.

"It's not too late, just so it's not another goddamn he-walks-on-water story!" laughed Burr. "Besides, he isn't here, so let's get 'em over with!"

Sam began, "You can rest assured he sure as hell don't walk on water. For about five minutes in the Coleen he wished he could walk on water! We'd been working our way down river for a few days, picture taking, fishing, and just enjoying the wall-to-wall sunshine and the fantastic Alaska weather. It was the second or third of September and temperature in the mid fifties, with the nights in the twenties. The water of the Coleen was frigid cold, being ice melt from the mountains and it was cold on this day. We were wearing snowmobile suits and hip boots. Will had his pistol belt on and his wife's camera hanging from his neck. Our life jackets were right where they were supposed to be. In the bottom of the raft! We'd just come around a bend in the river and our raft got hung up under a pine sweeper."

"What's a sweeper?" Linda asked.

"It's where the current in a bend cuts the rock and soil out from under a tree, the tree tips over in the river, but the current doesn't pull it out. The water flows under it with the strong part of the current. You can get dragged under the tree if you don't pull out and away from the edge fast enough, as you're carried around the bend," Sam explained and continued.

"It was my turn at the oars and of course when you row you usually have your back to the direction you're headed, so you've got enough power to pull. But, when you're rafting down stream you have to turn the raft to steer it so fast water don't carry you into trouble. We were yakking at each other and I didn't get the raft turned quick enough when we came to some fast water. Our raft went under a pine and got hung up. We were tilted down on the upstream side, overloaded with the boned-out meat of two caribou and all our gear. It was extremely dangerous, since if the raft rolled, we'd lose our gear and more'n likely, both drown.

"Will was caught at the back end and had to push down even more on the raft and up against the pine. When the raft broke free, his feet were in it going fast down stream, as he was pushin' up on the tree. We could see what was going to happen and as he spun in mid-air, I lunged to the rear of the raft and grabbed for my good huntin' buddy! Christ, it was too damn close, that one!" Sam shook and bowed his head. "I need another shot of that Harvey's," he said, reaching for George's bottle.

Taking a long pull on the Bristol Creme and catching his breath, Sam continued, "As Will spun and reached for me, we locked our left wrists like trapeze acrobats! Will went completely under, but we hung on and when he came up, we were face to face and he screamed, 'Don't let go, don't let go Sam'! Well, his wife hadn't offered a high enough percentage, so I hung on! His body went numb and we had to drift down river until we came to a shallow enough area so he could touch bottom and push into the raft."

"I'll bet you hung on 'cause you didn't want to be in grizzly country alone!" laughed Kevin.

"You're probably right, Kevin. But I'll tell you one thing, no one wants to die and it was a situation where Will had time to think about it. He was absolutely terrified!" Sam exclaimed. "If we'd hit another sweeper . . ."

"I was in a situation like that in Viet Nam and any normal person would be terrified," spoke up Burr.

"When you grabbed Will, you must've known it could kill you, didn't you?" Bob asked.

"Didn't have time to think about it and don't think of it as being a hero. It just happened. I reacted and I believe most people are heroes when these circumstances occur. It's not something you plan. You just do it—the best you can. This time it worked and if it hadn't, you might've read about it seven years ago, but you wouldn't 've heard it around a camp fire."

"What's this story about Will's Hill?" asked Bob.

"Oh no," Sam replied, "it's too long and I'm tired."

"Go ahead, Sam. Make it a quick one," said George.

"All right, but I'm going to keep it short," Sam promised. "I think it was in seventy-eight when we went back to the same camp in the Wilderness Area in central Newfoundland. To spend his night out, we left him on a little knoll in the middle of a large, flat, boggy area about eight miles from camp. He'd faked a severe knee pain and there was no way we could carry him back to camp. I told our young guides he'd be okay with his wet suit and his thirty-ought six.

"A polar bear sow with two cubs, they were probably two years old, had been sighted in the area and he wanted to get pictures at daybreak, if he could. The sow'd had her cubs and apparently been stranded on the peninsula, up around St. Anthony, when spring ice broke up. We were told later they won't swim out in the open sea and they'd wandered south to the Wilderness Area.

"It was warm, in the sixties when we left Will, but the weather there changes faster'n in Michigan. Before we got back to camp, the wind shifted and was coming straight out of the north. It started in a howling, freezing rain that was blowing so hard it was coming in horizontal! We damn near got lost!

"This is a much longer story, but I'm tired and so I'm going to cut it short. Will was able, with absolutely no protection, to keep a small fire going and using heated rocks against his kidneys, kept his body temperature up to avoid hypothermia. The hot rocks actually melted the back of his wet suit top! The weather changed just as fast the next day. We started out at daybreak expecting to find his frozen corpse. Well, it'd turned warm and there he was, about a mile north of Will's Hill. Bare-ass naked as the day he was born, laying on a rock, sun-bathing and watching the humpbacked 747s flying overhead on their way to Shannon, Ireland!

"We passed by that hill on our way back to camp and Will showed me his stone fire pot. He'd tied one of those red plastic, game-marking ribbons around a small hemlock bush, that most likely's still there. Then like Sam Magee, the bastard made me promise in front of our guides, that if he gets killed and I'm around, I have to take some of his goddamn ashes back to his hill! That's it, I'm going to bed. Good-night to all," said Sam getting up and walking toward his tent.

"He'll be back in time for breakfast and we'll all have another great day tomorrow," said Burr, as they headed for their tents.

———————

"Honey," Linda softly began as they lay together in the limited privacy of their tent, "what was that look all about over Kevin's toast?"

"You've never let your hair down when we're up here with strange men," Bob replied, a tone of jealousy clearly in his voice.

"My God, I don't believe what I'm hearing! Oh for heavens sake—he's a big flirt, that's all. He and Kevin were both fishing and I climbed up on the rocks. I think Will took a picture with a telephoto—that's as close as he got! We watched the eagles doing their aerobatics again. Quite a sight, aren't they, honey?"

"They sure are. They were really going at it Sunday!"

"Talk about soaring in unison—get over here, I'll show you unison, my mountain man. Jesus," she whispered, as he thrust deep into her receptive body. Together, with the vigor of youth and superb physical fitness, they sailed among the mountain peaks, each enjoying the bursting stars. Their deep passion reaffirming the conjugal bliss of a very special relationship. Slowly they glided down to the firm reality of the hard, mountain plateau; a mattress far above the low-landers. "Honey, you know, if something happens to Will out there, we're going to be in deep shit for letting him go off by himself"

"I thought about that, Linda, but for Christ sake, what the hell, he can handle Baldy and from the tales we heard tonight, he'll do all right. I like to go off by myself and heck, your ride to town was as dangerous. We can't always be in the safety of a group."

"I guess you're right, honey. I don't think we'll have to worry too much about him. Did you notice the tone of voice Sam used when he declared that Will would be back okay?"

"Yeah, now that you mention it. He sure isn't worried about him. So I guess there's no point in us worrying!" Bob exclaimed.

"You know honey, this is a real fun bunch. They all have a great sense of humor. And did you see Sam blush when he said 'sweet ass'? That was funny!"

"Will probably wouldn't 've."

"Don't get started on that again, damn it!"

"Okay. I promise. When he believed that Cutthroat was going to die, I thought he was going to cry."

"Honey, that's the bad part of this job. We spend a week out in the field. We get to know and like each other real well. Then they go home and we never see 'em again. Oh, they write—send pictures—tell us what a great time they had—send other friends, but we'll never see 'em again. And you know, I really like these guys. It's our job, but I'm really going to miss 'em."

"I agree, Linda. You know, Tex and I have really hit it off and they're all so much fun. Oh well, we make a living."

"Honey, that's not all we make."

"What's that supposed to mean?"

"Well, it's been three years now. You finally did it right!"

"What?"

"You're going to be a daddy!"

"What! Really! Oh my God! Wow—yippee!"

"Bob—quiet—you'll spook the horses and wake up everyone. You can tell 'em all at breakfast."

"My boy Bill," he started to hum.

"Our girl Jill," she whispered, giving his hand a tight squeeze. And together, as it was meant to be, they drifted off with warm thoughts and pleasant dreams of the joy filled days and years to come. Known only by her husband, she had never been exposed or touched by evil. Her youth and innocence gave her a soul still glowing with 'that flower of purity, which, in women, survives the first fall'.

6

'the morning of the fourth day'

The black earth
Was sown with bones
And watered with blood
For a harvest of sorrow
On the land of the Russ'
The Armament of Igor

Tuesday evening
Union Mountain

Leading the way, Lee brought the team of predatory hunters to a small lake, hidden in a depression above and north of the fishermen's camp site. With his binoculars, the camp fire was visible, though the distance made any practical observation all but useless. Enough information had been gathered to assure their success.

"Lee, you've been in and around the camp several times, so why don't you go over it with us one more time."

"No, John, this is to be your operation. I want you to lay it all out, putting together everything I've shown you and all the details I got on surveillance. You're the captain. If there's something Guy or I think should be changed, we'll speak up. I'll describe the area for you again, though.

"Simpson Lake's about two miles long, flowing south to north. It's fed by a stream known as Jakeys Fork. The camp's about an eighth of a mile southwest of the south end of the lake and on a plateau approximately thirty feet or so above it. To the south of camp is a small stream where they keep beer and other beverages cold. The camp's in a grove of scattered pine with visibility fairly open, but there are a few scrub pine and bushes that provide some cover. The horses are tied among the pine at the east edge of the camp and provide more cover for an approach from the east. The area south of the lake has a great deal of tall willow that would give complete cover, but it's difficult to move around in, unless you're a moose or on a horse.

"By the way, there's a big bull moose that hangs out in the area, as

well as a cow and a fairly large calf. Moose can be very unpredictable. They
have terrible eye sight, but their hearing's excellent. I wouldn't want to be
trapped in those willows with that bull in a bad mood."

"Where'd you learn all that, Lee? We don't have many moose in Virginia!" laughed John.

"Sam and Scumbag were watching the cow and calf across the valley
Monday morning before breakfast and were giving Bob a lecture on the fine
points of moose hunting. I don't know if they were bullshitin' or not, but they
seemed to know what they were talking about. Back to the layout of the area.
Both the east slope of Union Mountain, that's where we are now, and the west
slope of Shale, that's the mountain east of the camp, are forested and the trees
come down nearly to the edge of Simpson. In fact, you wouldn't be able to
walk along the east side of the lake at all. On the west side there's a flat area
and of course, the other camp with the kids I told you about, is approximately
a mile north of here in some pine. Any questions?" Lee asked.

"Yes," Guy spoke up. "What about light? How early?"

"Good question, Guy. Of course it's light enough now with a full moon
and all these stars. It starts getting daylight around five thirty in the morning.
But it's quite light out long before sunlight hits camp. They usually finish
breakfast about the time the sun breaks above Shale's crest. Sunrise and sunset
are quite a sight, since there's a sharp line of bright light that moves down the
side of Union in the morning and up the face of Shale in the evening. Does
that answer your question, Guy?" asked Lee.

As Guy indicated satisfaction with a nod of his head, Lee continued,
"There isn't anything else I can think of at the moment. If something comes
to mind I'll speak up, but for now, why don't you take over, John?"

"Okay—here goes. I've gone over all my notes of what you've already
told us Lee. As you've always told me, deception is a key and the starting
point, then the element of surprise. Each morning just before breakfast, Tex
goes up the hill and takes a dump. He may be armed, but even if he doesn't
have a gun he should be considered dangerous, and taken out without any
noise. This means Lee should do him and come into camp from the west side
with Guy. At all times, it should appear to the tourists as though Lee is no
threat and even as though he's not in on it. That way we'll have an ace-in-
the-hole."

"That's a very good idea, John!" exclaimed Lee. "I hadn't even thought
of that!"

"Guy and I'll have the radios and rifles. Hell, Lee doesn't need one any
way."

Oh yes he does, thought Guy. There's no fuckin' way they'll ever let
me back in the truck. I've got a surprise for both these cocky hillbillies when
we get on top.

"Guy, you take the nine millimeter and I'll take the lightweight. They'll be taken by surprise and we won't give 'em enough time to react. If they don't obey you immediately, shoot whoever hesitates. That'll get their attention!"

The Colt AR-15A2 rifle is as deadly a semi-automatic hand-held weapon as there is. To be available to law enforcement and other authorized government agencies, they had, as part of the Colt dealer's duties, been modified to fire on full automatic, as well as semi-automatic.

"Guy'll take the three—Bob, Tom and Kevin—to the east edge of the camp, right at the tree line, make 'em lie down and tie their wrists behind 'em. I'll do the same to Linda, Sam, George and Scumbag. Guy, when you've got 'em tied, cough and when you hear me cough, shoot each of 'em in the back of the head, at the base of the skull. From what I've heard you can handle that, right?"

"Oh, I think so," he replied, ignoring the dig. "When do I get to fuck the bitch? That was sure some video. I'd kind of like to see it again."

"Hell, man, you get to see the real thing tomorrow," Lee replied. "Since this is our caper, John should get a crack at her before you make it a canyon with that horse of yours!"

"Fuck, that's fair enough. They're all tight when I first get 'em!" he exclaimed, with a smirk.

"Back to the plan," said John, resuming his outline. "We went over the video enough to have everyone memorized. But for sure, we know the chick a little better'n the rest! Damn what a sight—her taking a bath by the fire— I'm getting another diamond-cutter just thinking about it! Anyway, after Guy wastes the three with pistols, of course they won't have 'em with 'em, he joins us, we do the girl—in the proper order—watch Lee entertain Scumbag for awhile with his hunting buddy, and then do him. Guy and I'll probably be ready to do the chick again. We load up and head back to the truck. The whole operation shouldn't take more 'an hour or so and we'll have a couple of days to get away. Any questions?"

"Yes," said Lee.

"What?" questioned John, with puzzled look.

"What if something is wrong or different than I've scouted out? Say for instance, what if someone just happens to come by, or someone happens to sleep in, or Tex doesn't take his morning shit, or Linda comes back later'n usual with her horses. Any of a bunch of things I can't think of now?"

"Do you want to call the whole thing off?" asked John, a little exasperated with his kid brother.

"No, I'm just saying what if?"

Watching his notes burn, John pondered his answer, "I think that in any operation, a lot of unexpected things can happen, or can certainly go wrong. The only thing you can do, is be as prepared as a team as you can be, and then go with your gut feelings. If you have to look at your notes when you're in the middle of your speech, you're going to blow it."

"Very good, John! You sound just like some of my instructors at Fort Campbell," said Lee, with a big smile. "We're all going to be pumped up. It's almost midnight. Why don't you both try and get a little sleep while I go down and check things over one last time. It's only a couple of hundred feet below us and about three-quarters of a mile away, so I should be back in an hour or so."

Like a cat, only a smooth, well-oiled shadow crept among the tents, checking to confirm they were all in ignorant bliss and having sweet dreams of giant trout. Shit—Lee froze, three tents—six; one tent—one. Where in hell's the fucking Scumbag. There was no doubt in his mind it was Tex snoring and there was no body heat on Dean's side of the tent. Moving back into some shadow, he froze; for thirty minutes he remained in frozen silence. Every nerve taut, listening for the slightest sound and watching for any motion. It's either the longest shit in history or the son-of-a-bitch has left camp, Lee thought.

Linda always lets some of the horses graze at night, so there's no way to count 'em, he thought. Wait, count saddles, maybe he went off on a lark. The son-of-a-bitch does like to ride and maybe he went off to beat his meat, Lee thought, laughing to himself. If that's the case, we'll just have a welcome home party for him! Moving quietly among the tied horses and carefully checking the tack, he confirmed his theory. Well I'll be damned, just like I guessed, seven saddles. He won't ride back at night, but the bastard's always eating and I'll bet he'll be back in time for ham and eggs. I'd better get back and fill John in, he's the captain.

———————

4:30 A.M., Hidden Lake

"John, Guy, come on men, breakfast at the Simpson Lake Hotel! Got some news for you. You're not going to believe this, but Scumbag's not in camp!"

"Where the hell is he?" asked an astounded John.

"My guess is he took a bottle of booze and rode a horse up to Dead Horse or Sandra Lake to spend a night by himself. He tends to be, how shall I say it, kind of a loner, even when he's with his friends. It's something I've noticed, but didn't think much about until now. What'll you want to do, John?"

"Nothing's really changed. I say we make the hit as planned, keep our eyes open and have a welcome home party for him."

"Those were my thoughts, exactly! What do you think, Guy?"

"I agree. But what about shootin' those three? Maybe I should just cut their throats?"

"No, I don't think that'll matter. Just don't do it until I give the signal,"

John replied. "Shooting 'em will give the others somethin' to look forward to!"

"There are a couple of changes," Lee interjected. "It becomes real important in my questioning of Sam that you don't kill George, unless you absolutely have to. They should be separated enough so they can't hear my questions. When I question Sam, I don't let him know I have any information at all. That way I can play what I know, as George's answers, against Sam's. Basic interrogation."

"Well," said John, "let's start down and get in place. The curtain is about to open men." I don't like Scumbag not being in his tent, but forewarned is forearmed he thought, following as quietly as possible, Lee's silent lead.

6:25 A.M.
Wednesday,
Simpson Lake Camp,

"Hey, Tex, where's your roommate?" asked Bob, the breakfast cook, as Linda returned to the fire, her horses rounded up and tied, ready for the adventures of a new day.

"Morning dudes," she said, with a big smile as the others gathered around the hot pot of coffee.

"Morning," they replied, almost in unison.

"Adorable, where's my huntin' buddy?" asked Sam.

"He's not in the tent. I guess he must've overslept," Burr replied, to answer both Bob and Sam. "I'm going to do my morning thing. He'll be back by the time I am. You know he'll smell the sausage cooking clear to Dead Horse and probably come thundering across the valley yelling 'Hi-yo-Silver'!" he laughed, heading for the trees.

"Bob, what the hell's the matter with you? You're grinning like a Cheshire cat. What's up?" asked Kevin.

With a grin a mile wide, Bob looked at his beaming wife, who, with a big smile, said, "Go ahead and tell 'em, honey."

"Well, men, Linda's going to have a baby next March! This is the happiest day of my life!" The happiness shared among friends, meant hearty handshakes around, with plenty of warm hugs and congratulations.

Hidden in the trees, with his back to the safe forest and facing his friends, the opposite of his field training and combat experience in Viet Nam, Tex wondered what joyous occasion he was missing. His thoughts were cut off as the base of his skull was shattered and his lifeless body slumped to the ground, twitching in his fresh feces. The force of the blow with the blunt pointed rock, separated the *pons* from the nerve stem to the brain and shattered the *cerebellum*. Death was instantaneous.

Utterly amazed at the skill and speed of movement he had just witnessed, Guy pushed the radio switch open and whispered to John, "One down as planned."

"Okay," came the soft answer. "Let's move in." And with one starting from the east, and two from the west, the vice of armed hate and pure evil closed on the six remaining, happy, totally unsuspecting and unarmed campers.

Daylight
Dead Horse Lake

Oh my God, I've overslept, thought Will, as he crawled out of his sleeping bag. The morning light was in full bloom as he saddled Baldy for the short ride to camp. The line of light from the rising sun had started its slow descent down the face of Union Mountain as he rode north out of the canyon. The plateau and camp area were just coming into view when he heard a shot followed by a piercing scream—cut short—followed by two more shots.

———

"Lee, are you sure you don't want some of this?" John asked, having completed his rape of the young woman. "It's good and tight, you'd better get some before Big Guy opens her up!"

"No! You know I don't want anything to do with any of this shit!" he loudly exclaimed, in mock seriousness.

"Okay, go for it, Big Guy." Needing no urging, Guy pounced on the helpless and grief-stricken young woman and began his rape with brutal force as the others walked away. In agony, shock and grief, it would be several minutes before conscious thought would return.

"Lee, find out where the fuck that lawyer is. I want his ass. Work the big one and Will's buddy over, but leave Sam with a little left for Scumbag's entertainment," he added.

"No sweat, they'll sing, sing, sing, in a matter of seconds," Lee replied. "No point in saving the big one is there?"

"No."

Lee in anticipation, walked over to the two helplessly trussed tourists. "Well, lookee here! My, my, are we in a little bit of discomfort?" With his mouth stuffed with the towel, the screams of agony were only gurgling groans as Lee quickly popped Sam's eyes. Passed out with the pain, Lee left him and as deftly did the same for George. They were far enough apart to not hear his questions and he returned to the now conscious and struggling Sam. With a short jab, he got his attention and began to speak.

"I'm going to give you a short burst of severe pain. When I stop, it'll stop, understand?" he asked.

Sam's mind raced. At least three were dead and probably Burr. He'll question two. That's George and me. One of us'll get it twice no matter what we say, he thought, and nodded in the affirmative.

Lee began the demonstration of his professional skill. Helpless and unable to prevent it, the thin blade of George's knife entered Sam's body, parting skin and muscle, but barely nicking small blood vessels. Searching, its point quickly found the target. Sam's body shook with intense pain, but gagged, only his brain could scream as the point turned and toyed. Jolts hit every nerve ending, yet through the burning-screaming-agony he suffered the curse of consciousness. Seconds passed as if they were days—no, weeks—and then slowly the thin blade withdrew; partially. Sam went totally limp, his bowels and bladder evacuating, but he knew one thing, his only hope to save himself and maybe George and Linda, was to protect Will.

"Whew!" Lee exclaimed. "I knew that would happen, so don't let it bother you. I'm going to ask you just a few questions and I'll know if you're lying. Believe me, I will, and the pain'll be doubled for twice as long. Do you understand? I want to know where the guy is, that the big guy said left camp, and his name."

In extreme pain, Sam's brain still functioned. He'll want to know about the gun. He'll do me twice no matter what I say. And George, George doesn't know about it. Again, Sam nodded the affirmative, his body now shaking.

"Okay, I'm going to take out the towel, but the knife is above that nerve—don't cry out," he advised. "Just whisper your answers. Who is he and why isn't he here?"

"He's at Dead Horse Lake. He goes out one night—every trip—woods—swamps—hills. His name's Will Dean," Sam murmured.

"Does he have a gun?"

I have to lie thought Sam, "No."

"Are you sure?"

"Yes," Sam sighed, quivering in silent dread.

"When will he be back?" Lee asked, satisfied about the gun, remembering his surveillance.

"Breakfast," Sam groaned.

Satisfied, but wanting confirmation, Lee stuffed the towel back in Sam's mouth. "Just to be sure, we're going through this again."

Groaning in agony, Sam helplessly shook his head from side to side. More severe pain netted no change and moving over to George, Lee repeated the process. Bored with the same answers and not wanting to waste time and smell the stench of fear and bowels, he quickly slit George's throat with his own knife. Walking over to John, he smiled in satisfaction at his professional success.

"What'd they tell you, Lee?"

"Well, it seems as though every trip he heads off by himself for a night in the woods, swamps or wherever," Lee replied, as he removed the thin, painter gloves and dropping them in the fire, glanced at the brutal rape in progress.

"Without a gun?"

"Yeah, and that confirms what I heard," Lee answered. "He'll be back for breakfast. Come with me for a moment," and walking to the north edge of camp, he pointed east across the valley. "See that opening over there?" he asked.

"Yeah," John replied.

"He'll be riding out there. Dead Horse Lake is to the right and up in a canyon behind those trees."

"That just shows how stupid lawyers are. Did you finish the big guy?"

"Sure, why wait?"

"Did you pop 'em?"

"What do you think? It's my mark isn't it?" Lee replied with a grin.

"Before or after, Socket?"

"During, of course!"

"Lee, you and your damn enucleation. It's going to get you in trouble," John admonished his kid brother.

"My what?"

"E-new-cle-a-tion. Eye ball popping!"

"Oh, sure, like rape, murder, torture and kidnapping are no big deal! Where'd you get the big word?"

"I looked it up after you popped that couple back in Tennessee."

Their exchange was interrupted by a muffled groan of agony as Guy raped the woman again, this time—sodomy.

"You know, Lee, I'll be damn glad to put that bastard down with the two horses, like you suggested. What do you think?"

"I agree. But keep your eyes open on the way, he might be thinking along those lines himself."

"How's Will's buddy doing?"

"He's one damn tough son-of-a-bitch. Christ, when you tied 'em up and gagged 'em, what'd you do, stick dirt in their eyes?"

"Yeah, I didn't want 'em to see what was goin' on."

"Well, he sure as hell can't see what's goin' on now, but he's all right. There's a lot left in that guy. Scumbag'll enjoy watchin' what I can do and what he can look forward to! The good ole U.S. of A. trained me well!" exclaimed Lee.

Dead Horse Lake

Stopping Baldy, and taking out the binoculars, Will could make out three forms on the ground—still twitching as he watched—a man in camouflage was walking away from the bodies and toward the camp fire, the muffled reports barely stilled.

Shock—horror, shock and horror—a scene from a macabre movie—a triple replay of a reporter in Nicaragua. They were his friends. He couldn't tell for sure, but from the way they were dressed, it looked like Bob, Kevin and Tom, apparently dead.

I have no choice, thought Will. As he started his fate-filled journey into chaos, the immortal words of Georges-Jacques Danton, a leader of the French Revolution, rang through his head. *'De l'audace! encore de l'audace! et toujours de l'audace!'* To dare! and again to dare! and without end to dare! Shaking with fear, Will knew in his heart King was right, '. . . if a man has nothing worth dying for, what does he have worth living for?'

These were his best friends in camp. In the slow ride across the valley there was time to remember a cold-cold river and a cold-cold hill. To remember Trish—the airplanes and the cars—his children and little grandson; there could be no turning back.

His plan was simple—deceit—the first rule of warfare. One shouldn't provoke a war when the enemy's strength is unknown; my own little strategic reserve, he thought, taking his pistol out of the vest's side pocket. If I can make 'em believe I've been on a binge, just maybe. Taking out the paper sack, he carefully secreted the small, worthless at any distance, but deadly in close quarters, semi-automatic pistol. Positioned crossway, to have his finger on the trigger and to tilt the top of the sack, a handy *slick,* toward his mouth, it might work. Will was confident of his ability to control Baldy, but not the bullet's path. Bob unexpectedly shooting at a coyote during the ride in, caused Baldy not a twitch, though he had been startled and jumped in the saddle.

If only I had my .357, he thought, that was a real weapon. In a sack at close range, one of 'em, maybe both, will be near enough. There has to be at least two of 'em, he thought, and I have to have luck, lots and lots of good luck. The initial shock and horror faded to the background of his mind as his plan developed. Space and time—barely enough—control fear—ride slow—distract 'em—let 'em know I'm coming. They wouldn't want to shoot toward the north camp, if they know it's there and this was planned. Sing a drinking song—start with your favorite—let it ring out. You're a drunken fool—an easy role he thought. What the hell are they after? Linda for sure. What a horrible price women pay at the hands of men who can't control their cocks. If the spoils of war could only be burning and plunder. It's the cruel rape of women and children since the beginning of time that has bathed the cheeks of angels.

Here goes he thought, beginning at first in a choking—breaking voice—blending slowly to a drunken, heavy, cockney accent;

> "Oh Monday night I kissed her
>   on the ankles,
> Tuesday night I kissed her
>   on the knees;
> Wednesday night, with some success
>   I lifted up her underdress;
> Thursday night we had a jubilee!
>   Oh Lord eee;
> Friday night I kissed her
>   on the boobies,
> Saturday night she give
>   me balls a tweak;
> But it was Sunday after supper,
>   I rammed the ole boy up her;
> And now she see's the doctor
>   twice a week'!"

———————

"Jesus, listen to that—here comes the bastard—drunker'n a skunk! See there—east—heading down to the crossing. John, go get Guy and let's get ready. This is going to be fun—wow—fun-fun-fun!" exclaimed Lee, clapping his hands in glee.

———————

God—I hope this works, Will implored of an unseen—and not to sure he believed in—force. With a drunken shout he began again . . .

> "Oh I didn't want to join the air-corp,
>   I didn't want to go to war;
> I just want to hang around,
>   the Pickadilly on the ground;
> An' make my livin' off the high class ladies,
>   I didn't want it up the arse hol;
> I didn't want me buttocks shot away,
>   I just want to live in Ingland,
>   in jolly jolly Ingland;
> and fornicate me bloomin' life away!"

———————

'I should have bawled the bastard out:
A yellow dog he slew;
But worse, he proved beyond a doubt
That—I was yellow too.' Robert Service

Jesus I'm scared, but I don't want to live a coward, he thought, as Baldy waded across Jakeys Fork at the inlet to Simpson Lake.

The sheer wall of Shale Mountain's west side rose above the valley due east, approximately one-half mile from camp. Their camp, at nine-thousand seven-hundred feet above sea level, was some twenty-five hundred feet below the crest. Shale's north-south crest line, peaking at some twelve-thousand four-hundred feet at Burro Point, shielded the camp from the rising sun until late in the morning.

Will knew he could force Baldy, who wanted to make a beeline to the horses in camp, in a northerly direction along the base of the plateau; out of sight of whoever was in camp. An approach from the north would give him a clear view into the camp without the sun in his eyes. It would be close, since the bright line of the morning light, cast by the rising sun, was already creeping down the east face of Union Peak.

If the attackers were experienced with horses, they would know instantly what he'd done and that he couldn't be drunk. He had to have luck—lots of good luck. With his heart pounding it would be tough to sing another drinking song. Cresting the edge of the plateau, at about two hundred yards out, and north-easterly of camp, Will took a quick look with his binoculars. Concealed in his right hand, they confirmed his worst fears. With a hammering heart and a dry mouth, he dropped the binoculars to the ground and lifting the sack of 'whiskey', tilted it to his mouth for another pull. It would be tough to sing another drinking song, but with a breaking voice he began . . .

"Oh the night that Patty Murphy died,
    I never will forget;
the Irish got so stinking drunk,
    they haven't sobered yet!
The only thing they did that night,
    that filled my heart with fear;
they took the ice right off the corpse,
    and put it on the beer!"

His voice cracking, he took another pull from the sack of 'whiskey' and plodding forward could see enough. One to his left was in camouflage gear with a rifle slung over his shoulder. A second, to his right, also in camouflage, was standing with hands on his hips. His casual indifference, the progeny of ignorance—a few feet away, a rifle leaning against a tree. The third, in ordinary clothes, was a short distance further to the right, with no weapon in sight. They were all standing—watching his performance—it had to ring true.

Will could see Linda peering over the log seat, obviously in stress. Closer, he could see all his visible friends were down; one, apparently George, his throat cut. Surprise—the element of surprise—shit, no other way out. Maybe some were alive, at least Linda was, so he began again, his voice slurred;

> "Oh they had to carry Harry to the ferry,
> Oh they had to carry Harry to the shore.
> Now the reason that they had to carry
> Harry to the Ferry,
> Was that Harry couldn't carry any more!
> Dead drunk!"
> "Singing glorious, glorious, glory be to
> God that there are no more of us.
> Singing Glory be to God,
> That there are no more of us.
> For one of us could drink it all alone!
> Damn near!"

Intently, Lee watched. A charade? No—it could not be. Not privy to the camp tales, he did not know of their bonds—nor Will's past. Sunburned—lower lip split and swollen—rocking gently to the horse's gait—four days of salt-pepper whiskers—Lee perceived a drunk.

His hammering heart subsiding, Will passed into the cold, intense, uncomprehendable zone of the 'charmed state'. Slowly he rode forward, eyes squinted shut to hide as much as possible. As he entered camp the horror-filled scene unfolded; to his left, Tom, Kevin and Bob, like three inert logs. Sam trussed like a dead hog; forms still in the dirt—only Burr nowhere in sight. He would not submit to their control, 'perish with the sword', you bastards.

Bringing his horse to a stop, as the one to his left approached, Will turned in the saddle, "Would ye half a nip, ole boy?" he slurred, in his best cockney accent.

"Naw, just let me help you down," John replied.

Will turned the sack toward John's face and in the flight of a millisecond, John realized his dupe. The knowing was no help, as no more than one is able to beat the puff of air from the optometrist's tonometer, his reflex action closed his eyelids—late. With a muzzle velocity of approximately one-thousand feet per second, the .380 caliber, Silvertip Hollow-Point bullet slammed through his left eye orbit, and in seven ten-thousands of a second, exploded his cranial nerve mass, ending without pain his personal grief. Stilled forever—

the raging hatred of the forces that cost his parents' lives and gave him an obsessed existence.

Rounds are counted in movies, and what Lee—a professional—counted; Guy felt. Will's second shot ripped into his lower gut, the third took his right lung—shock masking pain—the fourth, a miss.

Guy knew he was dead—eventually—fuck you mother-fucker, he thought, fatal doesn't count in a shoot-out. A deer can run a mile and die of a fatal hit; a man can make a will and seek absolution. Time's the real issue, he thought, as he grabbed the fully automatic, nine millimeter rifle and swung the muzzle toward Will—his hand tight around the grip—finger ready on the trigger.

At thirty feet, the central nervous system of a moving man is incredibly difficult to hit—a fact well known to any *shooter*. Targets are stationary or moving in a predictable orbit. A jerking, moving man's central nervous system would be like hitting a woodcock on the wing—something even Annie Oakley couldn't do with a pistol.

Murphy shrugged his shoulders and with a puff of air, bumped the inside of Will's right wrist as Guy swung the barrel of the deadly automatic toward him. The fifth shot, on the heels of the errant fourth, caught Guy through his throat. Crashing downward at the edge of the seventh cervical vertebra, it delivered enough shock to his spinal column to end any threat; he would die slowly, with time to feel, and, to think about it.

Mia, like Murphy unseen by mere mortals, with a big grin across her face and knowing it was wrong, clapped her hands in glee.

As Will wheeled his horse toward him, caught totally by surprise, Lee's only thought was to stop the shooting; to gain time and thus an advantage. "Don't shoot—don't shoot," he shouted, falling to his knees, his arms raised in phony surrender. "I didn't want it done! I couldn't stop 'em! I don't even have a gun!" he pleaded. He's only got two shots left in that pea shooter, he thought.

Turning his horse and carefully dismounting, Will kept the Mauser semiautomatic trained on the torso of the kneeling Lee.

"Don't move," he ordered.

A glance revealed Linda straining to see over the top of the log and staring in his direction. The lifeless body of George, lying still, a few feet away. His cut throat gaping open and a great dark stain—his future life of travel, hunting, fishing, and fraternity—spilled in a fly-gathering pool of blood on the matted grass. Three friends shot in their faces and the backs of their heads blown away. Another friend, Burr, missing, but probably dead, and nowhere in sight.

"Oh God! Sam, oh God!" He saw his life-long friend, who at great risk to himself, had saved his life, trussed like a butchered hog, blood on his face, apparently dead. "Oh God, Sam. I can never save you now," Will cried out loud. "You bastards! You worthless, fucking bastards! You killed my friends!" he screamed.

"Please, please don't shoot me!" Lee begged, his mind racing. A military tuck—his best friend, Sam, yet tent-mate, Tex—special forces, a common bond?—Korea—a kay-mag?—he couldn't be—he'll never shoot an unarmed man.

"Give me one good reason, you bastard," snarled Will.

"You can't shoot me in cold-blood," Lee pleaded, in a faked snivelling voice. "I wasn't part of this! I don't have a gun! I couldn't stop 'em!" If I can just get a little closer, this stupid slime doesn't have a chance.

As Will shifted his gaze in the direction of Linda, now out of sight behind the log, the dead mountain man and his close friends, a feeling of intense loss and sadness came over him. The motion Lee made, inching closer on his knees, drew Will's focus again to the man in front.

As if in slow motion, Lee lowered his arms to a parallel position. Raising his left knee and shifting his body weight to his left foot, he knew he could take Will. Only the look of supreme confidence gave away his intent.

That flash—that god-awful instantaneous fragment of time dreaded by every police officer—to shoot or be shot. Is it 'my life or his'nd, what will I do'? And with the involuntary wash of adrenalin sweeping through every cell in his body—the primordial defense mechanism, coupled with the higher intelligence of the species, *Homo sapiens,*—the officer reacts.

The pupils of the eyes. The uncontrollable dilation every poker player knows cannot be stopped—the royal flush on the last down card—the pupils of Lee's eyes dilated.

Will saw—that—and Lee's mistake.

The slight smile caused by the knowledge he could kill Will, was a violation of years of training. An *IT* should know better—Viet Nam, Rhodesia, Angola, Afghanistan,—*primus inter pares*—a mistake.

Will reacted, he did not think—there would not have been enough time—his index finger tightened. With blistering speed the .380 caliber hollow point ripped away the aorta of Lee's heart as the recoil pushed Will's right hand backward—the space, then occupied, now vacated for the swift passage of Lee's right foot.

Balanced on the ball of his left foot—with turning motion rotating his body—the bullet's kinetic energy was sufficient to knock Lee over. Spinning in a full circle he landed on his back. Lee knew the hit was fatal and he would not survive, nor would he ever get Orlov, nor did he care. His sixty seconds or so of consciousness would be better invested in prayer than in wasted attack on Will.

"Forgive me, mother," he whispered. More than a *tuck,* he thought, and, as he closed his eyes, he smiled at Will—who didn't see, wouldn't have cared and could not have understood. An innocent and gleeful little boy ran from the yellow school bus—that very first day—and leaped into the open arms of a smiling and loving Beta. Death came quickly as an eerie silence swept over the camp.

Believing Sam was dead, Will started across the tragic arena toward Linda. To his right and a little behind, he heard groaning sounds and looking around, could see Sam twisting against his ropes. Running to him, he pulled the towel from his mouth and holding him in his arms cried, "It's over, Sam. Sam, it's over. Hang on, old buddy. I shot the bastards, they're all dead." Sobbing, Will cut his friend's hands and feet free.

"*Naio mota mota shita itanda,*" whispered Sam, with a sigh, his body relaxing with a shudder into a state of semi-consciousness.

"*Oodu siyu,* Rustovitch. I'm going to help Linda."

"Linda, oh God, I'm sorry, I'm sorry." Quickly he cut her ropes. Naked and bleeding, but with no shame or embarrassment, she ran to clutch to her breast the lifeless body of her beloved mountain man. With a quick glance around the area, Will located her shirt and jeans scattered on the ground.

"Hey, what the hell happened here?" a man hollered. "Jesus Christ, Hank, get that camera going."

Looking up, Will saw Gary Smith, the outfitter from the northern camp along with his helper, who was in the process of recording the entire scene on video. Using some common sense of decency, he did not direct the camera on Linda and Bob.

Will still shaking, walked over to Linda. "Here," he said, "put these on, come on, Linda." But she wouldn't leave her dear husband and in shock, held him tight to her breast.

The two, heavily armed men dressed in camo-gear, were easy for Gary to understand. Will, again holding Sam, was either not willing or was unable to explain what had happened.

Linda could not understand how Will, in spite of what had happened, was able to shoot the unarmed Lee. She had not seen him hurt any of the party—he certainly had refused to rape her. She remembered his statement that he did not want to hurt anyone and briefly, she explained what she had seen. How upon hearing Will sing, she realized he was aware the camp had been hit and had a plan.

"Linda, did you see Will shoot the guy in sweat pants and tennis shoes?"

"No, Gary. Had to hold my head up—to see over the log. When I last saw'm, he—he was on his knees—begging Will not to shoot. Said—'I don't have a gun—I didn't want to hurt anyone,' she answered, body shaking.

"Did he appear to be with 'em?"

"Oh, yes. The one Will shot first and the one in sweats, had the same southern accent. They sounded exactly alike. They came into camp when Bob'd just told everybody I was preg . . .," breaking into body racking sobs, it was several minutes before she could continue. "They separated us—we—we never had a chance to resist. The one that must've come in from the east, had his hand on the back of my neck. When I heard the first shot, I screamed. And— and the next thing I remember, I was staked down and he—he was raping me."

Gary's helper continued to film the conversation. "That bastard shot my husband," she screamed, breaking into sobs and pointing to the now lifeless form of Guy.

"Joe, I think I'd better get Lander and some people from DCI. Why don't you check the area and see what more you can find. I'll call and see if the Highway Patrol can get the sheriff up here in one of their new choppers. And I guess we'd better have BLM send up the big Sikorsky, there're a lot of bodies here. Look around and photograph everything. Linda, I only see five here. I thought I met six, down at our camp, Monday?" Gary asked.

"Yes, Tex went up the hill to the bathroom. I haven't seen him since. One of the bastards in camouflage came into camp from that direction with the one in sweats. It's that bastard over there," again pointing to Guy, "that shot Bob and the other two. He's the bastard who raped and sodomized me—he hurt me real bad. The other guy in camouflage raped me first, but he wasn't brutal. The one in regular clothes said he didn't want to hurt anyone. He said, 'I don't want anything to do with this shit'."

"Okay. I'll call the sheriff. I'm sure he'll want Beckwourth up here. And then I'll start looking around. Linda, aren't you glad I've got one of these cellular phones?"

"I guess so, Gary. Not much to be glad about. I just can't understand Will shooting that last one. He shouldn't have shot him. The man was begging for his life."

"Did you see it?" Gary asked, for the second time.

"No. I put my head down just before Will shot."

"Well, the Sheriff and DCI'll be able to sort everything out."

Within an hour, the sleek, Bell 222 UT of the Wyoming Highway Patrol followed by the less elegant, but far more powerful Sikorsky S-76B of the Bureau of Land Management, came sweeping down from above the crest of Shale Mountain. The first carried the Fremont County Sheriff and his top investigator, Lieutenant Ronald Beckwourth; the second a pile of polyurethane body bags. The Sikorsky, with a pilot and copilot, could carry at least twelve passengers, or bodies. Today necessity, as it had in the dim past and far away jungles of southeast Asia, would once again dictate its distasteful mission.

The Bell's pilot, Captain Bradley McKinnon of the Wyoming Highway Patrol—experienced and disciplined in duty as a combat pilot in Viet Nam— brought his craft through a smooth descent to a gentle touch down on the plateau, just north of the edge of the camp. The thump—thump—thump of the rotor, a more alien sound than the rhythmic pounding of Baldy's hooves. Slowly the engines quieted and deathly silence once again swept across the beautiful valley of Simpson Lake.

As the second and more detailed statement of Linda was completed— again on video—Investigator Beckwourth, turned to the Sheriff, "Why don't you go back with him," pointing at Sam who had been given a painkiller and medication by McKinnon, "and Linda and—what's your name?" he inquired of Will.

"Will Dean," Will softly replied, his voice flat.

"Take 'em back to Lander," said Beckwourth, "and we'll put the bodies in the BLM chopper."

"I stay with my husband," Linda declared, in a tone that left no doubt of her determination.

"Okay, Linda. Okay. I'm sorry, I should have thought. Take it easy, Linda. I've known you both for years. Bob can go with you in the Bell and Dean can ride in the front seat. Maybe I'll need the Sheriff to help me with my investigation. Is that okay with you, Sheriff?"

"Certainly."

"Brad?" questioned Beckwourth.

"Sure," said Brad, who did not have a crystal ball. "Glad to meet you, Will. You got the bastards all right!" In silence and with a look of overwhelming sadness, one Brad had seen long ago, Will only nodded. "We'd better get cracking," Brad warned. "Those clouds will be coming in from the northwest. The report calls for afternoon rain and we're up here on VFR."

"Okay, you and BLM load up and go, I don't want to hurry the site exam. Sheriff—how about riding out with Gary and me?" Beckwourth suggested, as he worked at securing paper evidence bags over the intruders' hands.

"That's a good idea, Ron. I'll go and help Gary bring that body down from the hill."

Photographed where he lay to preserve the record, Linda's beloved mountain man was carefully placed on a stretcher, his distorted head wrapped. Linda would be able to clutch his strong, gnarled hands, now cold, on their journey out of his beloved mountains. As Bob's body was carefully secured to the litter bench, Linda, and Sam guided by Will, were strapped in the two remaining seats.

Felled before their time, the bodies of the remaining seven were carefully photographed by Beckwourth, placed in body bags and loaded aboard the Sikorsky. The four dead fishermen and the evil-sick prison escapee could be placed in boxes that were, at least for the events on this stage, easy to label. Two, appearing as twins—one a possible victim—were far more difficult to comprehend. Shaped by forces beyond their control, yet nevertheless having made choices, final judgment, as it must for all, would have to be made by a higher tribunal.

Warming its engine, the Sikorsky, its huge rotor slowly turning, waited patiently to follow the sleek Bell out of the fate torn canyon. Silent logs in a gently moving stream—the physical remains of eight dead victims would soon embark on the first leg of their final journey home.

As McKinnon strapped himself into the pilot's seat, the Sheriff helped belt in Will, who had climbed into the left front seat. The Bell could be flown from either front seat and even when flying on instruments, did not require a co-pilot as did the larger Sikorsky. Will and the pilot would become casually acquainted during warm-up procedures and the flight to Lander. Neither would give a thought—one knew and one didn't—that Captain Brad McKinnon was an expert shot and co-commander of the Wyoming Highway Patrol's elite, twenty-member, Special Services Squad.

———————

PART TWO

Uncle Remus

"Ole Brer Possum, he tuck a runnin' start, he did, on he come lumberin' 'long, en he lit-kerblam!-right in de middle er de fier, en dat waz de las' er ole Brer Possum."

"But, Uncle Remus, Brother Possum didn't steal the butter after all," said the little boy, who was not at all satisfied with such summary injustice.

"Dat w'at make I say w'at I duz, honey. In dis worril, lots er folks is gotter suffer fer udder fokes sins. Look like hit's mighty on wrong; but hit's des dat away."

Joel Chandler Harris

7

Extradition

August 26, 1991
Office of Robert J. Reising
Fremont County Prosecutor
Lander, Wyoming

"Sheriff Arce, thanks for coming over. Things are happening too damned fast," declared the Prosecutor, as they shook hands in greeting. "Have a chair. Here're the tickets for Beckwourth and Deputy Warren," said Reising, handing the folder to the sheriff. "We sent the Governor's Warrant out yesterday. Joe, there's something I'd like to do, but I feel we should discuss it first. I wouldn't want to create any problems with your department."

"Go ahead, Bob."

"I know how you feel about this case, but the Grand Jury indicted him. The physical evidence and those two witness statements were overwhelming proof he shot a man, begging for his life, in cold-blood. The outfitter who taped Linda's statement really iced it. Those damned videos can be a double-edged sword. I'm sure there're some in LAPD who don't like 'em. It's a cinch Dean won't! I hope what I'm going to ask will be okay and you don't think it'll cause any problems in the department. I know there's been some heat over the Ramshorn incident."

"Oh hell, that's history. Spit it out," replied the Sheriff, thinking to himself how hard it was for some lawyers to get to the point.

"I want to put Steve Strong on it, if DCI will let me. I want him to work the shit out of this case from the defense point of view. If there's any evidence to support Dean's contention he acted in self-defense, I want it. My duty's to see justice done, especially since we're going to certify under the new guidelines for the death sentence."

"Oh my God! Why?" asked the stunned Sheriff, color draining from his face. "My God, I was there. Who could blame him?"

"It's no different from any other first-degree murder case, but under the circumstances, at least it was a Grand Jury indictment. I told the Attorney

General I didn't want to be accused of seeking a publicity trick with elections coming up. We felt with Dean being a Michigan attorney and the unusual circumstances, the decision should be made by twenty-three citizens. Not just by a prosecutor and a judge. Now the indictment's the decision of ordinary people from the whole county. If there's a conviction of first-degree murder, we normally seek the death penalty from the jury that hears the evidence."

"Shall I have Beckwourth tell him?" asked the Sheriff.

"There's no point in that. I'd rather do it when he's here. I don't think he'll fight extradition and Michigan doesn't have the death sentence. He may not know about PREP. I can explain it when he gets here."

"Back to your question, Bob. Go for it! Have Strong do the best he can and I'll discuss it with Beckwourth. Most of my deputies know Steve. He's from Rock Springs and we work closely with DCI—some of the time. We've had some more leads. You know Beckwourth though, he's a hell of an investigator, but he's a loner. He'll share what he comes up with, but he'll want to handle this his way. He won't want anyone getting in his way, especially not someone from DCI. You know, he's a marine Viet Nam veteran and he personally believes Dean's as guilty as sin. He'll keep after Dean until he pays the piper. Let's face it, he can be a little arrogant at times. He's proud of his ancestry!"

"Hell, wouldn't you be, if you were him?"

"Damn right!" the Sheriff exclaimed. "That's some Black blood anyone'd be proud to claim!"

"If Beckwourth runs into any problem in Michigan have him give me a jingle. It just happens the prosecutor where Dean lives and I met at a national convention a couple of years ago. He'd hunted out here—up in the Absarokas—and looked me up."

"I doubt Beckwourth will have any problems," replied the Sheriff. "You let Strong know. I'll talk to the Undersheriff and have 'em start out. Beckwourth's got a knack at getting information while talking about a sunset and he'll size Dean up real good. This whole mess isn't going to be any fun. I tend to think that third one—what was his name?"

"Lee Mackintosh," the prosecutor answered.

"I still think he was just as guilty as the other bastards."

"Well, Sheriff, that's why Dean should've brought him in. Mackintosh had a right to his 'day in court'."

"Maybe it was self-defense, like Dean said."

"I hope it was, Sheriff. I really hope Strong can come up with something to support Dean's claim. Call me when they get back. I don't know what the deal will be on defense attorneys, but I sure hope Dean gets the best there is. I doubt he'll want to bring in an outsider, since he's a defense attorney himself. We don't want anything but an absolutely fair trial and shit, with PREP in place we'll all be under a microscope!"

"That's for sure! Well," sighed the Sheriff as he rose from the chair, "I'd better get these tickets over to Beckwourth, the Riverton flight leaves in a couple of hours."

"Thanks again for stopping over, Sheriff. I'll call DCI in Cheyenne and see if it's okay for Strong. Then I'm going up to the ranch and talk this all out with my grandfather."

As so often happens, circumstances over which he had no control and that he had absolutely nothing to do with, would nevertheless thrust him front and center stage of a drama, that in the end would gain national attention. A tragic situation, the irony of which was a first-degree murder charge, a substantial portion of the local populace believed to be wrong; possibly resulting in one of the quickest executions since the days of Judge Roy Bean.

The entire matter called for wisdom and counsel beyond his years, and he had a resource. As he started the drive north to the Sunlight Basin, his thoughts drifted back to his youth. The tragic death of his mother when he was only twelve; the move with his father to Chicago to escape the haunting memories; summers with his mother's parents at the Morrison Ranch. Loyola University—*summa cum laude*; University of Chicago Law School—Editor of Law Review; the corporate law firm where he punched a clock, yet was required to submit certain time billings; his dissatisfied rupture and return to Lander— the hometown prodigal son returneth; his private practice and unopposed election to the office of Fremont County Prosecuting Attorney. And then the call, and the inspection of the killing ground; the video and decision to call for a Grand Jury. The indictment and the pressure to let a jury decide Will Dean's fate.

How close he was to his grandfather. The times riding, hunting and more importantly, fishing in the mountains; time without pressure. Gramp always felt like a warm, shaggy, old dog who would love him no matter what he did. His father was as kind and close as a father could be and he knew his dad would always be there when he needed him, but a grandfather was special.

A bear of a man, with his dark, bushy, John L. Lewis eyebrows, he should have been named Richard or John or some other kingly name. But no one ever kidded him about his name. Had he been named Sue—he would have commanded equal respect. That his grandmother, certainly one of the world's great cooks, had the patience of a saint, could be certified as fact, if only half the legends of his grandfather's younger days were true.

Morrison Ranch
Sunlight Basin
Clark's Fork—Yellowstone River

"Bobby, you came here either for my advice or a sounding board for your ideas. Right?" asked Marion.

"I guess so," Bob sighed, at his beloved grandfather's sometimes brutal frankness.

"Which would you prefer?"

"Advice, Gramp."

"Okay. You've given me a lot of legal stuff like witness statements, photographs of the scene, a letter on ropes. These are things lawyers work with and evidence the jury'll see and hear. They may well decide the case on evidence or the lack of it. But, you've studied *Rousseau* somewhere along the line, haven't you?"

"Sure. The 'social contract'—I remember that. What's that got to do with it, Gramp?"

"Well, Bobby—the gut—sometimes it's in the guts. It's what you feel. *Rousseau* had a strong belief in the natural goodness of man. He favored feeling and emotion over reason and logic, as the main force in human behavior. Think how boring life would be if reason and logic decided who you married or the car you drove! Would reason and logic ever buy a Ferrari to drive?"

"I guess you're right. At least as far as what I've seen!" Bob exclaimed.

"Obviously this case could go either way, since there's no evidence, other than Dean's testimony, that you know of, to support his claim of self-defense. Lee may have been guilty as sin, but the system, though not perfect, does work and evidence, or lack of it, may well decide the issue. Your duty, but you don't need a lecture from me, is to go after Dean.

"Here's one way I see it, Bobby. With logic and reason, it looks like Dean shot Lee in cold-blood, is smart enough to come up with the explanation he gave and it's a contrived fabrication. If he'd shot in the heat of passion, at the horror of what he'd seen and all pumped up because of the other shooting, he might not've been indicted. Maybe he'll go with a plea to second-degree, reduced because of the emotional state. Any chance?"

"No, Gramp. I doubt it. He said very clearly, in the sworn statement he gave in Lander, that what he said happened, happened, and he was telling the truth. He even insisted on being put under oath. I just don't think he'd ever plead guilty to committing a wrongful act. I imagine we'll offer second-degree with a twenty year cap, in view of his age. But, he said very firmly, he'd never 'trade with the truth'. His exact words."

"Well, so be it. He'll be forced to make his choice soon enough and he may be telling the truth, but without something bad on Lee or evidence to support him, Dean's in deep shit with reason and logic. So now you have to go for his guts and the jury's gut. You have to go for his guts before Vickers takes that argument and runs with it, assuming he ends up hiring him."

"How, Grandpa?"

"I've read many soldiers don't shoot to kill even when they're being shot at. Now I realize Dean had to shoot to kill, at least the first two or they'd all be dead. But what is it about Dean that made him one of those people who can shoot to kill? Find out all you can about his background. Did he hunt as a small boy? Did he live on a farm that raised animals? It's not that he would be cold and not caring, maybe just the opposite, because killing was a necessity, very often a humane necessity. They Shoot Horses, Don't They?. That's what I mean, the killing of Lee became a necessity that overrode Dean's basic goodness and his awareness of his duty to bring Lee in. Do you follow me?"

"I sure do. Do you have any other ideas?"

"Let's look at the duty angle a bit. Just how ingrained in his character is it? In his guts and the jury's, it may boil down to just that, necessity versus duty. How old did you say he was and what do you already know about him?"

"He was born August 28, 1935. Are you psychic, Gramp? He lived on a farm near a village called Wacousta, in Michigan. His father and grandfather farmed with horses until after the war when they got a tractor. He can ride and it's obvious he can shoot. He quickly came up with a plan that let him get close enough to take out two killers armed with automatic rifles, and if he's telling the truth, to take out a trained killer. There's no question but he got lucky when he hit the second one in the neck with his fourth shot."

"No, I'm not psychic. I read the reports about how he rode into camp and what happened. He didn't sound like a city kid did he? And lucky? You know, Bobby, I often wonder about luck. What about Dean's military service, did he catch Korea?"

"He enlisted in the regular Air Force on January 4, 1955, under an Air Cadet two year enlistment and was Honorably discharged in early December, 1956."

"In 1956, that's strange," said Marion, with a surprised and puzzled look. "The Chinese were shelling the offshore islands of Quemoy and Matsu and the Russians invaded Hungary that fall. There was a problem developing with the communists in Japan and it's my recollection all military leaves and discharges were put on hold. Why don't you see if there's something there. Getting a military record that old may be tough and probably not worth too much effort."

With a big sigh, Bob shook his head, "There's not much more Wyoming can do to insure a fair trial. Beckwourth is working with me and I put Steve Strong, one of the best in DCI, on it to see if he can come up with anything to help Dean."

"Once the bell rings, you and Vickers, if that's who he ends up retaining, ought to be able to bring out everything there is and let the jury settle the matter. That's the only way you'll ever be able to sleep, especially if they decide to execute him and it should turn out wrong."

"Well, Gramp, two of 'em for sure were as bad as they get, and the one from Michigan is about the worst I've ever read about. He goes way beyond the sick ones who seem to target certain groups or types. His brutal rape of the little girl in Duluth is not much worse than what he did in Phoenix to the poor trucker who'd helped him. For God's sake, he raped him before he slit his throat! Hell, he was only twenty, with a pregnant wife and twin daughters. Of course the Judge is going to limit the case to what was done in camp or evidence about Lee to support Will's defense."

"You just called him Will!" Marion exclaimed.

"It's only fair, Gramp, if we call Lee by his first name."

"True, but you'll be calling him Mr. Dean if he gets sent to the chair."

"Lethal injection," Bob corrected.

"I know—just a figure of speech. I can't imagine anyone going through that. Not when they know it's not a hernia operation!" Marion exclaimed. "Bobby, another thought occurred to me."

"What's that, Gramp?"

"The Lone Ranger."

"Grandpa, you pull the damnedest rabbits out of your hat! Now tell me, what the hell does he have to do with anything?"

"Well, in 1945, any ten year old boy who had a riding horse and could shoot, who lived in Michigan, or for that matter, in most of the rest of the country, worshipped the Lone Ranger. They also knew he never shot anyone. He always shot the guns out of the bad guys' hands and brought 'em to the 'bar of justice'."

"I should've known you'd make a connection. That's what this case is all about! It's why I came up here to talk, Gramp."

"Flatter me if you want to, Bobby, but deep down inside, you and I both know you came up here for some of your grandma's homemade apple pie! Let's go see if she's ready for us to throw steaks on the grill. Just remember son, anyone, or at least a lot of people, could kill attacking wolves. Go for his gut, so Vickers can't win it with emotion and you show the jury that Will is one of those people who could shoot his horse. That's what'll win it. Lee was Will's horse with a broken leg. Only Will had a duty to bring Lee in, and, he knew it. That's the heart of your case!" he exclaimed, and together, the white haired rancher and his only grandchild, headed for the ranch house.

———

4:00 P.M.
Monday, August 26, 1991
Office of Thomas Herrick
Eaton County Prosecutor
Charlotte, Michigan

"Hi, Chuck, thanks for stopping in—glad you were in the building— have a chair," Tom spoke, his voice somber in greeting, as he reached out to shake the Undersheriff's offered hand. His look and tone quickly let the officer know this was a most serious occasion; the problem or cause of which he had no idea. With retirement due at the end of the week, a feeling of apprehension crept into the pit of his stomach. He was set for some quiet time fishing and was not at all interested in being talked into any new project by his good friend.

Apprehension was replaced with shock as Tom outlined the content of papers, moments before spewed into his secretary's hands by their Panasonic fax machine. "Jesus—my God! Tom, he and I went to high school together, I was only a year ahead of him. Hell, he took over for me in fifty-two as cadet commander of the Civil Air Patrol—we're good friends."

"Chuck, he and I are friends too. That's why I want you to go with me. The Sheriff received the warrant yesterday, but you were gone. That's why I waited. I knew you'd be over today. I'm sure he knew it was going to the Grand Jury. We don't want to do it with people he barely knows, do we?"

"No—I guess not. Shit—shit—shit! I thought from the papers it was self-defense?"

Shaking his head in the negative, Tom replied, "I talked to the prosecutor this morning and he told me to watch for the fax. He said he had no doubt but that Will can get a fair trial."

"Tom, doesn't Wyoming have the . . .?"

"Yes," Tom interrupted, "lethal injection."

"Oh God, not that!"

"Well, that's a long, long way off and while they're asking for it, I just can't believe a jury would recommend it. If you want to, why don't you stop by around eight-thirty or so in the morning and we can go over to his office. He was in court today and one of my assistants heard him say he was going to be in all day."

"Have deputies started out from Wyoming?" inquired the Undersheriff.

"Two Fremont County deputies will be staying at the Sheraton tonight. They'll be here later, since I told the Prosecutor that Will would waive extradition. It was a gamble, but I'm sure he will."

"Oh yes," said the Undersheriff, nodding his head in agreement. "He wouldn't want to be lodged in jail here. You know, Tom, he's going to want a couple of his kids to go out to snoop around about a defense attorney. Is there any chance we could pick up some extra tickets for the flight back?"

"Great minds think alike!" Tom exclaimed. "I've already got a couple!"

"People predictability makes our jobs a little easier, sometimes," observed the Undersheriff.

———————

9:25 A.M.
August 27, 1991
Office of Will Dean
Grand Ledge, Michigan

As his work day swung into its second hour, Will grabbed the phone at the ring of the intercom beeper, "Yes, Helen. What is it?"

"Tom Herrick and a deputy sheriff are here. Mr. Herrick called earlier and said he was going to be in the area. I told him you'd be in. And oh, attorney Smith is on line two about the divorce trial set for tomorrow."

"Have 'em go back to the lounge and get some coffee and then would you come back here please?" I wonder what this is all about, he pondered, punching in the waiting call. Something's up, that's for sure.

"Helen," Will inquired as she entered his office, "did Tom ask you not to say anything to me when he called this morning?"

"No. Why?"

"Just curious. Tell 'em I'll be right out, okay?" What the hell, Will thought, as he moved some of the clutter of files on his desk.

"Chuck, look at this, 'To Will Dean—Good Luck Always—The Lone Ranger'! I wonder how in hell he ever got that!" Tom exclaimed.

"I don't know. But see the newspaper clipping. It's a promotion photo for the radio program. It's Brace Beemer, the old WXYZ Detroit radio station character. You're too young, Tom, but he was our hero in the time before television '. . . from out of the past come the thundering hoof beats of the great horse Silver . . . Hi-yo-Silver, away!'. Hell, on television it was just another horse, but in your imagination it was a huge horse! From what you've told me, that's what this case is all about."

"How's that?" asked Tom.

"Don't they claim it wasn't self-defense—that Will shot in cold-blood? Heck, the Lone Ranger never shot anyone. Not that I can remember. He always shot the guns out of their hands with his silver bullets and brought 'em to the 'bar of justice'."

"I guess you're right. Do you know who did this pastel of the mountain valley? It's dated 1947, Jan."

"Sure. It's his older sister. She was a year ahead of me in school. He's got a kid sister, five or six years younger, but I've never met her."

The lounge, unfinished and obviously not open to the general public, contained in various nooks and crannies the memorabilia of a time now past. Several old, wooden rope-pulleys, a hand-cranked corn-sheller, steel grapple-forks and a rusted two-man cross-cut saw—all bearing witness marks of pigeons and sparrows, their constant barn companions. In the shadow of one corner, a bull moose head, surreal in its lifelike mount intruding through the wall, eyes glaring in anger over his wrongfully interrupted tranquility. In a barn-wood alcove, pinned to the wall, a piece of paper hung in silent warning.

"Chuck, how would you score this?" inquired Tom, inspecting the paper.

"Well, it's easy to score, but it's a lot more difficult to evaluate. Let's see. Four cutting the eight ring, one seven and a ten. That's a forty-nine with one x. It's a fifty foot, slow-fire, pistol target. See here Tom, it's dated 'April 1, 1990', and he's written, '.357, S & W 4″, double action, 30 feet, right-hand rapid-fire, windy'. Not bad for a fifty-five year old paper chaser. It might not win a Bianca Cup, but it'd sure work in the field. But I'm real surprised!" exclaimed the Undersheriff.

"Why?"

"I knew he could shoot rifles, even though he doesn't shoot in competition, but I've never heard he shot pistols. I wonder what he shoots left handed?"

"Chuck, we're not here to spy," said Tom. "And I'm not about to volunteer what I see in my friend's lounge!"

They were soon interrupted as Will entered the room, "Sorry about the delay, guys. Damn phone. A divorce case coming up in Charlotte tomorrow. Sometimes I'd do about anything to get the hell away from that fricking telephone. What's up? Jesus, have both you guys been fired?" Will exclaimed, at the look of doom on their faces as they shook hands in greeting.

Will sat in shock; the greeting and walk to his office blotted from his memory banks.

Tom paused, then began again when he could see he was getting through to his friend, "Will, they're seeking extradition."

"Tom, I've been a defense attorney for twenty-six years, but heck, I have never been involved in an extradition. They either ship 'em out or bring 'em in and I defend 'em. So talk to me. What am I facing? Just a moment please," said Will, picking up the intercom. "Helen, would you please come back and take some notes?"

Following the introductions and a brief explanation, Helen, seated and somewhat in shock, began, as best she could, to record the meeting.

"Here're the mechanics," Tom began. "First, the Grand Jury indictment. Normally they use a Prosecutor's Information and a preliminary exam just like we do. Second, Wyoming's Governor signs the extradition warrant. Third, the warrant is forwarded to the county Sheriff of the defendant's residence—or where the defendant is to be found. Fourth, the prosecutor requests a fugitive warrant, which is then signed by a Judge."

"I'm a fugitive?" Will asked, his voice quivering.

"Technically yes, even though Wyoming consented to your returning to Michigan. It's just the procedure," Tom replied. "Fifth, the arrest on the fugitive warrant."

"Oh, Christ," said Will, visibly shaking. "Now?"

"We don't have any choice, Will. You know that," Chuck answered with a sad sigh.

"Sixth, you're taken to the District Court for an extradition hearing. If you want it, Paul will handle it. The only issues at the hearing are whether or not there's a valid governor's warrant and whether or not you're Will Dean. Unless, of course, you wanted the Governor of Michigan to stop the extradition for some other reason, such as you couldn't get a fair trial in Wyoming. If you give up your right to the hearing, Paul will sign an extradition order."

"Hell, Tom, there wouldn't be any point. I'm sure I'll get a fair trial in Wyoming."

Nodding his head in the affirmative, Tom continued, "And last, we'd normally call the county Sheriff in Wyoming who'd send a couple of deputies to pick you up."

"Why do you say normally?" asked Will, a little puzzled.

"I know you pretty well, Will. You wouldn't want to be locked up in your own county jail. Right? You'd waive extradition. Right?" Tom asked, sadness shading the eyes of all four.

"Yes," said Will, putting his head down on his arms, folded on his oak desk.

"I figured as much. So a Deputy, an investigator by the name of Beckwourth, from Fremont County, is here along with another deputy. The hearing'll be held at 12:00 noon. Trish and your partner can be there, if you want 'em to. Chuck an' I've cleared our calendars so we can wait in my office."

"Thanks, Tom. That's damn decent of both of you."

"Will, we're all in shock over this. It's just not like you, even under stress. I know how much you believe in every defendant's right to their day-in-court. Shit, it's in all your passionate closings!"

"You'll start out of Lansing on United Flight 2789 for Riverton at two thirty-five this afternoon," Chuck interjected.

"Will, I've got to tell you something," Tom quietly continued.

His voice gone, Will, his mind once again reliving the horror only four weeks removed, could only respond with a stare.

"I've met the prosecutor. It's just one of those coincidences. It was at a convention and since I'd hunted up in the Absarokas, I looked him up."

"Good or bad?" asked Will.

"Very professional," Tom replied.

"Did you ask him?"

Knowing full well the first thing Will would want was a name, Tom was ready, "Yes, but I'm going to wait. Chuck and I can both guess how you'd go about it. So, I'll just wait and see who you come up with."

"Just a minute," said Will, reaching for the phone as he pushed a tab on his well marked and ever changing pad. Quickly he tapped in a number and waited in silent shock, his mind racing over the recent tragedy. "Mark, hi . . . your dad . . . not worth a shit. Sitting down? Pen and paper? Okay, I'm going to give it to you slow—I've been indicted. Mark—Mark—wait Mark, listen, you can be a real help. The first few days are critical, so I'd like you to help, if you can. Listen, Mark. It's going to be very important that we pick the defense attorney, that way I'll have faith in him or her. Okay?"

"Sure, Dad," Mark replied. "What'll you want me to do?"

"Just a minute. Christ, I was just there, but I don't know. What the hell county is it? Where's the courthouse, Tom?"

"It's Fremont County and the courthouse is in Lander. You'll be flying to Riverton," answered the Prosecutor.

"Hold on, Mark. I want to check the map. Be right with you."

Somewhat familiar with the area, Will knew what he wanted his son to do. Checking the back of the road atlas—he knew it was the last state—the main towns were obvious. "Mark, I'd like you to fly out to Wyoming, rent a car and hit every bar with a pool table in Lander, Riverton, and of course, Dubois. See who the locals would want to defend 'em if they'd been drinking and were in a car accident that killed someone. Those are about the toughest cases of all to defend."

"When, Dad?"

"Today, if they'll let you go," Will replied.

"Hold a second, I'll ring my boss and tell him it's an emergency. Hold please." The minutes passed in silence as Will, phone in hand, stepped to the window to stare out his second story office at a street scene he had viewed for a quarter of a century. His thoughts were interrupted as Mark came back on the line, "Dad—no problem."

"Just a second, Mark. Yes, Tom?" said Will, looking at Tom who had raised his hand.

"Could I talk to Mark?"

"Sure. Mark, the prosecutor, a friend of mine, Tom Herrick, wants to talk to you. Okay?" and reaching across the desk, handed the receiver to his friend.

"Hello, Mark. Tom Herrick, here. We're doing all we can to make it as easy as possible for your dad. Sometimes he's so predictable! I've already booked two extra tickets on the same flight. I knew he'd want someone to go out. Okay?" and nodding his head, returned the phone to Will.

With tears running down his cheeks at the totally unexpected act of friendship, Will, in a broken voice began, "See if Zack can go—I'd like you both to be there."

"Sure, Dad. Anything else?"

"No. I'll give a durable power-of-attorney to Trish to get a retainer around." With a nod, Helen left to prepare the document, as Will continued,

"Thanks son, love ya. 'Bye," said Will, slowly hanging up, his hand shaking. "Marital assets," he said softly, tears again welling in his eyes.

"What?" asked Tom.

"Children—if they still love you," Will replied.

"That's true. Let's go back to my office, Will. I've got some information for you. The prosecutor faxed me everything. He even had Investigator Beckwourth bring me a copy of the video. Christ, what a mess! A killing ground. A 'harvest of sorrow'!"

"I'll never get it out of my mind, Tom," said Will. "I relive it daily. And it's worse in my head now, than at the time it happened. I didn't have much time to think, it all just blended together. I'd been had by Lee and knew it. But, there's no evidence to support me?" Will questioned, with a discouraged look and quivering chin.

"No, I'm afraid there isn't," Tom quietly answered. "Not at this time."

"Could I win this one?" Will asked, as the three friends prepared to leave for Charlotte.

"No," Tom replied in a somber tone. "I'd beat you on this one."

"What makes you so sure?"

"Their clothes, Will. It's the way they were dressed. It's going to look like you shot a guy who was out jogging. Tennis shoes, sweat pants and a pullover. You know how important dress is to a jury."

"Jesus, Tom! Combat boots, survival knife and a camouflage suit don't make a person a killer."

"I know. That's why I'd win."

"Why?"

"Well, proving who were killers is going to be the burden of both lawyers. Forget that 'burden of proof' crap. Hasn't the prosecutor already met his burden? Now your attorney is going to have to prove Lee was a killer. Right?"

"I guess so," Will sighed. "Thanks for being honest, Tom. Maybe something'll turn up on the bastard," said Will, with a weak but hopeful smile. "They've got the death sentence. Are they going to be asking for it?" he inquired, signing the power-of-attorney Helen had prepared.

"I don't know," Tom lied the best he could, signing the document as a witness. And the three, each a different part of the system they deeply believed in, started for the door.

Capital City Airport
Lansing, Michigan

Shifting in the cramped airline seat, the six-foot three-inch Beckwourth turned toward Will, his left wrist cuffed to Will's right and broke the silence as they waited for the first leg of the westward flight to begin. "Will, I'd like to talk to you on the flight, if you want to, but I'd have to give 'em to you again."

With a nod, Will confirmed his consent to talk and as the deputy reached for his worn, yet memorized card, Will's mind went back in time—back to a rumor he was not sure was true.

'Here are your Miranda Rights'. Upon hearing his name, Ernesto Miranda, bleeding from a mortal stab, pulled himself to a sitting position on the bar room floor. The officer, reading from his newly printed card, began, 'You have the right to remain silent. Any statement you make may be used against you in a court of law'. Ernesto's alleged assailant stood cuffed, the officer's monotone heard but not registering, as the blood of life slowly seeped from one of the most famous individuals in modern criminal jurisprudence.

On March 13, 1963, Ernesto Miranda had been taken from his home to the Phoenix, Arizona, police station. Identified and following established procedures, questioned without an attorney present, he gave a confession and was soon convicted of kidnapping and rape. Rooted in Judeo-Christian principles as far back as the Book of Judges and aware of the history of the Star Chamber Oath, the Warren court, on June 13, 1966, ruled the confession inadmissible. Remaining in custody throughout these legal proceedings and retried with admissible evidence, Miranda was convicted, served his time and released.

'You have the right to have an attorney present during any questioning'. Weakening, Ernesto drifted near uncon-sciousness.

The Warren court, using in part Scottish case law declared in *Chalmers,* recognized that interrogation of a person in custody can be very dangerous. In *Boyd,* an earlier court had opined that '. . . illegitimate and unconstitutional practices get their first footing . . . by silent approaches and slight deviations from legal modes of procedure.' In *Giddeon,* the Warren court decided 'due process' required an attorney.

"If you cannot afford an attorney, one will be appointed for you at public expense. Do you understand your rights, Will?"

Will, returning to the present, nodded his head in the affirmative. "Officer, my mind was going back to Miranda."

"I wish you'd call me Ron, Will."

"Okay. I heard he died while 'his' rights were being read to the killer who stabbed him. That's sure ironic!"

"It's also bullshit, Will. He was stabbed twice in the chest at the La Amapola Bar in Phoenix, Arizona, the afternoon of January 31, 1976. Apparently he'd got the best of two guys in a fist fight started over a three dollar dispute in a card game. When Ernie went to the bathroom to wash blood off his hands, one of the two gave a knife to the other and left the bar with his girlfriend. The guy with the knife got Ernie when he came out of the bathroom."

"Didn't the police get there and grab the guy?" asked Will.

"Oh, hell no. The suspect fled before a fire rescue unit got there. They took Ernie to Good Samaritan Hospital, but he was flat-line-dead. Good old Ernesto Miranda, DOA!" exclaimed Beckwourth. "Actually he wasn't so old, only thirty-four when he was killed. He was born the same day I was, March 9, 1941."

"Did they catch the guy?"

"The Phoenix Police Department did a hell of a job. The investigation came up with Eseziquiel Moreno Perez as a prime suspect and a warrant was issued. I don't know how it ended."

"I heard Miranda was traveling around the southwest selling autographed, Miranda Warning cards," said Will.

"I guess that's true. However, the rumor about his rights being read to his killer while he lay dying, was spread by some New York writer who didn't have his shit together. It's totally false. Ernie was probably dead before the rescue squad ever got there. For God sake, do people think all police are stupid, or don't care?"

"Do you want me to answer that?" laughed Will. "I don't," he continued. "It'd be a damn jungle out there without the police. A few bad ones make it real tough on a lot of good ones. But what is it you wanted to know officer? I'm sorry, Ron. I told you every detail I can possibly remember back at Lander. Heck, if I remember right, I even gave you my life history!"

"Oh, nothing about the case, Will," Beckwourth replied. "I'd like to talk and felt I'd better give you the *Miranda Warning* anyway."

"I'd rather not talk about this summer. It was too horrible. I suppose we can talk about other things. Maybe that'll take my mind off it a little," said Will, with a deep sigh.

I just want to find out what makes you tick, Will, Beckwourth thought to himself.

And he did.

8

Digging moats and fletching arrows

Tuesday afternoon,
September 3, 1991
Office of John Vickers
Riverton, Wyoming

Events happened fast following the uneventful, but traumatic and humiliating handcuffed flight on commercial airlines from Lansing to Riverton. With changeovers and waits in Detroit and Denver, the curious stares of strangers at Detroit, included, as chance would have it, two attorneys who had been victimized by Will's closing arguments. Their smug grins adding insult to injury at this bitter twist of fate.

Two days of investigation quickly led Mark and Zack to the modern, one-story, dark-brick, office building of the law firm of Vickers and Vickers. Located on North 3rd Street, the building sat to the east and below the four watchful bug-eyes of U.S. West Communications Center's microwave tower. The building's design and decor spoke of quiet confidence. Retained the preceding Thursday evening, 'Big John', as the senior partner was affectionately known, had already displayed his competency with the smooth and well prepared argument he presented at the Friday afternoon hearing, in obtaining a reasonable bail, coupled with the newly instituted electronic-tether program.

"Will, you've got to understand—and I don't think you need a lecture—this is going to be tough. This is going to be real tough on all of us. You come in here, thanks to the tether program, and you become more of a person. It's not like I can walk out of your cell or out of the attorney's conference room and close the door. And I don't mean those clients are not people. It's just in a way, I guess I see myself across the table if I'd been in your shoes that morning. I believe you and I hope I could've done as well. But, we don't have any evidence at this point to support you, and that's real tough to deal with."

"John, Trish and I are aware of what you're saying. It's why we can't socialize or go out around here. It would almost be better if I was locked up.

159

We stay in our apartment, watch television and read. Hell—Lander and Riverton—the edge of my world. It sure as hell isn't a vacation!" exclaimed Will.
"That reminds me, where are you staying?" John inquired.

"We've rented a kitchenette at the Silver Spur Motel in Lander. It was only five-hundred a month and with all the hunters in the area, we thought it was reasonable," Trish replied. "Here's a card with their number," she added, reaching across the desk to hand the card to John. "It's on the west side of town and has a spectacular view of the mountains."

"I don't look up there too often," added Will, his voice flat.

"You know, our defense is only going to fly if we can come up with something on Lee. You realize that don't you?"

"Yes, we're aware of that. John," Will inquired, "who's the detective working with the prosecutor? He looks familiar. He brought me here, but there's just something about him I can't put my finger on."

"Beckwourth, Investigator James Ronald Beckwourth. The counties in Wyoming don't call them detectives. They use the term investigator."

"Is he Black or maybe Indian? He just looks familiar. Beckwourth—oh my God! Not Jim Beckwourth! Not the *Medicine Calf!* It can't be!" Will exclaimed, a look of excited-shock on his face.

"What? What is it, Will? Are you two going to let me in on your little secret?" Trish asked, as John gave an affirmative nod of his head.

"Will," John inquired, "do you want to tell her or shall I?"

"Go ahead, John. You obviously know the old as well as the new."

"Here goes, Trish. And this is all well documented and probably true. In about 1810, a Sir Jennings Beckwourth, who I believe was an aristocratic Virginia physician, moved to St. Louis. He brought his wife, who was a former mulatto slave, and their twelve year old son, James. Because of his love and moral convictions, they'd left Virginia due to the miscegenation laws. To make a long story short, their son became a Mountain Man and when he was about thirty years old, he was captured by Crow Indians, the Amahabas. Their territory includes the Absaroka Range north of here."

"Trish," Will interjected, "that's why I said he looked familiar. He's got that distinctive, straight, lip-line with no upper lip showing, just like the pictures of the *Medicine Calf.*"

"Anyway," John continued, "the Amahabas believed he was a fulfillment of an ancient prophecy, so he was treated with kindness and respect and became a great warrior. So good he became a chief and given the name *Medicine Calf.* He's probably the most famous of all the Amahabas, even though he wasn't one. Certainly, because of his unique history, he was one of the most famous men on the frontier. His adventures have been the subject of several books. There's a monument to one of his battles south of Cheyenne. It's at the natural stone fortress, just off I-25.

"He testified against Colonel Chivington at the military tribunal following the massacre of a peaceful Cheyenne village at Sand Creek. They made a movie of that called *Soldier Blue,* staring Peter Strauss and Candice Bergen. Anyway, in 1865, Beckwourth returned to the Crow Nation and married a young woman by the name of Sue, who, according to tradition, had a son she always claimed to be *Medicine Calf's.* Beckwourth, one of his descendants, was raised on the Crow reservation, joined the Marines, fought in Vietnam, went through the FBI school at Quantico and then worked for DCI in Cheyenne. He decided to come back to western Wyoming however, so he could be near his people and his mountains. The ties were too strong."

"Wyoming has a CID?" asked Will, a look of surprise on his face. "I thought that was only military."

"It's DCI, the main investigation organization in Wyoming. The Division of Criminal Investigation is a part of the Attorney General's office. DCI has original jurisdiction over organized crime and drug cases. They're called in by the counties or cities to assist in criminal investigations and their crime-scene analysts do the work-up at the scene. They have a very modern lab facility in Cheyenne. The staff is not made up of police officers, but experts in the various research fields. The investigators are more like police officers, but are not under control of the Highway Patrol, or of the County sheriffs. They're a little more independent of the police agencies. They have a good reputation, even with the defense lawyers."

"What kind of person is Beckwourth?" inquired Trish.

"Trish, he's honest and thoroughly competent. I'm sure he believes Will's guilty, but he'll give us everything he can find, even if it shows him wrong. He's already checked Army records and obtained a complete profile on Lee. There's nothing we know of yet to support your claim of self-defense, Will. He's done everything possible to show Lee was linked intentionally with the hit on the camp. If he comes up with anything, I know he'll share it with us."

"And look at this. He even did his research on the knots the three were tied up with!" exclaimed John.

"You know, I guess I shouldn't 've cut George's hands loose. I never thought. He just looked so twisted, even though I knew he was dead," Will sighed, with a shudder.

"No problem, Will. Everyone understood. Here, read this letter Beckwourth received awhile back. He did this on his own, with one of the knots he obtained from DCI."

Reaching out, Will took the letter and began to read.

Honorable James Beckwourth
Investigator—Fremont County Sheriff's Department
Lander, Wyoming 82520, USA

Objective: Knots
With reference to the above-mentioned objective.

My colleague, Angelo Iafrate, and I wish to thank you for allowing us to examine this most interesting knot. We first must compliment you on your wisdom in removing the cord while maintaining tension on the knot, as without this, a proper analysis could not have been made.

In our opinion, and we would so testify, this is a unique knot. As best we can describe, it is a variation of a double Spanish bowline, that slides and tightens much like a slip noose, but will not loosen by backsliding, and yet, may be instantly undone by simply pulling on either end, like a hitch knot.

From the structure of the loops that are formed in the bight, we both believe that it may be possible that the knot can be created with one hand, although we have not been able to accomplish that feat as of this posting.

It is our opinion that the knot may have been developed, invented if you please, by a fisherman, possibly Portuguese. They often are forced to work with one hand and much spare time is spent working with ropes and playing with knots.

We take this opportunity to give you our regards for allowing us the opportunity to examine this unique work of cordage art. We send our most sincere hope that we have been of some assistance.

Distinti saluti
Mario Calderoni
Angelo Iafrate

"They've published several books. They're world famous rope experts who live in Italy. Here," said John, handing Will a copy of a recent fax, "this just came over the wire from Lander."

Deputy Ronald Beckwourth, Investigator
Fremont County Sheriff Department
450 North 2nd Street
Lander, Wyoming 82520

RE: Guy Gerlach #48325

Dear Deputy Beckwourth:
    Per your request, we have reviewed all records for cell mates of the above-named inmate who may have had experience in sailing, climbing or fishing.
    From July 3, 1968, to February 12, 1969, Guy Gerlach was cell mates with Antónnio Jose de Gusmào. Mr. de Gusmào was seventy years old and was incarcerated for life for the rope strangulation death of his wife and her paramour. He had tied them up so that they strangled each other. His papers stated that his occupation was 'fisherman'. Mr. de Gusmào hung himself in 1969 while Guy Gerlach's cell mate.

Mr. Gerlach was paroled in 1970, violated parol by going to New Mexico and returned to Marquette prison. He was due to be released soon when he left Marquette and committed his first crimes of violence, three murders. We understand you have been provided with his recent history.

If we can be of further assistance, please advise.

Very truly yours,

Robert Harley, Director
Michigan Department of Corrections
Lansing, Michigan

"Jesus! I guess we can't ask for much more!" Will exclaimed. "Of course it'll help hang me."

"Beckwourth, if he's related, would be *Medicine Calf's* great-great grandson," John ventured.

"You know, some coincidence isn't it? My great-great grandfather, Enos Wheeler, went through South Pass in 1852 and died in the Humbolt Valley, Nevada Territory. He was buried and covered with sticks and dirt to keep the animals from digging him up."

"Oh yes, it was common in those days and out here, we've all heard about the practice. Chief Washakie and the Shoshoni were famous for helping emigrants on the way to California. Several hundred signed documents attesting to Washakie's help. Maybe Mr. Wheeler signed something like that?"

"I've never heard of that," Will replied, "but I doubt it. I think he just went through, got sick, got buried and they continued on! Let's get back to our case, John. What about those AR2s? The report indicated full-auto. Those are as illegal as hell! What did ATF say about 'em?"

"Lee was a Colt dealer's representative and held an AO-2 license. The tax was paid and according to Internal Revenue Service, everything was proper with the Alcohol, Tobacco and Firearms people. Colt has given Lee the highest praise an employee could get. Most of the time he works with police departments and his record and reputation are squeaky-clean, both here and in Virginia. He's even been pushed around a couple of times, but just flat refuses to fight."

"It's going to boil down to the video and Linda's statement at the scene. Isn't it?"

"Yes, Will. I'm afraid that's the smoking gun, at least unless we come up with something," John sighed.

"Sure, John. Linda told it to the Grand Jury like she saw it. Hell, I don't blame her, *res gestae*—spontaneous declarations—admissible anywhere. An honest person. What she said, was what she saw and heard. Hell, it happened so fast, if she'd been watching she might not've seen it. Christ, watch pro football instant replay. Shit, three or four cameras, slow motion and sometimes they still can't tell! Sorry—John Madden and Pat Summerall just didn't happen to be there! I'm telling you John, the man exploded with the same speed the pistol fired. Oh hell, you've heard enough about it. John, why don't you give us this PREP stuff again—slow and easy if you please."

Parallel Review Evaluation Panel

The Constitution—mandates established as if set in stone—reliable—good—reasonable, yet changing times and new technologies provided and allowed changes in procedures and even upon occasion, changes in the very rules themselves.

Witness—Lord Mansfield's Rule set forth in 1777, one of the most sacred rules of the English common law, as a prime example. The paternity of a child born to a married couple could not, except in a few extremely limited circumstances, be challenged. A matter of public policy springing in large part from the lack of a method of proof. This citadel of rigidity was to fall however to common sense and the laboratory of the scientists who had developed highly reliable blood tests to enable organ transplants. It could now be proven—to virtually an absolute certainty—that a specific individual could not be the father, and the walls of Mansfield came tumbling down!

The reasons for a change in the rules of appellate procedure, in cases where the death sentence was sought, demanded a change be made. Having reversed the decision creating the decade-long hiatus in carrying out the death sentence, the Justices of the Supreme Court became persuaded by common sense and a few tragically long delays, that waiting years to be executed was in and of itself a cruel and unusual punishment.

A procedure of parallel review in place of subsequent review, was a concept now technically possible. It was believed that PREP would protect defendants' basic right to 'due process of law' as mandated by the Constitution of the United States of America.

"Sure, Will. Here's how it works. A panel consisting of six distinguished jurists, including one from your state and one from Virginia, the *victim's* state, is able to monitor the trial. They'll have hard copy within minutes of the words being spoken. They will also have audio, which can give an insight—voice inflection—sarcasm *et cetera* never before showing up in a verbatim transcript.

"They're not given video since it's just designed to replace the normal appeal procedures. To run parallel with the trial instead of subsequent to it, but still to provide all of the 'due process of law' protection. New technology gives almost instant cross reference to the latest decisions, interpretations and any issues where the law might be in conflict or where a unique point of law would require a full appellate review. In other words, if it's a *clean* case and there are no new or unusual principles involved, and you have a *fair* trial, from jury selection to closing instructions, and no jury tampering, it ends here.

"The panel has sixty days to submit its findings to the Justice of this Federal Circuit. Remember, four panel members are judges from the Wyoming bench and they monitor the federal as well as Wyoming standards, which may be higher than federal in some cases. The Supreme Court justice of this Federal Circuit—we're in the 10th, so that would be Justice Murphy—reviews PREP's findings and then within thirty days, either gives the green light to Governor Deloney, or finds that a full, normal appellate review should be held. If PREP's finding confirms the trial court proceedings and the jury recommendation—note, they don't substitute their judgment—the Governor has thirty days from receipt of the justice's notice, to grant clemency and commute to life or carry out the sentence. "PREP is only in place when it's requested. The panel only goes to work after the jury recommends the death sentence and the Court, following the recommendation, orders the death sentence."

"Mr. Vickers," spoke up Trish, "do panel members actually sit and listen to the trial?"

"Good question, Trish. But I wish you'd call me John. No, no more than appellate judges would. But each judge assigns a law clerk who's a member of the bar to sit in on the trial proceedings—they're known as the trial review group—at the remote venue. They also have an experienced attorney selected from the Appellate Defender's office, who specializes in appellate work.

"This trial review group, has a side effect of making sure nobody goes off half-cocked, and the court and lawyers go by the book. Do the very best they can. Remember, the cameras are on, whether we like it or not. Just look at the William Kennedy Smith trial. It's going to be on camera, at least that's what I've read, and you can just imagine the type of coverage that trial will get! There's one other major advantage, of course, like a good sword, it cuts both ways. Both sides are given daily hard copy of all testimony and court proceedings within one hour of each day's adjournment."

"John, do the parties have any input to PREP, like normal appellate briefs?" inquired Will.

"Yes. Given daily transcripts, each may file a brief limited to thirty pages to be submitted within twenty-one days, but there are no reply briefs. The procedure assumes a certain level of competency all along the line. Remember, there's a member of the Appellate Defender's office in the trial review group and it only takes *one* vote in the Parallel Review Evaluation Panel to set aside PREP! There are three options for the panel. If at least four agree, a new trial is mandated and the reasons why are explained. It must begin within sixty days, unless good cause is shown. If one or more request it, full appellate review is required. And of course, if unanimous and confirming, that ends all appeals. If new evidence is found, and *only new evidence will stop it,* it better be convincing and it better be found within the one-hundred and twenty day period! Do either of you have any other questions?"

"Not at this time," answered Will.

John, acknowledging Trish's slow, negative turn of her head, continued, "Will, I've got a court hearing tomorrow that can't be changed. Could you come back here the first thing Thursday morning so we can go over our defense strategy?"

"Sure, John. Do you want Trish to come along or not? This is tough on her."

"It's just as tough on you, Will. Of course I can come with you!" declared Trish.

"Well," said John intervening, "it might be a good idea Trish, if I spent some time alone with my client. We may have to butt heads a little to establish what we're going to do and just who's going to do it," said John, with a smile at his older client.

"Don't worry, John, you're the lawyer!"

"Glad to hear you say that, Will. But don't you worry. It's your case and your ideas are more than welcome. Okay, I'll see you both here about eight Thursday morning. Here's your copy of my file to date. It includes transcripts of the testimony of Linda and Sam before the Grand Jury, as well as all of Beckwourth's work. I know how you'll go over it!"

Shaking hands they parted and with no bounce in their steps and sad, dejected countenances, Will and Trish started for the van and the drive to the recommended restaurants in Hudson, on the route to Lander.

"Honey, what do you think? Are you satisfied with John? Do you have faith in him?"

"More than faith, Trish. He's good, really, really good. That came through at the bail hearing. I'm sure he believes me, but he's frustrated by the fact there just isn't going to be any evidence to support my claim and he and I can both feel it. Sometimes you know the final scene before the curtain ever rises."

"Honey, don't be so pessimistic. Something's going to turn up, I just know it will."

"I hope you're right and it turns up in time. Things are moving forward awfully fast. That new procedure sounds good. It'll sure keep everyone honest. I've seen and heard a lot of non-verbal judicial communication, sarcasm and facial expressions, that never show up in a transcript. But, I've got a strong feeling I'm riding a short trail and there's not a damn thing anyone can do to make it longer. Trust me, honey. I don't have any 'death wish', it's just my gut feeling."

"Will, John mentioned a massacre at some creek. Was it the one with Dustin Hoffman, ah—what was it, *Little Big Man?*"

"No, that was the Washita River massacre Custer carried out in 1868. The one he mentioned, Sand Creek, was a whole lot worse. I think it was about the worst that's ever happened in our country's history. Thank God it wasn't the U.S. Army. It was carried out under the command of a colonel by the name of Chivington and as I recall, it happened in October or November of 1864. I visited the site once after taking William back to Colorado."

"Where is it?"

"It's down in the southeastern part of Colorado. You have to drive a few miles north of the highway and it's on some private land. There's a bend and depression in the rather bleak countryside, with a dry creek bed called Sand Creek and a bunch of cottonwood trees. You can 'listen to the murmur of the cottonwood trees'. Trish, when I was a kid, *Don't Fence Me In* was my favorite song. 'Wild Cat Kelly, a looking mighty pale, was settin' by the Sheriff's side, and when that Sheriff said I'm sendin' you to jail, Wildcat bowed his head and cried, oh give me land lots of land . . .'. I'll spare you my singing! It's a very quiet, lonely, sad place with a small marker. It makes you shiver just to stand there and go back in time. It's completely barren—no town, no McDonald's, no Indian-doll souvenir shops."

"Do you have to pay to go in there?"

"No. There's a small donation box on a post. Anyway, this large encampment of Cheyenne, led by Chief Spotted Wolf, had moved there as directed by a Union general in charge of that military district. The attack was by a National Guard unit and they really lost it. The army went out the next day and cleaned up the mess. From what I've read it was real carnage—men, women, children, babies—nearly five hundred wiped out. A dark, dark page in our history."

"Was anything ever done about it?"

"There was a military tribunal, but nothing came of it. The Civil War was going on and it was in the midst of our westward expansion. Bad things happened on both sides, but this was about the worst," Will sighed, reaching for the radio switch. Set at 97.5, KDLY Lander, and the friendly voice of J.J. McKay to mask their fears, the journey down highway 287 to Hudson was a far cry from their joy-filled Wyoming visit a year earlier.

Hudson, declared population of three-hundred ninety-two and home of the 'World's Finest Food', soon interrupted their quiet soul-searching. "Well, honey," spoke up Will, breaking their silence, "if they have fresh Apalachicola oysters on the half-shell it may be the finest. What do you think?"

"Ugh! That raw oyster you shamed me in to eating at Gulf Shores was the size of Maine! I'll pass on raw oysters, but let's give them a chance. I've never had Serbian food, or do you want to start with steak at the El Toro?"

"Flip a coin and let chance decide."

"Okay—that settles it—it's *sarmas* at Svilar's," Trish grinned, slyly peeking at the hidden penny deftly palmed on her slender wrist.

———————

Thursday morning
Office of John Vickers

"Will, I think you're right. It's all going to boil down to one last question put to Linda and whether or not they're going to accept your version. You know, good character witnesses can be a big help, but again a jury can just as often go with the so called 'experts'. It isn't your word against someone else's. It's going to be your believability against the experts and no evidence of anything bad against Lee."

"John, are you going to have co-counsel at trial?"

"Yes, I think we should. I talked to Bob Reising yesterday and he advised me he'd have one assistant and of course, Beckwourth. We won't gain a thing by trying to appear as underdogs and the jury is going to expect us to be thoroughly prepared. I'd like to have a friend of mine, Richard Jenson, of Lander, work the trial with me. He represents a lot of business people in the area and would be a big help in jury selection. And, Jennifer will be there to help. She's a brilliant paralegal and is going to be one hell of a good lawyer as soon as she finishes school."

"John, my future's in your hands. I take it back, my actions and fate put me here. You'll do the best anyone can, but I know it's my burden, not yours."

"Thanks. I'm glad you feel that way. As you know, not all defendants do. I'm also glad Trish decided to stay in Lander. We may have a problem, Will."

"How so, John?"

"Do you remember how I told you Bob has always seemed sort of laid back on this case, he even put Strong on it to work our side?"

"Yes. Now what?"

"Will, you've got to level with me. What did you do after you got washed out of flight school?"

"First, I drank a fifth of whiskey and nearly killed myself with alcohol. This escape lasted quite awhile, maybe a month and then . . ."

"No, Will," John interrupted, "I mean after you went to Reese Air Force Base in Lubbock, Texas. What did you do there?"

"Just did odd jobs around the base, waiting out the rest of my enlistment. I'd gone from a Cadet Major on Wing Staff to an enlisted corporal standing in lines," Will answered, a puzzled look on his face.

"Will, God damn it, you're not leveling with me! For Christ's sake Will, the State of Wyoming is going to strap you to a table and shoot you full of a chemist's cocktail if you let 'em surprise me in court!" John shouted, his voice filled with raw emotion. "Damn it, will you listen to me? I'm trying to get through that thick Scot skull of yours! Are you going to hear me?"

"Yes, John—I'll hear you. This sounds like one of my lectures coming."

"Will, be serious. A few months from now there's a drive I don't want to be making. Do you know anything about Rawlins?"

"No, is it a place or a person? Or something to eat?"

"Jesus, Will, it's a place and let me describe it. I'll get in my car and take a real scenic drive about thirty-six miles down 135 to 287 and then about ninety miles southeast to Interstate 80. I'll take a short drive back west to exit 214, Higley Boulevard and go south through a couple of high berms. And there it sits, right in the middle of some of the most godforsaken land in Wyoming, the Wyoming State Penitentiary. I'll show my ID at a gate, hang a left, park my car, walk through a steel gate, take another short walk and check in. They whisk me over with one of their buzzing, black, Garrett scanners and in I go. They'll walk me across the yard to a small prison within the prison that's ringed with another steel fence topped with coiled razor wire. Are you with me?"

"Yes, but I don't think I'm going to like this trip!"

"I won't like it, God damn it, you'll already be there! I'll be taken through a steel fence sally-port and inside the building. This area of maximum security is on the west side of the main prison and in the southeast corner of the building is an area maybe twenty by twenty feet. There's a glass wall there so the people can see in and watch the show. We'll all be standing around, some sad, some happy, lots of small talk to calm their nerves. There'll be a couple of reporters, maybe some of Lee Mackintosh's friends and relatives, they come sometimes. And, Will, they're going to wheel you in strapped to a God damn gurney. Oh, you'll be all relaxed and smiling. Hell you'll have just enough *thiopental sodium* in you—you know it by its trade name, Sodium Pentothal—to make you goofy. Hell, you won't know what planet you're on!"

"At least it won't hurt!" Will exclaimed.

"Will, it'll hurt, it'll hurt a lot of us," said John, his voice dropping to a slow calm level. "It'll hurt Trish, it'll hurt your kids and it'll hurt me. And right there in front of me, with not a God damn thing I can do about it, some masked physician, some unknown the prison physician brings in, is going to shoot you full of *pancuronium bromide*. This will totally relax your muscles, heart and lungs, causing *apnea*. You'll stop breathing. And mixed in with it is a dose of *potassium chloride*, which goes after your nervous system. It'll cause cardiac arrest. And right there in front of all of us, you're going to die! Do you hear me?"

"John, those drugs sound expensive. Do you think they'll let me use my Visa card?"

"Jesus H. Christ, Will, I give up!" John, extremely agitated, exclaimed, getting up from his desk. "I'm going to get some coffee, do you want some?"

"No thanks, John. But when you come back, there's something I want to say, if you'll hear me. Okay?" Will quietly asked.

"Okay. Fair enough, Will. I'll be right back." It was only a matter of minutes before John returned and resumed his seat in the somewhat cluttered, but relaxed, western-decorated office. "Okay, Will. I'm listening."

"John, I'm sorry if I seem too, what can I say, smart-ass? John, I have to joke all the time," declared Will, his voice breaking. "I was there! This wasn't some actor's goddamn wantabe *Rambo-Diehard* wet-dream I could get up and walk out of! The reality of the camp was a scene straight out of *Dante's Inferno*. It was hell in a half-acre of one of the most beautiful places on earth! When I get serious I go back there and relive it. It was blood and brains and eyes gouged out and bleeding rape and cut throats and ropes and knives and gun powder and screams. And these were my closest friends. Jesus Christ, John, I was in an emotional hurricane! I was scared shitless, but as well as I knew I'd been had, I know I'm going to be had and there's not a goddamn thing anyone can do to help me. Not unless something can be found on Lee to support my defense. Something to show that he could do what I know in my mind he did do! If you'd seen his kick, you'd know we'd all be dead, so as far as I'm concerned I'd be dead anyway. And now Sam's alive and so is Linda, and Bob's and her baby. That baby's got a lot more life ahead of her or him than I'd have! It's not a bad trade, John. There won't be any more girls like Mia. Not by that other bastard," Will whispered, in closing his short, but extremely emotional speech, tears running down his cheeks.

"All right, Will. I hear you," John quietly responded. "But now, what happened at Reese?"

"Jesus, John! There's not one damn thing I did there that's remotely relevant to what happened at Simpson Lake!" Will swore, highly agitated.

"I thought you said I was the lawyer trying this case? Don't you want me involved in what's relevant? Jesus H. Christ, Will, you're making these choices in your stubborn Scot head. What's relevant is what the prosecutor can get admitted and what the damn jury believes is relevant. You're a lawyer, Will. You know that!"

"Nothing happened there," Will softly replied.

"Will, do you want me to withdraw?"

"No, John—my whole future . . ."

"Don't lay that shit on me!" John snapped. "Will, just level with me. You just said 'nothing happened *there*'. That's a negative-pregnant and you know it. What happened somewhere else?"

"Nothing."

"All right. Maybe you're telling me the truth, or all you can tell me. I wanted it from you. Shit—some more coffee now?"

"Yeah—something tells me I may want it laced!"

Pushing the intercom, John a little more calm, spoke with a pleasant voice, "Lora, would you please bring us two cups of black coffee? Too early to lace it Will—I think. Okay, here's what Bob laid on me yesterday when I bumped into him over at the Courthouse. He's pissed—his whole attitude has changed. He obviously now believes, that somehow, you were able to pull off what you did just a little too easily. Taking out two armed guys and one who, according to your version, had the ability of a trained killer. Granted he was a Colt dealer and had served in Viet Nam. But there's nothing, not a shred of evidence to show he'd had any professional karate or any other hand-to-hand training beyond the normal military. He's never even held a passport."

"Not good for me," Will muttered.

"Will," replied John in a deadly serious tone, "it's worse for you."

"What do you mean?"

"All right," John sighed, as he continued his inquiry. "Bob knows you got out of the Air Force in December of 1956 on an Honorable Discharge, with all of your appropriate service ribbons and honors. He also knows most military leaves and discharges were canceled or put on hold due to the Soviet Union's invasion of Hungary, the Chinese conflict brewing over the islands of Quemoy and Matsu, and serious problems developing in Japan with the communists. Beckwourth contacted a retired General by the name of John J. Bodenheimer, who was the base commander at Reese. Bodenheimer lives in Fort Collins. When he was given your name and shown your flight-school press-ops photo, according to Beckwourth, he lit up like a Christmas tree. And this is thirty-five years after the meeting!"

"What meeting, John?" questioned Will, a look of serious concern on his face.

"It seems the General remembered you because of your being named after Will Rogers. And, because of the visit you'd had by a bird-colonel from the Inspector General's office, who flew in from Washington. Apparently someone wanted you to do a *special job,* since they knew you weren't going to reenlist when you couldn't fly. And so now good buddy, do you want to tell me what the fuck you did as a corporal for a God damn full colonel who came all the way from the Pentagon to talk to you in a private office for over an hour while a base commander sat on his ass twiddling his thumbs and pissing his pants or not!"

"For Christ's sake, I audited files!" exclaimed an exasperated Will.

"Will, the base commander transferred out a week or so after the visit and doesn't have any idea what you did, nor does anyone else. Your morning-report cards were destroyed and the record, from the time you left Hondo until you got out of the Air Force at Reese in December, doesn't show shit. You were never around. It's just a big blank. And if I tell Bob that a bird-colonel flew from Andrews Air Force Base to Reese Air Force Base to meet with a corporal who was getting out of the Air Force, just so you could *audit* a few files, he's going to laugh me out of the office."

"John, I told you what I did. But let me tell you, to a twenty year old corporal, the words of a bird-colonel from the Pentagon couldn't have carried more weight if they'd been delivered to me on a stone tablet on top of Mt. Sinai! I'd 've strafed Toronto's Younge Street if he'd 've asked me to! Let it go," Will ordered. "I'm telling you, it's what I did. I audited officer leave records against the morning-report cards."

"Well, it may be the truth. But it's only your word and in this age of double-speak, for all anyone knows, 'auditing files' could be just another euphemism for interrogating or eliminating individuals—here, there or anywhere. Reese was an air base, and there was plenty of time to teach you. You'd been through regular Air Force basic training, the cadet tiger-program, and you could fly—without puking—if you didn't do barrel rolls. You were grounded for landing on a closed field and washed out for motion sickness. You were never pink-slipped and there's even a note in your file that you flew through brush! And from your records, I think you were in just a little better shape back then!"

"That's for sure—boxing, cross-country, hockey, low-hurdles, tennis, handball. 'Those were the days my friend'!" Will laughed, in a singing voice at the memories.

"And, you had a reputation some of your old neighbors reported on. Beckwourth obtained a copy of your FBI security check prepared for flight-school. You were a crack shot. And by the way, he also got your physical and test scores at Chanute Air Force Base in Rantoul, Illinois. Right eye dominant, twenty-ten vision. Left eye, twenty-ten. Coordination scores, ninety-fifth percentile and they didn't break it down any finer!"

"Jesus, I forgot about that. Is Beckwourth always this thorough?"

"Yes."

"My shoe size?"

"Nine and one-half D," John answered. "It's in the report. Will, you of all people should know it's not what you did, it's what the jury may think you did, if this gets in. In my opinion, we can keep it out and there's no way they can get it in unless we somehow open the door. We can have an evidentiary hearing if we have to. But let's move on. Bob has given us until the first of October to decide on a *nolo contendere* plea to second-degree murder with a twenty year cap."

"John, I've told you how I feel about plea bargaining. It sucks. Most of the time it's a cop out. It's not what the defendant did or didn't do, but it's what they may get convicted of even if they're innocent, or less than they did if they're guilty. But the state or the defense hasn't got the nuts to try the case.

"John, I'm fifty-six and I've had a good life, the usual ups and downs. The last thing I want is to be locked up like a rabbit in a hutch with my wheel of salt, tray of pellets and a water bottle. Most of my youth was spent out-doors—you name it. It's where I spend most vacations—rivers, swamps, mountains. To be cooped up would kill me. My God! Can you imagine what that would do to my children, to my grandson? And for God sakes, to Trish?

But beyond that, I will never sell my soul for my life. Can I tell you about a case I had a couple of years ago?"

"Sure, go ahead."

"As you know, lawyers don't like to talk about their cases unless someone will pretend to listen," he began facetiously. "This was a cocaine case I defended on the west side of Michigan, the Grand Haven—Holland area. Ottawa County to be exact. It's an area where there're a lot of very conservative, straight-laced Dutch Reformed. They're good, honest, hard-working people, but I'll cut a long story short. Two Hispanic Americans . . ."

"You mean Mexicans?"

"John, my client wasn't an American Indian. His Spanish ancestors had lived in the New World a lot longer'n any of those Hollanders. He was born in Holland, Michigan, and before this incident he'd never even been accused of any crime, let alone arrested. He was, is and will die an American, I don't think he's ever even been to Mexico. . . ."

"You made your point, Will," John interjected.

"I'm sorry, it's a bad habit. Anyway, there were three defendants involved. One of the two he knew casually from high school, although they didn't hang out together, the other one he'd never met. It was a sting operation set up by a narcotics team. They had a local dealer by the *cajones*, who by the way, had never even heard of my client! Ortega didn't know about the kilo of cocaine coming in, nor was he present when any sales were attempted. Claimed he was innocent and didn't know they'd brought it to his apartment. I'm not carping about the trial, there was evidence to support the verdict. It's how the system works sometimes that makes me puke. The guy who brought the shit in from Texas pled to a reduced charge and agreed to testify against Ortega. He ended up with one year in jail. Ortega was offered a one year if he'd plead, but he maintained his innocence and wanted a trial.

"John, the jury got him on 'aiding and abetting' and because he had to go on the original charge, state law required a mandatory minimum of twenty years in prison! He has a trial and gets nineteen years more than the guy who brought the shit in and tried to sell it!"

"Does that surprise you, Will? It's the system."

"John, that young man—he was only twenty-one—had the right *cajones*, maybe the wrong lawyer. But if he could face a twenty year minimum instead of a reduced charge with a one year cap, I'm damn well going to testify as to what I know happened. I'll not plead guilty to shooting that man in cold-blood. It's not how it happened and they can hang me if they want to. I'm not any Tom Horn, but damn, I can take it, if that's what they have to do."

"Well, we've got thirty-nine days until the trial starts so let's get our asses in gear and get ready. It's going to be a classic battle-royal. One thing you should be pleased about, Judge Waters will give us a level field. She's a cracker-jack and the trial had better run smooth as silk or someone's fat'll fry!"

"John, what about Lee Mackintosh's military training?"

"Both Beckwourth and Strong ran complete and independent checks. Strong using the same channels Beckwourth used in digging up the information on you. Lee had the normal training and a regular tour in Nam that was interrupted by a trip home shortly after his parents died. He completed a second tour, taught French and military history at a community college in Virginia and was a manufacturer's rep for Colt Industries. He'd never been in any trouble, had excellent references, worked with the police a lot, was quiet and well liked."

"I've read they weren't working on a regular basis. What was their financial status?"

"Beckwourth went full time on this case right from the start and launched one hell of an investigation. They'd both accumulated a lot of money from the sale of the family estate and their earnings. They were very frugal and lived modestly, almost like they lived off the land. Total asset accumulations have been reviewed by accountants. The report indicates no illegal collateral sources and no lump sum deposits. There's no evidence at all of spending any unreported income. Both were squeaky-clean with the IRS."

"Have those assets been seized for Linda's damages and for the wrongful death of Bob?"

"Oh, yes. Linda's attorney is a friend of mine and he's had a firm in Alexandria, Virginia tie up all of the assets under a conspiracy and joint-venture theory. And not just the outfitters are claimants. Everyone injured, or family of those killed, will be protected."

"John, I went to GW. What's the firm's name?"

"It's a branch office of Hannibal and Draco."

"Oh yeah. They're one of those mega-firms that specialize in billing and are trying to break the ranking of Covington and Burling. I hope there's something left for Linda and Bob's baby and for the rest of 'em!"

"There should be. They'd accumulated about one and a-half million in blue-chips and CDs. Lee's property, if his estate gets it, would go to various charities and to a cousin who owns some land in a place called Hayters Gap, Virginia. Lee taught at Highland Community College and John blue-printed automobile engines for an engine shop in Abingdon."

"When and why did they come out west? Were they on vacation?"

"No. According to the Abingdon Police Chief, they'd said they wanted a change of scenery and they kept up their contacts with the people in Virginia. They'd moved to Rock Springs, that's over near Pinedale, in the fall of 1989. Seemed to do most things together, but not always. John had the hots for a chick in Pinedale."

"What else do you know about Lee?"

"Not a whole lot more to know. According to his medical records, Lee'd had a bilateral *orchiectomy* in the late sixties. The autopsy notes indicate it was surgically performed. Also, he had a bad scar on his left arm from a wound in Viet Nam."

"Okay, I'll bite, John!" Will exclaimed. "Just what in hell's a bilateral or-key-ek-toe-me?"

"I knew I'd nail you on that one, Will!" laughed John. "Do you want to take a stab at it?"

"Hell no, I haven't the foggiest!"

"Well, *orchis* is the Greek word for testicle. He'd had his nuts cut off! I had to look that one up myself."

"John? Sam and I've been good friends for a long, long time. He explained in detail how slick and efficient his torture was. That couldn't 've been done by an amateur and from the accent, one of those two from Virginia had to be the one who did it. Sam's a trained observer and he wouldn't make a mistake about that. He's certain in his mind it was John, who was the only one close to him, tied him up, and put dirt in his eyes. But Sam could be wrong. Lee was in Vietnam and a lot of that shit has always gone on in the military. Has any attempt been made to try and find out where either John or Lee got that training?"

"Will, Beckwourth's a pro. That information was not used in the Grand Jury, but it's been done and it'll be in a supplemental report we should have early next week. Bob doesn't cheat on continuing disclosure. He and I were both wondering about it and as it turned out, Beckwourth had already started on it. It seems one of John's best friends, who played with him on the varsity baseball team in high school—Virginia state champions by the way—went on to become a well-known neurosurgeon. He and John remained close friends and they spent a great deal of time fishing. Everyone in the community near Abingdon knew they were friends. However, the doctor, his wife and two of their three children were killed in 1986. A bad accident caused by a drunk driver, on a highway near Bluefield, Virginia."

"Fate cuts both ways! Shit—shit—shit!" exclaimed Will. "John, I've an idea about this hit. Do you want to hear it?"

"Of course I do. Shoot."

"I did! That's why I'm here!"

"Sorry, Will."

"No problem. Anyway, Lee was good. Far better than he was supposed to be. That means a professional and maybe a planned hit. There are two basic hits. Simple, one on one, like in *The Day of The Jackal*. And complex, a team of two or more, like Hoffa or maybe Kennedy. In a simple hit, the assassin plans the hit and the backdoor. While in a complex hit, there's a team, a backdoor, a patsy like Oswald and maybe a Judas goat. The brothers were clean, on the record, and it's my guess, were using Gerlach. He was a stranger at the Longhorn, but it was just a little too convenient. Of course that's a major problem. When it's a pro and planned, there's no evidence. Signs are left, but often they're too thin to hold up."

"Who are you, Will?" inquired John, in a low voice.

Shrugging his shoulders, Will's mind scrolled back, "Who am I? Who *ever* knows?"

"Well, lets start digging. We've got lots of work to do," declared John, realizing he had reached a dead end.

––––––––––

Friday evening
Silver Spur Motel

"Will, is something the matter? I know yesterday was difficult for you. Can you tell me about it?"

"I don't know, honey. Yes and no. It's just that I don't know how far they're going to go to convict me."

"What do you mean?"

"Well, I know I'm going to get a fair trial. That doesn't worry me. It's just that sometimes circumstantial evidence can be relevant, and thus get admitted to the jury. Then arguments will be made on those circumstances and can create an inference that really hurts."

"Oh, Will. Obviously something happened yesterday that you haven't told me. What is it? Tell me."

"I guess I can, Trish. John's going to file a motion *in limine*. That's where you get a ruling from the judge before the trial starts, to keep out matters that may be far more unfair than relevant or helpful to the jury."

"What came up, Will?"

"Oh nothing," replied Will, with a big sigh.

"There's something to bring on that humongous sigh."

"Not really. They just went back to my days in the Air Force. And I didn't do a damn thing back then except audit some files."

"What do you mean 'audit some files'?"

"Just what I said," snapped Will.

"You don't have to yell at me. I'm just trying to help," Trish pleaded, tears welling in her eyes.

"Oh darling—I'm sorry," said Will, reaching out to take Trish in his arms, clutching her close, his body shaking. "I just want a clean trial. If the judge grants John's motion, it'll be clean. But that doesn't mean John can win it."

"Think positive, Will. I know John has faith in you. I know he thinks it can be won. He has to have faith in himself or he can't win. Don't cut the ground out from under him with a defeatist attitude," pleaded Trish, giving a rare lecture.

"Trish, I don't think things are going to work out—I'm really scared."

"Honey, don't be so pessimistic . . ."

"Trish," Will interrupted, "no matter what happens I can see into the future enough to do some planning. If I get convicted, I'll never get out and if they were to grant the prosecutor's request for the death sentence, then we can *never ever even see* each other again! Not unless you want to come and watch 'em do me."

"What! Why for God sake?"

"John told me when you're on death row, there's no visiting at Rawlins, except for *immediate* family. I called today, while you were shopping. Only immediate family and once a month. I talked to a man by the name of Austin Blackwell, a major, the head of maximum security."

"Once a month, that's ridiculous!"

"You could visit if we were married. We'd at least be together, not together together. But he said a spouse could visit in a small room with an officer present. Get this, one hug and one kiss at the start and one hug and one kiss at the end! He said they're flexible on the once a month rule if there're no problems. Only one other guy's in there now and he's been there some twelve years!"

"How long?" Trish asked with a grin.

"Twelve years."

"No, I mean the kiss."

"I doubt long enough! Anyway, their policy is a lot more open than most places. In maximum at Marquette, we'd be on a phone and talking through the glass. Zero hugs and zero kisses!"

"Then let's get married!"

"Do you mean it?"

"No,—of course I mean it!"

"I was going to ask, but I think I was afraid you'd say no."

"Oh, Will, I love you so much. Don't you know that? What do we have to do?"

"I called the county clerk's office. A lady said there's no waiting period, but you'd have to be tested for Rubella and have an RH test. That is, unless you're over forty-five or have a statement from a doctor that you can't have children . . ."

"Well, I'm not and I can!" Trish exclaimed.

"The Sheriff would have to grant permission—I didn't tell her I was out on bail—and the District Judge would have to write a letter authorizing the Clerk to issue a license. John's cleared it all along the line."

"How long did all of this planning take?"

"Just an average shopping trip, Trish!" Tears again became Will's contact lens. "Oh darling, I'm scared."

"We've got lots of time before the trial, so let's arrange it. Come on, let's go to bed. I believe this needs consummating!"

————

"I'm sorry, honey. That's never happened to me before," said Will, with a long sad sigh.

"Oh, heaven, don't worry about it! We've got lots of time, darling."

"I hope so. I guess my mind's on that new procedure. Maybe they'll find me not-guilty and then we can really celebrate!"

"That would be nice. I'm confident they will."

"You know, Trish, it's about time they came up with something like PREP. I'm opposed to the death sentence, but where they have it, the delays are ridiculous. Gacey was convicted of the torture and murder of those thirty-three young men and he's been on death row nearly twelve years!"

"That's sheer nonsense! That is not *justice!*"

"I guess you're right. In *Magna Carta*, King John agreed '. . . to none will we sell, to none will we deny, *or delay*, right or justice'. Perhaps delaying justice is as bad for the victim's family, and society, as it is for a defendant waiting for trial."

"Well, that's certainly how I feel about it. But, I'm not worried. John will win this one. Just hold me close, honey." And, with a slight tremble— her expressed optimism, a fragile shield for a deeper fear—she snuggled against her fiancee.

Time raced with fate.

————

9

Trial

'for the odds are better in mortal combat than the defendant's in a murder trial'.

M.W.

Monday, October 14, 1991
Ninth Judicial District Court

Filled with apprehension and foreboding of a dreadful time to come, Will sat waiting for Judge Waters to enter the crowded courtroom. Seated to the left of his attorney in a unique role, he stared across the room at the empty, but soon to be filled, red upholstered chairs in the jury box. The ultra modern courtroom, central in the new county-building complex, was filled to capacity behind the 'bar' with prospective jurors. Directly behind him sat his new wife and two of his five children.

To his right, at the table nearest the jury box—they had the burden of proof—sat Prosecutor Reising, Investigator Beckwourth and an assistant prosecutor. The young Jason Cogswell, filled with the thrill of pending battle, looked forward to his first capital case with the zeal of youth, confident in his team's ability. After all, wasn't this courthouse built on the very site of the old courthouse that sat the only jury ever to convict Robert Leroy Parker, alias Butch Cassidy, of a crime? Jason's inexperience rendered him totally unaware of how often life or death could be decided by little quirks of fate, in or out of court. The court clerk, seated at her desk in front of Will; the Court Reporter, Al Bernstein, in the center immediately in front of the bench; and the empty witness chair to the right of the bench, as one faced the bench, completed center stage. To Will's left sat co-counsel, Richard Jensen and to the left of him, Jennifer Stevens, law clerk.

The door to the left of the bench, directly opposite Will, opened and out of years of sheer habit, Will stood up, waiting with trust. For he knew from her reputation and earlier court hearings, that the tall, proud woman approaching, who wore her beautiful grey hair as a regal crown of experience, would guarantee him a fair trial.

"All rise," the Court Bailiff ordered in a stern, loud voice, and with a hard bang of his gavel, began the traditional call to order. "Hear ye, hear ye, hear ye, the Ninth Judicial District Court for Fremont County is now in session, the Honorable Vivian Waters presiding. Be seated."

"Ladies and Gentlemen," the Judge began in a soft, yet filled with strength voice, "I wish to welcome you as prospective jurors to the Ninth Judicial District Court for Fremont County. My name is Vivian Waters and I will be conducting this trial. You may hear me referred to as 'Her Honor' or as 'The Court'. Any other names I may or may not be called are usually kept private." A few muffled snickers were quickly suppressed and not noted, though heard by the Court.

"I would like to say at the outset that we all understand this is a most serious, no, *the most serious* occasion a person can face. From earlier pre-trial matters I also know that Mr. Dean, the defendant in these proceedings, has not lost his sense of humor. He would rather have these proceedings go forward in a natural way and knows that the spectrum of emotions are what make us human, no matter the circumstances."

That's sure a personal touch a defendant's rarely blessed with. If it's not a level field, it's not tilted my way, thought the prosecutor to himself.

"As I am certain you are all aware, the case those of you who are chosen will be asked to decide is *The People of the State of Wyoming-versus-Will Dean*. Mr. Dean, would you please stand and face the jury panel."

Rising and turning to the panel from which the jury would be selected, as he often had in a far different role, Will smiled as best he could and in a barely audible voice murmured, "Good morning."

"Thank you," said Judge Waters and continued. "I am sure most of you have read about the camp-incident, but I am equally certain only those at the scene are able to tell what they saw happen. I make this statement to you at this time because I have been formally notified that the defendant is going to take the stand and testify as to the events he observed.

"Both counsel have informed me they would rather have this matter heard in this venue, the jurisdiction where it happened, than somewhere else. Both attorneys and Mr. Dean would prefer to have jurors who have read about the incident than a jury made up of people who cannot read or do not read. So without further comment we will begin the jury selection process. Madam Clerk, will you please call the first prospective juror."

The process began.

As it had since 1215, A.D., decided by battle on a small meadow on the south bank of the *River Thames,* three miles downstream from Windsor Castle, at a place called *Runnymede,* the Anglo-Saxon system of the common-law selected as best it could in keeping with changing societal standards, a jury of fourteen peers. The jury, with two alternates to be removed by chance prior to their final deliberation, would decide the fate of Will Dean and was to the surprise and satisfaction of all, promptly seated.

With both sides well prepared, witnesses on stand-by and the Court uninterrupted by collateral matters, the trial proceeded at a smooth and rapid pace.

The Prosecutor would present the State's case against Will Dean with strict and good faith loyalty to the rules of the system.

The defense team, with equal good faith and dedication, would likewise cross-examine the prosecution witnesses and present the defense. All *available* evidence relevant to the issue—'did Will Dean kill Lee Mackintosh in pre-meditated cold-blood?'—would be produced, received by the Court and sub-mitted to the jury. It would be a clean and a fair trial.

The court, following the end of testimony and after the attorneys' final summations would, without unfair emphasis on any point, instruct the jury on the law involved that they had a duty to follow in deciding the case.

The jurors, as was their duty, would decide which facts were true based upon properly admitted evidence, apply the law as given to them by the court and reach a decision.

The umbilical cord, the precious supply line of the miraculous system that passed the genetic blue print of all physical characteristics and possibly, the memories of ancient skills, was the line of life that created the defendant. Now, its electronic counter-part would pass all information gleaned from these proceedings as well as the procedures used and conduct of the parties, to de-termine after detailed scrutiny, if there was compliance with the accumulated wisdom of hundreds of years of Anglo-Saxon Judaic-Christian standards of 'due process of law'.

Should it be decided the standard had been met, then this umbilical cord would be the electronic supply line to convey the ideas and concepts that in one-hundred and twenty days might terminate Will Dean's existence on planet Earth.

Ready for the seriousness of the charge against the defendant and the intensity of the proceedings at hand, Al Bernstein, the official court reporter, sat ready with the absolute latest in technology at his fingertips. The 'courtroom of the future', they called it, but in fact it had been installed and working well in Judge Waters courtroom for almost three months.

As the testimony began, Al's fingers moved to the beat of the spoken word, endlessly striking the keys in steno code. As if by magic the words were translated to the English text and appeared on the Toshiba 3200SX laptop. The umbilical cable joined the computer steno, proceeding word by word, second by second. As the pages were completed on screen, Al's scopist set the laser printer in motion.

In a small room, far from the main courtroom, the printer resumed its daily task of generating verbatim testimony so the team of lawyers, paralegals, and investigators could begin devouring the transcript. Now came requests to create litigation support diskettes of testimony, that the legal team could insert in their computers for swift, accurate, search and retrieval of all proceedings. Orders came in for ASC II, Discover ZX, Catlinks; on it rolled.

The next step incorporated real-time translation with video, where Smart-Writer and Toshiba laptop were serially cabled to a PC-VCR, and then, not only the word, but video and voice became synchronized for instant identification and cross-indexing.

Al sits for a moment, his fingers still, as the Judge ponders her ruling on the latest objection—his thoughts drifting to the scribes of ancient Egypt and their methodical way of recording the spoken word. Never ceasing to look with awe and wonder at his high-tech surroundings, he waits.

The Judge explains her reasons—for the record—and overrules the objection. The trial rolls on . . . .

There are throughout the country—on every working day and occasionally on Saturdays—trials in progress where the proceedings go forward with the smooth precision of a fine Swiss watch. Those ordinary cases out of the scrutiny of mass media, where, the participants are, as common decency and the canons of ethics require, seeking to find—in an imperfect system—the truth.

Trials where honest, hard working detectives and investigators follow every lead and report their findings to each side; where both adversaries are thoroughly prepared and follow the rules of evidence; where the court properly instructs the jury on the laws of the jurisdiction, and does not, by subtle leanings, often subconscious, attempt to influence or steer the outcome.

And the—JURY—the collective conscience of the community; proven time and time and time again to possess an insight and understanding of the forces that make ordinary people tick. The collective judgment that defines the duties and responsibilities of a 'reasonable person' under the circumstances and situation of the event in question. Not perfect—of this world and not the heavens—yet in most cases, no defendant would want a different method.

The unheralded—the ordinary—the empty courtroom—the slow methodical not to compete with the choreography of a daytime soap opera, but where on rare occasions—the drama—the emotion—may reach a level of intensity such that breathing is held in abeyance. Where all eyes and ears are riveted on the witness—days or weeks of foreplay building to a climax—a point where every heart—every fiber of their bodies and even the souls of those who care—know that the answer—sincerely and honestly spoken will dictate the outcome—even if the answer is, in fact and truth, wrong.

Linda Caldwell, the outfitter's pregnant wife, having been ruled a 'hostile witness' due to her close friendship to Will, entitled the Prosecutor to ask in culmination of her description of the entire incident, a leading question and he did. "Witness, at any time during this entire tragedy, did you see any actions by, or hear any words or sounds from Lee Mackintosh—*which at that time—*you interpreted to be threatening to anyone in camp or toward Mr. Dean?"

All breathing stopped. Cotton fiber attempting to form dust balls lay silent. It was as if this tiny portion of the universe froze in place. With tears streaming down her cheeks and unable to look at Will, softly, yet in one syllable to be heard by all, air pushed from her lungs through her larynx, was formed in a whisper by her lips and tongue to crash with the force of a cannon against the eardrums of all in attendance.

"No."

Silence reigned supreme as the Prosecutor, careful not to break the moment, quietly took his seat.

The verdict was sealed. Quirks of fate.

Friday, October 18, 1991

Will and John Vickers sat in solemn silence in the attorney conference room of the Fremont County jail. Convicted of murder in the first-degree, Will's bail and the tether-program were immediately canceled and he was remanded to the custody of the Sheriff to await the sentencing hearing scheduled to begin the following Monday.

"John, now what?" asked Will in a subdued voice, his world shattered by events completely beyond his control.

"Well, under Wyoming law, evidence can be brought in which can be used to mitigate the offense. The trouble is, all of the circumstances anyone knows about were brought out at trial. Both sides can introduce just about anything. Except, the Prosecutor can't introduce anything negative about you or your past that makes you look bad, unless we were advised of it prior to the trial. Character witnesses, past good deeds, things like that can be brought up."

"Oh that's just great," laughed Will, his sense of humor wounded, but still alive. "Why don't you tell the jury about all of the people I've defended who various Michigan prosecutors were trying to lock up and the juries refused to find guilty over the last twenty-six years. Let's see, how about a few drug cases, two or three wife beaters, a couple of rapes, toss in a couple of murders, and then for good measure a bunch of drunk drivers! They'd hang me, draw me, quarter me and put my head on a stake in the middle of the town square!"

"Good God, Will. How can you joke at a time like this?" John laughed, in spite of himself.

"Hell, John, what else is there? Do you think you can smuggle Trish in here?" asked Will in reply. "Or at Rawlins?"

"I guess not," John answered. "We might as well get started and see what we can come up with."

4:00 P.M., Wednesday
October 23, 1991
Fremont County Courthouse

Prisoners to the final courtroom scene, they sat waiting the Jurors' decision. A courtesy extended to the defendant allowed him to remain in the Courtroom with his counsel, family and friends. The Deputy, seated discretely to the side, remained an ever-present talisman of Dean's prisoner status.

"John," Will began, "we both know what the recommendation is going to be, we can feel it. You've been around the block enough and I've strolled it a bit myself. They're not going to come back with a recommendation of community service!"

A deep sigh confirmed John's agreement in spite of his reply, "Oh, I don't know, Will. We both know better'n to predict what a given jury'll do."

"John—John, sometimes it's written. Just hear me out. This is something I feel very strongly about and I want you to do everything you can to help me. I know you will. Trish and I met with Tim Hutchinson in September, not because of any lack of faith in you or Dick, okay?"

"I know, Will. What about?"

"There are some things I want and thanks to those Thomas hearings in Washington, the media has left us alone so far. But, if I'm going to be executed, and it's a quiet news week, they'll swarm to Cheyenne and Rawlins along with both sides of the death sentence groupies like flies on a dead dog!"

"You're probably right."

"John, I want to be executed by a firing squad and at Dead Horse Lake like a human being, not in a back room or on some doctor's hospital slab. Tim said the Governor's a decent sort and all it would take would be a rider on that popular, Bighorn Preservation Bill. Tim knows Ben Crabtree, the rancher who made the big donation to the Highway Patrol for their helicopters. Crabtree believes that if the Highway Patrol would've had the choppers, his daughter might've been saved. He said Crabtree thinks the indictment was a bunch of crap. Tim said Ben now blames the Department of Interior for the spread of *brucellosis* east of the Divide, that he claims has hit his herd and is causing his cows to abort. Tim thinks Crabtree would put in a word with the Governor to see if it could be granted and to hell with Interior."

"Well," John replied, "perhaps it can be done and I'll sure do everything I can. You know that."

"Yes," said Will, with a smile. "You guys, and Jennifer, did one hellofa job. I'll tell you something, John, that I haven't said anything about before. The prosecutor back home is a friend of mine. We've always gotten along, even on opposite sides. He'd gone over all the evidence used before the Grand Jury. Told me he'd beat me on the facts on this one. Sometimes, in spite of lawyers, the evidence does decide the issue!"

"I guess you're right," sighed John, in agreement.

"*If* they give me a choice, and *if* it can be at Dead Horse Lake, then Tim will fly my body to Ogden and my ashes back to Riverton so my family can catch the early flight to Denver. If it can all go down that way and the media can be kept away from Trish and my kids, at least until they can control the situation, I'd be happy. If there's a spirit out there to be happy!"

"Will, here comes the bailiff. The Judge'll be sending 'em home until tomorrow morning."

"All rise," the Bailiff ordered.

Thursday, October 24, 1991
Ninth Judicial District Court

Helen Malenkowski, the elected Foreman of the sentencing hearing, spoke up, "You know it seems to me it's really a racial issue."

"How so, Helen?" Thorton Thompson, Foreman of the trial jury asked. "They're both Scots. That came out in the background profile at the hearing."

"Well, stop and think about it," she replied. "Isn't that what we've been talking about? Showing the country it isn't just poor people or the Blacks, Indians and Mexicans who have to worry about the death sentence? You know, Hopkinson's been on death-row twelve years and he hasn't had to answer yet. None of us seem to really want to see Dean die, but we're all afraid to let him live! Basically because of racial injustices done in the past and what we're afraid will be done in the future."

"Helen, I think we can all agree with what you're saying. But you know, there's a verse in the Bible that this case brings to mind from the Song of Solomon or maybe it's a Proverb. I think it goes 'woe unto them that call evil good, and good evil'. But maybe I can deal with this if we just stick to the facts and the court's instructions on the law. It's the only way I'll ever be able to sleep and no matter what we do, this case will always haunt me," Tony sighed, "because I really wanted to believe Dean."

"Can you believe the Prosecutor being able to get Dean to admit the Lone Ranger was his hero and he never killed anyone—always brought 'em to the 'bar of justice'!" exclaimed Tom.

"Yes," Helen replied. "And the defense was just as good. Bringing in a retired Judge who Dean had testified against, to say Dean's reputation was to go by the rules."

"You know," Henry interjected into the discussion, "our state stands for equal rights, that's our motto and really in a larger sense everything we stand for, not just women's rights. It seems to me it's part of our belief in capital punishment. If you take someone's life who had an equal right to live, or at least to have a fair trial, then you forfeit your right to live. It isn't an eye for an eye revenge philosophy. But more like everyone has an equal right to live. And as part of that, there's an equal responsibility that you just can't take another person's life! If you do, and it's first-degree murder, then you must pay. I don't think of it as a deterrent, or even as justice being carried out. It seems more like it's just there. Do you know what I mean? It's hard to describe, but it's just there. You have to accept responsibility for taking another person's life. And that's my speech."

Candy spoke up, "We all accept the death sentence, that was in our questioning by the prosecutor. We all found Dean guilty based on the evidence. Or, in this case, because of the lack of evidence to support his defense. We swore to do our duty and that's hard sometimes. Just think of that poor soldier, Manuel, they buried over in Gillette this summer. He was killed in Iraq doing his duty and by friendly fire at that! We all know Lee had a right to his day in court. We've been over it and over it. And we all know Dean has to answer for what he did. If he'd said he didn't remember what'd happened, we would've found him not guilty. Or at least, only of second-degree. Or maybe even manslaughter, but I didn't mean to lecture."

"Candy, other than a few words now and then, that's your first speech!" Thorton smiled. "And you're absolutely right. I think we all know what our duty is. If there'd been just one goddamn shred of evidence this was planned, or that the three of 'em had done something bad before, or that Mackintosh ever had any skill or special training in karate."

Thorton continued, "I think the one expert, the psychiatrist, laid it out best. Remember, he said, '. . . I listened to Dean's description of the crucial moment. Dean testified he saw Lee's eyes—the pupils of his eyes—dilate. He knew he'd been had. Well, that *story* would justify his acting in self-defense, but in my opinion, as an MD and psychiatrist, for Lee's eyes to dilate like Dean described, Lee *would have to know* he could beat Dean. And for Lee to *actually know that as a fact,* he would have to be an expert with *actual experience* in this type of combat and in this situation . . .'. That is right out of his transcript.

"The prosecution then showed, virtually proved the negative. First, that Lee was completely unknown in the karate field in Canada and Mexico as well as in the United States. And secondly, Lee'd never held a passport to go where he could get that level of training. And third, he'd never had any highly specialized military training. We all accepted that Gerlach was probably the instigator. And according to the evidence, all the bad things that were done, were done by him or Lee's brother. If Dean had just said he lost it and shot him. But no, it had to be a complicated story of self-defense that we just had absolutely no evidence to support. In fact, just the opposite! Like I said at the start of this speech, if there'd been just one goddamn shred of evidence for Dean's defense."

Helen stood up and looked around the table at the other eleven members, "Thorton, that's the first time in thirty years I've ever heard you swear! Lee had a right to his day in Court. We all know it. And we know what our *duty* is. Our sworn oath. This is not a vigilante state. It's not the frontier like it was for Jake Spoon in *Lonesome Dove*. They had no choice but to hang Jake. Dean had a choice. He could've brought Lee in and maybe Lee would have been convicted and maybe he would have been acquitted. *But it would have been a jury*, not a cold-blooded execution. We found Dean guilty and have we heard anything from either side that really makes any difference? We never believed or heard anything bad about Dean. We assumed he was a good person, a good father, had all the normal human strengths and weaknesses. But does that really change anything? We heard and tried the case over the facts in evidence, on what happened on the morning of the fourth day of their camp. That's what this trial was all about.

"You know," the Foreman continued, "we really do represent the rule of law. I've never forgotten the motto on the old Territorial seal, *Cedant Arma Togae*, 'force must yield to law'. Does anyone want to add anything?" As they all shook their heads no, Helen softly and with a deep sigh requested what they all dreaded, "Let's vote then and get it over with. Waiting has got to be hell on earth for Will Dean and his loved ones."

4:25 P.M. Thursday

As they had at the close of trial, a somber jury returned to the courtroom following nearly a day and a half of sincere and serious deliberations.

The people in the courtroom—all one-hundred and twenty seats filled with family, friends, the staffs of both legal teams, many local citizens, numerous courthouse personnel and a few members of the press—resumed their seats and waited in silence. Only Will could hear the hammering of his heart. He had seen the faces before, he did not need to hear the words. I have had a good life he thought.

In a soft voice—emotion filtered through her sad awareness of what the answer would be—the Court spoke, "Ladies and gentlemen, have you decided upon your recommendation, and if so, will the jury Foreman please declare it to the Court?"

With all eyes on the jury and all jurors' eyes on their laps, Helen Malenkowski, juror number five counting to the right from the far end and seated in the back row of the jury box, located to the left of Judge Waters, looked up and slowly raised her right hand. Well-dressed and in her mid sixties, her stately bearing conveyed to all present an awareness she had been in charge of a deliberation that could not have been conducted with more thought or seriousness.

"Juror number five, Madam Foreman Helen Malenkowski, would you please rise. What is the Jury's recommendation to the Court?"

"Your Honor, it is the Jury's recommendation that the Defendant, Will Dean, receives the penalty of death."

There would be no outburst in this Courtroom, the rules of conduct had been well established prior to the trial; the hush of agony punctured only by a few gut wrenching sobs of those closest to the defendant.

"Members of the Jury," the Court spoke softly, as the Foreman resumed her seat, to continue the proceedings and rupture the silent hush, "I am required by our rules to poll the Jury. I shall call on each of you by juror number and your name, so please state clearly, 'yes' or 'no' to the following question. Was and is the recommendation delivered by your Foreman, your individual recommendation at this time?"

Will, his outward calm a phoney facade for hidden terror and anger, waited. Gut churning like a swarm of writhing snakes—bile in his mouth—why?—is the final scene deserved? To lose Trish—my children—the quiet time—all I've worked for—why? Why, God? Why?

There are questions that can not be answered, murmured Murphy. Time will tell.

All in the Courtroom sat in silence as one by one, each of the twelve quietly delivered their individual "Yes" answer, that hammered tightly shut with twelve spikes, the coffin's lid.

Like desert flowers following an early spring rain, an acronym called PREP came to life. Tragically long delays frustrated the will of the people in states with capital punishment and shocked the conscience of most people, even in those states that did not choose to have the death sentence.

The fact that the taxpayers were paying the bill for lengthy appeals was not mentioned, but certainly not forgotten. As a result, the Supreme Court of the United States together with a collection of prominent scholars, attorneys of both the defense bar and the Prosecutors' association and selected judges, devised a plan.

Called PREP, its formal name was the Parallel Review and Evaluation Panel and its goal was RED, Rapid Execution of Defendants. Modern technology in court reporting and computer retrieval of information made PREP an alternative to the normal appeal procedures. It was now believed possible to have a rapid execution of the convicted defendant and comply with the constitutional protections of 'due process of law'.

PREP certainly would not be used in all capital punishment cases. It would be called into being only when the Prosecutor or States Attorney involved knew the state would be seeking the death penalty. In all probability this would only be done when there were gross facts or in the case of very strong evidence with a high degree of public attention.

The Panel would consist of six members selected by the Judicial Tenure Commission or similar body of the State where the trial was being held, if the victim and the Defendant were from that state. If the victim was from another state, one panel member had to be from the victim's state of residence. The same right would be given to the Defendant. There would always be at least four from the state where the alleged crime took place.

Since PREP would require multi-state cooperation in certain cases, federal funding was the carrot for compliance. If a citizen involved was from a state that did not have capital punishment, provision was made for payment of actual expenses.

At least one panel member had to be of the Defendant's racial background. If this could not be provided from the legal community, they would be selected from civic organizations whose members had the same racial background and from their cultural community in general.

The panel would be located in an appropriate facility not disclosed to the public and at a different venue than the trial, though within the same state. A review of the Court proceedings would commence on the first Monday following the recommendation of a death sentence. In addition to the standard matters guiding the nation's appellate courts, some juror input was sought, anonymously. The juror questionnaire was designed is such a fashion so it would be simple, to the point and easy to read. The form, when returned in the pre-addressed and machine stamped envelope to PREP, could not be identified to any individual juror.

It asked basic common sense questions that only required a yes-no box to be checked.

Parallel Review Evaluation Panel
—Questionnaire—

1. Did you understand the Judges' instructions?	Yes	No
2. Do you feel the Prosecutor was fair?	Yes	No
3. Did you feel pressured by the Judge?	Yes	No
4. Do you believe the Defense was well prepared?	Yes	No
5. Were you able to see and hear witnesses?	Yes	No
6. Did anything happen during your deliberations you would not want to happen if you or someone you loved was the Defendant?	Yes	No
7. While judging a fellow human being is always difficult, are you satisfied with the verdict given all the facts, law and argument you heard?	Yes	No
8. Was there anything you wanted to know about that was not presented?	Yes	No
9. Did anything happen outside of the Court room that may have swayed your decision?	Yes	No
10. Did the Trial appear to you as fair?	Yes	No

The questions were staggered in such a manner so as to preclude a string of unthinking yes or no answers inconsistent with a conscientious juror. With twelve jurors in deliberation, a perfect trial score would be seventy-two yes boxes checked to questions one, two, four, five, seven and ten; and forty-eight no boxes checked to questions three, six, eight and nine.

On the basis of the juror PREP questionnaires, Will Dean had a perfect trial.

The same basic format was used for juror input on the sentence recommendation hearing; the result, the same.

———————

10

'unwelcome solitude'

Tuesday, December 3, 1991
Wyoming State Penitentiary
Rawlins, Wyoming

Completed in 1980 and located south of the city of Rawlins, the Wyoming State Penitentiary was one of the most modern prisons in the United States. Remote from urban sprawl, it's domain was at the end of a southbound exit from Interstate 80 on some of the most barren land in North America. And, unless the jackrabbits and coyotes could pay taxes, the property, with no oil or other known commodity of value beneath its surface, was as totally worthless and without beauty as land could be. Could it be found, shifting sand would be a scenic wonder.

As such, it was an ideal locale to serve as the site for the state's main prison and maximum security cell block. In the unlikely event of an escape, the unfortunate soul would be an easy target—day or night—for any of the posted security guards.

Following the Court's entry of Judgment on the jury's recommendation, Will had been immediately transferred to maximum security. Allowed one monthly visit by his new wife, two weeks earlier, he looked forward to his pending visit. He knew Trish would know where to find him.

Escape, or any attempt, was the last thing on Will Dean's mind. It was not in his character—since right or wrong—he still believed in the system. The visiting area, as was the lethal injection room, was as modern and efficient as money could design. In hope of preserving the family, the Wyoming Department of Corrections provided facilities and allowed conjugal visitation, except on death row, between married couples. The philosophy, while acknowledging the need for certainty of punishment, was to promote rehabilitation and return to productive society, as quickly as possible, all they could.

Warden Blyth Steward, was a fair and considerate administrator. He had earlier approved biweekly visits under watch of the security guard, whose eyes were far more lingering on Trish than her convicted husband. One firm hug and a warm kiss, passion clouded by the agony of pending doom, began the visit.

The concept of lethal injection, was, for Will, a punishment worse than death itself. Four major surgeries on his wrists had left him with a morbid phobia that would strike terror in his heart. To go out this way would not be his choice, if choice he could have. Without much to smile about, the look on Trish's face immediately conveyed to Will there was some good news, however slight.

"Will, Governor Deloney had a choice of execution method rider attached to the Bighorn Watershed Bill and it went through without a hitch. John said he'd heard one legislator had raised an objection because of all the money spent on the facility. But the speaker just shrugged his shoulder with a so what and called the question. It became effective immediately and gives a choice—firing squad or lethal injection. John said the Governor wouldn't have Wyoming put anyone through the horror of gas or by an electrocution. And they didn't have anyone qualified to carry out a humane hanging."

"Trish, if there's good news at a time like this, that's good. So let's keep this all in perspective, honey. We've had some wonderful times together and that's sure something in this frantic world. I've had a good life and my children are healthy. When I think of the accidents of clients and the endless suffering of innocent children, I'm fortunate. I'd just like to be strong enough to keep my dignity—my head up. To look at the heavens. Not down in fear, looking where all the mud and dog shit is."

"We'll all be with you if it happens, but it isn't over yet. John said the prosecutor is following the American Bar's standard for disclosure of information that might be helpful to you, or even might lead to something. John and Investigator Strong are still digging. Strong for some reason—I don't know—is like a driven man. He flew to Hartford at his expense and talked to people at Colt. He went down to Taos because of a restaurant napkin they found in the pickup. Will, he's doing his damnedest and maybe he'll come up with something. By the way, Linda sends her best. She really believes you, Will. She just had to answer that damn question truthfully. You can understand, don't you?"

"Of course, honey. It went down just the way she testified. She didn't say Lee didn't kick. She said she put her head down and then heard the shot. It was that—no special training—no passport—no karate schools—and the medical experts that led to the verdict. That, and maybe my own testimony. This has had such an effect on me. I don't know. Maybe I just wasn't believable. I felt tired, wrung out. I don't know, resigned," Will sighed.

"Boy, that medical expert, that damn pathologist Fred Robinson and his 'I'm a doctor and how can I be wrong attitude'. Damn he made me angry! How could he say Lee was stationary when the bullet hit him?" asked Trish.

"Qualified experts are allowed to give opinions and that was his opinion. Don't forget, the karate expert gave his opinion the kick could be developed and the torso might stay squared at the start of the kick. It was just if

Lee'd had the ability, he would've been known in the karate community, if he was trained in North America. And don't forget, Beckwourth was honest, and Reising more than fair. He gave us Strong, and didn't use smoke and mirrors. But most importantly, he didn't beat on a distant drum. What about Dead Horse?"

"Oh, right. John said the Governor would not even discuss it. He said the Governor wanted to wait and see if everything was confirmed by PREP and to get back to him by the middle of February. He didn't close the door."

"What about Ogden?"

"Do you really want me to fly over to Ogden and visit a crematory? That's going to be a little difficult for me to do," Trish declared, her face drawn and sad. Would she ever again be able to wrap her body around her condemned husband, she thought, tears welling in her eyes.

"You said Hutchinson was willing to fly you over. It's just that I'd like to know about it—what happens—how long it takes. You could tell me all about his plane. Maybe it won't happen. But if it does, I'd just like to have everything taken care of. You and the kids out of here—away from the media. Maybe they won't be around. Who'll give a shit if I get popped anyway? God, just think of all the lawyer jokes out of this!"

"Stop it, Will, or I'll go. My time is up anyway. I'll see you in two weeks, honey." Quickly she gave him a firm hug and a kiss and turning, with tear filled eyes, fled from the hated room.

December 18, 1991
Longhorn Saloon
Pinedale, Wyoming

Steve Strong, a third generation resident of Wyoming, was a dedicated member of Wyoming's Division of Criminal Investigation. He supported the concept of the death sentence for first degree murder, but was even more dedicated to the concept that it should not be applied if there was any reasonable chance the person did not commit the murder or there was a valid defense to the act.

He was most mindful and sensitive to the role played by his grandfather in the Horn incident. His grandfather had always maintained Horn was innocent of the murder of young Jimmy Nolt. The execution of Tom Horn by the State of Wyoming in 1903, was not without controversy. There could be no doubt that the circumstances surrounding the case were less than clear and he did not want another such controversy to occur on his beat. If anything could be found to support Dean's defense, he would continue his search, at least until the execution.

"Hi, Steve," said Betty Lou, with a big smile in greeting. "What brings you to this neck of the woods?"

"You, of course. You know that!" he exclaimed.

"Bullshit—don't you bullshit me, you hunk you. Your old lady would have to be planted for five years and you know it! Come on, what gives? Some coffee?"

"Sure. Sounds good."

"At the round table?" she questioned with a grin, knowing he'd sit at the opposite end of the empty bar.

"It's the Dean case, Betty," Strong sighed.

"That's right. They're going to put him to sleep in a few weeks aren't they? Christ, Hopkinson's been waiting twelve years and Dean gets it in four months!" she exclaimed.

"Yeah, the end of February if everything's affirmed. Unless the Governor commutes, and all the smart money is he won't. Shit, they're even giving odds down in Vegas. I think that's sick."

"Well, they convicted him, that's history. But, why are you here, Steve? You usually head south for a couple of weeks, this time of year."

"Oh, I was just hoping that you'd be able to remember something you forgot to tell Beckwourth or me. Something that might help Dean. Can you think of anything at all?"

"Wait, Steve," she replied, "let me go and get the notes I jotted down for Beckwourth. You know, I didn't want to get involved, because I really liked Lee and John. But then that other bastard, and what John and Troy—I mean Guy—did, I guess I couldn't blame Dean. It's too bad they didn't have any evidence to support him. His execution won't bring Lee back. Oh well," she sighed, "like they all said afterward, 'it was our duty'. Back in a minute."

Waiting, Steve's mind went back to the haunting photo of Tom Horn hanging from the scaffold in Cheyenne and his grandfather's role. If it's wrong, I hope I can stop it, he thought.

"Here," said Betty, returning to the table and sitting down, "let me glance over these. You know, there was something they told me that I just can't remember, but I know it's there. Damn. You know, I wasn't real relaxed when Beckwourth threatened Ken's license. Wait, they said they were camped in the Pinon area, but there was something else."

"We went over the Pinon with a fine-tooth comb. We must've checked out every damn trail and possible camp site there was. Nothing!"

"Wait, I've got it! John said Lee wanted to climb some mountains up in that area and one was a name I should remember. I'm not a native here, Steve, help me out."

"Well there's Union, Sheep, Gypsum, Flat Top, Osborn . . ."

"Wait, I think I've got it! Johnny Horton's song, *Sink The Bismarck*. Is there a Bismarck?"

"That's it, Lou!" Steve excitedly exclaimed. "That's it! 'The biggest battleship that ever sailed the sea'! You've got it, kid! Battleship Mountain! It's a beautiful mountain just south of Gypsum Creek, near the headwaters of South Fork. Both areas would be great places to camp if you wanted to ride horses up there. It'd be a damn tough hike though. That's not going to help Will now, Betty. The area has too much snow cover this time of year. I'll go up and nose around, but I doubt I'd find anything until spring. What I was more interested in than where they were, is if you can think of anything about Lee? His mannerism, anything at all that you might've left out or overlooked?"

"One thing, I don't remember if I told Beckwourth or not. Did you know about the run-in Lee had with that clod, the Hanson bully?" she asked.

"No," Steve replied. "What happened?"

"It was last November—no—it had to be a year ago last November, in '90. Somehow they must've bumped into each other by accident. At least it would've been an accident on Lee's part. Well, 'Bully' Hanson called Lee down on it, gave him a shove on both shoulders and pushed Lee against the bar."

"What happened?"

"Lee refused to fight. He just kept his hands down at his sides. I think a lot of the guys thought he was a coward, maybe even a queer. Since he never will—you know." A smile and a nod confirmed the unspoken meaning. "Anyway, I didn't read him that way, because there was something in his eyes I can't describe, but it was something I've never seen before. Just a cold, intense, piercing, burning, something that told me Lee was not afraid of anything. Bully called him a 'fucking faggot', but Lee didn't even blink. It was kind of like his face turned to stone."

"Whew!" Strong exclaimed. "I wish we could back that up. Damn! Not fighting or not arguing doesn't mean your afraid or dumb. There wasn't a shred of evidence he had any special training at all. I'm still working on it. And, I'm going to stay on it until, well, until it's over," he said with a sigh, his voice dropping. "Here's my card. If you think or hear of anything call me collect, okay?"

"Sure, Steve. I won't forget," she said, smiling as she gave him a hug and a quick kiss on the cheek.

"See ya," said Steve, with a smile, and walking out the door, exchanged the dark saloon for the brilliant, crystal-clear winter afternoon sunlight. Maybe there's something up on that mountain, he thought, climbing into his GMC 'Jimmy' 4 x 4, heading for Cora and the Bridger National Forest. For three days his winter search proved only that cold is not warm.

Tuesday, January 28, 1992

"Hi, honey!" Will exclaimed, as he reached out to give his wife the first half of their now weekly allotment of two hugs and two kisses. The seconds passed all too quickly and there was no point in a public display, if only before the security guard.

Sergeant Santos—by now familiar with the couple's tragic plight and secure in the knowledge they would cause no trouble—averted his eyes to allow them, at least in his mind, a moment of private solitude.

"How was your drive down, Trish?"

"Oh the usual, the wind up toward Muddy Gap was blowing out of the west. It's difficult to hold the van on the road. There's a sign up there the highway department has got all wrong."

"What's that, honey?"

"It says 'High Winds Possible'. I have never yet driven across Wyoming without it blowing hard. It should read 'Probable'!" exclaimed Trish.

"Well," said Will, his voice quiet and with no touch of his usual humor, "I guess your right."

"Will, everyone around here seems a little subdued—sad even. What happened? I've been over to Ogden and haven't been watching the news, or even reading the paper. I am sick and tired of the darn speculation—the pro and con crap. What's up, anyway?"

"Trish, I don't think there's much hope for me," Will replied softly.

"Will, don't. I still think the Governor will grant clemency, even if PREP has confirmed everything. Why are you so pessimistic and down? You always said that PREP would confirm. What is the matter?"

"They did Mark," he answered, his voice quivering as he burst into tears.

"Oh, no! Oh, God! Will—I'm sorry!" Knowing full well the implications to her husband's case, Trish began to shake and cry, collapsing in his arms. He held her tight. Sergeant Santos, aware of the repercussions of the Hopkinson case, did not count it as a hug. As the couple wept in silent agony, Santos himself could not help but understand their deep and not unfounded grief.

The Governor would not intervene and put himself between the jury, the appellate courts and the laws of Wyoming to stop the execution. Hopkinson, at the time of the killing, was in jail. In his jury trial, he had been convicted on circumstantial evidence of conspiracy to commit murder in a cold-blooded torture killing. The fact that the actual killers had not been arrested nor given testimony, along with the fact that an internationally famous 'top gun' had been appointed special prosecutor in the Jackson Hole trial, troubled many.

In the end however, and while still asserting his innocence, Mark Hopkinson, on January 25, 1992, became the first person executed by the State of Wyoming since 1965. At least Dean did shoot Lee Mackintosh, thought Santos, and the second time in his lifetime, a lot like adultery, would probably be easier than the first.

"Trish—Trish—Trish, honey," said Will, breaking the silence, "it isn't going to change anything. I've always felt it was going to happen. So tell me, how was the flight? What kind of an airplane does Tim have?"

Wiping her eyes and blowing her nose as she struggled for composure, Trish began, "The flight was very smooth and everything went without a hitch. Let me look at my notes. Okay, his plane is a Beechcraft B36TC. I think he said that meant turbo-charged, with a low wing and retractable tricycle gear. It's white, with brown and gold stripes. The inside is white and it was a lot quieter than I ever expected. He even let me fly it for awhile!"

"How fast does it go?"

"I think he said it can cruise at around two hundred and thirty miles an hour. We flew from Hunt field out over South Pass, which is a little south of a straight line and then southwest to Ogden."

"Why didn't you fly straight to Ogden?"

"Tim said we were too close to the mountains and it would take longer to climb above the peaks, which are over thirteen thousand feet. We could cut over the pass at eight thousand feet much quicker. When we came back we flew straight from Ogden to Riverton and then back to Hunt Field. The mountains are very beautiful. Everything was snow covered, but it was a beautiful, dazzling sight," Trish stopped when she realized that Will was crying. It was a sight he would never see, unless a miracle happened.

"Tell me about cremation, Trish, I want to know," Will softly requested.

"Let me look at my notes. Okay, it's an I.E.E. high-temperature refractory, natural-gas oven . . .," her voice breaking, she paused and caught her breath. "They'll put the body in a cardboard burn-box and I think it goes in on cardboard rollers. The unit is just a huge box-shaped oven with a stainless steel front and a control panel on the right side."

"Did you look inside?"

"Damn it, Will! Yes, I knew you would ask," Trish replied, with an exasperated sigh.

"The chamber is nine feet long, lined with fire bricks and it has a cement floor. The opening is about three feet high," and pausing to look at her notes, caught her breath, "and thirty-three inches wide. I believe he said they can cremate a body with the coffin, but Tim said it was quicker with the cardboard burn-box. There are two gas burners that bring the temperature up to about twenty-six hundred degrees. There is nothing left except a fine gray ash and some of the main bones, like the thigh bones and the skull. They break them up in small pieces."

Again pausing to catch her breath and giving a shudder, she looked at her notes and continued, "They use a crusher to pulverize the bones and the pieces look a lot like the crushed oyster shells they feed chickens. That's what the man said!" she exclaimed.

"What about the gold in my teeth and the metal rods and pins holding my wrists together!" Will laughed, in a weak attempt at graveyard humor.

"He said the temperature is so high the teeth and fillings just vaporize, they're gone," she replied.

"I find that hard to believe! Gold gone? I'll bet!" Will exclaimed. "Well, dental gold nowadays isn't worth anything anyway, unless of course you're paying for it!"

"That's what he said. He said things like steel hip joints and rods are just tossed. Anyway, it takes quite awhile to cool down the oven and if they open it too quickly, hot air would blast out and damage things. I forgot just how long, but I think he said around three hours for the entire process."

"That's about how long my mother said it took me to get born!" said Will, with a feeble laugh.

"How big are the packages of ashes?"

"Let me check my notes. He told me—depending on the size of the bones—they're in a box four by six by eight inches and weigh about eight pounds."

"How much does it cost?"

"Tim said they charge him around two-hundred dollars, but it's included in his fees, since they can only cremate under direction of a licensed funeral director."

"I suppose they don't want people driving around with bodies in the trunks of their cars shopping for discount ovens!" Will laughed, thinking of all the morbid joke possibilities. "Just think, Trish, like some of the shoddy lawyer television commercials. 'You die—we fry', or maybe 'a turnabout's fair play—we grilled a lawyer today'! Or better yet, 'you get the blame—we'll give the flame'! Now that's good!" Will laughed.

"Enough, Will, enough! It's not funny," Trish pleaded.

"Honey, I've only got two options."

After a moment passed and it was clear he wouldn't explain his comment, Trish inquired, "Yes?"

"To laugh or cry, and I'm tired of crying. But I'm afraid it's not over yet. Say, were you able to ask him any questions?"

"Yes, but it was a little morbid."

"What did you ask him?"

"Well, the opening didn't look real big, not anywhere near big enough to accommodate an obese person. So I mentioned it and he said really big people have to be buried."

"Let's see, that ought to be easy—ah—yes, too big around—you go in the ground!" On this one even Trish burst into the welcome relief of laughter and together the couple embraced in a laughing, but uncounted hug, joined in the brief merriment by Sergeant Santos.

"Oh, Will, it isn't settled yet. Just because PREP has affirmed everything, it doesn't mean the Governor won't grant clemency and commute to life," Trish declared, with her customary optimism and 'let's put our best foot forward' attitude.

"Trish, it's not PREP that settles it, Mark settled it. Besides, I absolutely don't want to die, don't doubt that. But even more than absolutely, if there can be more, I don't want to live in a cage. Honey, you'd better go 'cause I'm about to lose it," and reaching out, they clutched each other for the counted, second half, of their weekly allotment.

February 13, 1992
Wyoming Highway Patrol Headquarters
Cheyenne, Wyoming

John Vickers opened the door and slowly entered the Wyoming Highway Patrol conference room, "Gentlemen and Miss," he said, noting with surprise the lone female member, "thank you for letting me meet with you. I'm John Vickers and I guess a couple of you know me. There's no need for introductions unless you want." Pausing to catch his breath and noting they all remained silent, he began, "We know this may be tough on all of you. Mr. Dean said to tell you 'he's just a defense attorney.' The guy still has a sense of humor.

"He's asked for special rifles and when I called to schedule this, Captain McKinnon informed me they'll be set up by your armorer. I delivered Dean's rifle to the Sergeant just a few minutes ago. Dean asked me to read a letter to you, and I'll leave it with the Captain. I'd like to meet with you, Captain, briefly if possible, before I leave." Eye contact and a barely perceptible nod confirmed the Captain's willingness and John continued, "Well, here goes."

To the Captain and Members of the Firing Squad
In the Matter of the Execution of Will Dean

Dear Captain:
   Gentlemen, and Ladies if there be any on this squad in this great state of 'equal rights'; first, let it be known by each of you that my friends, if I still have any, my family, my heirs and I, forgive you for all time.
   If subsequent discoveries bare witness to my asserted defense, that is of no moment to you, for I have requested your assistance in exiting our planet

with dignity. I cannot abide the clinical and physically painless sterility of lethal injection and would be equally terrified of the agony of electrocution or some noxious gas.

To hang like a sack of oats twisting in the wind, my feet turning like a wayward needle on a compass, likewise is not my choice. So thank you, and please grant my wish. I am informed that Sergeant O'Doul can provide some Springfield '03s, which can be loaded quietly.

Captain, I would like you to use my rifle, if you will. You will find it well balanced and true. I have always tried to make clean and quickly-fatal shots when hunting and trust in your skill. My counsel would like to have a private word with you.

Gentlemen, and I apologize in advance to any women among you— actually I hope there are, for they do have steady hands—you should not find it too difficult to shoot a criminal defense attorney, who, upon occasion, has had to rag on police techniques. Remember, I will not be filing any Federal Court complaint for violating my rights! You'll probably be envied by every cop in the country! If that's not enough, pretend you'd just discovered I'd nailed your wife, or worse, your girlfriend!

Please keep your sense of humor through these proceedings and I'll try to keep mine. I've had a good life, and still believe with all my heart in our system. Wyoming gave me a fair trial and that's all any defendant can pray for.

Sincerely,

Will Dean

In spite of the seriousness of their pending and generally distasteful task, the team could not help but break out in laughter at several points during the reading of Dean's correspondence.

"Well, that's it. If this new procedure works, then state law requires that he be executed one hour before sunrise—of course that wasn't followed in the Hopkinson case—that's if there're no delays. It appears as though it's going to happen and if there are no questions, I'll go," John concluded.

There were none and without again being asked, Captain McKinnon rose, walked over, and gave the attorney he had met once before a firm handshake. Together they walked toward the coffee urn and held a private conversation.

Monday, February 17, 1992
Office of Governor John DeLoney
Capitol Avenue and 24th Street
Cheyenne, Wyoming

"John, you're asking an awful lot," Colonel Sheldon Ackels, Commissioner of the Wyoming Highway Patrol declared. "To grant his request would take all three of our choppers and that's a risky place to go. It just seems as though . . ."

"Sheldon, wait, don't forget."

"I know, I know, you did appoint the new Highway Commissioner and he appointed me at your request."

"That's not what I was thinking about, I was thinking about the choppers."

"Oh all right, you also pressured that through. I give up—my job and the choppers!"

"What are friends for?" John laughed. "And, Sheldon, there's another way to look at it."

"How's that, John?"

"Add it up. We were able to use the tether program until after the conviction and Dean paid his own defense fees. PREP has meant he'll only be housed by the Wyoming taxpayers for about four months and there won't be the god-awful appeals and years of imprisonment. What could've cost millions—maybe even as much as the choppers—has been saved. Hell, he's even going to pay for his own cremation! My God, just look at the years and years the Hopkinson case dragged out.

"And, Sheldon, that's just part of it. That old codger, Ben Crabtree, put up half the cost and even with the deal we got on 'em, it was still a three million contribution. Don't forget, he's on a first name basis with every rancher in the state and most of the outfitters. He's hot over the verdict, but understands the jury has spoken. Hell, he and 'Tex' Morrison, the Prosecutor's grandfather, are fishing buddies."

"He's a tough old nut, but he does carry a lot of clout," Sheldon acknowledged.

"Apparently Vickers' co-counsel, Jenson, saved Crabtree's ass with the EPA a while ago and was able to bend his ear. Ben called me the afternoon after my meeting with Vickers, setting out Dean's request."

"Well, John, I guess I was being a little uptight about it. One thing though, I don't want to put our men at any undue risk. If the team's willing, and if the pilots say the trip is safe and the weather's okay, then it'll be a 'go'. Fair enough?"

"Sheldon, I won't risk anyone over a convicted murderer. It's hard to think of Dean as a cold-blooded killer, in spite of the jury verdict. I wish something would've surfaced to support his defense. Listen—make sure we're in direct and constant radio contact both to the warden and to the team captain—right up to the command, okay?"

"Sure, John. By the way, I know how you feel about the death sentence—we've never agreed on that—and how you'd like to grant clemency, in spite of the problems. I'll make sure we're in direct contact, may even go along."

"Thanks, Sheldon. It's not necessary, but I guess there's plenty of room. That's up to you. I'd like to know you're on top of everything, just in case we've got a chance to blow the whistle."

"It's done, I'll go! I'm going over now and meet with McKinnon. I'll want him to educate me on these. Hell, I've never even had a chance to go up in one of the damn contraptions, and hell, I'm the one who wanted 'em for the department! Don't worry, Governor, I know McKinnon and not a whisper of this will get out."

"Thanks. I'm going to grant a couple of Dean's requests and in view of the circumstances, this is one I couldn't agree more with." The two long-time friends shook hands and parted. God, time speeds by sometimes, thought John.

3:00 P.M.
Wyoming Highway Patrol Helipad

Stately cottonwoods lined Warren Avenue, as driving north, the Commissioner soon merged with Central Avenue traffic, passed the Governor's residence at Walker Road, crossed over Interstate 25 and entered the state's new governmental building complex. Sprawled on the northwest edge of Cheyenne, only a five minute drive from the State Capitol, it provided a breath-taking view of sunsets behind the north-south crest line of the distant, snow-covered Laramie Mountains.

The modern, russet and sand colored brick buildings, with their white and pale blue trim, housed the new headquarters of the Wyoming Highway Department, the Wyoming Highway Patrol, and to the north, the Wyoming Game and Fish Department.

Fifty-three hundred Bishop Boulevard was now home-base for one of the three previously owned helicopters purchased through Bell Helicopter Textron, Inc., as part of a three-way transaction with the State of California. With new factory paint of white—with brown and gold accent-strip colors of the University of Wyoming—they were a welcome addition to the Highway Patrol's people-help program.

Ford, and others built cars—Ferrari built the 308 GT; Sikorsky and others built helicopters—Bell built the 222 UT. Fast—sleek—quiet—the twin Lycomming jet turbines with their high pitched whine—quickly ascending through the power curve to liftoff speed, they provided modern-day mobility the Patrol needed for the wide open spaces, often only accessible by horses. The interior, thickly padded with sound absorption material, afforded a quiet environment to conduct business, sleep or as it soon would for Will Dean, to contemplate the finality of his ride; his journey to the edge of the platform.

The view, unobstructed by wings and aided by the sport car slope of the front cockpit, was unparalleled. Never used by the military, they had been the rapid-fire fighting-platform heros of television's *Air Wolf.* They were a favorite of corporate America, air medi-vac units and certainly, of well-heeled police departments.

It was amazing to Sheldon how far helicopters had progressed since that first practical use by the Gannett Newspaper Company of an early Bell, a model 47, in 1947. Coming of age during the Korean War, they greatly improved military mobility, especially that of medical units and rescue operations. Now, in wide use in a variety of corporate, government and private ventures, they would be of great assistance to his department.

The main hangar and helipad was located approximately two blocks northwesterly of Patrol headquarters on a small parcel of land acquired from Warren Air Force Base in exchange for other state land.

Colonel Ackels, while not unique, was one of those rare government employees who felt no need for direct 'good strokes'. He was secure in the knowledge that excellence in performance by individuals to whom he delegated authority, in the end, would be his greatest reward. He was not often disappointed.

Bradley McKinnon, co-captain of the Wyoming Highway Patrols' Special Services Squad and in charge of the newly acquired helicopter fleet, given *carte blanc,* had designed the headquarter facility. Protected by a short berm from the constantly blowing west wind, the sixty by eighty-foot building provided ample space for storage and maintenance. Its long north side was equipped with interlocking sliding doors that allowed for direct towing access to the sixty by sixty-foot concrete helipad. Located a short distance north of the hangar, the helipad was unprotected from the westerlies for a reason. The wind, like it did for the winter grass that fed the country's largest herd of Bighorn sheep at Whiskey Basin, swept the concrete clean.

Entering the facility through the east-end office door, he knew where the chief pilot would be found—a polishing cloth in hand. "Hey, Captain, how's it going?"

"Great, everthing's going great," the officer replied, walking over to meet his boss and giving him a firm handshake. "They're sweet birds!"

"Brad, I guess I need an orientation. But first, a question—full confidence—okay?"

"Certainly," Brad replied. McKinnon, an experienced combat pilot, kept his counsel. Quiet to a point of appearing shy, he was generous and would share without reservation—on a need to know basis—and on his terms. If a pair would win, he would bury a matching pair.

"Brad, the Governor wants to grant Dean's request to be executed at Dead Horse Lake. It's located a little above Simpson. He said he wouldn't grant the request if there was any real risk. I don't want our three choppers to go up there in the middle of the winter for the sake of a damn murderer, even if he did save lives. Can you stop it in good faith?"

"No," Brad replied without hesitation. "Only if we can't fly VFR, or if there happened to be some icing conditions. If it's clear out, there's ample hemispherical illumination, altitude is no problem, fuel and weight would be no problem, and the landing—even in deep powder snow—is no problem."

"How about the icing?"

"That's more likely to be a problem in Michigan or Buffalo, New York, but it's not much of a problem in cold, dry Wyoming!" Brad exclaimed. "In fact, the cold, dry air is the optimum condition for flying since it's heavier, more dense than warm moist air. Even if it doesn't feel that way."

"I'll trust you to call the shots on safety conditions and to organize your team and the mission, but we don't want to go up there if it's not safe."

"I won't, Colonel," the captain declared in a quiet, authoritative tone. "I wouldn't lead a dangerous mission, not under these circumstances, but I want very much to go," he replied, dropping his voice to a whisper.

"Why?" asked the Colonel, somewhat surprised.

"I was there—I flew in, helped bag the bodies and flew Dean and his blinded friend out. It was as bad as it gets, Colonel. Yet I know the jury convicted him and I'll do my duty on the rifle squad, but he deserves to go to Dead Horse."

"Can you fly in to Dead Horse Lake?"

"Oh yes. I took the prosecutor and Beckwourth back up and we checked out both areas. Where Dean spent the night, his ride back, everything. Let him go out in his canyon, Colonel. It's a corner of heaven," the pilot softly pleaded.

"We will, Brad," the Colonel quietly promised, his opposition completely extinguished by his top officer's poignant plea, "and I'm going in with you. Come on and give me a crash course and a flight."

"All right. The engines deliver approximately seven-hundred-fifty shaft horsepower to the rotor and that's the 'Jesus' nut," Brad declared, pointing to a large nut located on the rotor drive shaft.

"Why do you call it that?"

"It's what you scream when you're flying along and the rotor comes off! 'Jesus! I forgot to check the nut!' And then of course you crash!" he laughed.

The two hour indoctrination course in the details of the Bell and thrill of helicopter maneuverability ended as the 222 UT slowly settled to the heli-pad. Following the mandatory two minute cool-down period at idle, the rotor came to a stop and the two men exited the aircraft. Their silent admiration of the department's newest acquisition was broken by the Colonel, "Brad, that was pure pleasure! I can't get over how quiet it was!"

"They're a smooth machine. And the nice thing for our department, as well as hospital medi-vac units and the corporations that can afford 'em, is that this model doesn't require a co-pilot. It can be set up to carry nine pas-sengers besides the pilot. In terms of manpower operation costs and being able to quickly go on a mission, one-pilot operation, even on instruments, is a real plus for a chopper this big. Do you have any questions?"

"Yes, I do have a few. Why is it they can't go over a certain speed forward?"

"Well briefly, as they move forward faster and faster, the tip of the rotor blade moving forward in its circle approaches the speed of sound, while the blade moving backward is of course going a lot slower and vibrations set in."

"Just as clear as mud, but I think I understand. How about service ceil-ing?"

"Flight characteristics degrade as you go higher, since the air is so much thinner. In fact, they can fly higher than they can hover for that very reason. Twenty thousand feet is pushing helicopter operation."

"Explain the cone-of-visibility again, if you will."

"Right. In dust, or as you saw in powder snow, the downblast thins it out and blows it away as you're settling down. Of course, you can't see to either side and when you're taking off, you have to go out on instruments until you climb above it. That's why we'll have to land one at a time and go out one at a time, since we'd be too close to each other."

"Why the thump, thump, thump?"

"It's caused mostly by the pitch of the rotor changing as the rotor goes through its revolution, which becomes necessary to equalize lift. Remember, one air-foil is moving forward through the block of air faster than its partner, that's swinging back around the circle when the helicopter is moving forward. We call it 'dissymmetry of lift'."

"Okay, that seems logical. Why is it so smooth when we're going for-ward and so much vibration when we're hovering?"

"That's caused by the bite of air the rotors are grabbing. It's getting smoother air as we were moving forward, but it's all roiled up when we are in hover mode. Of course, it's much worse where you're close to the ground. Just the nature of the beast!"

"Gosh, Brad, you've given me so much information that I'll be seeing 'slugs per cubic foot' in my sleep! Bernoulli's Principle, dissymmetry of lift, dynamic rollover, ambient temperature, ambient pressure, ambient air density.

I think I'll just ambient home and have an un-ambient scotch on the rocks!" laughed the good-natured Colonel.

"I know," Brad replied, with a grin, knowing he'd been on a roll. "It's a lot of new information and sensations in a two hour span. And don't forget the 'fred figure' and the 'deadman's curve' either!" he exclaimed. "It was all Greek to me when I started in the program. Do you have anymore questions?"

"I can't think of anything else now. If there's a change, I'll get in touch. Oh, by the way?" the Colonel questioned, with a smile.

"Yes?"

"Aren't free lessons a perk?"

"You've got 'em!" Brad replied, with a smile as the two co-command-ers—one past, one current—of the elite, Special Services Squad, shook hands, the first lesson over.

———————

11

'power, options, choices and decisions'

2:00 P.M., Thursday,
February 27, 1992
Office of Governor John Deloney
Cheyenne, Wyoming

John Deloney, formerly a United States Representative from Wyoming, was now finishing his second term in the Governor's chair. Many considered he had an excellent chance as a presidential candidate, or at least for consideration as the candidate's choice for vice-president, in the not too distant future. With strong support from Jerry Anderson, the immensely popular Secretary of Defense during the Gulf War, his hat could definitely be in the ring inside the beltway.

With him at this most private meeting was his wife, the vivacious and very supportive Katherine; his long-time press secretary and confidant, James Livingston and his personal attorney, Thomas J. Haversack. Tom, a good friend of the defense attorney, was a graduate of the National Law Center at The George Washington University.

Unlike Vickers, Tom was not content with the general practice of law; the incredible highs in winning a tough case and the heart breaking lows of losing a case you believed you could and should have won. The equally uncertain cash flow and overhead of a modest law practice did not provide the regular pay and security he needed.

Money and power were of more concern to Tom. This was not to detract from his moral character and reputation of being an honest, loyal and thoroughly conscientious person. Tom was an astute judge of the mood of the country and with his eye on a role in Washington, maintained a steady reading diet of bellwether publications. National Law Center contacts remain carefully nurtured; the 'good ole boy' networks were well intact.

It was clear without being spoken, that the decision now being forced on the Governor could have an immense impact on their future. In spite of the jury verdict, clearly technically correct, there was strong local demand to not execute Dean. It was well pointed out in the local press, that at great risk to himself, Dean had returned to camp and saved, in all probability, the life of the outfitter's wife, Linda, as well as one of his companions. The jury had made a tough decision, but made it nonetheless. This case was entirely different from the Hopkinson case, which, after twelve years of delay, had in January, been Wyoming's first execution since 1965.

For the Governor at this hour, to come to the rescue of a convicted white attorney, who had actually shot an unarmed man, would be strong evidence in the eastern and California press that he would be a white man's president in spite of his local reputation for fairness. It would reinforce the perception held by many, that the poor, the uneducated, Blacks and Hispanics were the only convicted defendants who would pay the ultimate price. True, serial killers like Bundy and maybe Gacey and Evans might answer, but those were special. Everyone, except a few die-hard, anti death-penalty people, wanted them to be fried.

"Tom, will you please bring in the two reporters selected to pool the coverage to the rest?" he quietly requested.

"Sure, Governor," Tom replied, and left the room.

While Haversack was gone, Katherine and James, each intimately aware of what was going to be said, having been privy to the meeting in John's private study at the DeLoney residence the evening before, embraced their mentor.

Livingston, unopposed to the death sentence, was fully aware of the political ramifications, as he knew even Will Dean would be. He could feel the honest struggle that John—who he knew was privately opposed to the death sentence, especially in this case—was going through.

As the Governor resumed his seat—waiting for the two reporters—he considered again, as he had for many days, his options and the choice of this conference room to deliver his final decision. In the Hopkinson case he had merely provided a written statement to the media via his press secretary. This matter was far different, and, required face to face contact, in view of granting Dean's unusual request.

The conference room—located close to his second-floor, southeast corner office—served mainly as a space to pass through, between his office and the reception-secretarial staff area. He would be far more comfortable surrounded by the more personal decor, or the shirt-sleeve familiarity, of his working conference room.

Formal, with its large oak desk and thick carpet with the Great Seal of Wyoming, it provided a reminder of the authority of his position. The surroundings would help to buttress this power, the actual choice of life or death over another human being. The power was not something he had sought out; it came with the turf. Two large brass ceiling fixtures, each with six globes of light, provided soft but sufficient illumination to avoid the necessity and brightness of the available recessed lighting.

John strongly believed he had been elected to represent all of the people and not just his personal philosophy. To reverse the jury's verdict and decision to grant the state's request for the death-sentence would add considerable flame to the increasing racial tension existing in many, if not all, large urban areas around the country. The people who wanted it, wanted it and even the people who didn't want it, agreed that the extended delays PREP was designed to avoid, were an even more cruel punishment, not to mention a waste of millions of their precious taxpayers' dollars.

Wyoming was a state where, both as a territory and as a state, the death-sentence for murder had always been accepted by a strong majority of the population. Only during the decade-long hiatus mandated by the United States Supreme Court ban, as cruel and unusual punishment in violation of the Eighth Amendment to the United States Constitution, had it been suspended. To Wyoming residents, this was a clear violation of their state's right to punish for crimes committed in their jurisdiction.

It was a state wherein the population was not all that willing to kowtow to the power of the Federal Government. Many people feared pending gun control legislation and in fact, it was ranked number one among the contiguous forty-eight states in terms of the percentage of its population as members of the National Rifle Association. Many of the populace were still rankled by the action of the Congress of 1872 taking approximately three thousand square miles of some of the most beautiful part of the territory to create, under Federal control, Yellowstone Park. There were a large number of residents, especially in western Wyoming, who believed that some of the other huge tracts of federal land controlled by the Bureau of Land Management should be returned to the state for private use and development.

The state was independent enough to be the only state in the Union to thumb its nose at Federal highway money, rather than to enforce what it considered to be the ridiculous, fifty-five mile per hour energy speed limit. Finally and reluctantly giving in to the Federal purse and power.

In reality there'd be few, if any, cases like Dean's. And for the rest on death row, much of the public would be damn glad to get rid of. The hour of the liberal left had clearly passed. If only there'd been a shred of evidence to support Dean's contention he'd acted in self-defense, the jury would surely have acquitted him. His private thoughts were interrupted when Haversack and the two pool reporters entered the room.

Representing the Gannett Newspaper chain, the main paper in Dean's home state, was Michelle Harper and representing United Press International, Colin Richards. Both had been selected by their associates at a meeting of news media held in Cheyenne the day before, hosted by the Wyoming Press Association and the Wyoming Association of Broadcasters.

It had been well reported that the execution was to take place on the morning of the following day, at 6:00 A.M. Mountain Time, an hour before sunrise. Unless of course the Governor exercised his right to grant clemency and commute to life in prison, the jury's recommended death-sentence. The news media could not help themselves or prevent, nor should they in a free society, the extensive analysis of political pros and cons of commutation by the governor to life imprisonment. In view of the Hopkinson case, the wise money was on death, only the how was in doubt, since Rawlins, the site of the state penitentiary, was the where.

A locust cloud of media had descended on Cheyenne. It had been a relatively quiet news week around the country and for some reason, this execution of an obscure, stereo-typed attorney in the south center of Wyoming, had become the media event of the moment.

The pool reporters, as previously directed, had arrived at the Governor's office earlier and were now introduced to Governor Deloney, Katherine Deloney and James Livingston, by Thomas Haversack. They quickly took their seats since it was obvious to them and would be duly passed on to the rest of the media, that this event was causing emotional pain to the Governor, certainly a humanistic person.

Tom Haversack spoke by way of introduction to the Governor and to Katherine and James. "Governor and Mrs. Deloney and Jim, I've been advised the press corp and broadcast media held a general meeting chaired by the Editor of the Cheyenne Times. It was felt a man and a woman should cover what happens. Michelle Harper, as you know, was asked to be present by Will Dean, but she wasn't aware of that. Several at the meeting recalled she'd covered one of Dean's cases and also represented the newspaper chain in his home state. She and Colin Richards were nominated and selected by acclamation. Thank you," he said and sat down.

Clearing his throat, the Governor prepared to address the gathering. Thinking to himself, I'll answer all conceivable questions in this speech and hopefully I'll be in control of my emotions and not lose it to some dumb-ass, stupid question like 'will it hurt'?

First taking a sip of water, he began, "Ladies and gentlemen, I've reached a decision and mind you, this is difficult. Any decision that sends or will send people, whether soldiers or defendants, to their death is tough. This speech is practice for my press conference tomorrow," he added. His reference to soldiers was a quick clue to all he had not lost sight of a greater role. "The jury has spoken and it was certainly a fair jury. Tom and I," nodding to his friend, "have reviewed in detail the PREP findings. There's absolutely nothing known *at this time* to justify a delay of the Supreme Court guidelines or to stand in the way of the Jury's decision. 'No free man shall be taken or imprisoned . . . or any ways destroyed unless by the lawful judgment of his peers . . .' granted by the *Magna Carta*, signed by King John on June 15, 1215, in the seventeenth year of his reign, in a meadow called Runnymede, is my history lesson for the day.

"Last fall, a fair and honest jury hearing the evidence, the Court's instructions, and the closing arguments of learned counsel, reached its verdict. I want to add something here, and not because he's your friend," looking again at Haversack. "The closing argument Vickers made should be required reading in every class of history, psychology and humanities in every high school and of course, law school in this country!" he exclaimed. "It was videoed and should be seen by everyone. It was clear, concise, did not twist the facts and yet brought before the jury all they could possibly absorb of the various conflicting values and emotions they had to be feeling. This was not a hanging jury and the Judge was eminently fair. I've said enough about the history of this matter and Dean must,"—his voice breaking with sincere sadness—"answer for what he did.

"And now the details. Some of you know about the rider attached to the Bighorn River Watershed Preservation Bill. That bill had the support of everyone, including the Native American community. I requested the rider when the Attorney General sought certification last October, asking for the death sentence. Vickers had notified Tom that Dean was terrified of using injection and he wouldn't be able to control his bowels—didn't want to go that way," John spoke softly. "The rider, somewhat like Utah's, gives the defendant his choice of lethal injection or firing squad." The reality of what was going to happen struck home, John's voice broke and pausing, he took another sip of water and taking a deep breath, continued. Katherine's eyes filled with tears at seeing her husband's honest grief.

"Dean, through Vickers to Tom, has made a couple of unusual, but not unreasonable, requests. Granting these will demonstrate to the family and press that we have compassion and flexibility.

"Ladies and gentlemen, I will not grant clemency and commute to life the jury's decision. As Governor, under my inherent powers, I'm granting a couple of Dean's requests that we believe reasonable and humane, taking into consideration the public's right to know and Dean and his family's right of privacy. Let me outline what's going to happen—when, where and how. There isn't going to be a media circus and the entire group of interested people, candle burning and so forth, won't be able to see anything in Rawlins.

"The points I'm going to spell out are Dean's requests that my attorney, Mr. Haversack, along with the Attorney General, the Warden, the Highway Patrol Commissioner and I have reviewed and approved.

"First, you're here at Dean's request that only two pool reporters cover the scene. By the way, this has been our policy, so his request is nothing special. Ms. Harper, for some reason Dean asked that you be added to the pool reporters. I assume he wanted someone from the newspaper in his home state and we're pleased you were selected by your peers.

"Second, and again this is a right Dean has under our law. Death shall be by a firing squad of six members from the Special Services Squad of the

Wyoming Highway Patrol and will be led by a co-captain of the squad. Except for the Captain, they were selected by lot from those who indicated they were not opposed to the death sentence. All have the highest rating, expert, and are experienced riflemen. At Dean's request, they met with his lawyer earlier this month. One rifle will be loaded with a special round that has the sound and recoil of a standard round, but disintegrates. Each rifleman can believe it is in his or her rifle. There are women in the Wyoming Highway Patrol." Pausing, the governor took a sip of water and continued, "The rifles are all pre-examined and loaded by the State Police armorer, Sergeant Patrick O'Doul. At Dean's request, the rifles they'll be using are Springfield 1903, 30–06s, with standard military issue ammunition, along with Dean's own special rifle. They have quiet bolt-actions, and, in Dean's opinion, are more accurate than the modern, military M-16.

"Third, and this is really the only *major* concession we've granted Dean, the execution is to be carried out at the edge of Dead Horse Lake. The lake is located in a box canyon above Simpson Lake. This is the place where Dean spent his last happy hours before this tragic event occurred," John paused, and took another sip of water. "I can sympathize with Dean's request.

"You, and I mean Ms. Harper and Mr. Richards, will fly in my personal plane to Lander. There, you'll be met by the Fremont County Medical Examiner and Father Andrew Stoll and go by helicopter to the canyon. Dean, John Vickers, Major Blackwell and the Fremont County Sheriff will fly by helicopter from Lander to the canyon. I'm assuming both of you want to fly to the site. Is that correct?"

"Yes," both replied without conferring.

"Dean, in State custody, has been moved to the Fremont County Jail by Major Austin Blackwell, head of maximum security, so he can be with his friends and family tonight. There'll be no long wait standing around while some clock ticks away. The site's been picked and the riflemen and Sergeant O'Doul'll be there at approximately six-thirty in the morning with everything prepared.

"Let me interject something here. Since this is taking place in the Fitzpatrick Wilderness area of the Shoshone National Forest, I personally met with Jerry Anderson over the holiday. Attorney Vickers had relayed Dean's request in the event PREP affirmed the jury and I wanted to touch base with the federal authorities. Secretary Anderson cleared this with the Secretary of the Interior, the agency that manages the national forests. While there may be some flak over it, the word was, if it's to be done, just go in, do it and get back to Rawlins. There's no question but that most of the locals would want Dean's request granted.

"Those are the basics. Each of you," looking again at the reporters, "has pledged to not divulge the site until after you return to Cheyenne. You should be back here before ten o'clock and I leave it up to your professional judgment and your pooling agreement as to when, where, and what you divulge. I'm sure Secretary Anderson and the Secretary of the Interior can take the heat, if there should be any.

"Finally, I know we're all concerned about these last details and I haven't discussed this with any of you, I guess it just never came up. The team will be located about seventy-five yards from Dean and is instructed by radio through private head sets. Dean won't hear the order and it should be over before the sound ever reaches him. My physician has told me that with five shots to the heart, the shock'll be so great there should be little pain and of short duration. Dean can be blindfolded if he wants. I've no idea one way or the other. Do any of you have any questions?"

Michelle raised her hand, "Governor, is there any chance this has leaked out and some enterprising photographer is in the area secretly planning on filming the execution?"

"An excellent question, Ms. Harper," he replied. "It's doubtful. Secretary Anderson and the Secretary of Interior certainly don't want it known. Except for McKinnon, neither of the other pilots, nor the team will know the exact site until airborne. Those going, you here, the Attorney General, Dean's attorney and his family are the only ones as far as I know, who know. They're all staying in Lander where Dean is being held, and Dean's being in Lander is known to only a couple.

"You all are aware of the great deal of snowmobiling in Fremont County. That activity is well outside the wilderness area and there are no trails going in. There's simply no reason anyone'd be in the box canyon this time of year. I'm told there's no hunting or trapping in the area and the horse trails are under deep snow. The helicopters are often fitted with skids this time of year instead of wheels. Does that answer your question?" he inquired.

"Yes, but a follow up if I may?"

"Certainly, Ms. Harper," the Governor replied.

"The best made plans do go astray. What if?"

"Well, we've thought about that. If there is a hiker or even a group, they would have to be on snowshoes. It's a dry, powder snow in the area. There'll be three helicopters on site and I've been assured by the Captain, a former Viet Nam pilot, that a cloud of snow that would obscure everything could easily be set up. If there are people in the immediate area, then the Highway Patrol would not allow them to film the execution. The area is open to the public and there's always a chance this could be a problem. We hope not. Does that answer your question?" he asked.

"Yes. Thank you," Ms. Harper replied.

"Any other questions? No—then Katherine and I are going home. Jim and Tom will wrap up any details on transportation and so forth. Oh, there is one other matter. I've granted Dean's request that Sam, his closest friend outside family, be allowed to go. As you may know, Sam was blinded in the attack on the camp and he wants to be with Will. If the execution was to be held at the State Prison in Rawlins, then Wyoming law allows the defendant to have up to ten of his friends and family present. It's kind of hard to imagine sending out invitations to something like this!

"You may think I've granted too many of a convicted man's requests, and maybe I have, but this is the first actual use of PREP in the country. It's also a most unusual case. Remember, Will did go back and save lives. But, he's been found guilty and must 'pay back', as the jury decided. However, don't lose sight of the fact he was an officer of the court and a respected attorney in Michigan for a quarter of a century. His request isn't unreasonable in my opinion." Without realizing it, he had slipped and was calling Dean by his first name, something he always avoided doing. "Tom, please call Vickers at his office. He knows, but the family's waiting for my official decision. Also, let him know about Sam."

"Sure," Tom replied.

"Ms. Sharp and Mr. Richards, you can let the media know I'll meet 'em at ten o'clock tomorrow morning in room 1699 of the Herschler Building and explain what's been done. You should be back here by then and can answer their questions. Okay, there being no other questions, good afternoon." Katherine and the others rose, and together, John and Kate left the room.

2:15 P.M., Thursday
Lander, Wyoming

"Hello, Troy? Tim, here," the owner of Hutchinson's Funeral Home announced.

"Hey, man, how the hell are you? What's up?" Troy asked.

Troy Brock was the owner of a crematory located in Ogden, Utah, on the west side of the Continental Divide. His only competition for the western Wyoming business was in Cheyenne, about the same distance from Lander. He and Tim had been business acquaintances for many years.

"Been doin' any fishin' lately?" Tim asked.

"No, not for awhile, not that business is all that great. How 'bout you?"

"Well, we got our limit of Rainbows and a real nice Brown last Labor Day weekend up on Warm Spring Creek, above Dubois. My son and I had a great time."

"Tim, what's up? Your tone of voice is a little strained—stressed shall I say?"

"Anyone with you?"

"No. Why?"

"I've got a problem, Troy. Think you can help?"

"Sure, old buddy. Thought it might be someone else who had a problem
and now needs me!" he laughed.

"Serious, Troy. You alone?"

"Yeah, go ahead."

"Dean."

"Holy shit! How'd you get him? Shit! You mean they're really going
to do him? Christ man, he saved that girl and his buddy. Jesus, man! Half of
Wyoming thinks he's a goddamn hero!" Troy exclaimed. "Hey, when you were
over here last December and I missed you, Joe told me you had some good-
looking little blond, a foxy blue-eyed lady with you. Dean's squeeze?"

"Don't be crude. Not any more! Yeah, he wanted to know all about
what goes on. We showed her the oven, but I didn't want to ask Joe a lot of
questions. You know, I'm afraid he's going to get it. Now that they finally
did Hopkinson, the ice is broken. Troy, like the paper said last fall, 'it can't
just be the poor, the Indians, Blacks and Mexicans' that get it and he probably
didn't have to pop the guy. Not like in the time of *Lonesome Dove*. Bring him
to trial was the argument. Will and his lawyers, by the way one of 'em is my
attorney, don't want the media around and . . .."

"Wait, Tim," Troy interrupted, "they've already called to see if ar-
rangements have been made! Get this—I just got a call from Steve, over in
Cheyenne—they even called there! Shit, it must be a quiet news week. Isn't
Dean in Rawlins?" he asked.

"I don't know where he is. They want me to pick him up at Hunt Field
after it's over, but here's the problem. If I fly the body to Ogden, have an
ambulance meet me and drive out to your place, how quick, and I mean *Will's*
ashes goddamn it, can you hand me the urn? Body weight 150 pounds. He
hasn't been eatin' too good lately!"

"Let's see. It'll be a lot quicker if we meet you there and get the body
the minute you stop at the ramp and load into the burn-box. It'll take me about
eight minutes down 31st Street to Washington Boulevard, two minutes to get
in here and if we have the furnace temperature up—cardboard burn-box—cool
down time, that's the big delay. Scrape, crush bones and pack, I'd say about
two hours and twenty-five minutes at best. If I had gear and have the room
temperature up, maybe a little quicker. I'll have to be real careful about opening the oven too quick, but hell, I'll see what I can do. The ashes'll still be
very hot, so I'll get an insulated container."

"Troy, this is very important. I think I know how the Governor feels
about this one, but he's not likely to put himself between the jurors and stop
it. I'll call later tonight or by seven in the morning, okay?"

"Sure."

"Take care, Troy. I'll call back soon."

"Good-bye," said Troy, hanging up the phone. Well, he thought, it's
a good thing I don't agree with the jury. There's five hundred out there if I

get wind of anything. Shit—so I'll always be poor. I guess Dean's family needs all the help they can get, he sighed, resuming the attack on his monthly stack of bills.

———

2:30 P.M., Thursday
February 27, 1992
Office of John Vickers

It had become clear to thinking individuals that modern, highly specialized societies could not function without the development of acronyms. The reduction in the amount of paper alone through the use of these space-saving codes would result in the preservation of a significant portion of the world's forests. For Will Dean, PREP meant his earthly existence would be limited to fifty-six years, six months, four hours, thirty minutes and just slightly more than six-hundred and fifty-two ten-thousandth's of a second, Eastern Standard Time, from the moment of his birth.

As John Vickers entered, a hush fell over the already subdued quiet of the conference room of Vickers and Vickers, P.C., in downtown Riverton.

Present were Will's wife, Trish, and three of his four sons, Mark, William and Zack. His oldest son, Thomas, was out of contact with the family and thought to be exploring in the Peruvian Andes. His daughter Tanya, his lifelong buddy, the blinded Sam, and Linda Caldwell, the seven-months pregnant widow of the murdered outfitter, completed the gathering.

The look on the attorney's face and his drooped shoulders were enough body language to clearly convey to all, what Will's counsel was about to relate. There was no need to inquire to confirm the obvious. Muffled sobs were slowly stilled as John cleared his throat and began.

"Friends and family, God bless you for your support. You know how tough this is for me and I can only imagine how difficult it is for you," his voice breaking. Taking a deep breath, John began his explanation of what the small group before him could expect. "We sincerely believe Will, an experienced defense attorney, knows the trial was as fair as humanly possible. With PREP in place, we know both sides bent over backwards to be prepared."

"We don't believe there was a shred of evidence we wanted in, that didn't get admitted. At least we couldn't find it, if it was out there. There were just a few objections, a complete record made and the Court ruled correctly on all. None of these concerned matters of any significance and both sides agreed they were only to control the flow of testimony.

"I'm speaking for the defense team when I say we are devastated by what happened and is going to take place," he paused as several broke into muffled sobs. He found his voice and continued, "You know the first case under these new guidelines was appealed through the normal procedures to the United States Supreme Court and that tribunal affirmed what Texas had done and allowed the execution to go forward.

"Unless there's some unforeseen miracle, Will's case will be the first where the . . .," he couldn't finish. "I know all of you went over PREP in detail at the time of trial. Well, the Panel's certification's been reviewed and approved by Associate Justice Kendall Murphy, the Supreme Court Justice for the United States Court of Appeals for the Tenth Circuit. The execution warrant's been signed by the Governor, who will not set aside the Jury's sentence recommendation."

"John?" asked Mark, interrupting and asking for the group, the question all needed to know and that John was obviously avoiding. "When?"

"Christ, Mark! I would've talked for hours to avoid the only thing you all don't want, but have to know. It's set for tomorrow, Friday—six-thirty or so in the morning," he added.

"How?" Tanya asked.

"Will's choice," John replied and continued, as talking, his profession, seemed to make it easier. "You all know Will had his personal ghosts and the Governor has granted his request. Will's several surgeries made lethal injection unacceptable. Will, as you know, has a great sense of humor. How he can joke is beyond me, but to tell the truth, he really wants to go out with rifles.

"He knows in his own mind he acted in self-defense, even though there was no other evidence to support his testimony. Thus, he believes all the birds and animals he's shot, that maybe he shouldn't 've, will believe he's been punished enough and won't get him at Firelake! He described his view of the scene with the birds and animals and had Dick and I laughing so hard we were in tears.

"I want to relate something to you Will said during the Jury deliberations. He said 'John, I don't think it matters. The script was written late at night, on old U.S. 16, in the summer of '54'. I asked him what he meant. He said he was driving back to Rockford, Michigan, where he was working a summer job for the Michigan State Highway Department. He was heading west and fell asleep driving his 1948 Studebaker Champion convertible, went across the highway and hit an east-bound semi head on. An empty car-hauler headed for Lansing and another load of Oldsmobiles. It completely totalled his car, but he didn't get a scratch!

"He told me how a man came up to him, put both hands on his shoulders, looked him in the eyes and said, 'You must have a guardian angel looking over you son, and you should thank God because you're being saved for something'!"

Zack spoke up, "You know, Dad seemed tired on the stand, maybe resigned, kind of like he expected this to happen."

"I know what you mean, Zack," John replied. "Will *honestly* believes he was saved in his close calls with death so he'd be able to be in position to actually put an end to a sick, evil force. It's not so much he has run out of luck as it is that the purpose for his dodging the bullet—shit—wrong word—has been fulfilled. By the way, Sam. You are totally absolved and released from the 'hill pledge'. Will said you'd know, but that he couldn't explain it to me."

With this, Sam and the others broke out in tears. William spoke up, "We'll see, 'a promise made is a debt unpaid'."

"John, can you tell us where?" asked Mark. "Is there anything we can do?"

"The second part, just be close for your dad, he loves you all very much," he added. "The Governor has granted Will permission to go to Dead Horse Lake, in the box canyon where he spent the last night of peace before this tragedy and horror unfolded. Will has written a letter to the team and explained that he absolutely forgives them. They have a duty and to not get weak knees. He also gave some special instructions to the Captain of the team. He told them, 'hey guys, look at it this way, you get to shoot a defense attorney and not get sued in Federal Court for violating his rights! You'll be envied by every cop in the country!'.

"Then he told them, pardon me, but I'm paraphrasing your Dad, 'if getting to shoot a lawyer wasn't enough, to just relax, listen to the radio count and pretend they had just found out he'd nailed their wives'!" he said, grinning in spite of himself. "How he could get the team to laugh with a letter, and laugh they did, is beyond me."

"That's my Dad!" spoke up Tanya, the others nodding.

"Well, I have nothing more, any questions?" John asked.

"Where are we to be?" asked Trish, her voice breaking.

"Oh hell, I'm all shook up, there's a lot more we have to cover. All of you should stay in Lander, where Will is being taken now and during this—situation," he answered. "At the canyon, can only be myself, Warden Steward, Major Blackwell, who's head of maximum security, Sheriff Arce, the team and Sergeant O'Doul. He's the Highway Patrol armorer. Then two members of the press and maybe an attorney from the Attorney General's office. Father Stoll, who's also a physician and can fill out the certificate, will be with Will. Oh, by the way, Sam, I almost forgot. You can go to the site in the helicopter, with Will.

"The Team, by Highway Patrol helicopter, is to be in place early in the morning and all preparations made. Will and the rest are going to be flown in, in separate choppers. Sam and I go with Will, Major Blackwell, the Sheriff and Father Stoll. Two from the press and the others will go in the third chopper. There may be some changes on flying out, I just don't know.

"After it's over, two of the choppers are returning to Cheyenne. Father Stoll, the Sheriff, Sam and I return to Lander with Will's body for cremation.

The family doesn't have to make any formal identification since Father Stoll, as a physician, does that and the cremation will take place immediately, as requested. As you're aware, Will's last 'trial' is his desire that what he calls 'the media locusts' don't get a hold of any of you until this is all over, then it'll be up to each of you what to do. This has been very difficult to accomplish. Tim Hutchinson told me he met with you in Lander, right?" he asked.

They all nodded in the affirmative.

"Well, some media have even called the crematories in Cheyenne and in Ogden!" he exclaimed. Tim's as careful as it gets. He takes custody of Will's body from the Medical Examiner at Hunt Field and puts it in his airplane. He'll fly to Ogden where he'll be met by the crematory operator. He'll take Will's body to the crematory where his assistant will be waiting and ready to proceed. There'll be about a two and a quarter hour wait and then they'll bring the urn back to Tim. He'll have his plane ready to fly directly over to Riverton, where the scheduled flights will get you east.

"If possible, you might be able to make United Flight 2284 that leaves Riverton at one-twenty in the afternoon for Denver. My secretary has booked you four," looking at Will's children, "on that flight to Denver. It's an American built Beechcraft, which would please your dad. In case it doesn't work out, a friend of mine has booked five tickets on Continental Flight 2408 at four-fifty in the afternoon to Denver.

"Tim's going to fly Trish and Sam to Dubois, but if the airlines don't workout, he'll fly the four of you to the Kremmling, Colorado, airport which is only thirty miles down the Blue River Valley from Dillon. You may want to do that anyway and tickets can be fully refunded. Whatever works out best. We'll have at least three options, so it's not really any problem at all. Since the media'll be in Rawlins or in Cheyenne, it may work. The long delay's going to have 'em out sniffing like a coyote on a sheep trail," he added.

"Who's the urn to be delivered to?" John asked.

Mark spoke up quietly, "Trish'll take it, but we'll all be there."

"Okay, I'll be there, Mark. I think you all know how we feel about what's gone on," John replied. "Is there anything else?" As they all shook their heads in the negative, John continued. "By the way, Tim will be at the Mount Hope Funeral Parlor this afternoon if you want to meet there for a brief memorial service. He thought around five-thirty would be a good time. Well then, Sam, I guess I'll meet you at Hunt Field in Lander at about six a.m. and see the rest of you at the Riverton Airport, probably sometime around one o'clock. Good-bye for now and God be with you," he said, and turning left the room.

Slowly the assembled family and friends filed out of the conference room. As they started out, Linda grabbed Sam's arm and held him back. "Sam, I can't go to Lander. My heart would break for Will. Our baby is due in mid-April and I think it's just too much stress. You and I both know Bob'll be beside Will talking him through it. I wish I could be—but the emotions—I just can't. Can you explain it to them?" she asked.

"Of course, Linda."

"Good luck, Sam, and maybe someday we can get in touch. For a life-time, the memories are going to be painful. Do you understand what I'm say-ing?"

"Yes, I know," he answered.

Wiping away the tears, she gave him a warm, firm hug and they left the room to join the others.

3:35 P.M.—Thursday
February 27, 1992
Gypsum Creek—Bridger Wilderness Area
Bridger National Forest

Approximately eleven miles southwest of Dead Horse Lake, as a crow flies, and west of the Continental Divide, the two cougar hunters were taking a rest break. From the brush cuttings, the area appeared to be that of an old camp site. Signs in a nearby cave indicated human usage, but disclosed no recent evidence of the presence of any cats.

"Well, Joe, the season's about over. A lot of fun—some good chases, but no luck. I hope the cats don't kill too many Bighorn lambs this spring."

"It's been fun, Brian. Sometimes the chase is better'n the kill. But I agree on the lambs. If we didn't get a few cats now and then, there wouldn't be many Bighorns around. The department's mortality-quota system's worked out real good. Three seems a little tight for Wyoming west of the Divide, in view of the amount of sign we've seen. I guess they know what they're doing though."

"Speaking of seasons being over, Joe. What about that lawyer, Will Dean? I guess his season's about over!" Brian exclaimed with a laugh.

"Yeah, and I'll bet there'll be a bunch of new lawyer jokes out of that one!" laughed Joe.

"How da ya feel about the death-sentence, Joe?"

"Oh, no problem, Brian. It seems a little tough in Dean's case. But you know, it seemed even tougher in Hopkinson's case. Christ, Mark was in jail when it was done and they don't even know who tortured Jeff Green to death. In my humble opinion, that nobody gives a damn about, old hot-shot Spencer just bamboozled the jury. Shit it could've been another drug case and not even connected to the motive they thought Mark had."

"You're right on that, Joe. I always liked Mark. He was a wheeler-dealer, but he'd never been convicted of any violence. At least Dean killed the guy and the jury decided it was cold-blood. Shit, when you're in a shoot-out,

your blood's not too damn cold! I'll bet if they'd 've had a couple of experienced cops on the jury, they'd 've understood cold-blood!"

"Well, Brian, Vickers did a hell-of-a job. If he couldn't win it, who
the hell could've? Hey, what's that!" Joe exclaimed. "Look, the dogs are diggin' for something. What the hell—I never seen 'em do that—let's check it
out. Here, Taz, get back! Brian, hold 'em if you can. Brian—look here! Look
at these sticks under the dirt! That's not natural, let's tie up the dogs."

"Joe, I'll get my hatchet and start diggin' while you tie 'em." The small
area had been blown clear of snow and the daily increasing sunlight had softened the ground. "Look, Joe! It's just a few inches of dirt over some sticks.
This is new, look at those cuts. Couldn't be more 'an a few months old. My
God, Joe, I've heard of this. It's how they buried people in the old days to
keep the wolves and coyotes from diggin' into the graves! Their paws hit the
sticks and they give up," Brian explained.

"Brian, we can kick most of the dirt away. My God! Holy shit! There
must be a body buried under here—see, a blanket!"

"There's got to be foul play here. Let's take pictures before we dig any
more. Do you want to look?" asked Brian.

"God, I suppose we have to," Joe replied. "Shit, what the hell should
we do now? You're the deputy sheriff, Brian. What do you want to do?"

"Well, Joe, we just can't do *nothing*. It'll be dark soon and we can't
leave the body here where a bear or other animals might get it. Quick, you
take some pictures of the area so we can pinpoint the scene in case of a storm,
while I try to get it out of the dirt. Let's hurry, I'd like to get back to the
Newfork Lodge before dark."

Working fast, the sticks made a quick opening possible. Pulling the
corpse out by the blanket, the deputy rolled it over to stare at the frail, wasted
body. "Oh, God, Joe! It's a young woman! Christ, she's wasted. My God,
she's just skin and bones! I'll carry the body down to the snowmobiles. You
control the dogs, if you can."

"I wonder what happened?" Joe questioned. "Let's go. We can call the
Sheriff from the Lodge and they can get an autopsy tonight or first thing in
the morning."

At 4:15 P.M., and as fast as possible on snowshoes, they started out of
the Wilderness Area of the Bridger National Forest. Unknown to them, their
burden—a silent messenger of hope.

The clock continued its relentless beat as planet Earth slowly rotated
away from a setting, and toward a rising sun.

12

'time flies and sad good-byes'

4:00 P.M.—Thursday
Weapons Room
Wyoming Highway Patrol
5300 Bishop Boulevard
Cheyenne, Wyoming

Sergeant Patrick O'Doul, official armorer for the Wyoming Highway
Patrol, was charged with the duty to inventory, clean, repair and maintain in
good supply all weapons and ammunition in the arsenal. O'Doul, the son of a
New York City cop and grandson of an Irish immigrant Boston cop, truly hated
four things in this world—only the order was uncertain. They were; the English, protestant Scots, scumbag lawyers and the clap. His Northern Ireland
relatives were still suffering at the hands of the first two and he had been
victimized by the last two.

A bad case of the clap had, together with his wife's attorney, cost him
his family and most of his property, along with half his paltry, future retirement
plan. That he had put the mighty O'Doul Tool in the honey trap never crossed
his mind as the cause of his suffering. With obvious glee he once again carefully inspected and prepared to load the rifles he now considered to be his
closest friends and allies.

Three years earlier, his harsh methods led to his being removed from
road patrol. His last four arrests had resulted in two not-guilty verdicts following humiliating cross-examination and two dismissals, in his mind, on technicalities. He clearly considered the constitutions of Wyoming and of the United
States of America as mere technicalities, when used by attorneys. After all,
wasn't this the view of many law-abiding good Americans? Of course if used
by police officers, who were occasionally prosecuted—in his mind wrongfully—they were fundamental rights! That his oath of office as a Highway
Patrolman was to uphold those constitutions, had, like his marriage vows, been
long forgotten.

It was only due to Colonel Ackels' experience and understanding the
stress of road-patrol that O'Doul had a job. Their loud and heated argument
suddenly ended and some staff had seen O'Doul quietly leave the Commis-

sioner's office. The rumor started a few days later when an officer mentioned seeing their personal vehicles take the Snowy Range exit from the Interstate; heading quickly for the Laramie Mountains.

The Commissioner was assumed the victor when his unexpected fishing vacation lasted five days, while the huge, rock-hard O'Doul's vacation required seven days. Nothing was ever said, but no further arguments were heard between the hard-headed Irishman and the obviously, tough-as-steel Englishman.

Two of O'Doul's difficult to swallow defeats had been at the hands of the most despicable, in his mind, of all attorneys, John Vickers. The fact John had defended and won cases for several patrolmen didn't matter, since they were obviously innocent. Laughing, he turned to his new assistant, the young trooper Anderson, "Hey, Tom, did you hear the one about the Corporal in Kuwait?"

"No. Is this another one of your lawyer jokes?" Tom asked.

"How'd you guess? 'Cause I'm gearin' up for good ole Will Dean?" he laughed, in his deep rolling Irish brogue.

"No shit! Where you get all those lawyer jokes is beyond me. I'll bite— no, I haven't heard it—go ahead."

"Well, this Corporal see, he jumps into this bunker in Kuwait and sittin' there at a table next to a lawyer, is Saa Demm Hussain with a pistol pointed at the Corporal's belly. Right next to the Corporal on the floor is the biggest, fuckin' Cobra snake he's ever seen. Its fangs are dripping poison, its head flattened and reared up, ready to strike. The Corporal realizes he's only got two rounds left in his rifle. What should he do?"

"I'll bite, I couldn't guess," Tom replied.

"It's easy, dummy! You don't take any fuckin' chances at all! You shoot the lawyer twice!" he roared, in a belly-shaking laughter.

"Sergeant O'Doul, you're something else!" Tom declared. I don't want to be like you, he thought to himself, but boy, if I ever get in trouble, I'd sure want you to be on my side. At six-foot six and two-hundred forty-five pounds, the red-headed Irishman was, at fifty-two years old, hard as a rock and about as open to new ideas.

Well, thought O'Doul, as he prepared to load the weapons, I ain't takin' any fuckin' chances! There ain't no way that fuckin' Viet Nam Veteran murderin' scumbag-lawyer is only goin' to get five of these. Who's goin' to count the slugs and who'll give a shit? Scumbag won't be filin' any complaint, he chortled. If they don't like it, they can have the other half of my fuckin' pension. "Tom, will you do me a favor and get me another cup of coffee? It's going to be an up all nighter anyway," he declared.

"Sure, Sarge."

When Tom left to go upstairs, O'Doul put the phony round in his pocket and kissing the rounds he'd prepared a few nights before, quickly loaded the six rifles.

His mind drifted back to the two evenings previously spent at his private workshop, in pleasant preparation for this historic moment in his life. He was not surprised at all with Dean's choice of the Springfield '03 rifle, as directed by the Governor's order. There was no way however, that Highway Patrol Armorer, Sergeant Patrick O'Doul would trust the outcome of this all important event to the chance of standard ammunition. He was the official Armorer and as such, it was his duty to prepare the rifles and load them. An armorer he would be! This was an ancient and much respected tradition, long preceding even medieval times and not necessarily of British origin.

To O'Doul's credit, while his harsh methods ran him aground on the rules and guidelines of the times, he had a reputation for absolute honesty, which pertained to almost all matters. Without regard to the consequences or costs, he would be scrupulously truthful, excluding only those facts, that he evaded if he possibly could, connected with the O'Doul Tool.

In this regard he had the respect of all, and many, including even John Vickers, held great admiration for some of O'Doul's traits. Likewise, O'Doul did not know or personally dislike Will Dean. He respected many attorneys as individuals. His feelings toward Dean somewhat softened when he learned of his choice of the old Springfield, bolt-action, Model 1903, 30–06 caliber army rifle. After all, hadn't the weapon been good enough for Sergeant York?

This rifle, while not an automatic, nor even semi-automatic, possessed several characteristics not present in the modern-day military rifle. The most important of these was instantly apparent to O'Doul, and he felt a twinge of sympathy at the thought. Dean would be dead, or nearly dead, before the sound of the shots ever reached him. But in the confines of the newly prepared Rawlins firing-squad execution site, the sound of loading an automatic or semi-automatic weapon would hit his eardrums like a cannon boom and be more frightening than the shots.

The Springfield Model 1903 could be loaded quietly once the action was cocked. Although the bolt action could be opened, whether the safety was on or off and the round checked, it was not quite as good as the silent cocking and loading capabilities of the famous double-lug bolt-action German Mauser. Maybe Dean didn't think I could scrape up five of 'em, he thought, or maybe he just wanted to go out with American made rifles! If that was the case, maybe he wasn't that bad after all. O'Doul softened a little bit more toward Dean.

O'Doul had acquired, at a long forgotten gun and knife sale, a case of brand-new and still unused Springfield, Model 1903s. Manufactured for the United States Army by Smith-Corona, the receivers were stamped:

U.S.
SMITH—CORONA
MODEL 03—A3

A later model of the Springfield 1903, the A3s had been manufactured in great quantities by a number of companies for the United States military buildup prior to World War II. Many professional soldiers, with years of shooting experience, still preferred them to the newer M-1 Garrand. Dean won't care.

Although they were collectors' items, would there ever be another time like the present to break their cherries? Since they're mine and being used at the Governor's request, they'll still be mine and worth a fortune as 'the rifles that killed Will Dean', he thought, with glee.

Dean, given the choice of method of execution by the new law, had been granted his wish to select the rifles. Along with the Springfields, Dean had requested that the squad captain, the acknowledged best shot, would use his rifle, which O'Doul assumed was also a bolt-action 30–06. Being bolt-action rifles, they could handle much more powerful ammunition than any of the hand held automatic or semi-automatic, modern, military rifles. Will Dean was obviously a fellow rifleman, and thus a cut above the usual New York City scumbags he'd dealt with before his move to Wyoming.

After cleaning, checking, test firing and sighting in each of the five new Springfields, with military issue ammunition, he had turned to the task he looked forward to the most—preparing the ammunition that would be used. Since he had never seen Dean, he was not able to visualize his face. During the locally publicized trial, he had been at his private retreat in the Bighorn Mountains, with a very nubile young woman, who had taxed his bighorn to the limit. The week had passed all too quickly and the absence of television had been well appreciated. He would just pretend Dean had the snarling face of Vickers, as he was tied to the chair.

Each round would be hand-loaded with precision on the latest equipment. New brass cartridges would first be fitted with primers. These primers, the heartbeat of any round, would, when struck by the firing pin, ignite the rapid-burning, smokeless powder. The expanding gases would push the bullets of his choice spinning down the spiraled lands and grooves of the barrels' rifling and into the heart of Will Dean with blistering speed.

Careful thought had to be given to the metallic breakfast he planned on serving the scumbag lawyer. The standard military issue 30–06 ammunition would travel at about 2,500 feet per second, which was definitely not fast enough to suit O'Doul! In his opinion, this historic event should happen much much quicker!

The .223 caliber varmint rifles could use the 60 grain Remington, Hollow Point Match rounds capable of being safely loaded to kick along at 4,300 feet per second. This of course was for a varmint rifle with great speed and accuracy and weren't they going to shoot vermin? There was available, the store made Remington 30–06, 55 grain Accelerator round. Travelling at more than 4,080 feet per second, it was a varmint round in a thirty caliber *Sabot*.

They would be good, but the sport of hand-loading would be the thrill of knowing he would be custom building the rounds specially for scumbag Dean.

After reviewing the manuals, his choice of bullets had quickly narrowed down to the very popular 180 grain Nosler Partition bullet, with its excellent mushroom capacity, and the deadly, 110 grain Sierra Hollowpoint Varminter #2110 bullet. The Hollow Point Varminter definitely caught his fancy, it just plain sounded good!

Checking the latest handloading guidebooks, he had computed that by using fifty-five grains of fast-burning, Hodgdon's #322 powder in new Federal brass cases, and using the heavier, Winchester primers, he could safely push the speed to nearly 3,500 feet per second. At this speed and across a distance of seventy-five yards, the six, one-hundred-ten grain bullets fired simultaneously, would deliver six-hundred sixty grains, or about one and one-half ounces of metal in approximately sixty-four thousands of a second into the heart of Will Dean.

By comparison he thought, the .470 caliber Nitro Express elephant rifle round would only deliver the 500 grains of the Weldcore Soft Point bullet at 2,150 feet per second and with a kinetic energy of 3,965 foot pounds at 100 yards. The energy he was building would deliver the small chunks of metal into Dean's chest with a combined force of approximately 8,200 foot pounds. Well more than double that necessary to stop a charging bull elephant!

After preparing eighteen rounds, again test firing and sighting each of his Springfields with two shots using his hand loads, he had confirmed that the average bullet muzzle velocity, displayed on his Pro Tach Chronograph, was 3,502 feet per second. Turning his attention to Dean's rifle he had walked over and expecting to find a scope-fitted, modern bolt-action 30–06, opened the case. Jesus, he'd exclaimed as he looked in and carefully removed the rifle. The plain and well-scratched stock, a sporter replacement for the original, cradled in its well fitted form, in mint condition, quite possibly the best bolt-action rifle ever built.

Adolf Hitler used the German engineering genius of *Mauser-Werke* to equip his riflemen. In the end, it would be the ordinary foot soldier and his rifle that would take and hold the new territory of his thousand year *Reich*.

With reverence he again held the Model '98, 8mm Mauser. Its forged and hardened steel breach and frame, with double-locking bolt lugs, made it virtually accident proof. Designed to load an empty chamber and work the safety in absolute silence, it was the pinnacle of German hand-weapon engineering.

Stamped on the breach, 1939, with the serial number 243, it was rebored to the 30–06 cartridge and modified with a new bolt handle and safety to permit attachment of a scope. Though tapped for a scope, for some unknown reason it was now fitted with a Williams, open iron sight.

The plain stock, sling and sight told a story of use. It could not compete in the show salons with rifles of intricately checkered, exotic-wood stocks and artistic engravings inlaid with gold and silver to show off the wealth and status of their owners. But as a rifle, built to do what rifles were designed to do, it feared no challenge to its premiere rank.

If only it could talk he thought; what tales of combat and adventure— heartbreak and triumph. With its past war and hunting stories, it would soon have a new tale to tell—the hour of the scumbag. Test firing and sighting the perfectly balanced weapon, he knew that a 'shooter' could drive a nail at seventy-five yards. It alone could easily take care of Dean, he thought. Sergeant O'Doul had gone to bed that night beside himself with joy.

He finished the last of the wire seals and placed the cutter in his pocket as Tom walked in. "Thanks, Tom. They're all set and sealed. I'll box 'em, and if you'll go get the car, we can head out for Rawlins. Warden Steward wants us to be ready to go at five in the morning."

"Why so early?" Tom asked.

"I do not know, my son. I understand it's the Guv's order, and as I am ordered, so I obey. Okay?"

"Guess so. I'll go and get the car, Sergeant."

Well, thought O'Doul, now I can make plans. I will declare the anniversary of the twenty-eighth day of February to be an O'Doul National Holiday from this year forth. So be it! I reckon it'll be another lonely night in a motel. Oh well, some of Tennessee's finest will keep me warm.

———

5:30 P.M.
Dean's holding cell
Fremont County Jail

"Will, this is Major Austin Blackwell."

"I know, we met several times over at Rawlins and he brought me here. Hello, Major."

"Hello, Will. Nothing we can do, Will. You understand don't you?" said the Major in a quiet voice, as he reached out and shook Will's hand with a firm grip.

"Sure, Major, I understand. Can I, Joe?" Will asked, looking over at the sheriff.

"No problem, Will. The Major's going with us. But turn around, we do have to hook up the chains."

His desire to see his last sunset forced Will to submit one extra time to the hated ankle shackles, waist chain and having his wrists manacled at each hip. Belted and harnessed in the passenger seat of the new, white, Chevrolet Caprice sedan, with the unarmed sheriff behind the wheel and the head of maximum security for the Wyoming State Penitentiary seated behind him, they pulled out of the parking lot and headed south on First Street.

"Will, we go south here a couple of blocks to 287, hang a left and then we're going to go north on 789 toward Hudson. There's a friend of mine who has a house up on Skyline Drive just past the Lyons Valley Road."

"Oh heck, Joe, know right where it is!" Will laughed.

"Sorry, Will. Just making small talk," the Sheriff replied.

"No, Joe, I wasn't kidding. Trish and I have driven this road a bunch— mostly up to John's office and of course to the El Toro and Svilar's—Worlds Finest Food—right? We ate there several times before the verdict. Joe, it's hard to imagine there are two restaurants that good in a town of three-hundred people. Maybe the Major could get those cooks to come down to Rawlins now and then!"

The knowledge he would be viewing the splendor of his final sunset only a couple of miles north of the situs of Tim Hutchinson's memorial service for Sam, Trish and his children, provided a point of contact, if only a spiritual sharing of the beauty of nature. A few minutes after six, Mountain Standard Time, in western Wyoming, with a breath-taking sunset, the sun gave the illusion of sinking behind the jagged crest of the not too distant Wind River Range.

"Gosh, what a beautiful sunset!" Will exclaimed. "Well, let's go back. It's going to be god-awful tough sayin' good-by to everyone. At least tomorrow won't hurt."

Oh, Christ, thought the Major, as I understand it, Gary Gilmore took almost four minutes to die with five rounds in the heart.

Rotating toward the east, the mountains sped to warm their face by a rising sun, now less than thirteen hours away.

The Sad Good-Byes

7:00 P.M. Thursday
Fremont County Jail
Lander, Wyoming

"*Ata moonò mo ney*, Russtovitch," said Will, tapping his temples with the tips of his fingers, his hands flattened. Sam, his lens to the world gone, could see in his mind's eye, his longtime friend's expressive gesture of futility.

"Yes, Pierresan, you've got a big problem!"

"Sam, we've had some good trips, but things sure went down bad up in those mountains. I'm sorry, but guess there wasn't any way to stop it sooner.

If I'd 've come racing across the valley they'd 've had me covered. I'm sure sorry about George an' the others."

"Will, if you'd come back sooner, we'd all be dead. I knew you'd have a plan. Haven't we always worked things out? It worked the only way it could've. Listen Will, if tomorrow goes down, I'll be there. Nothing I can do, but I'll be with you. Linda said to tell you Bob knows you saved her and the baby. She believes real strongly there's another side and that Bob'll be walking beside you—waiting for you to come over."

"Well, Russtovitch, old buddy, at least there's one good thing about it," said Will, his grin unseen, but sensed.

"What, Pierresan?"

"I won't have to worry anymore about you double-skunking me!" Will exclaimed, with a laugh.

"Oh, I wouldn't be too sure about that, Will. Maybe they'll have cribbage boards on the other side. Get one set up. I'll be over someday! Will, I'm going now. Trish and your kids were just coming in the hallway when they brought me in."

"Sam, okay—thanks—I'll see you in the morning. And oh, Sam, thanks again. I guess we were too busy for me to say thanks back then for hanging on."

"What?"

"The river, Russtovitch, the river. You gave me seven more years."

"Oh hell, Will, I had to. There were too goddamn many grizzlies in the area! Besides, you still owed me ten dollars for the cribbage games! And thank you, Pierresan," Sam added.

"What for?"

"Life," Sam replied, shaking Will's hand. And with a firm embrace, the long-time friends, with many warm, happy campfires behind them, parted and mentally prepared for a cold, sad morning.

Carefully checked for security, it was a sad quartet of young adults led by Major Blackwell into the visiting room to be with their father for a final visit. A circumstance generally reserved for the terminally ill, with a blessing of a peaceful sleep and gentle parting prayed for, it was a healthy though somewhat emaciated father who tearfully greeted them.

"Come on, kids, some hugs please," and packed tight around him, their bodies gripped and shaking in grief, the floodgates opened. Major Blackwell, his recent experience in the Hopkinson case a sad memory, could no longer watch and without fear, tightly closed his eyes.

The gates finally closed. "Hey, kids, how about one last lecture for the road?" Will asked with a grin, wiping away the salty water and his running nose.

"Go for it, Dad," said Mark and Zack in unison. William and Tanya, still shaking, nodded their heads and tried to force a smile.

"First, let's clear up a little matter. I know you can't understand why we threw in the towel after having climbed so many mountains for thirty-two years. Maybe someday you will, but I can assure you, it wasn't Trish and it wasn't the grounds we occasionally handed each other either. Those slips and falls from grace were forgiven, even if not completely forgotten. Maybe we wore each other out with our constant arguing and maybe I gave up when I shouldn't 've, but I did. Let me tell you a story an' maybe there's a moral in it, okay?"

"Sure, Dad. I think tonight we'll all listen," said Tanya, with a smile.

"Atta girl! Never-never-never lose your sense of humor, even if it's graveside! It's what puts us up the scale! Well, strange as it may seem, this story starts in Wyoming a few miles southeast of Cheyenne."

"How's that, Dad?" asked William.

"I'll get to it, Shining Dollar" Will replied, and a quick burst of tears, upon hearing his childhood nickname, was soon quelled.

"Have any of you ever seen your Mom or me fry a steak in a pan?" Will asked.

"Ugh—God no!" Zack exclaimed. "Grill mine medium rare, just like yours, Dad!"

"Well, one of our first and most volatile arguments was over how to cook steaks and they've always been grilled since that day. But you kids have never had a good steak. They don't feed the steers and sell 'em the way they did years ago, too much cholesterol."

"What's the difference, Dad?" asked Mark, a little more relaxed with his mind temporarily off the pending trauma.

"When I was a kid we raised real herefords—not polled mind you, ours had horns—that we sold as breeding stock, not for beef. They were too good for that, *crème-de-la-crème*, the best that could be found. They were all WHR Domino stock, the blood-line of Prince Domino. The bull whose offspring made the Wyoming Hereford Ranch one of the most famous hereford ranches in the world. Seventy-thousand acres of some of the most beautiful ranch land in America.

"Prince was calved in the fall of 1914 and died in the spring of 1930. They have a monument to him at the ranch, off Interstate 80, a few miles east of Cheyenne. 'He lived and died and won a lasting name' is the inscription. Actually, Prince didn't do all that much, it was his offspring who won the awards that made the name famous.

"You know, kids, being a parent can be a real roller-coaster. It's kind of like Newton's law of physics—equal and opposite—or like the *Claymore,* the Great Sword of your Scot ancestors, it cuts both ways. You suffer in unbelievable emotional agony when your children are injured or killed or make serious mistakes in judgment. Yet, you swell with pride and your head rings with joy at their triumphs! I wouldn't delete a day—nay not a moment—out of the lives of any of my children. Of course I might like to change a few moments!" Will exclaimed. "So just remember, I don't care how good you are or how good your children are, try not to throw the first stone at another parent, because sooner or later you're likely to be tested. Maybe not as much as Job was, but you'll be tested!

"Anyway, you've heard me mention Quell Domino. She was the bad-ass cow always chasing me out of the barn yard, the ungrateful bitch! She was one of Prince's many grand-daughters. Every spring she'd go down and we'd have to pull out her calf with a block and tackle. She never did thank us!" added Will with a laugh.

"Dad, the steak?" Tanya admonished, steering her father's memories back on track.

"I wander around in those fields sometimes, don't I?" Will replied and resumed his tale. "Whenever a bull or heifer calf didn't have the correct white and rust coloring, they were destined for the locker-market or the steak-houses in Detroit. We'd pen 'em up in separate pens so they wouldn't fight—the bulls, now steers—and sock the corn to 'em. At around a thousand pounds or so they'd be butchered and now you'd have a good steak! We're talking young, tender, cured, marbled with fat, prime-grade plus, top-of-the-line, direct descendant of Prince Domino, melt-in-your-mouth Porterhouse!" Will exclaimed.

"And you and Mom argued over those?" inquired Mark.

"Oh no, not over the steaks. We argued over how to cook 'em. My mother would take one of those Porterhouses, cover it with flour and pound the piss out of it with a steel steak mallet, turn it over and beat the piss out of it from the backside. Then she'd fry it well-done in home-made butter, turn it over and fry it well-done again on the other side! Your Mom and I argued until I gave in and grilled one medium-rare, without the flour and with the piss!"

"And that's the way we've always had 'em ever since," said Zack.

"Right, Zack. I can't imagine doing one my mother's way. I guess the moral of the story is, be open to new ideas and be willing to try new ways. There was no need for the big argument."

"Dad?" questioned Tanya.

"Yes, Princess?" And again the tears welled.

"How did Grandma's steaks taste?"

"Well," said Will, and pausing, went back to a happy, crowded, dinner-table at their eighty-acre farm near Wacousta, Michigan. Back to sweet, Dunlap strawberries, warm short-cake and melted, home-made butter; to mashed potatoes and the world's best country-fried steaks. "They were good—pretty darn good, Tanya."

"Dad?" Tanya inquired. "Did you ever stop and think that maybe we would've liked to try 'em Grandma's way?"

"No, I guess not—sorry—I wish you could've. You know, maybe arguments like ours were, are not really about 'this or that', or 'your way or my way' or even about 'right or wrong'. But, I'm sure they were destructive struggles for position or power. Come on, kids, we had some great times in our family and you all survived my lectures. Now go with my love and let me spend a few moments with Trish. I love you all very very much." It was a sad—sad—sad, love filled, final separation.

———————

"Will, darling, I talked to Emily a few minutes ago. She said she was going to pray all night and would be sending warm and calm feelings. You've become a part of her life. She'll miss you."

"Tell her I've had a good life and I'll try and watch over things. Maybe good things can be sent from the other side."

"I will, honey. She said the story has hit the international press and news people have called the house. I guess they are even having what they call, 'Mackintosh kick—Dean shoot', contests. And with big prize money, some have been able to do it."

"Well, that's not going to help me. Game playing is always different. It's like playing capture the flag with paint guns. Emotions change things when it's real. I don't think there's goin' to be any last minute knight-in-shining-armor with a reprieve. If there is, he'd better get saddled up in a hurry!"

"I'll keep praying, darling. Oh, by the way, Emily said there was a strange call on the machine. Some man—she said he had a foreign accent—left a message. He simply said he was coming in Thursday afternoon, at 2:45, on Northwest Flight #12, to Detroit Metro and to meet him. But, it was already too late."

"Was it a crank call?"

"I don't know. She said he called me Trish and left his name. She said it sounded like Sergei Chewy-cough or something like that. She couldn't make out part of the call, but she said it sounded like the words 'late' and maybe 'help'. I called the Riverton Airport and that flight is a daily non-stop flight from Narita, just outside Tokyo, to Detroit. Does his name sound familiar to you?"

"No, but whoever he is, he can't help me. Honey, I can't stand it anymore. Give me the world's best hug and go." Grief, like the gray—white—black—slate—boiling clouds of an approaching tornado, swirled around the silent clutching of Trish and Will, as together they braced for their final moment of parting. "I love you very much, but we have to let go. Darling, don't be afraid of life, go for it. We've had a great time together. My karma says there's work in another place. I'll see you on the other side—sometime. Go, darling, I love you."

Like ecstacy, there exists grief beyond description and knowledge before the act compounds even that.

8:15 P.M.
New Fork Lodge
Cora, Wyoming

"Sheriff, here, take a look," said Deputy Brian Stokes, as he unwrapped the corpse.

The body was face down, but Sheriff Coulter could see it was a very wasted young woman; naked.

"Do you want me to turn her over?" Brian asked.

"No, I've seen enough haunting faces of the dead. Just wrap her up and try to get a hold of that new forensic pathologist over in Lander. Have him come right over as quick as possible. If he's not in, leave a message with his wife or on his machine and tell him I'd like an autopsy report by six tomorrow morning. Did you take pictures of the area?'

"Yes," replied Brian.

"Good. Get 'em developed as soon as you can and I'll notify DCI in Rock Springs. Take Deputy Hawkens up at daybreak and report back to me as soon as possible. There've been so many hikers hit throughout the Rockies—innocent and unarmed—they seem to think the bears are all Yogis and Jack-the-Ripper is long dead!" he exclaimed with a sigh.

"You know," said Brian, "those guys in the 'camp affair' were up on Pinion Ridge. That's a long way north and I doubt they were involved in this. There had to be a thousand roughnecks in here for the Rendezvous and probably one of the hookers got wasted. She may be tough to identify, unless she'd been arrested."

"Well, check out the grave and the area real good. I'll bet you'll find something up there. I'll take the body down to the parlor in Pinedale and Doc Robinson can do the autopsy there. Why don't you guys go and get some rest. Brian, there's work to be done. Remember, crack of dawn! Good night, Brian and Joe; catch you later." And shaking hands, they left for the evening.

'seed time and harvest, heat and hoary frost,
shall hold their course.' - Milton

"Will, before I forget," said Father Stoll, "I received a call this afternoon from a doctor in Grand Rapids. He said he'd been following your case and for me to tell you to be in peace and he knew you would walk among his trees."

"That was certainly nice of him. He rebuilt my wrists. He's an orthopedic surgeon and one of the best in the world. Alfred Swanson's his name."

"Will, Sam told me you've had several very close brushes with death. He said you sounded resigned at the trial—kind of like you expected it. Do you feel like talking about life and death?" Father Stoll asked.

"Yes, I guess so. Talking is how I made my living, maybe it'll help. I don't want to die, whether I was 'saved' to end evil or not," weeping again, he stopped for a moment. "Where the hell do these tears come from? Do they ever dry out? It doesn't seem like I've had that much to drink!"

"Take your time, Will, we've got all night. I think I know you well enough by now—you won't want to sleep. I'll be right here with you, so tell me if you want to."

"Okay. Yes, I've had several close calls and should have been killed, but those are not the worst. The worst thing that ever happened was an emotional incident. Hell, bones heal."

"First, about the accidents. Most of my close calls were cars, a river incident, things like that. Lots of my family and friends can tell you about those and I don't want to bore you. Everyone who drives or is active has had close calls and thinks they've been saved. The cars, the river, a bad night in a swamp, those are risks of life and chances we all take, if we're out doing things. Hell, if I hadn't been driving tired, I wouldn't 've fallen asleep and needed saving! It was my fault. Why should God or anyone else try to save me? The more molecules bouncing around, the more collisions. Some survive—some don't!"

Murphy, somewhat surprised, nodded in agreement.

"I guess you're right."

"There was one incident though, that I've never forgotten. Shouldn't say forgotten, I haven't forgotten any of 'em. I mean it was one that I never understood."

"Can you tell me about it?"

"Sure. I was in pilot training—an Air Force Aviation Cadet, not the Academy. The class of '57 Kilo. That was before they broke the Tiger Program. I got washed out for motion sickness and landing on a closed field, but that's another story. I'd been on Wing Staff at Lackland, and to be a fighter-pilot was my life dream. A neighbor of ours, Harvey Hughes, was a fighter-pilot in World War II and owned a P-38 that he raced in the *Bendix* after the war. A couple of times he brought it roaring down over our farm. Heck, I'd started flying at sixteen in the Civil Air Patrol. Anyway, we were in the downwind-leg of the traffic pattern, shooting touch-and-go landings, at the time."

"What were you flying?"

"A primary trainer—a Beechcraft T-34—like a Bonanza, but a tail with a verticle stabilizer and a horizontal elevator, not the V tail of the Bonanza. That was in the days when propellers were on the nose instead of on top! My instructor, a Mr. Allen—civilians taught us—was in the back seat. It's a two seater, red-lined as I recall at a hundred and sixty knots on aerobatic setting. We were only up about a thousand feet or so."

"Where was this?"

"An auxiliary field called Alkali, just north of D'Hanis and a few miles west of Hondo, in south-central Texas. About forty miles west of San Antonio. The traffic pattern was extended out several miles on the up-wind leg. There was a control tower with radio contact, but no instruments like radar, so we were all flying VFR. That means visual-flight-rules. It was a hazy, west Texas afternoon. Apparently, one of the student pilots climbing out on the up-wind leg—we were all in a line, in a huge, long, but narrow rectangle pattern— saw the plane ahead of me on down-wind leg and thought that plane was the end of the line. It almost was for us! Well, he was in a climbing right turn to cross-over to the down-wind leg and then a climbing right turn to get in line."

"What happened?" asked Father Stoll, as Will caught his breath, reliving the past.

"Well, on VFR, at least when your instructor's behind you, you're constantly looking all around and ahead of you. That's where danger is, you don't have to look below and behind you. What nearly happened to us, happened a few years ago in California. I think at Lindberg Field, when a climbing, right-turning, small plane impacted a jet airliner.

"Back to the four of us. The instructor and student pilot couldn't see us, we were in their blind spot and Mr. Allen didn't see them. It was kind of funny at the time. Mr. Allen, I think he got to like me as I slowly conquered my motion sickness—I never was able to do a barrel roll without puking— was in the back seat. He was puffing on his cigar, relaxed, all was right in his world. When for some reason, I just happened to look down to my right and to the rear. There was the other propeller ready to chew into the side of our plane! We all had chutes, but we were way to low to get out and open 'em. As a reflex, I hit hard left stick and left rudder, and Mr. Allen's head hit hard right canopy! He started screaming at me, words he'd learned as a B-26 pilot at Ploesti, in World War II! I couldn't talk, just pointed!"

"I take it no one got hurt?"

"Just a hot cigar in Mr. Allen's lap and a bruise on the side of his head! Tower control saw it developing, but didn't have time to contact us. The control officer, I think his name was George Rucher—who always attested to my flight time—told us they'd written off the four of us."

"That was a close one!" exclaimed Father Stoll.

"I've no idea why I looked in a place I'd never looked before!"

'You're welcome,' said Murphy with a smile.

"The worst thing—the one that affected me the most -hell I'm always taking chances, that won't change—well, I guess it will tomorrow—was an emotional trauma."

"Does it bother you to talk about it, Will?"

"Oh no, it was just a bad scene—a wake-up call."

"How's that?"

"Well, Father Stoll, I sure hope I don't bore you."

"Sometimes that's my job!" he laughed. "But you're not."

"All right. I'll try not to digress, it's one of a bunch of bad habits I'm told. As a kid, I got older—not sure I ever grew up—on an eighty acre farm in central Michigan, that now's just a part of Interstate 69. We were Methodists. My parents took organized religion with a grain of salt, but strongly believed in the golden rule. I'm fifty-six. We're about the same age?"

"Yes, I'm fifty-eight."

"Did you ever get Luxed, Father Stoll?"

"Yes, Will, a couple of times."

"My dad was never mean, but he did Lux my mouth out a few times. I still don't like bar soap! Anyway, one day I said n-i-g-g-e-r—still can't say it—and there came the Lux! If my Dad had any prejudices, he kept 'em to himself.

"On January 4, 1955, thirty-three other Air Force enlistees and I left Detroit by train for Lackland Air Force Base in central Texas. There was one Negro in the group. This was after n-i-g-g-e-r, and before Black. In my little world I'd shot and killed hundreds of crows. There were huge flocks of 'em and the Conservation Department tracked 'em and put the information in the daily paper. I also knew that Old Crow was a whiskey, but I'd never had the pleasure of being introduced to *Jim Crow*.

"We all got along real well on the trip and by the time we arrived in Palestine, Texas we were a fairly tight group. All nerved up, some drinking and a few hangovers. Apparently because I was going into pilot training, I'd been put in charge, which meant hanging on to the group ticket and to just try and keep things cool. In Palestine there was a train change or layover or something. About a two hour wait as best I can recall. We were all hungry and had walked a few blocks down the street to an open restaurant. It was very cold, six o'clock or so in the morning. But for some reason, about eight, including the Black—I've long forgotten his name—came into the restaurant after we'd ordered.

"Man was I hungry, hell I'm always hungry. The bacon was sizzling, bread was toasting, eggs frying on the grill and in came this real nice black guy with seven or eight white friends. Well that woman—I think she must have been the owner as well as the lone waitress—got a look of horror on her face and came flying around the counter with the back of her hands like she was shooing chickens, yelling 'shoo nigger—shoo, shoo—nigger—shoo'! She obviously'd never been Luxed! My dad would've used two bars on her!" laughed Will.

"I stood up and said he's in the Air Force and he's with us. But a hellofa lot of good that did. She screamed at me, 'I don't care if he's with the Holy Ghost! He's a nigger and the niggers eat around in back with the rest of the niggers!' I'd never heard that word used three times in one sentence and said if he can't eat here, I can't eat here, and started out. Well, you know how crowd psychology works. First one, then another and finally everyone—even the white guys from Detroit, who I doubt had ever been Luxed—got up and left.

"A police car with one patrolman arrived, so I explained what'd happened and asked him to please go down to the restaurant and straighten her out. When I walked away, he apparently gave me the finger. My buddies saw it and wanted to roll his car. They were as hungry as I was!

"Well, I went into a self-righteous rage and told the officer my buddies wanted to roll his car and break windows and he should never've given me the finger. I was so mad for missing breakfast—that was always my big meal after farm chores—and his giving me the finger when I was in the right, that I rocked his car by pushing an' pulling on his door. He had a white-knuckle grip on the steering wheel and never reached for his shotgun. It's amazing how tough you feel when you've got thirty-three or so pissed-off buddies to back you up!

"He said he was sorry for giving me the finger. I calmed down a little and said I was sorry about such a bad place, but flying was more important 'an Luxing his rotten little town. We got on the train—went to Lackland— and never went back to Palestine.

"If the car'd been rolled, we all would've been famous! And dead! I've never forgotten the back of her hands or the look on his face. Christ, how totally mortified and angry I felt. It was against everything I'd ever been taught. Hello, *Jim Crow*. I'm Will Dean. Not at all pleased to meet you!"

"That must've been quite a shock."

"It was an incident—feelings got hurt. It didn't seem like I was in America. I'd heard Texas was different, but this was sure a shock! Later I realized this was the way of the South. Like I said, 'wake up Will'! I'll never forget the look on that kid's face and how horrible it made me feel. I guess it was a lunch counter sit-out! And by whites at that!"

"Tell me about your background, Will, if you want to."

"Oh, there's not much to tell. The most important part was that my parents let me do lots of things at an age that today would be considered 'too risky'. The high school had boxing—won six and lost three. Losing isn't any fun! It was horses—flying—trapping—track—shooting—symphony—fishing—hockey—tractors. Just did a lot of things. They supported me and let me make my own mistakes. I was exposed to a lot of different things. But probably the most important, was that my Mom and Dad read all the time. We did things together and with the neighbors. Remember, I was born 11 BN."

"What's BN?"

"Before Nagy. His name was John Nagy and he had the first television show on the air. It was in 1946. I believe it was *Let's Learn To Draw*. But my folks didn't get a TV until after I got out of high school."

"We didn't have a TV then either," said Father Stoll. "Will, why did you request the firing squad?"

"You want more of ole Will Dean's 'he's not going to be around much longer so it won't matter anyway' philosophy?"

"Oh—it may matter, Will. You haven't put me to sleep yet—oops—sorry about the choice of words!"

"Heck, no problem," Will replied, laughing at the cleric's *faux pas*. "Talking's like shooting pool, it takes my mind off it a little. Well, it's a lot like my views on meat eaters—if you can't chop off their heads don't eat chicken! Today's supermarket shoppers buy bits and pieces washed, colored, treated and wrapped in plastic. Most of 'em couldn't knock a young steer in the head and gut it out. We jumped all over Lt. Calley for killing civilians face to face and pilots did it every day with their video screen gun sights. I don't think it meant a bit of difference to Qadaffi's little five year old girl, who probably didn't have a whole hellofa lot to do with bombing the nightclub in Germany!"

"Most people seem to think the raid on Libya was the right thing to do," Father Stoll replied.

"Yeah, just like eating oatmeal wasn't it," Will cynically rejoined. "College, Father?"

"Yes. Above the 38th Parallel. Violence *is* a prolific parent," sighed the cleric. "Were you there?"

"No." Will smiled, as it was easy for him to see that Father Stoll was not offended by his views. "I pray to God I'll have enough strength to let 'em do their duty. The five seconds of my 'last time' aren't going to be as much fun as the five seconds of my 'first time'!" he laughed.

"I've got something for you Will, it's *Lanoxin*. It's made from a plant called *Digitalis lanata*. The Indians used it and it grows about everywhere. It'll help with the heart palipatations. A side effect is diarrhea, but you're on a fast, so that shouldn't be a problem. Are you still lightheaded?"

"Yeah, a little. It's the third day and my weight's down to one-fifty now. It's a piss poor reason to diet, just so they can get me cooked down in a hurry!" he laughed.

"Will, how can you joke at a time like this?"

"Easy—humor helps. What's the point in not laughing? Those last few minutes will be tough enough, but until then. By the way, will you see if you can get me a black felt marker? There are a few things I'd like to jot down. Tell the Sergeant I'll be good and not try and escape with it, at least not from his joint! But, Father Stoll, you asked me why rifles. I knew if the Governor granted my request to go to Dead Horse, it'd be the only way they could do it. Out in the open—the only way to go out. Not like a piece of shit in an electrician's closet. Or strapped on some lab-slab gurney and rolled out in front of a bunch of people to be squirted full of some chemist's cocktail. And, I've done a lot of killing with rifles. So what the heck, if you can't take the heat, stay out of the kitchen! I want to be in the open. To look up at heaven."

"Do you believe?"

"Perhaps," Will sighed. "But I don't believe in foxhole religion. I don't accept Hitler being saved at the last minute and not being punished for what his system did to innocent children. It's hard for me to understand how there can be atonement for the cruel suffering of Mia at the hands of that bastard. I know Tolstoy had a hard time squaring a 'just God' with the suffering of innocent babies, who couldn't have sinned."

"We mortals can never solve that question. Clerics have struggled with that one for centuries. As a man of the cloth, I have to assume that God can work it out.

"Will, we talked earlier about the death sentence and I think we basically agree. There are times however. And then of course, once you have it, it tends to be used on a broader basis. But what about this new procedure, PREP? How do you feel about it as a candidate and as an attorney?"

"Father Stoll, I support it one-hundred percent. Let's take that case last fall in Texas and apply it to me. He was an accomplice in a robbery where one of the other guys shot a teller. He was on death row eleven years and executed on the 14th of November, or it was fourteen years and he got it on the eleventh.

"Hopkinson claimed he was innocent to the end and he was convicted of a conspiracy on circumstantial evidence. A guy was tortured to death, but they never did convict the ones who did it! He was executed last month at Rawlins, after twelve years of emotional hell. Can you imagine what that would do to me? Or to anyone who cares about me? Everyday I was here, they'd be forced to emotionally deal with it. Hope—fear—anger—hate—guilt. Guilt at not being able to visit. Guilt for wishing it was over and wanting to get on with their lives. Hell, it's punishing the tax-payers, the lawyer who lost and wants to try to get it set aside, everyone."

"Gosh, Will, those are things I never even thought about. I've always just thought about the one on death row."

"Those are just some of my feelings. What would I do? Write to Trish and tell her I love her and how are you doing? Have you met someone who wants to hold you? Do you need more hugs? Do you miss—oh God!" Will couldn't finish, breaking again into tears.

"Will, let's change the subject."

"How, Father Stoll?"

"I guess you're right," he sighed.

"Father, he must've done something bad before—there's gotta be a record somewhere, or someone knows about him. But you know, I just don't believe any sky-God is going to come to my rescue."

"Well, it won't hurt for me to pray for it anyway, Will."

"Father, everyone believes I shot an unarmed, innocent man in cold-blood. My acquaintances will believe the jury and my closest friends are dead. Sam, Trish and my children, *if* they believe me, it's fueled by love. But their doubts, which I sense, are based on reason. I told the truth, but it wasn't believed, and that's tough to live with. Maybe this is the best way out," said Will, his face drawn and sad. "Back to PREP," Will continued. "If it's a fair trial, if everyone did their job and the jury was selected properly, then let's get it over. You know, it's like a new ruler killing one of the opposition a day for three-hundred and sixty-five days. Shit, Machiavelli would say it'd be better to round 'em all up and get it over with in one day. And then get on with being a good ruler. Maybe he was right. Get it over with."

"Yes, Will. In the abstract it sounds good. But what about in your case? You claim you're innocent. Don't you think this is going to happen too quick?"

"Absolutely not!" Will exclaimed. "Let's say something is found that proves I'm right. It may be found the hour before or twenty years later. If I had a fair trial, and I did, what's the point in a long delay if you're going to have the death sentence in the end? It's never going to be a perfect system—hindsight's always going to be twenty-twenty. And I just don't want to finish out my life in a damn cage waiting to be executed. Those are my views and I'm sure there're lots of people who'd disagree. But then, I've never had trouble finding people to disagree with me!" laughed Will. "Oh well, my days are swifter than a weaver's shuttle, and come to their end without hope," whispered Will with a long sigh.

"Job seven, verse six," said Father Stoll, with a smile.

"Father, they showed an old movie on television the other night. Maybe the last line would be something to pray for."

"What was it, Will?"

"The movie was *Once Upon A Time In The West,* and the last line was spoken by Jason Robards—who'd been gut-shot—to Charles Bronson. He said, 'Hey Harmonica, when they do you in, pray it's someone who knows where to shoot'," related Will with a sigh. "Chaos, the oldest of the Greek gods. Chaos, Father. It was flukes of fate that brought us on a collision course. Shakespeare said it best, 'fortune brings in some boats that are not steered'."

The night waned as the planet slowly rotated on its axis toward a direction, to give order to this corner of the endless universe, named East. His skin, slack due to the rapid loss of weight, pulled by gravity and deep depression, gave Will's countenance an increasing look of hopelessness. "Father, have you ever taken apart a large, grandfather clock?" he asked.

"No, Will, I haven't. What about them?"

"Oh, I was just thinking as we sit here about 'time' and how it can seem to drag and yet race all at once. Kind of like a hot-fudge sundae, hot and cold. Old gravity pulls on the center weight night and day, day and night, and the pendulum, using some of the energy, swings back and forth. There's a little double-pointed lever, called a *verge,* attached to the top end. With each swing it lets the escape wheel turn just enough to move a couple of gears and tick-tock, a second is marked 'as the world turns'. I believe that tonight, time has become my merciless adversary. You know, my trail's getting short fast!"

"Will, I'll be with you. I'll ride as far as I can," he replied softly.

"Father, as I set here turning back the pages, it's either skip, skim or savor, and I've been incredibly fortunate. For the most part, it's savor. When I'd clean up behind Charly, I'd generally spend more time currying her. Changed a lot of diapers, but remember the giggles more 'an the poop! Ugliest woman I ever met, had the most beautiful eyes. Never'll forget those eyes!"

"Not a bad point of view, Will."

"You know, Father, I guess nothing's perfect. I've tried to do the right thing, but I've sure not been perfect. If I hurt anybody, just hope they can forgive me. Never intended to. There were a few things to grin about if I could've reached the rockin' chair!" laughed Will.

"Anything to share, Will?"

"Oh no. I've got no use for those celebrities who 'kiss and tell'. Human beings should keep their mouths shut about private matters."

"I certainly agree with that, Will."

"There was something cold and intense in his eyes. Something I can't describe. Then that smirk—his eyes dilated—a flash—then that smirk. They just didn't believe me. It's not fair, Father, he'd 've killed me," said Will, breaking once again into muffled sobs.

"Hang tough, Will. I'll be with you."

A few moments passed before Will, breaking the heavy silence, his voice quivering, began. "I was just thinking, Father, sometimes you don't get a fair deal. There's no place on your birth certificate where it says 'life will always be fair'. It's like those people who want children and can't have 'em and then try to buy one. I don't care what they call it, someone always gets hurt.

"You know, Father, if you listen carefully you can hear a card being dealt off the bottom of the deck. I think somewhere along the line, someone slid John and me a card off the bottom, and there wasn't a damn thing either of us could do about it."

"You may be right, Will. That's why I keep praying and will keep on praying. It's all I can do," whispered the cleric.

"Oh well," began Will, with a deep sigh, tears welling in his eyes, "perhaps it's a just payment for the wrong bill."

———————

3:35 A.M.
7850 North Skyline Drive
Lander, Wyoming

With a start, Fred sat up in bed, mind churning, "That's it!" he exclaimed. "There could be a link!" Arriving home exhausted a little after midnight, he'd heard his message, but decided to try and grab a few hours of rest before starting out. Sleep had been difficult.

"What is it, honey?" his wife asked, coming up out of a fitful sleep. "My God. What time is it?"

"It's almost four. I'm going over to Pinedale and do that autopsy. Grab me some coffee, please. I just thought of something! The old noggin's problem-solving in my sleep!" he exclaimed.

"What's the rush? I've never seen you run to an autopsy before. I'll make some instant coffee."

"Wasted, the deputy used the word *wasted* and he didn't mean killing. He said the body was wasted. If she was a hiker she'd have good muscle tone, but she'd be wasted if she'd been held captive. Hurry, I think they're going to execute Dean this morning and hell, part of it was my testimony that the guy was stationary!"

"Can't you call and stop it?"

"No, Jenny. But if there's some evidence on the body that's similar to the camp autopsies, I can. Write down the Warden's number and the Sheriff's and stick 'em in my wallet." Ready to start, he took the hot mug, "Thanks honey," and giving her a quick kiss and a gentle rub on her bare rear, headed out into the dark, bitter-cold morning for South Pass and the hundred and forty mile drive to Pinedale. If the road's as clear and dry as it was last night, he thought, I'll be there by a quarter to six—plenty of time.

As the miles of empty road raced past at a steady speed of ninety-five miles an hour, Fred had time to reflect. Should I have been so certain in my opinion? There was no doubt about the bullet's path, but could he have been moving up toward Dean, his torso squared? Well, it was the psychiatrist who really iced Will, that and no evidence of any special training. Christ, the crime-scene analysts from DCI did everything they could to find support for Dean's version. There wasn't a shred of rope fiber on Lee's hands—no blood—no skin—no hairs. The torture of Sam must've been done by John. He had rope fiber and a hair from Sam on his hand and the rope on Sam was different than on the other men killed.

Fred Robinson, as a Board Certified Forensic Pathologist, was unique in Wyoming—he was the only one in the state. His recent move to Lander had been made only a few months prior to the camp incident and he had often been called from Colorado to testify in the Wyoming courts. The growing number of killings in the Rocky Mountains had been a most troubling development. Forest service personnel were scattered and only recently, decided to work armed. The trouble was, bad people never seemed to give good people a fair fight.

Wasted, a different way of describing the body. If they were camped in the Bridger area and held a hiker captive—to be used—she would be wasted. His mind scrolled over the evidence, which, due to the complexities of the case, he had reviewed in detail. He knew the devastating effect his testimony would have on Will and the great weight jurors always seemed to give so-called 'impartial experts'. Bullshit he thought, we do our best, but we still come at it from a point-of-view. Could I have explained it as convincingly from Will's version, if I had wanted to?

Wait, the light again went on in his computer brain. Too young to be affected by those tiny bugs that go racing around inside the heads of older people with their little bottles of white-out, it clicked. They all had hunting licenses and the waitress from Pinedale testified that Gerlach had mentioned going hunting for 'camp meat'. Of course then it didn't have any connection to the attack. But if? What if *camp meat* had meant something far more sinister and diabolical?

South Pass, at an elevation of only seventy-five hundred feet, was a historic gap in the Rockies for western travelers who followed the North Platte to present day Casper, trekked to Salt Lake City and on to northern California.

As he approached the pass, seeing lights askew, he slowed, then braked hard and pulled off the totally blocked road. The head-on collision—a sleepy driver?—a drunk?—was a bad one. First on the scene, he reached for his car-phone and called the Rock Springs zone post of the Wyoming Highway Patrol.

There were people hurt, badly hurt, and he was a doctor. He had to help. He could see there were children. Oh God, save the little boy! And, bending over, began to restore life. He could still make the autopsy, hopefully in time.

Sometimes the windshield—sometimes the bug, he thought.

13

Canyon

'. . . and though you want to last forever;
you know you never will,
you know you never will;
but the 'good-bye' makes the journey harder still.'
Cat Stevens

Daybreak
Dead Horse Lake
Fitzpatrick Wilderness Area
Wind River Range-Rocky Mountains
On the Continent of North America
The Third Planet in the Solar System
An incredibly beautiful globe called Earth

The pristine silence in the wilderness cathedral of the canyon was shattered as the two, sleek, Bell 222 UT helicopters swung high above the confines of Dead Horse Lake. In separate intervals, two minutes apart to reduce the effect of whiteout, they made the rapid descent and cut their engines to idle. The last of the huge clouds of powder snow settled slowly to the surface, the temporary whiteout passed and silence again became master of the house.

As the planet Will loved so much continued its relentless spin through space, memories of his past life wandered about his head like rabbits on the soft, pine-needle carpet of the Hartwick Pines. The consciousness that he would, within minutes, absolutely and forever cease to exist, pulled at every fiber of his being. Like a heavy, wet, wool blanket it draped over every cell, hanging like an anchor from his very soul.

As the rotor came to a stop, with the nose of the helicopter pointed toward the people assembled at the edge of the lake, McKinnon opened the doors, assisted his passengers out and started for the rifle team to assume his dual role as Captain. Curse the word duty he thought, something is wrong about this one, but it cannot be stopped. No more than to stop an avalanche, the wheels of justice had rapidly ground forward; the result decided—reviewed—confirmed—planned—carried out. And now it would be completed with the

245

absolute finality from which there could be no appeal, nor would there be any hope of undoing that which was about to be done.

Will and Father Stoll, having exited the helicopter followed by Sam and the others, made the short walk across the frozen lake. The pace slowed by the demeaning and pathetic shuffle of Will's chained ankles. At the edge, the team and the other 'witnesses' watched in solemn silence, as with tears streaming down his face, Sam embraced his friend. Thinking to himself, 'Your luck has finally run out', there was no need for words.

"Will, just a minute," said Sheriff Arce softly, his voice breaking. "You're okay, Will. I'm sorry. Here, you don't need these and neither do we." And with trembling fingers he unlocked the hated ankle cuffs, released Will's hands and removed the waist chain. Small acts of friendship often carry enormous feelings.

His physical shackles removed, Will now embraced his life-long friend and whispered in his ear, "Sam, maybe something'll turn up someday and clear my name. That's all I can pray for. Russtovitch, old buddy, you forget about that hill pledge!"

"*Oodu siyu,* Pierresan. *Keo skide,*" Sam whispered. "We've had a good ride my friend. That was sure a sweet song to hear when you came riding in. I knew you could take 'em. Go with Bob and our buddies. They're waiting with *Charlemagne* saddled—ready for you to ride, my son."

Giving his friend a firm embrace, Will turned and with Father Stoll, began the trek along the snow packed path of earlier visitors. With fear and heart palpitation, in spite of the drug he had been given, Will recalled the evening before, after his final parting with loved ones, spent with Father Stoll. They had discussed many things into the morning hours.

"Will, do you remember *A Place In The Sun?*" Father Stoll had asked.

"Yes," he had replied. "I remember Montgomery Cliff was executed for the murder of his pregnant girlfriend, Shelly Winters. As I remember it, she accidentally drowned after falling out of a boat, when they were arguing about his new love, Elizabeth Taylor."

"Right. It wasn't that he killed her. The moral question was, did he want her dead and didn't save her when he could have?" Father Stoll had reflected.

"I know," Will had answered. "It was the same with Karamazov. He had reason to hate his father, had the opportunity and might have killed him, but he didn't. Though each was innocent of the act, nevertheless, the jury convicted in both cases."

"You're right, Will. The basic question. If you kill a person in your heart, aren't you guilty? Could you have stepped back?"

"I'm not sure—physically—maybe. I'll never know, Father. As he shifted his weight to his left leg—the look on his face. My choice, if ever there was one, was to pull back or shoot—to beat him—to end it all. I just don't know.

At the instant I pulled the trigger, I knew if I didn't, he had me. It showed on his face. I'll always be opposed to the death sentence, but my views won't be around much longer!" he had laughed. "Whether guilty or not, not because of me, it's *The Ox Bow Incident*, Chessman, the guy in Chicago where the girl lied, the old man in Florida who didn't poison the kids. New evidence. You just can't undo it. And, if it's the wrong person, which occasionally happens, who ever looks for the right one?" Will had asked. "You know, Father, if I have to make it, this is an awful payment for a debt I don't owe."

Not fully aware as he walked along in the snow, toward the tree standing alone at the edge of the lake, Will grabbed Father Stoll's arm. "Father, please pray—I really don't want to go. I really, really don't want to leave this beautiful planet," he cried.

"No sane person ever does, Will."

"It's the 'platform over the abyss', isn't it?"

"You're right. No sane person ever jumps," Father Stoll replied.

"Well, it's going to happen, so please help me. Oh God, I'm scared!" Will cried, his voice breaking.

"Anyone would be."

Terror, cold clammy terror crept through Will's body. It came rising up his legs as if gleaned from the crunch of the snow. Up through his spleen, his liver, his stomach. His breath shortened, the pressure causing microscopic blood vessels to burst in his eyes, his vision blurred. His mind raced over the past. His loves, his pains, his children and grandson, his daughter's child to be. His mind screamed in kaleidoscopic turmoil and drenched with an instant cold sweat, his mind raced back to an earlier canyon—*ack-ack-ack, the staccato burst of radio gunfire snapped over his earphones as his unseen cadet buddy, diving through the broken clouds, parked on his tail. The scattered cloud cover at eight-thousand feet and the brush-covered rocky hills of west Texas goat-country were to provide the sandwich layers of their prearranged dog-fight venue.*

"Buzz, you cheated on altitude to come out of the clouds like that!" Will chided, using his friend's private code name.

"So watch out for cheats! All's fair in love and war, Coyote!" came the laughing reply.

With no electronic scoring, one or the other would have to get so close or so low that the opponent would beg off. Flipping his T-34 on its back, Will pulled the stick toward his gut and starting a split-S, raced straight down for the hills. "Buzz," he challenged, "I'm taking you in."

"I'm tucked in your wake, Coyote," his best friend replied, giving him another burst of radio ack-ack.

Quickly, Dean pulled a hard right snap-roll into a diving right-hand turn as the two best friends courted death beyond the watchful eye of Hondo control. The tower, breaking in on their channel, ordered them to knock off the dog-fight and practice their maneuvers. Isn't that what we're doing, thought

Dean, as he pulled out of the diving right turn. Making a hard left turn, he leveled out and pushing the nose down, his propeller clipped the tops of the brittle, drought-dried brush as he raced for a narrow opening between two high hills.

"Coyote, you're crazy! I'm going up!" Buzz exclaimed.

Grinning to himself as he banked to his left, going between the hills— Oh God!—his silent scream went unheard as he realized the valley was a box canyon. Oh-God—the wall was way to high and much to close. With no room to turn—it would cost lift anyway—he leveled out and pulled back on the stick. Already above the red-line, he felt the shudder of a high-speed stall. Back-off, pressure, back-off, pressure, back-off, pressure. The plane finally made it to a nearly vertical climb, his flight suit drenched with cold sweat, as shaking in sync with the T-34, together they rode the 'edge of the envelope'. With his heart hammering—propeller once again chewing brush—his plane broke through at the top of the ridge and soaring for the clouds, his 'hour-long journey of terror'—actually only seconds—ending as the friendly sound of Buzz's voice stilled his shaking.

"Christ, Coyote! I thought you were going in, you dumb shit!"

Wing-tip to wing-tip and cruising at 90 knots, just above stall speed, Dean opened his canopy, "I've got to dry out a bit, it's a little stinky over here," he declared, grinning over at his friend, his white silk scarf flapping in the breeze. Their conversation heard, but not identified by control tower, the Cadets often did crazy tests of nerves. No one dies when you're twenty. "That's got to be closer to the 'edge' than 'G's' eighteen spins! Support me at the club tonight?" asked Dean.

"Hey you two, knock off that dog-fighting and get back to those maneuvers," ordered control.

Ignoring control, Buzz, the 'class' of 57-Kilo, replied, "You got him on that one—'G'll buy!"

"Control's an old fuddy-duddy! Let's follow SA home Buzz—over and out." They both tuned their radios to KTSA, San Antonio, Texas and music for their Chandell and Immelmann filled dance back to Hondo—and then calm, a warm soft calm, as if the very soul of love gently descended over him.

"Please God, help me walk to the tree, my legs are shaking."

"Will, would you like to pray with me to our Father in Heaven?"

"Or the Great Spirit. Does it matter?" Will asked.

"I'm not sure," the cleric responded, cutting Will some slack. "If your head's in the right place, maybe not. Let's pray silently as we walk," he answered. Taking Will's left arm and firmly gripping his hand, with the Sheriff following, they continued slowly toward the pine.

Standing tall and still in the cold winter morning, a beautiful monument of nature, the great smooth-trunk lodge-pole pine waited silently for its unexpected role of giving strength and support to Will in his time of need.

"Will, do you want an eye shield?" Sheriff Arce asked, tears streaming, as he carefully placed the strap around Will's chest, hugging him firmly to the tree.

"No," Will replied, his face white and drenched with cold sweat. "I'd—like—to—look up—at at at—the the—sky," he stammered, his entire body shaking.

The broad strap, with velcro locking ends, had been tailored to Will's size and showed a black circle centered over his heart. Father Stoll, holding Will firmly by each shoulder to calm his trembling and hoping he could hear, whispered softly, "Save a place for me, Will, and say hello to Mia. He'll work it out." He kissed Will's forehead and without hesitation, turned and walked with Sheriff Arce to the side, behind a large outcropping of rock.

The squad captain, in clear view of Warden Steward and Major Blackwell, watched intently for a sign reprieve had been granted. The slow, negative shake of both of their heads was a clear sign it had not. Carefully holding Dean's perfectly balanced rifle at the ready, the radios checked, Brad waited for the awful moment he was certain Dean would not delay. Cursed be that word—duty.

All too often on this venue, Murphy was forced to close his eyes and bow his head.

His shaking slowly subsiding, Will tilted his head in a dream induced state to stare above the canyon's ridge where eagles on a better morning soared. A small black spot, under the point of his chin, was revealed to the team that held a special interest to Brad and the cool, expert-shot Theresa, now standing to his left. The team ready, the radio count was given, and, with one sharp crack, Will's head snapped back against the tree, his earthly sojourn through this time frame ending; instantaneously.

His spirit, like an eagle in an updraft, slowly climbed the canyon wall. His body relaxed, his head fell forward, and, as if in a final communion with nature, fresh flecks of bright red blood drifted gently down to meld with the waiting virgin snow.

Mia, knowing it was not proper to feel or show such happiness for what he had done, broke away from her mom and dad, and quickly ran forward to welcome him. Somehow, inexplicable, Will understood why, as she floated into his arms to give him a big hug and a kiss. To the side, waiting patiently on their horses, were five friends; George holding the reins of a beautiful, long-legged buckskin mare, named for a king, her mane and tail feathered in an ethereal breeze.

1:05 P.M.
Riverton Municipal Airport

John Vickers and Tim Hutchinson entered private suite 203 of Western Executive Air's building where Trish, Sam and Will's children had gathered. The room's large window, more like a gleaming, living photograph, disclosed to the west, the awesome, snow and ice-covered crest of the Wind River Mountains. Earlier, the brilliance of the morning sun, reflected like a field of diamonds from the ice-glazed peaks, had been a stark counterpoint to the dark event hidden from their view.

Fortunately, the media had yet to ferret out their grieving refuge. Trish, obviously in a state of extreme anguish, caused John to turn to Will's second oldest son. "Mark, your dad's ashes," said John, handing over the urn. "You can be proud. He refused to bargain with the truth."

"Thanks, John. We, and I speak for Dad and all of us, we all know you did not lose Dad's case. Maybe it was the times. As Dad said, 'Maybe it had been written'. Dad did shoot Lee and there was simply no evidence to support his claim. We know Linda and Sam testified to the absolute truth as to what they knew. Each of us has a copy of your closing argument and nobody could've spoken better for Dad. We all want you to know that."

"Thanks, Mark. It's been tough on everyone," said John, as together they started down the stairs to head for the Denver-bound flight. "What are you going to do now?" he asked, as they gathered at the edge of the ramp.

"Well," Zack answered, "we're going to Denver with William, who's going back to his family. From Denver, the rest of us are flying to Michigan."

Taking the urn from Mark and holding it close to his chest, as the tears ran down his face, William spoke up, "We're going to get together with Sam, in September, and try to find a small hill, in a bog, in the middle of Newfoundland." Handing the urn back to John, so he could deliver it to Trish, they shook hands and parted. Four devastated young adults walked across the tarmac and boarded United Flight 2284 for Denver.

A short distance down the parking strip, the door of a chartered, twin-engine private jet, opened and unloaded some camera laden media, who headed toward the airport entrance. "Hey, John!" Dick exclaimed. "Look over there— the media—hell man, hot on the trail! Will's beaming somewhere. He won his last case!"

"It's over, Dick," said John, as they started for Jenson's car, "at least this part. You know, handing that urn with Will's ashes to Trish was the most difficult thing I've ever done in my life. There's something wrong though. I really believe Will's testimony. It's just not like him—not the person I've come to know."

"Don't beat yourself on this one, John," said Dick, trying to bolster the spirits of his depressed friend. "You did one hellofa job and there's not a defense attorney in the State who isn't proud of you. Your argument will go into the classics, in spite of the verdict!"

"It helps to hear you say that, Dick. Still I wonder. I guess I always will. Thank God things like this don't happen very often. Usually it's just crooks and the triangles," John sighed, with a strained and sad look as he climbed into the car to begin the five mile ride back to his office.

The cellular phone rang as they pulled out of the parking lot and Dick picked it up.

"Is John with you?" the voice inquired.

"Yes. Is this Lora?"

"Yes."

"Here, John, it's your secretary," Dick stated, handing him the phone.

"Yes, Lora. It's over. What's up?"

"John, I just got a call from the Sublette County Sheriff. He thought you should know. Some cougar hunters' dogs found a body of a young woman at a camp site over in the Bridger. The pathologist was held up early this morning by a bad accident at South pass. He called the sheriff when he started the autopsy and realized that—that . . ." her voice breaking, "both—both of her eyes—her eyes were gone," she sobbed, hanging up.

"Oh God! Oh no!" John groaned in anguish.

Epilogue

'. . . truth will out . . .'
Wm. Shakespeare

March 25, 1992
Office of Detective Matthew L. Jaeger
Marion County Sheriff Department
Jasper, Tennessee

The small, white building located at the corner of West 1st and Oak, in the center of Jasper, was about as spartan as a county sheriff's jail and office facility could be. What the department lacked in physical assets, it compensated for in integrity and skill. Problems in the county were, as in many areas of the country, in inverse proportion to its wealth.

One of the department's key assets was Detective Matthew L. Jaeger. A native of the county, Matthew knew its people; he knew their strengths and their weaknesses. Fifty-five years old, five-foot ten and one hundred seventy pounds, with graying hair growing thinner, time had taught him you rarely learned anything while you were talking. He listened and with an ever present toothpick, pumped out information with a frown or a smile.

"Come in," he beckoned, in response to the soft knock on the jamb of his generally open door. "What's up, son?" he asked, as the new detective in training, Joseph Brandon, entered his tiny and badly cluttered office. When you're fifty-five, everyone is young he thought. "Hey man, what's the matter? Don't tell me Bledsoe County of all teams, beat the Warriors last night!"

"Oh no, they've played four games in the last five days, but still beat 'em fifteen to one. The umpire called it after the fourth inning under the mercy rule. At least baseball games have a mercy rule. How's Martha feeling?" Joe inquired.

"Fine. But hey, the look on your face tells me you're not here to talk about your boy's baseball team or my wife's operation. How about a cup of coffee and we can talk? You look like shit," he observed.

"I feel like shit and I'll have coffee number five and probably six'n seven," Joe sighed, as he dejectedly slumped into an old, battered, easy-chair.

"What's on your mind, Joe?"

"You'll get pissed again, Matt?"

"Oh shit, not that goddamn case again. It's a damned obsession with you. What the hell's the matter with you? We're in the middle of depression around here, we're up to our ass in crime and you're still worked up over the Prentice-Cooper case. Never going to find 'em!" yelled Matt, who rarely raised his voice. "Joe, listen to me a minute, then you can talk and I'll try not to be patronizing. You're new here, you're from Knoxville and lived all your life in the city. These natives 'round here, in the hills and valleys, don't like outsiders. They're good people, and no different from people anywhere who live out in the hills. I don't care where you're talking about—Maine, Michigan, Montana—you name it. They tolerate outsiders. They want the tourist dollars, but deep down inside, it's always 'them and us'.

"An awful lot of these locals hate off-road vehicles, even when it's locals on 'em! No matter how you skin the 'possum, those three were outsiders and the locals, *if* they know, are just going to let sleeping dogs lie. I know it happened while you were on patrol up at the Crossroads, but you did everything that could possibly be done. It'll take hard physical evidence. Okay? Now talk to me."

"All right," Joe quietly began. "You know I've been doing some time on the phone and fax?"

"Yeah. So what've you got?" Matt asked, with just a note of curiosity in his voice.

"Matt, this is tough—real, real tough—as I read it, a damn tragedy! Matt, I guess our case can be closed, but I'm not too happy about it," said Joe, his voice breaking.

Matt could see Joe was real shook up, so he hollered down the hall to the Sergeant on dispatch to cut off all calls; he and Joe would be out of contact for awhile. "Okay, Joe, take it slow and easy," he said, seeing Joe was on the verge of tears.

"Remember the case last month where they executed that lawyer from Michigan under the new guideline, PREP?" Joe asked.

"Oh sure! Who doesn't? First case, white man, attorney, execution, equal justice, no delay—everyone's happy. Just imagine all the lawyer jokes out of that one!" he laughed, in spite of the sad look on Joe's face. "What's the connection?"

"He was innocent, or at least he had a good defense no one knew about," Joe answered, in a low voice.

"Christ! Imagine standing there looking at the sky with five rounds coming down the pike at your . . ." he couldn't finish. "*Cojones* to stand there and take that. The poor son-of-a-bitch never knew what hit him."

"You're right on that. And probably it was just a little bit quicker than anyone expected. Here, Matt. Look at a copy of the death certificate they sent me with the other papers I'd requested. Take a look at the cause of death!" Joe exclaimed.

STATE OF WYOMING
DIVISION OF HEALTH AND MEDICAL SERVICES
CERTIFICATE OF DEATH
///////////////////////

IMMEDIATE CAUSE (Final   Approximate Interval
disease or condition   Between Onset and Death
resulting in death) →

a.   *Cardiac Respiratory Arrest*   *Instantaneous*

DUE TO (OR AS A CONSEQUENCE OF):

b.   *Exacerbation — CNS Destruction*

DUE TO (OR AS A CONSEQUENCE OF):

c.   *Two Gun Shot Wounds 4cm Superior Larynx*

DUE TO (OR AS A CONSEQUENCE OF):

OTHER SIGNIFICANT CONDITIONS—Conditions contributing to death but not related to cause given
Gunshots through chest & heart

AUTOPSY (Specify yes or no)   *NO*

WAS CASE REFERRED TO CORONER (specify yes or no)   *NO*

DESCRIBE HOW INJURY OCCURRED   *Execution*

LOCATION (Street and Number of Rural route Number, City or Town, State)

Dead Horse Lake, Fremont County, WY

"Wow! Destruction of the central nervous system."

"Matt, he was supposed to get five in the heart and that takes several minutes to do the trick. Somehow he must have set this up, but I doubt we'll ever know how he did it."

"Explain it, Joe. Talk to me. What's the connection to our case?"

"Well," Joe began, "the day before the execution some Wyoming cougar hunters' dogs found the body of a young girl who was buried at an old campsite on the west side of the Continental Divide. They didn't realize what they had until shortly after the execution. Even then it didn't really prove anything bad about the one Dean was executed for killing. The autopsy doctor made the connection on the similarities, but there wasn't a shred of evidence to link the killing to Lee Mackintosh. DNA tests on semen did link the case to the other two.

"I'd followed Dean's case and remembered that Lee Mackintosh and his brother John, both from Virginia, and a third man, the guy who'd escaped from prison in Michigan, had driven up an old jeep trail and hiked down to the site of the 'camp affair'—as it became known. It never ever occurred to me there might be a connection to our case. But when I heard about the hiker, and we've had a few hit in the Smokies, I just got curious and called the officer in charge of the girl's case. He faxed me a copy of the autopsy. No eyes!"

"Oh piss—shit—fuck!" Matt exclaimed. *Taking The Pelham 123,* was one of his favorite movies.

"I called and got the autopsy reports on the camp victims along with a bunch of other papers. Somehow the news reports had just said rape, torture and murder with no mention of eyes," Joe continued. "Will's best friend's eyes had been popped and so had one of the other victims!

"Remember, the trial was in mid October and didn't get much national coverage by the media since most of 'em were busy in Washington covering the Thomas hearings. They jumped on the execution however, like flies on a dead horse. The Cooper enucleations were kept secret so only the real killers could confess and no law enforcement information network made the connection. I called the detective in charge of the Dean case—an investigator by the name of Beckwourth. He told me Will's only defense to the shooting was he shot when he realized he'd been tricked, that Mackintosh's foot only missed the pistol due to the recoil. It was totally unconfirmed and you know the rest.

"The jurors and PREP had a clean Nam veteran, there was no rape, torture or killing in camp on his part that anyone saw. No prior record and nothing negative on him in any way. They argued he was unarmed and dragged into it, not a part of it. Kind of like Jake Spoon in *Lonesome Dove.* Dean's defense . . . ," he stopped and drank some of his now cold coffee. "Of course Jake had a gun."

"I then called and got a copy of Mackintosh's military record. Fine, but an odd code I hadn't seen before. Remember, I'd worked in central records when I was in the Army, before I went to the police academy. I called a very close friend with access to *complete* military records and she checked it out. While she was working on it, I got prints from Wyoming. And sure enough, John Mackintosh's prints matched those on one of the beer cans!" Joe exclaimed. "And we weren't even sure that any of the cans found at the Prentice-Cooper crime scene were involved!"

"Joe, didn't we have a bunch of cans at the Prentice-Cooper crime scene?"

"Right. We ran ten fresh cans through NCIC, that's the National Crime Information Center . . ."

"Joe, I'm a detective," said Matt with a smile.

"I'm sorry. Sometimes I'm back in the classroom. Anyway, we had five sets with no record and the others were cleared. The two Wyoming detectives went to NCIC with the Mackintoshs' prints, but they were both clean. With no pattern or similarities—the weapons were different—there was just no connection made to our case. If we hadn't kept the enucleations secret . . ."

"Ifs and should haves, Joe. It's always twenty-twenty!" exclaimed Matt. "Lee must've been the one who helped move the bodies and vehicles."

"Right. Anyway, a couple of days later my friend called me back and said Lee was a graduate of Special Forces. The 'Ultimate Human Killing Machine', to quote the old Fort Campbell recruiting poster. It gets better—or worse—depending on how you look at it. Lee went to Grad School," continued Joe.

"Grad School?"

"Right. After Fort Campbell, a select few went to Langley and became *ITs*."

"*ITs?*" questioned Matt, a puzzled look on his face.

"Yeah, *Intelligence Technicians*. It's the euphemism special forces teams called the select Special Forces volunteers, who, at the Central Intelligence Agency in Langley, were taught by doctors how to extract information a/s/a/p without giving away their position in hostile territory. Exquisite masters of extreme pain. After Viet Nam, some of 'em may have worked in Rhodesia or Angola, Afghanistan or maybe other places and I've got a hunch some of 'em may be working for the Drug Enforcement Agency."

"What makes you say that? That's quite a serious allegation, Matt."

"Do you remember the Kiki Camareno story that was shown on television?"

"Yeah, I saw it—tough!"

"Do you remember when the DEA official from Washington was listening to the tapes of Kiki being tortured?"

"Yes. A gut wrenching scene to show on television."

"Remember," continued Joe, "he turned to his partner and said something to the effect that, 'Kiki was letting go', that 'it was about over'."

"So?"

"How do you suppose he knew?"

"Christ—you're right!" Matt exclaimed. "Shit, and I just heard on the radio that the Director of the CIA doesn't object to releasing the Kennedy papers as long as they don't disclose Agency *methods* or *sources*. Our own little *schutzstaffel!* Obviously they're into some heavy shit, and don't forget who used to head it! You know, we didn't put an end to the cold war. *They* wouldn't even let Kennedy slow it down. It was an electrician from Gdansk and ordinary people in East Europe and Russia who just quit it. I suppose a lot of those special types are out of work now, unless you're right!"

"Now get this, Matt. Apparently as a *perk*, if you went to the grad school and had a clean military record, then any record of your going to Special Forces and of course Grad School, *at your option*, would be eliminated! Not deleted mind you, just blocked by the code in the interest of National Security! You would unofficially be an 'ultimate human killing machine', plus added skills, in civilian clothes," said Joe, with a deep sigh.

"Oh, one other thing. There was another code I didn't understand, it was PX. I didn't think it stood for Post Exchange, so I asked her about it. She said it was all public, but it really bothered her and she still didn't want to talk about it, certainly not on the phone, just that it stood for the *Phoenix Program*. She also said there was a code, that she was able to find out stood for Homestead Air Force Base. It was in his coded file a number of times over the last twenty years, but nothing more. She had no idea what it meant.

"I was able to make contact with a member of his unit in Viet Nam, who now lives in Nashville. I went up to talk to him and he decided to let me record it. He said he was dying from cancer, *agent orange,* and he might as well let it all hang out. He confirmed all my friend had told me," Joe smiled, flashing Matt the small tape.

"He told me Lee's nick-name was Socket, 'cause he always left 'em empty, a terror factor. Lee's calling card. Most Special Forces guys had one. He told me Socket always knew that if he got close enough, no one could shoot him. He described a skill Lee had. By the way, each Special Forces grad always had at least two specialties. They could be hand-to-hand, demolition, weapons, medical, language and so forth. Lee's were hand-to-hand and weapons, but here's the kicker—no pun intended. Lee had a *special trick*. Somehow he'd developed an ability to make a very deadly kick from a one leg kneeling position. No one knew he could do it until they had an incident in camp when a grunt went berserk and had Lee on the ground, on his knees, begging him not to shoot him. The soldier had lost it in the field and really wanted to waste someone—didn't even know Lee! He said Lee exploded from the ground with a spinning kick combination, first taking out the rifle and then hit the guy in the side of the head, knocking him colder'n a cucumber! They took the grunt away in a straight jacket. He said the guys tried to get Socket to show 'em with a cigarette in their fingers, but Lee just shrugged his shoulders and walked away. He said no one ever fucked with Socket after that.

"I then asked him why I had never heard a word about *Intelligence Technicians* before. He just laughed and said, 'Only an *IT* would be believable and because of Stonefish'. I asked him what he meant and he said he was certain I'd be able to figure it out. I haven't yet.

"I asked if he was afraid of my going public and he broke out laughing and said 'Hell no!'. He said he had no living relatives and then he asked me to wait at least two days. I agreed and asked him why. He said and I'll quote, '. . . there's a few things I'd like to take care of before I lend my cancer a helping hand!' I didn't need to ask him what he meant!

"I also asked him about *Phoenix*, but he clammed up. He just said, 'Eyes ain't nothin'', and that was the end of the interview."

"Dean's defense would've been accepted by the Jury," Matt stated, a little subdued. "Joe, what was the motive behind the killings in the Prentice-Cooper, if you know?"

"Well, a quick check with Social Security led to some banks. In 1968 the family estate of around six-hundred acres up near Winchester—an original grant from Lord Fairfax—was taken by the Commonwealth of Virginia for an off-road vehicle park. In the fall of '69, their father shot his invalid wife—who of course was the boys' mother—and then in his mouth with a twelve gauge. A real mess. To make it even worse, Lee was in Viet Nam fighting for his country when it happened and wasn't able to come home for their funeral.

"To top it all off, the banker in Abingdon told me he'd just informed Lee about a new recreation park being put in this remote valley, near Hayters Gap. That's about twenty miles northeast of Bristol. John and Lee lived near there. Some coincidence!" exclaimed Joe.

"No shit! That could get to a lot of people."

"I don't think it was any plan. I think one of them, because of the location of the beer can, probably John, just lost it. Then Lee helped cover it up and they split. Out west, things just got worse. But, talk about coincidences, listen to this. The big guy at the Cooper was a senior in law school. The young woman the hunters found was a lawyer and of course, so was Dean. I wonder if Dean was a target?" pondered Joe.

"Well, I don't suppose we'll ever know. Joe, what are you going to do now?"

"Well, Matt, for the sake of Dean's family and the families of the Prentice-Cooper kids, don't you think we've got to call a press conference and lay it all out?"

"You're right, we don't have any choice but to let the families and the public know," Matt agreed. "But Joe, I'll tell you one thing, if what you're saying is true, and with all the shit that's been coming out on Kennedy's assassination and about Marilyn, I don't doubt but that you're going to really piss some people off. Did you see the school play last week?"

"No. Hamlet, wasn't it?"

"Right. 'Their grand commission . . . O royal knavery!' You know, Joe, you'll be about as popular in Washington as Copernicus was in Rome! You're probably going to find a horse's head at the foot of your bed!" exclaimed Matt, with a laugh. "You'd better watch out for knaves and sit with your back to the wall!"

"You're right, but if someone wants to take me out, there's nothing anyone could do to stop it. Shit happens! I'm going to take it public and let the chips fall where they may."

"Good God, Joe—rape—torture—murder—execution of a lawyer—and now this. As long as you're going public, write a book. The 'pen is mightier than the sword' and this would sure make a hellofa movie!"

"Well, I don't know about a book. I'm sure someone will. Matt, you know, the pen may be 'mightier than the sword', but I'll say this, the eraser is the deadliest of them all. If you don't know about it, you can't deal with it," said Joe, with a deep sigh. "You know, Matt, if *it's* too quick, maybe *it* isn't."

"What isn't?" Matt asked, looking puzzled.

"*Justice.*"

'If my life-force, by death decree
  Could find green haven in a tree . . .

A viking trunk, a warrior tree
  A hostage to dark destiny . . .

Let others vision Heaven's gate,
  Dark Pine, I dream for me you wait.'

Robert Service

Author's Note

Should you, reader of this tale, be interested, I would share a few moments of my time with you.

This book is dedicated to the honest and hard working professionals, hopefully the majority, in the judicial system throughout our country. There are individuals in any society that the rest of the population needs protection from. In a perfect system, for which we strive yet fail to reach, we hope to apprehend and deal fairly with the guilty, and release the innocent.

This is a work of fiction with some facts and true incidents thrown in. There has never been a solo escape from Marquette's maximum security, level V. The actual Laundry Basket Caper was prevented by Murphy's Law number three. Any similarity to any persons, living or deceased, is purely coincidental. At this juncture I would add that the Wheeler Letters are true and verbatim.

While I am opposed to the death sentence, PREP is an idea that may or may not work. If there must be execution, I would support PREP, which has been some baggage knocking around in the back of my head for a considerable time, with no cart to carry it. Hopefully this is not a vehicle with four flats!

The idea for this cart occurred after the trek west and only after a long ride to the top of Shale Mountain disclosed the existence of the Union Mountain—Marion Lake jeep trail. Of coincidences too numerous to mention, the centennial celebration of Marquette Prison, revealed at my first meeting with prison authorities, in response to my disclosure of the date of the planned escape, was certainly incredible.

The reader can only imagine the reactions of Trish and 'Bud' Wheeler to a bit of unsolicited information tendered by an elderly gentlemen, in the remote hills of southern Virginia. Months after Walden Ridge had been drafted, and giving directions to Hayter's Gap (that's pronounced Hotter's) while standing in an early evening misty-rain at the side of our van, he informed us that a recreation park was to be built near Brumley Gap!

There have been so many people who have provided me with detail that I am reluctant to mention any, least the oversights offend. However, since it takes but little ink to give credit where credit is due, I'll apologize for my CRS condition, my bad note taking and proceed.

Wyoming: To the Honorable Mike Sullivan, Governor and of his most gracious staff, Tamala Plunkett and Dennis Curran, my very special thanks,— you made it all possible. Col. E. L. Ayers, Commissioner—Wyoming Highway Patrol; Warden Duane Shillinger and Major Stan James, Wyoming State Penitentiary; Sandra Mays, Deputy Director, Division of Criminal Investigation; Honorable Joe Lucero, Fremont County Sheriff; Butch Hudson, Lander; John Vincent, Esquire and Karen Clausen, Riverton; Judy Legerski, Lander;

Shane Larsen, Riverton; Helen Ward, Deputy Clerk—Laramie County; Dee Leimbeck, Dubois; Al Langston, Wyoming Game and Fish Department; Paul Fees, Curator, Buffalo Bill Museum, Cody; Paul Douglas, WHR; Dave Moore, Ogden, Utah; and to all those unnamed interviewees, my deepest gratitude.

Arizona: Detective Michael Meislish, Phoenix Police Department; thank you for setting the record straight.

Michigan: To Warden John W. Hawley and George Pennell, Administrator, Marquette Branch Prison; Jeffrey Sauter, Eaton County Prosecuting Attorney; Diane Spaniolo, Certified Court Reporter; Greg Forrester, U.S. Weather Service; Terry Tanner and George Kass, ballistics; Karen Beaton; Captain James Lynch, Michigan Air National Guard; Gary Frace; Randy Maloney; Tom Murray; Ken Morgan; Gerald Shane; Tim Brutsche; Mary Lou Fisher, Pine Mountain; Ted Bornhorst, Phd., Michigan Technological University; Bert Boyum, M.S., Isphpeming; E. Olaf Rankinen, Suomi College, Hancock; Lauren Conway; and Detective Joe Hartig, thanks.

Minnesota: To Lt. Jeffrey Grams, Duluth Police Department, thanks!

Virginia—Tennessee: To Allan Masuda, P.E., U.S. Department of Transportation; Anna Eagle, Virginia Department of Licensing, Richmond; Janet Rhodes, Dominion Bank, Winchester; Steve Williams, Jasper; and certain staff of the Marion County Sheriff's Department, Jasper, Tennessee; thank you.

Russia: Dr. Sc. Alexey V. Neyelov and Dr. Mikhail V. Sablin, of the Russian Academy of Sciences, Sankt-Petersburg, Russia; a special thank you. I'll work on my Russian and pray for a gentle winter!

Bell 222 UT: My special thanks to Fred Koenig of Bell Helicopter Textron, Inc., Fort Worth, Texas and to Tim McKenna, pilot and the great opportunity to learn about and fly this super aircraft. Wow, what a flight along Chicago's lake-shore!

Special thanks to the following: Robert Behnket, PhD, Department of Fisheries and Wildlife, Colorado State University; Arthur Adams, PhD., Retired-Professor Emeritus, Ohio State University; George L. Penrose, Phd., Hope College; Frederick D. Williams, PhD, Retired-Professor Emeritus, Kazuhiko Fukushima, PhD., and Leonard J. Rahilly, PhD., of Michigan State University; and Vincent Marazita, Italian Trade Commission, Los Angeles, California.

And it goes without saying, to 'Trish'; my lecture-suffering offspring; Mary; Debbie; to my fishing companions and to Wayne and Tania—outfitters of the greatest mountain-fishing trip ever—my sincere appreciation.

In closing, I must declare that none of the above individuals are aware of, or had anything to do with, the allegations expressed by the fictional characters in the Epilogue.

J'ai fini!

October, 1992
Grand Ledge, Michigan   Myron 'Bud' Wheeler

Bibliography

Bain, Robert *The Clans and Tartans of Scotland* Great Britain; William Collins Sons & Co.Ltd., 1968.

Bigon, Mario and Regazzoni, Guido *The Century Guide to Knots* London; Century Hutchinson Ltd., 1988.

Clark, Thomas D. *Frontier America* New York; Charles Scribner's Sons, 1959.

Florinsky, Michael T. *Russia* New York; The Macmillan Company, 1964.

Herr, Michael *Dispatches* New York; Alfred A Knopf, 1977.

Hotchkiss, Bill *The Medicine Calf* New York; W.W. Norton and Company, Inc., 1981.

Jelavich, Barbara *A Century of Russian Foreign Policy 1814 - 1914* Philadelphia and New York; J. B. Lippincott Company, 1964.

Karnow, Stanley *VIETNAM A History* New York; The Viking Press, 1983.

Kerr, Walter *The Secret of Stalingrad* New York; Doubleday & Company, Inc., 1978.

Murphy, Edward F. *Heroes of WW II* New York; Ballantine Books, 1991.

Roy, Jules *The Battle of Dienbienphu* New York; Carroll & Graf Publishers, Inc., 1963.

Service, Robert *The Best of Robert Service* New York; Dodd, Mead & Company, 1953.

Publications:

Golder, F.A. *The Russian Fleet and the Civil War* American Historical Review, vol. XX, 801–812 (1915).